Kay Nolte Smith's first novel, *The Watcher*, won great acclaim and an Edgar Allan Poe Award. Her articles have appeared in *Vogue* and *Opera News* and she is the author of five further novels, including *A Tale of the Wind* ('rich with historical detail' *Booklist*) which is also available from Headline.

Also by Kay Nolte Smith

The Watcher
Catching Fire
Mindspell
Elegy for a Soprano
Country of the Heart
A Tale of the Wind

A translation of Edmond Rostand's *Chantecler*

Venetian Song

Kay Nolte Smith

HEADLINE

First published in Great Britain in 1994
by HEADLINE BOOK PUBLISHING

First published in paperback in 1994
by HEADLINE BOOK PUBLISHING

This edition is published by arrangement
with Random House, Inc.

10 9 8 7 6 5 4 3 2 1

ISBN 0 7472 4556 8

Typeset by
Avon Dataset Ltd., Bidford-on-Avon

Printed and bound in Great Britain by
Cox & Wyman Ltd, Reading, Berks.

HEADLINE BOOK PUBLISHING
A division of Hodder Headline PLC
338 Euston Road
London NW1 3BH

Venetian Song

CHAPTER ONE

Of Marriage

On Ascension Day, every year, is the ceremony of the Marriage of the Sea. The water is strewn with flowers, and, cutting its way through their fragrant brilliance like a sickle of gold, the ship of state bears the Doge from the Piazza San Marco to the Lido. Around him sails a huge train of dignitaries, nobles, soldiers, civilians; and when he lifts a golden ring and throws it into the water, crying, 'We wed thee, O Sea, in token of our true and perpetual dominion over thee,' the crowds cheer with a voice like bells, and the bells ring like trumpets, and trumpets join in too – all singing the glory of Venice, which by this ritual proclaims its power over the water in which it lives.

In the conjugal bed Susanna Bardi lay waiting for her husband of six weeks. At dinner he had told her he would come to her; he had plucked a fig from the platter of fruits, smacked his lips mightily and suggestively, and said he would arrive at his pleasure. As if there were any question of hers. He visited her three or four nights a week, face florid above his nightshirt, a red moon above a pale sea.

'Are you mad?' her father had cried before the marriage when she once again begged him to cancel the contract. 'We must thank God for continuing to sink Ludovico Rossi's ships and sending him other difficulties, so that he thinks only of your dowry and not of your face. He has tolerated all your delays. No more!'

Her mother, weeping into a long handkerchief of ivory silk, had said, 'Signor Rossi expected a wedding much sooner, *cara*. And you know there is no one else, certainly not here in Venice. The saints were witness to how we tried. At eighteen . . . what other hope do you have?'

Footsteps came along the hall, hammers on the marble floor. Susanna clutched the sheet which trembled in sympathy with her. From habit so long-standing that her brain no longer willed it, her fingers crept to her face.

On the day of the wedding her mother had whispered, 'He is an old man. He will not live so very much longer.'

But he was fifty, only two years older than her father, who was healthy, strong, and still flush with appetites.

'Perhaps,' her mother had said, 'your husband will not spend much time in your bed. No doubt he has courtesans to serve his pleasure.'

There had been some comfort in her mother's words, but the feeling that suddenly coated them, like a pear dipped in salt, was surprising. It was common practice for wealthy men to patronize courtesans, while jealously guarding their wives, and common knowledge that Antonio Bardi was among them. Surely her mother did not mind?

As it turned out, however, Ludovico did not want courtesans.

There was silence outside her room; the footsteps had gone past. Susanna took her hands from her face and smoothed the coverlet, calming her heart. If only she could run away. But each time she thought of escape, she was stopped by the question: Where? A return to her family was impossible; already they had suffered humiliation because of her, and even if they loved her – her mother, at least – they would not accept the stigma of her returning to them. Her father had always been so insistent on the marriage; he would send her back to Ludovico. If she ran to a convent, she might hide in the shadow of a nun's headdress and behind thick walls, but how could she spend her days worshipping God when her heart was filled with bitterness because He had allowed her to survive the plague without a mark but then had let her be marked for life anyway, and had never shown the slightest sign of compassion? And what of the things that were said to happen behind convent walls? She did not have the courage for such a life. Or for its alternative, the brothel. In any case, what brothel would accept her face?

'Signor Rossi does not seem to mind the scar,' her mother had said hopefully when he first appeared.

How much better it would be if he did.

Of itself, the scar was not so long or large, but it lay just below the right eye, on which it tugged like a malevolent rope, twisting the skin around it and pulling down the lower lid to reveal permanently its red lining. If the scar had been on her brow, she could have disguised it with a jewelled headband; if farther to one side, she could have arranged her hair to cover it. But it lay in the centre of her face, of her being, like a stake to which she had been pinned in her ninth year.

Until then, grace and laughter and pride had filled her life as naturally as wine filled a goblet. As a child of noble family, nothing was denied her that gold could buy, and nothing was expected save that she grow into a creature of elegance and beauty, like her mother, and make a good marriage – so that, like her mother, she could be the object of a husband's boasting, if not his fidelity. Susanna had run through the halls and rooms of the upper floors of the great house of Bardi, sometimes even straying into the ground-floor hall where the business of the Bardi spice trade was conducted and where, before she was sent back upstairs, the merchants would pinch her cheeks and call her a little Venetian beauty; she had played happily in the inner court with her brothers and sister; and she had begun learning the wonder and skill of reading the marks on the pages of books and transforming them into ideas and pictures in her mind. She had a natural curiosity and the confidence that it would be satisfied, for she was a daughter not only of the Bardi but of the Most Serene Republic of Venice:

Venice, which lay impregnable and isolated in the lagoon and, alone of cities in Italy, had never been invaded or destroyed. Venice, which, as the sixteenth century drew to a close, remained the crossroads of East and West, accepting the homage and riches of both, treating gold and glittering mosaics as commonplace, and velvet, silk, and pearls as her birthright. Venice had the greatest of architects to build churches and splendid houses on the Canal, and the greatest of painters to immortalize her sights and her citizens. Venice had all Europe's admiration for her exotic beauty; she lived in such splendour that sumptuary laws were frequently passed and in such arrogance that they were usually ignored. To be Venetian, and a Bardi, was to feel in one's body, and to take it as much for granted as one's blood and bones, the assurance of pride and power.

One warm afternoon, Susanna had grown bored with leaning from the high windows of her room to watch the traffic moving past the water door along the Canal. She had wandered down the polished central staircase of the house and into the inner court, where two of her brothers were wielding swords at each other, their half-naked bodies gleaming and muscling like Arabian thoroughbreds', their voices loud with the sneering gravity they thought was an expression of adulthood. 'I shall remove your ugly head from your shoulders,' said the younger of the two. The elder made ready to lunge at him, but just at that moment a huge bird – a falcon, the brothers said later – flew overhead and swooped low, startling Susanna and both boys. The sword escaped the elder one's grasp, twisted through the air, and before striking the stones at Susanna's feet, sliced across her brow and near her eye. In her dreams, for years, she heard the singing of the blade.

Her brothers claimed it was the fault of the falcon; her mother screamed that they should have taken more care. Her father, whose capacity for sudden violence had always intimidated Susanna, raged so loudly that the noise penetrated her sickroom. He did not punish her brothers. Instead, he offered a ducat for each falcon killed anywhere within the next month and brought to his door. Word had seeped throughout Venice, and each morning people had lined up at the door, not all of them beggars, dead birds dangling from their hands like empty purses. Most of the birds were not truly falcons, but her father paid anyway.

Everyone had feared Susanna would lose her eyesight, if not her life. Her mother ushered in doctors from the College of Surgery. Representing different schools, wearing heavy black robes and caps, they stood on both sides of her bed and argued: crows cawing at one another across the trembling fence of her body, bringing it no peace.

'Clearly this infection is the product of an imbalance in the four humours.'

'Ridiculous! Only our new Paracelsian doctrine can explain and cure her condition – she must be treated with an ointment containing mercury.'

Surreptitiously Susanna's mother appealed to a woman who dealt in magics, even though to do so was to court suspicion of witchcraft and its punishments. Three spells were cast on three successive midnights, involving hot ashes and invocations to beings whom Signora Bardi did not dare ask about. In the kitchen one of the serving women produced a concoction from her native village, made largely of mashed toad; she smuggled it into a bowl of soup heavily seasoned with garlic and sent it up to the sickroom. When Susanna did not die, each of the parties claimed, in public or private, to have saved her. When she healed and the detritus of the accident became apparent, all claims faded into silence.

The brother who had wielded the sword started taking too much wine with meals. The other began talking increasingly of God and His will. For her part, Susanna studied her face in a small gilded mirror and pushed at the scar's edges for hours, hoping that enough pressure and patience might force its disappearance. She prayed to the saints to remove it, and spent weeks examining her soul to learn what weaknesses she possessed to make her unfit for their mercy. Everyone knew that suffering was God's punishment upon man and must be accepted. But what crime had she committed to warrant such a punishment? Eventually the gaping red lips of the wound grew paler and closer, but never did they meet. Between them lay the width of several straws; and around them, the frozen agitation of flesh that drew all eyes to it and, protectively, her own hands.

'Do not touch it,' her mother would say, 'you only make things worse.' But how could she stop? The face was no longer hers; it was a stranger's, affixed to her like a mask. No longer could she simply follow her desires to run, play, and dress as she liked; that span of several inches, half the length of her index finger, from tip to knuckle, had to be consulted, placated, before any public action could be undertaken. Sometimes she felt like Ludis, the Circassian woman who worked in the kitchens and who told of one day being a princess of her people, and the next a captive of pirates, with a chain around her ankles.

'I shall cover it,' Susanna's mother had said, going to her chests of lotions and creams and unguents and bleaches, which all Venetian women stocked to the degree their wealth and position allowed. But whatever thickness of paint she applied only enhanced the distortion beneath it.

'Great God,' Susanna's father had said, 'will the marriage contract be honoured?'

That contract had been written when Susanna was six and the groom five. He was a pretty boy; she had a miniature of him. In her child's notion, getting married would be like what happened at the Ascension Day ceremony. The Canal before the Bardi house would be strewn with flowers, the groom would throw a gold ring into the water, and they would go together in a golden boat, not to the Lido, as the Doge did, but to a great house in Mantua. She did not know – and if she had, she would not have worried – that the contract contained a proviso: She must develop soundly, without blemish.

When the groom's family heard of the accident, his

father and an elder brother came from Mantua to see her. Susanna's mother dressed her in red, fur-trimmed velvet with a train. 'No veil,' she sighed, and fastened pearls in the darkness of Susanna's hair, like stars. Susanna was led into a room where food and wine were laid out sumptuously and told to walk three or four times around the large, carved table. Her father had warned her that if she put her hands up to touch the scar, he would punish her afterwards. So she had pushed them into the folds of her dress, where they left damp, shiny tracks in the velvet, like small animals. Summoning the memory of how she had felt before the accident – of having something steady and solid at the base of her life and her body – she had lifted her head high and walked: once, twice, aware that the two Mantuans, seated at the table's head and foot, were studying her with narrowed eyes. On the third round, she saw that the father had a large wart to one side of his nose; she struggled not to look at it. After the fourth time around, and a shake of the Mantuan heads, she was led out. That night her mother came to her room, weeping; the Mantuans had demanded to cancel the contract.

Susanna had lain beneath her silk coverlet, unable to move, feeling something drain from her that she doubted could be replaced. Only later, with the perspective of distance and adulthood, did she realize what it was – courage. At the time she knew only that she had failed in the sole important task assigned a daughter: to bind her family to another family of wealth and power.

Influential as the Bardi were, with their membership of the Signoria, their house built of Istrian stone, their windows covered with costly panes of glass, they could not permit a rejection by one of the great houses of Mantua. Susanna's father undertook further, delicate negotiations and emerged to announce that the Mantuans would honour the contract, provided that the name of Susanna's younger sister Barbara be substituted for her own. Barbara had clear skin and delicate lips, and her hair was by nature *filo d'oro*, the gold colour that all Venetian women desired but many could achieve only by artifice. At the wedding Barbara, at fourteen, was beautiful in her crown of pale gold hair. The groom's was gold, too, framing a face with broad cheekbones and brown eyes, but Susanna's was as dark as ever, for she refused to bleach it. To what purpose?

'Wear a veil,' her mother said. 'Veils are as common in Venice as seagulls.' It was true. Young women saw the world from behind white veils; wives and widows from long black ones. But a veil was only temporary, Susanna had thought; sooner or later one had to lift it. And then what?

'By God,' her father said, 'she may as well be in a convent.' The daughters of many families were sent into convents as a matter of course, when they were very young, to avoid paying dowries for them. The Bardi preferred to marry their daughters into other great houses, but if Susanna was unmarriageable . . . Her mother had pleaded: 'Antonio, you know what happens inside convents. Let the poor girl stay here with us. With me.' Grumbling, distracted by bad weather that was imperilling several of his galleys, Antonio Bardi had acquiesced.

Occasionally, stubbornly, he would insist that she be 'shown' to a potential groom, like a piece of cloth or glass in one of the shops on the Rialto. But cloth or glass did not writhe with shame when it was declined, nor did all Venice know the story of its failure to be purchased.

As Susanna grew, her breasts swelled and ripened but her walk became careful, as if she carried within her something made of glass. Her spirit shrank farther behind the scar each year, both losing and finding itself in the pages of books: Horace and Virgil, the sonnets of Pietro Bembo, comedies by Plautus and Terence. If she laughed or cried, it was over her books, in private. Rarely did the world see her, happy or sad. Even at Carnevale, when the world was masked and she could have gone about unnoticed, she preferred to stay home. She seldom spoke to anyone but her mother. Sometimes whole days passed in silence.

Suddenly, when Susanna was twelve, her father announced that God had sent a miracle: Ludovico Rossi, merchant of wool and silk, was willing to sign a marriage contract. He was a short man, plump, though not distressingly so, whose first wife had died in childbirth and his second of the plague. He looked closely at Susanna's face, his own revealing nothing, squeezed her arm, and said, 'The little one will suit very well.'

'I cannot marry him,' Susanna told her father, who

looked at her long, hard and cold, and said simply, 'You will.'

Three times she had begged her father to postpone the marriage. He agreed, reluctantly: 'So that you may prepare yourself to become more accepting of the future God has provided.' But his patience, and Rossi's, lasted only so long.

Once more Susanna heard a heavy tread in the hall. This time it slowed outside her bedchamber. Her fingers ran to the scar.

If only she had the courage to kill Ludovico, to hide a knife in one of her chests, push his body into the antechamber that held her private close-stool, and run . . . But in the first week of the marriage, after fully initiating her into the rituals of his pleasures, he had said, 'I know you have married me without desire, Signora. I know what you think of me. Be warned. In your preference for life without me, if you should try to hasten that goal – by seasoning my food with poison, for example – you would succeed only in hastening your own end. In any case,' he had added, 'the slaves taste everything before I eat it.'

Ludovico entered the room, carrying a small bronze oil lamp. He held it above her, studying her, nothing moving but his lips, which smiled. 'Now then, Signora,' he said, 'take your hands from your face.'

The confines of fear closed around her, and she obeyed. Women always obeyed; she had first had the thought when she was a small girl, before it was properly a thought and was only the sense of a common element in the behaviour of her mother and sister and aunts and the nuns and of all who wore long skirts. Except courtesans and priests, who seemed to move to their own laws.

Ludovico held the light closer. She saw the grey hairs sprouting from his nostrils and caught the wind of his breath, like rotten onions. He put down the lamp and began stroking the scar. At first she had been unable to believe that he was not repelled by her disfigurement. Far from it. He was aroused by it, and by what it made her feel.

She could not look at him; her eyes went to the painting of the Madonna on the opposite wall, her nostrils sought the scent of the pastilles heating on the perfume burner. Sometimes Ludovico wanted to penetrate her; tonight his desire was to lift his nightshirt and thrust himself at her mouth. Fellatio. What if this was a crime? she thought wildly; if she posted an accusation against herself in one of the stone lions' mouths, she would be taken to prison . . . If only she had the courage to bite down, bite it off and leave him to drown in the blood that would come in gouts . . . Silently she begged the Madonna to forgive her thoughts.

By the time he heaved himself away, the candles had burned only the length of a thumbnail. The brevity of it was the only mercy.

As soon as the door closed behind him, she rose from the bed and went to the enamelled silver basin and ewer on a small carved table. She rinsed her mouth many times, swirling the scented water inside her cheeks. If only she could push back all the clocks and be again that nine-year-old 'little Venetian beauty' to whom life, and the Most Serene Republic, held out every promise. If only she had the courage to run away.

There was one alternative to the convent and brothel: to seek a woman who prepared magics, or an alchemist; to purchase a powder and drop it into a glass of wine; to wait for the stab in throat and heart, to battle for breath and finally lose . . . Would that be the hardest of choices, or the easiest?

She crawled back into the bed, wrapped her arms around her as if to hold herself together, and struggled to make her mind a heavy broom that swept away not only all physical awareness but also the bitter knowledge that in the city admired by the world for its beauty, she was desired for her blemish.

Hours later she awoke, heart pounding. She had been dreaming that she had a child, a daughter, fathered by Ludovico. 'Go, go,' the baby told her, 'go before he conceives me on your body . . .'

She rose, went to her wardrobe and took a fine black wool dress and a fur-trimmed jacket, for the air was often cool now, and a black veil. Into a *borsetta* she put two silk handkerchiefs, a pearl choker, and a ruby and gold brooch that was a marriage gift from Ludovico. She opened her door, listened intently to the quiet, went soundlessly down the stairs, and slipped into the street.

CHAPTER TWO

Of Mirth

To the man who was clutching his jaw in pain, his servant said solicitously, 'Master dear, I have a cure for you. Take an apple in your mouth and put your head in the oven. Before the apple is cooked, your toothache will be gone!'

The October sun shone a thousand times over, in the sky of the lagoon and on every golden surface of the Piazza San Marco, where crowds milled among temptations and distractions that fought for their attention like mongrel dogs over a bone.

Beggars revealed their sores, cripples held out their ruined limbs, a young man with a lute sang sweetly. Vendors, the spaces for their stalls marked out by white lines on the stones, touted their wares. Gold and silver flashed from the money-changers' tables. At the vegetable and fruit stalls, onions and peppers rose in tiers of gleaming yellow and green; grapes formed purple and glossy pyramids, and plums lay beside them, their velvet jackets tight with juice. One cart was heaped with oysters, and around a burly man's shoulders hung flat wicker baskets of fish so fresh that the sea still glittered on their scales. At the butchers', the carcasses were pearl-white still lives, except for a single motion: the slow dripping of red. Sometimes the crowd itself provided the temptation and distraction, for the breasts of many women puffed into moons above the laces of their bodices, and courtesans paraded freely, on heels so high that attendants had to trot beside them to help them walk.

The day before, the crowd had been drawn to one end of the Piazza, where a monk had been burned at the stake for begetting children by at least a dozen nuns. But the remains of the fire and its victim had been cleared away; in their place stood a raised platform before which people clustered to watch a troupe of travelling players. In bright costumes, some of them wearing masks, they portrayed characters that were known throughout Italy: a Merchant, a Captain, a Maidservant; young Lovers; and *Zanni*, or Clowns. The characters could be featured in many scenarios, and played better by some actors than by others, but their names and basic natures were always the same.

In the Piazza, while the clown called Pedrolino played his guitar, two acrobats vaulted on and off the platform with graceful leaps and somersaults. Bows, cheers, applause. Next, out swaggered a stocky man brandishing a long knife. 'The Captain!' cried the crowd, anticipating his stock in trade: lengthy braggadocio. He did not disappoint, thundering about his feats of swordsmanship – no man in Italy, or any other country, or the world, was as adept as he. Suddenly from his jacket appeared a bottle of medicinal oil. 'Never will your money buy greater worth!' he cried. 'No finer oil than this exists on earth!' A good deal more along the same lines. Then, flourishes of one arm, which he held out straight. Took the knife in the opposite hand and gashed himself a dozen times. Blood welled from the arm. Great flourishes from the other arm, with which he applied a cloth soaked in the oil. The flow of blood ceased. The mouths of the crowd hung slack before their hands started applauding this miracle, and as the Captain boasted and harangued, many dug into their purses.

Watching from behind the scenes, Teresa Laurano carefully studied the hands that reached up to buy, especially the men's. It was she who made the miracle oil, as well as the other elixirs and potions the troupe sold, using recipes taught to her by her mother. She also did acrobatics and played the small part of the Maid when necessary, but her real skill was with the preparations. Usually they sold well, but they were not the sole reason for Teresa's presence. The Captain, who also headed the troupe, had been a friend of her mother's and had promised to look after Teresa and keep her in the company. 'But,' her mother had said, 'one can never be certain people will keep their promises. Especially men. So you must see that you become a valuable member of the troupe.' Teresa had followed her mother's advice as carefully as she had her recipes.

The players began to enact a story, their third of the day. There were scenes between the two Lovers, blonde and beautiful, who wore no masks and spoke in an elegant Tuscan dialect, but much of the action involved the characters who were always masked: the doddering Doctor, spouting mock-Latin; the Pantalone, a rich old merchant in a long black gown and red breeches, who in this story yearned after the female Lover; and the two servant-clowns, Pedrolino and Arlecchino. The troupe had been in Venice only for a few days, but already, thought Teresa, it was obvious, just as in the villages where they played on the road, that the crowd's favourite was Arlecchino. Wearing jacket and tights with coloured patches sewn everywhere, he made people laugh before he said a word by walking in an odd, roostery strut that brought grins leaping to people's faces as if he were pulling them out on strings. When Pantalone entered, a cloth tied around his jaw and one hand held to it, Arlecchino swung his slap-stick, the *batte*, and offered medical advice:

> 'Hold your head in the Canal at high water, Master, and when the tide recedes, your toothache will be gone.'

The crowd roared, Pantalone groaned, Arlecchino strutted. Although his legs moved swiftly, they barely bent – 'I walk like a cock in a hurry,' he was fond of saying – and every now and again his head would sink inches down into his shoulders and then bob up comically, like an apple in a pail of water. He halted beside Pantalone and proffered more advice:

> 'Put a burr beneath the saddle of your horse and

ride him to Mantua. By the time you arrive, your toothache will be gone.'

One of the fruit vendors, who had been craning to watch, laughed so hard that he dislodged a pile of his apples; their gold and red globes rolled on the stones, among the lines that divided the stalls, like balls in a game of chance. Several were picked up and stuffed into sleeves. 'Hey!' he shouted at a boy, who thumbed his nose and ran, and at a veiled woman in a black dress who shrank into the crowd. The fruit vendor was ready to chase her, but Arlecchino distracted him:

'Master, here is a guaranteed cure. Stick your head into a hive of bees. By the time you take it out . . .'

'Your toothache will be gone!' shouted the crowd, including the fruit vendor.

Waiting for the next scene, in which she would chase Arlecchino around and across the stage, Teresa peered again at the hands of the crowd. Especially of the men. She did it everywhere the troupe went, but she did not truly expect it to be of use except in Venice, where they had not been for years. Not since her mother's death had driven them out. Now, she thought, surely now God would answer her prayers and let her fulfil the vow she had sworn every day since her mother died, trudging beside the players' cart as it rolled through the countryside, costumes and properties swaying, pots and pans rattling, the wheels creaking a threnody. She had whispered it to the sheep that sometimes stood watching them pass, eyes unblinking in the sad triangles of their faces: 'I shall learn why she died and who was the man that killed her.'

'Let's go!' hissed Arlecchino, and Teresa realized she had been lost in her thoughts and the scene was upon her. She swung her red hair, shook the skirt of her red and black dress, and ran on to the stage. She leaped on to a table, skirt high, taunting Arlecchino. He tried to leap up after her, but one leg refused to leave the floor. He tugged at it furiously, the bushy eyebrows on his leather mask waggling in frustration; finally the leg came free. But Teresa leaped over his head and sent him sprawling. Whistles and roars from the audience. She ran to the other side of the platform, thumbing her nose at him, and he, in eagerness, tripped over his own foot and went sprawling . . .

They had done it a hundred times, never the same – yet never completely different, the pace always controlled by Arlecchino, even though she appeared to be leading him. Sometimes he would mope and moan by the edge of the stage, so that she almost had to coax him to come after her. Sometimes he would be so zanily aggressive that she could barely keep her breath as they raced around the platform. To be the same yet different, that was the point, for they, the troupe, played *commèdia dell'improvviso*, working from a set subject or scenario but each time improvising most of what they said and did.

* * *

> Race across the platform, taunting Arlecchino, who comes after, swinging his wooden *batte* and muttering, 'I shall stop her, I shall make her answer me.' Let him get close then leap from the floor on to the table, skirt high, while he stops, surprise carved in every skinny line of his frame. Lift the skirt, vault from the table, thumb the nose at him, and race off. And in that moment before returning to the stage – that moment when Arlecchino is left alone, woebegone, his fingers flapping like ten sticks and the crowd roaring with laughter – suddenly take a deep breath and murmur, 'I shall find the man and make him pay.' And the thought is such a spur, sends her back on to the stage with so much energy, that Arlecchino cocks his head in surprise and does something quite new: hops after her like a great rabbit.

The mouths of the crowd widened; the bells of San Marco seemed to be pealing laughter.

After the performance the company packed up the properties and stored everything in the space allotted to them. Bruno, the leader of the troupe, who also played the Captain, counted the coins, nodded with satisfaction, and declared they would try to stay in Venice at least two weeks – longer if they could find a wealthy sponsor – provided the authorities left them alone and did not rescind their permission to play. As all mountebanks and players learned early in their lives, authorities bent the laws to whatever shape suited them, and would expel people for lewdness of performance or the practice of 'sorcery' with their potions – or for any other reason.

The sun cast long shadows, and the angel on top of the Campanile no longer dazzled but was softly luminous. Shutters closed over the shops at the tower's base, the vendors wheeled away their carts and stalls, and the crowds headed home or to supper, the international Babel of their languages floating behind them, merging with the lapping of water against the Molo. The company went off, along the sidestreets, across bridges and down alleys to have supper at their inn, where they sat around a table drinking wine and eating sausage and fowl and cheese, and picking over the details of the day's performance until every chicken bone of it was clean.

'You were a beat late on that entrance.'

'When I come to you, Pedrolino, move so close that our noses touch. The laugh should get bigger.'

'Isabella, you were splendid in the letter scene.'

'Bruno, why wait so long to pick up the ladder?'

The camaraderie at the table did not come from the free-flowing wine; it was a bond forged in performance between each pair of them and among all of them, so that each always knew what the others were going to do. Not literally, because of their continual improvisation, but each knew *how* the others would improvise. The rhythm of the sideways, shuffling gait Il Dottore used while meaningless Latin trailed from his lips; the way Pantalone would spread his arms wide, bend his right foot, and stretch the left behind him; the way Pedrolino always lifted and shook his hands before playing his guitar; the middle finger Isabella laid against her lips before she began a scene with her male counterpart . . . these things were known without needing words, as the moods of the sun and seasons were known: as matters underlying and governing one's life.

There were eleven of them. They had been pulled together into a troupe by Bruno and his wife Isabella, who was the female Lover. Bruno had known some of them for years, like Arlecchino, whereas Giulio and his wife had joined them only fifteen months before, when Bruno had seen Giulio working with some mountebanks from the South. Soon afterwards Bruno had announced they were now a company and would be known as 'I Favolosi', after the new fashion of choosing a symbolic name.

'The Fabulous Ones?' said Luca, who played the male Lover. 'And if we are not fabulous?'

'Then,' said Arlecchino, drawing a bony finger across his neck, 'we become "The Headless Ones".'

Teresa had been with them for six years, since she was eleven. 'Isabella and Bruno will look after you,' her mother had said. 'Bruno promised me. They will teach you things – to be an acrobat, to spin eggs on a stick, perhaps even to play in scenes.'

'I don't want them to teach me!' Teresa had cried, her words ricocheting in the black, stinking cell. 'I want to learn from you, only you!'

'Quiet, my little darling, quiet now. If my Teresa is

not strong, how can I be strong?'

Two weeks later Teresa had been loaded into the cart along with Isabella and Bruno's possessions, and nothing of her own – nothing of the pretty life she had had with her mother. '*Why* did she have to die?' she asked them, over and over. They had shrugged and looked away; the cart had rolled from the city and into the north of Italy. Soon afterwards Venice had issued a ban against all players and mountebanks, which it had lifted only in recent years.

Sometimes, from the wagon, they sang and clowned and did acrobatics as a prelude to selling their preparations or some printed love songs. 'Signori,' Arlecchino would say, 'one bottle of this wondrous elixir will double the size of your – (twirling the bushy eyebrows on his mask) – potency.' The Captain would chime in: 'Signorine, lovelies, one bottle will make your charms irresistible and draw the eye, the hand, and the lips to your breasts.' Gradually they began performing scenarios as well, especially in the larger towns, taking the plots from other companies or from books Isabella and Bruno had picked up.

For a time, when Teresa began to mature and her breasts to take a shape that invited a man's hand, Isabella had not believed she would be content to play the small role of the *servetta* and do her acrobatics and mix her preparations. 'You will be a beauty,' Isabella had said, her green-grape eyes wide in the perfect oval of her face, her voice a thread of honey. 'Soon you will want to play a Lover.'

'I do not want to be a beauty,' Teresa told her.

'You will have no choice,' Isabella said dryly. 'God has decreed that you will look like your mother.'

Teresa had been silent. Why say things Isabella would not believe? Why explain that she had another purpose to her life, and no wish to be admired by all the men in their audiences? So she had merely shrugged and gone on mixing potions and binding up her red hair in a cap or scarf when she went on stage.

It must be tiring to be a beauty, Teresa thought: always feeling the intrusive pressure of eyes upon one's face, always coaxing and teasing and posing, to make sure the fact of one's beauty never left people's minds. Even now Isabella was giving sidelong glances around the table at all the men. Why could she not leave Arlecchino in peace to eat his chicken? And why must he behave as he always did with her – smiling, his long thin face quite foolish with adoration?

'Come, my friend,' Teresa said to him sharply. 'The light is going, and you promised to walk with me tonight.'

Arlecchino lifted his sharp chin, scratched it, and nodded. 'The little redhead has spoken,' he said; he had called her that from the time he first saw her. He licked his fingers, as if each were a stick of sugar, picked a last leg of chicken from his plate, pantomimed lighting it like a torch, raised it above his head, and said, '*Avanti!*'

Bruno called, 'Remember, tomorrow we play *The Desperate Doctor*.'

In the gold and purple light that sank to the lagoon and painted it, they went to a nearby taverna where

Teresa walked among the tables, looking at hands lifting glasses, then wandered into San Zulian. Arlecchino chattered about the next day's scenario, the growing chill of the nights, the light of the cats' eyes in an alley. Teresa had never known him to want for words; everything on God's earth brought a thought to his mind. When the two of them walked behind the players' wagon, he had something to say, usually silly or cheerful, about every sight on the road. 'That cow has a face as long as a bishop's,' he would say. 'See those eyes? They tell us to obey or go to Hell.' 'They just look stupid to me,' Teresa would say. 'Stupid and rather sad.' If a cold wind came roaring at them, Arlecchino would shout, 'Hey, go back where you belong! Freeze the clouds, not the skins of decent players!' and stand up and shadowbox with it, teetering and yelling until she did indeed have to laugh. The two of them were an odd pair, Teresa thought as they stepped into the church where four faceless people in black prayed before the red-draped altar.

'It's nearly dark now,' Arlecchino said. 'Have you not had enough for the night, my serious little redhead?'

'Yes,' Teresa said. 'Very well.'

But she would never have enough, not until she succeeded. *I shall find the man who killed her*, she thought, vowing it again to the stones of Venice, with a feeling that was not happiness but something deeper: her soul hewing fast to its purpose, like a ship to its course.

'Will you never tell me what or whom it is you search for?' Arlecchino asked.

'Probably not,' Teresa said, smiling at the grimace he made. Although if she were ever to tell anyone, it would probably be Arlecchino.

The terrazzo floor was worked in heraldic designs, a majestic sideboard displayed pieces of silver and Murano glass, the heavy oak table had legs carved into caryatids, and set upon its cloth were intricate decorations made of sugar: merchant galleys in full sail. Antonio Bardi and his wife were dining with two of their sons, two other wealthy merchants, all accompanied by their wives, and a bishop who was a frequent guest. The women wore silks in dark, brilliant colours and many jewels. Liveried servants moved in and out with a stream of bowls and platters: wild rabbit, geese, dried fish, chickpeas, beans, fruit. Within the odours of meat and fish and their sauces hovered that omnipresence of spices – cinnamon, cloves, saffron, vanilla – underlying the treasures of the table just as they formed the foundation for the wealth of the house and the basis of much of the dinner conversation: the new tax laws handed down by the Senate which involved itself in every aspect of Venetian commerce, and the finances of the association to which all at the table belonged in order to share the huge expenses of loading cargo and fitting out and manning ships.

The bishop, who would soon leave Venice for a period of service in Rome, speared a forkful of rabbit.

Although some of his fellow churchmen still regarded the fork as an invention and tool of the Devil, Andrea Palma welcomed the ability to manage one's food with dexterity and cleanliness and believed that God must do so as well. He allowed the aroma of the sauce on the rabbit – honey, oil, garlic, and cinnamon – to reach his nose, and said to his hostess, 'Signora, which do you believe is more important to this dish, the rabbit or the sauce?'

Signora Bardi reflected. 'I believe I must choose the rabbit.'

'Indeed?' said the bishop. 'I would name the sauce.'

'I should like to know why.' Signora Bardi smiled and clapped her hands for attention. The diners turned to listen, for the bishop was known for his discourses.

'Consider,' he said. 'A dish may consist largely of fowl or game, like this rabbit, yet which of us would desire it without a sauce? And what would the sauce be without spices to establish its character? Therefore, are the spices not the chief ingredients, despite being present in relatively insignificant amounts?'

The bishop's gaze moved around the table. The men seated there were part of the hierarchy of powerful families which ruled Venice and – defying Rome's disapproval – took many religious matters into their own hands, including the election of their own bishops. 'I wonder,' Andrea Palma said, 'whether we appreciate the similarity between the role of spices in the kitchens of Venice and that of religion in her political life? Venice may declare that her secular authority overmasters Rome's, but who would regard her as civilized – who would obey her laws – were it not for the tempering influence of the church? Just as the dinners of Venice require spices to achieve their proper character, so does her political life require the church. In politics, as at the table, that ingredient which is the most critical is not necessarily most evident to the eye.'

As the piece of rabbit disappeared from the bishop's fork into his mouth, murmurs of appreciation rose around the table. Despite the independence that made Venice quarrel repeatedly with the Pope, a streak of piety underlay everything in the Serene Republic: her government, her commerce, her material splendours. The diners' coffers of silver ducats and gold *zecchini* made substantial contributions each year to Bishop Palma's projects.

'It is good to know,' said the Bardi son who was devout, 'that God is on our side.'

The bishop lifted his glass of dark Grecian wine, drank, and said in the resonant voice that had helped to elevate him in church councils, 'God is always on the side of those who honour Him.'

'When you are in Rome, Your Excellency,' said Antonio Bardi, 'we shall miss your company, and our ships will miss your blessing.'

'My associate's good offices are yours to command.'

'Yes,' said Signora Bardi, 'but your associate cannot provide as good company at dinner as you.'

The bishop smiled, imagining Fra Filippo, his faithful servant – and of course the Lord's as well – at the dinner table. Unfailingly respectful, Filippo would nonetheless feel an ascetic's disapproval in the presence of plenty. He had not even fully accepted the use of the fork.

'Signori,' said the bishop, 'for whatever length of time the Holy Father keeps me in Rome, I shall pray for the safety and prosperity of your ships.'

'We lost another galley last month,' said one of the guests, 'and we are now certain that it was Turks, not Spaniards, who sank it.'

As if a lighted taper had been tossed into a barrel of oil, talk exploded. Which brand of pirates was to be the more detested – Spaniards, Slavs, or Turks? Were they financed by the Archduke of Austria and the King of Spain?

'Pirates,' snarled Antonio Bardi into a luxuriant beard. 'May they all roast in Hell.'

Signora Bardi cast a worried glance at the bishop – as if, he thought, he might be offended by her husband's cursing. He? He who – in the church's interests – was dining by the light of bronze oil lamps in the shape of sporting satyrs? He smiled reassuringly at her, thinking there could be great beauty in an older woman, especially one who knew how to keep her hands soft and to apply colour to her mouth and cheeks so that it lay there artlessly. A woman, in her way, could have skills like Tiziano's or Tintoretto's, except that her canvas was small and soft, and could not survive her. The bishop contemplated his thought with a pleasure that many of his fellow churchmen would condemn as vanity, but he believed that cleverness of mind was a blessing from God, meant to be cultivated so it could be used in His service.

'Never mind sending pirates to Hell,' said another of the dinner guests. 'Send them to the Portuguese!'

The table, including the bishop, laughed. Decades earlier, the Portuguese had discovered a route round the tip of Africa that let them go directly to the suppliers of spices and thereby avoid the tariffs and other high costs the Venetians had to pay to Egyptian intermediaries. The news had spawned panic on the Rialto and badly affected the Venetian markets in England and France. The Venetian traders had managed to recover and prosper again. But the arrogance of invincibility had never fully returned.

Signora Bardi lifted an arm and, her sleeve swaying with its cargo of pearls and other jewels, beckoned servants to bring the bowls of fruit that would soothe palates after the heat of spices and prepare them for the next course.

Suddenly figs and pears and plums went thudding to the floor; the men carrying them were pushed aside by a plump, red-faced figure who might have been ridiculous if his agitation had not been so great.

'Bardi! Is your daughter here?' cried Ludovico Rossi. 'I demand the truth. You cannot hide her from me!'

One of the servants murmured apologetically to his master, 'Signor Rossi insisted on coming in and speaking to you at once.'

Antonio Bardi rose. 'Ludovico, what is the reason for this behaviour?'

'Do not mock me. Where is your daughter? Is she here? I know she is.' Rossi's stocky body struggled in the grip of his feelings like a fish in a net. His shoulders twisted in his velvet jacket, his neck fought the edging of his shirt, his hands clutched at the air.

Antonio said, 'It is for a husband to know the whereabouts of his wife.'

'It is for a wife to be where her husband expects! In his home! Do you imagine I shall allow your daughter to make a fool of me?'

'Do you think I shall allow you to behave in a manner that insults my family and my guests?'

Signora Bardi said, 'Ludovico, tell us what has happened at once, please.'

Her cool voice seemed to madden Rossi even more. 'She ran away! Three nights ago, like a slave creeping out. I learned it in the morning. I have waited three days for her to recall her duties and return, but she has not.'

Signora Bardi rocked as if someone had shoved her from behind, and raised her handkerchief to her lips. The guests shifted on their ornate chairs, and the servants' eyes slid from one speaker to another.

'Bring her to me now. At once!' Rossi shook off a spray of perspiration and, as if that act freed him to state his worst fear, cried, 'I shall be the butt of all jokes in Venice – abandoned by a wife with the Devil's own face!'

Antonio Bardi's brows met in one black bar. 'Susanna is not here. I would not permit her to return to us. It is a husband's charge to see that his wife does not leave their home.'

'You dare reproach me when it is your daughter

who delayed the marriage for years and now runs from her obligations?'

'If she has run, her brothers and I will deal with her. But I do not know that she has done so.'

'Signori, please.' The bishop held up a hand to prevent the two from advancing on each other. 'Signor Rossi, if your father-in-law gives his word that his daughter is not here, surely that ends the matter? Antonio, my good friend, why would a husband announce that his wife has run away if she has not done so?'

The tension between the two men slackened. The bishop felt it as a rope being transferred to his hands, which could fashion it into a harness. He had learned early that to be a conciliator of men was to acquire power from both sides, which could then be used to achieve a good neither was capable of alone. 'Is it not likely,' he said, 'that Susanna has gone to a convent?'

'Your Excellency,' began Rossi. He ran heavily to the bishop and knelt at his feet. 'You were at my marriage. You gave it your blessing. If my wife is in a convent, you can restore her to me, can you not?'

Bardi's eyes were also on the bishop. 'She cannot be allowed to hide in a convent. She must honour her vows, and our commitment. I too ask you to find her and return her to her rightful place.'

For a moment the bishop was silent, feeling the power of the rope. 'If Susanna is in any convent in Venice, then it is my duty to find her and restore her to her rightful place.'

'You will not find me ungrateful,' Bardi said.

'Nor I,' echoed Rossi.

The bishop bowed his head for a moment. 'I shall do everything in my power to serve both God and my friends.'

CHAPTER THREE
Arlecchino

I am clever – but also a fool.

Is that not why you love me? You who crowd into the squares wherein we set our stage, or run to greet us as we approach your towns, or hire us to perform in your palazzi*. Poor and rich alike, you love to laugh at the foolish and admire the clever. And when they combine in one person . . . in one tight-fitting costume, on which the squares and diamonds and ovals of colour are sewn as randomly as fate . . .* Che bel spettàcolo!

Twirling the wooden batte *as if it were alive, I am the most comical of the comic servants – whose cleverness is ever at his master's service; whose foolishness keeps him from seeing the consequences of an action even as they ensnare him . . .*

'Good night, little redhead,' he said.

'You are not coming in?'

'Not just yet.'

In the wavering light of the oil lamp above the door of the inn where the players stayed, four or five to a room but not many *soldi* out of their pockets, Teresa peered up at him. 'You will not do anything foolish?'

His eyes made mock astonishment. 'What a thing to say to Arlecchino!'

'I am saying it to you, Paolo, not to the mask.'

'Yes, yes,' he said, patting her hand. 'But remember that you are the little redhead, not the little mother.'

Teresa bit her lip. 'Where are you going so late?'

'I do not ask what you search for when I take you on your night-walks, so you must not question me, either.'

'But you do ask me,' she said.

He cocked his head. 'Ah, but do you answer?'

'You are impossible,' she said in good-natured exasperation.

'What a nice compliment!' he said. 'And now, I am off.'

She bade him good night and went inside.

What a serious, secret little person, he thought. He had loved her dearly ever since he had first climbed aboard Bruno and Isabella's wagon and seen a girl with sad eyes and hair as bright as fire leaping on a hearth. To be sure, he loved the whole company, even when he was upset with them for some reason, but perhaps he loved Teresa most.

And one other.

He gave a little skip, to remind himself he was a fool, and walked on along the *calli*. The night was chill and damp, but a melon of a moon hung over the city. In the quiet, a burst of laughter sailed from a window and seemed to land at his feet. He bowed deeply, as if he had earned it, and then smiled at himself. He loved laughter: the ripe-fruit sound of it; the sight of it, splitting cheeks, shaking breasts and bellies. What else could reduce men to helplessness without harming them? In the grip of laughter, he often thought, when the throat opened wide, the path to the soul was laid bare. If God had not made men able to laugh, would they not be dumb animals? And would God not then be imperfect? O impious Arlecchino, he chided himself. One of his siblings used to tell him how God would punish him if ever he sinned: 'The devils will build a fire hotter than any you have ever felt and will push you into it with their forks, and you will scream through all eternity.' Was that the brother later sent to be a priest or the sister despatched to a convent? In memory the faces of all his siblings, eleven of them, had blurred into a common pool of eyes and noses: a single face that mocked his own by recasting his features into quite ordinary lines.

He looked up at the full-bellied moon, along the roofs it silvered, and down at the Grand Canal, where its reflection rode at a dozen anchors. As he walked, water whispered at his heels. It was good to be in Venice again, he thought. The troupe had fled from it when Teresa's mother died and had avoided it for years afterwards, but they had had to return to it, for there was so much wealth in Venice. So much of everything: beauty and grandeur . . . mystery . . . courtesans and prostitutes . . .

He frowned and went on, thinking that when they played the next day's scenario he would have several scenes with Isabella, especially one in which they abused Pantalone for being a thief. He began plotting what lines he might throw her for a start, for she was a wonder at improvising. They were all good; it was their craft. But there was a special pleasure in scenes with her, in watching, seeing, and feeling her react to what he did, as he reacted to her . . . in knowing that if he sent a line or grimace or motion, she had to absorb it with her body.

Paolo halted, realizing which way his thoughts were leading. The way of the clown. Only a clown would allow himself to be roused by dreams of the body of a woman he could never touch, except in a scene. Yet he was a man, was he not? With the face and skill of a clown but the parts of a man, which could sometimes ache with the need to be plunged into the warmth of a woman . . . He shook himself and walked on resolutely, reminding himself of what he was, and had always been: a creature of blades and brushes. Thin as a knife, and too tall, so that no matter how much he ate, the food never stayed to pad his bones. Nose and chin fighting to see which would be sharper, thick lips keeping an uneasy peace between them. Hair like a black broom on top of it all. His brothers and sisters had laughed at such a creature, and so had the other farmers in the fields in the Veneto where, with his siblings, he went to work as soon as he could lift the tools. One day, when they were all resting and eating beneath a tree, watching the wind carve golden patterns in the grain, he had stood up, stretched elaborately, and begun strutting about, pushing out his chin, flapping his elbows like wings and making odd noises, half-belch, half-crow. Everyone, even his father and brothers, had been silent. His heart had beat so high in his throat that he feared it would leap out, but he had continued prancing and squawking, for what could he do but go on and on, until the weight of the silence crushed him beneath it like a shield?

Then he had heard a gurgle of high-pitched laughter from one of his brothers; others joined, and finally the older men began to laugh, too, booming sounds that made him strut higher and crow like a cock greeting the dawn. From that day he had known that he could be the master of laughter, not its slave.

Everything had come to him naturally, as if it had been sleeping within him, waiting. The first time he decided that since people often laughed when someone fell down, he could fall down in a way that would make them laugh harder, his body had quickly learned what to do. He had practised on a Sunday afternoon, in a field, regarded blankly by three crows, and by the next day he was able to pretend to trip over his own feet so that even his mother shook with laughter and forgot for a moment her perpetual, mysterious sadness. And his hands! The long, thin fingers learned – on their own, it seemed – ways of sticking straight up and out, each separate from the others, like a row of puppets making gestures. His face, too, had slipped without effort into one grimace after another. It had been easy to make himself into a clown.

So easy that he soon forgot what had made him do so: the fear of being laughed at.

He had assumed he would spend his life in his village in the Veneto. Even if his parents had wanted him to follow the brother and sister who were sent off to serve God, in effect as offerings, he did not want to go. He wanted to live in a world where one was saved by laughter, not threatened with tales of pitchforks and eternal fires. When the players' wagon had rolled into the village, in his fifteenth year, God had seemed to bend down from above the altar in the church, tap him on the shoulder, and say, 'There, Paolo, my son, there is the way for you to go.' He had attended each performance, watching the clowning, listening to the pitches, memorizing each motion, breathing in the air that surrounded the players, which seemed charged not only with the smells of their costumes and props but with the energy and strangeness of their being. He had hung about before and afterwards, helping in every way he could devise: grooming their horses, washing their linens, fetching water, bringing them bread he coaxed from his mother's oven and fruit he took from the fields. When the players' cart creaked out of town, he had watched it for a moment. Then, with a great leap, he had gone racing and panting after it, to announce that he must go with them, God had ordered it, he would work for nothing, all he asked was to share their meals, not even all the meals, one a day would suffice. He had capered and pleaded in such a mad fashion that Isabella had laughed. 'Paolo Bertoldo,' she had said slowly, in her golden voice, which seemed to caress the sounds of his name, as if she were pouring honey on a peach, or baptizing him into a new life, from which he had never looked back with regret. He did not even know whether his parents still lived, or where or how his siblings had scattered. If he thought of them sometimes in the lonely togetherness of the night, when the players camped in a field or slept in a barn, it was to tell himself that now it was they who were his family, who suited him better anyway. He who was born a peasant had been reborn as Arlecchino, by dint of hard work and by the grace of Bruno and Isabella. Isabella who lent him books, whose hair curled on her neck like golden feathers when she bent her head, whose glances were as fresh in memory as if someone had painted her and hung the portrait in his mind. Not that she meant anything by the glances. She was the sun, shining her splendour on all, and the moon, bathing everyone in the radiance of her skill. Isabella could no more cease twisting a man's heart by looking at him than the heavenly bodies could cease their passage through the skies. He felt a swell of need for her, hopeless, burning. It could never be satisfied, only blotted out for a time, in a certain place, in a certain way.

Around Paolo were the sounds of water, slapping languorously and playfully against the buildings, sometimes sucking at their bases as if it would take them into its mouth stone by stone. He began to walk faster. Sometimes one could not fight one's body any longer.

He slid from a *calle* narrow enough to have been tailored for that body and headed to the Rialto, where he knew many of them were to be found: the women and men who offered their services to all comers. Venice was the whores' capital, nearly fifteen thousand of them by the last licence count. He had overheard a man in the Piazza crowds say so. It might be shameful to be driven to whores – his priest-brother and nun-sister would say so – but God knew that men by the legions were so driven. One could see them by day and more so at night, entering the grand houses where the elegant courtesans reigned over their wealthy admirers, and the *calli* where the whores, much less expensive and more ribald, displayed themselves. The whores did not laugh if they saw him approaching; they cared only – what comfort in the knowledge! – that he had money.

But if he was comforted, then why, during a night he once spent with one of them – who had had olive skin and black lines around her big eyes – why had cart-tracks of tears run down his cheeks, so the whore had nothing to do but look on, puzzled, stroking his hair because it was all she could think of to do? Why should he weep, when he was a man who had geared his life to laughter?

He did not know. Sometimes a man was a riddle to himself.

A gondola passed, black like all others since the decree that had forbidden them ostentatious decoration. The lantern glowing within its cabin shed rivulets of light, and laughter trailed behind it like a hand in the water. Paolo crossed a bridge and walked briskly towards the sector of the Rialto called the Casteletto. The streets were crowded and noisy. In the light of the many lanterns he saw women leaning from the brothel windows or standing at the doorways and along the walls. Their breasts rose from their dresses like plump, eyeless faces; their blonde hair was twisted up into little horns above their pale foreheads. Under black-rimmed lids, their glances rolled over him in small, inviting waves. He knew that if he simply stood, he would soon be approached. That was part of the pleasure; to do nothing, yet be sought.

A solitary, veiled figure caught his eye. Leaning against a wall, she held a black dress about her as if it were a curtain. Although she did not move, Paolo sensed that she was shivering, like a reflection in the water. He started to turn away but instead found himself walking towards her, impelled by the certainty that she lacked the strength to approach him, or anyone else.

'Are you alone, lady?'

She nodded.

'Are you waiting for anyone?'

She hesitated. 'No.'

If she were a prostitute, she would not allow the dialogue to languish. She said nothing.

'What is your name?' he asked.

A pause. 'Anonima.'

'Do you wish me to go away?'

'No,' she said quickly.

'Yet it does not seem that you wish me to stay.'

'Please . . . stay.'

'Very well.' He did not know why he said it, for he felt no desire for her, only curiosity.

'I shall do . . . whatever would please you.'

After a moment he said, 'Lift your veil, so I may see your face.'

'Why?' She put up her hands to the cloth. 'Why should the face matter to you? Are we not speaking of the needs of the body?'

'Lady,' he said softly, 'Anonima, you will not please many men by that manner of address.'

She did not reply. He made a small bow and started away, but before he had gone three steps, she said, 'Please . . .'

He turned. 'Yes?'

'I will show my face, if you insist. But . . . only afterwards.'

He could have sworn that she tried to shrink back, but her body was already pressed to the wall. 'How many men have you been with tonight?' he said.

'I cannot see how such knowledge could affect your pleasure.'

'Do you dispute with me?'

'No. No. I promise you that I have been with . . . with men.'

'I do not believe you are a prostitute.'

'Why else would I be standing here?'

'I do not know. I merely wonder.'

She shifted against the wall. 'You seek such a woman, and I wish to be one, if you will help me.'

'And if I do not?'

She shook her head. 'I must be.'

'I am sorry,' he said. 'I did not come here to initiate anyone into the life of the brothels.'

'But I know what to do! I know how to use the . . . mouth and . . .'

'I am sorry,' he repeated gently, and started to turn away again.

She clutched his arm and lifted her veil. Even in the dim light he saw the twisted scar track pulling at her right eye like an anchor.

For a moment they stared at each other. Finally she said, 'Now you can leave without regrets.'

'You should not be here,' he said.

'Because no man will have me?'

'I do not mean that. I mean that this is not the sort of place where you seem to belong.'

'Where am I to go, then?' she cried. 'I have no money. I had a brooch and a pearl choker, but two *bravi* stole them, and my jacket and purse as well. Even my handkerchiefs are gone. I must earn some money. I must! And I know what pleasures a man. I swear I know.'

He wanted to be angry with her, for destroying completely the mood in which he had come to those streets, but the anger would not catch fire, merely lay sputtering in his chest. He reached into his jacket and took out some coins.

'This is all I have,' he said. 'Take it.'

'I cannot take your money without . . . without . . .'

'I want nothing from you. I only wish to be of help.'

She began to weep.

'What is it?' He was irritated, yet unable to leave. 'What is wrong?'

'If no man will have me, how shall I live?'

'Why do you not seek the help of God?'

She shivered as if something colder than the wind were touching her. 'If I go to God, I shall never . . . I cannot. Please do not ask me.'

Paolo sighed. 'Very well. I can offer you a place to sleep for the night and some food. In the morning you will have the strength to go where you wish. A convent, perhaps.'

He expected her to refuse. The prospect relieved him, yet disappointed as well. But she wiped her eyes and came closer to him. 'You have a kind face.'

He could have laughed. Instead, he gave a comic strut-step and one of his funniest grimaces.

She did not smile. 'What is your name?' she said.

'Arlecchino, lady.' He bowed, bending straight to the ground, like a folding knife. When he stood erect, she lowered her veil and took his arm.

They went in silence through the alleys and across a small bridge, their feet wringing little sighs and protests from the wood. The scent of the water was strong: moon-sweet, sun-salty, the breath of all life in Venice. For the first time since Susanna had run from Ludovico's house, she was walking without fear. She felt astonishment at her situation and, at the same time, acceptance: that she was following this strange, tall, thin man, his face all bones and angles and fish-lips, with a sensation of trust. How did she know that when they crossed the bridge and plunged into the next alley, he would not beat her or tear off her dress, which was made of expensive wool, or reveal some other sinister intent? Because she knew, that was all.

And because, after three days, she had no choice.

When the thought of conceiving a child by Ludovico had propelled her from his house, she had walked for a while, gripped by the urgency of the dream. Then there had been a time of exhilaration over her escape, but it had drained away, replaced by the stony light of dawn, the clangour of bells, and the cold reality of her situation. She had actually considered returning to the house, but her legs had taken her instead to a church, where she shivered for hours beneath the stone gazes of dead patriarchs. Finally she forced herself to walk to the Rialto to try to sell her choker and brooch; if she had money, she could stay in a lodging house and plan what to do next. But on the Rialto, where she had been jostled and shoved as no one would dare do to a daughter of the Bardi, she had seen a spice merchant who often dined with her parents, and, veil palpitating with fear, she had run away. Without coins, she could only hide in churches or slink along the streets, clutching her *borsetta* tightly, moving from the shelter of one doorway to another. Hunger had driven her to the Piazza in the vague hope of bartering her brooch for food, but she had no idea how to approach anyone; women of good birth did not go to the markets. Her father, and then Ludovico, made the household purchases, piling them in the basket of a market boy, who carried it to the house. Besides, she had been unable to shake the belief that Ludovico had spies in the Piazza – among the vendors, on a terrace of the Basilica – even though when she turned, she could not see anyone looking at her. It had been like trying to outrun her shadow in the courtyard as a child; she knew she could catch it if she moved quickly enough, but no matter how dizzy-fast she spun, the shadow was always right behind.

'We are not far from the inn now,' said Arlecchino.

She wanted to respond, to let him know her gratitude. But could one say to a stranger, even one as familiar as Arlecchino, *I think you are saving my life*? 'I saw your troupe perform in the Piazza,' she said. He nodded but did not comment. 'I was very hungry,' she said, 'but I could not help laughing.'

'Laughter feeds the spirit,' he said, not sententiously, merely as if it were a fact.

Perhaps it was, although in the Piazza, even while she laughed, hunger had worked at her with small, sharp teeth. In all her life she had never been hungry for longer than it took to ask for food, but now in three days she had learned that the desire for food could be more than a pleasant, anticipatory rumbling; it could be pain twisting above her waistline like a pestle into a mortar. She had considered begging scraps from a kitchen, or even scooping them from the canals. When some apples rolled from a vendor's stall in the Piazza, she had snatched one, stuffed it into her sleeve, and run behind the Campanile to devour it in panic: crisp red skin over sweet white meat, the juice fountaining down her throat, spilling on her dress because she could not get it into her mouth fast enough. She had gulped down the core as well, and then she had wept, not because the apple was gone but because she had eaten it like a savage, with no thought for the fineness of manner that had been bred into her. How could she live a new life if it made her a stranger to herself?

Even as she recalled the apple, water rose in Susanna's mouth, her tongue quivered with memory, and the pain of emptiness wrenched her belly. That pain had made her too weak to protest when, at dusk, footsteps had come up behind her in an alley with the suddenness of a squall and one pair of hard hands had gripped her elbows while another pair reached for her *borsetta* with brute impersonality. She had put up her hands to defend her veil, as her life, and then stood immobile, knowing she lacked the courage to resist whatever the two *bravi* might do to her, be it rape or murder. When they did neither, merely walked away with her jacket and purse as if they had picked them from a cart, not from a living creature, she had sunk to her knees on the cold stones. Recalling it, she could not stop a whimper.

'Are you all right?' Arlecchino asked.

'Yes,' she replied as firmly as she could. He had seen her at her lowest ebb, in the street of whores, and must not see her so again.

'There will be food soon,' he said.

After the *bravi* left her in the street, she had cowered there, feeling such contempt for her helplessness that she had yearned to scourge herself. But not with whips or nails. There was a better way to mortify her flesh: a brothel. The idea startled her, for she had always thought going to such a place would require courage. But kneeling on that dark street, its stones pushing the cold deeper into her whole body, she had realized that, for her, the necessary condition for a brothel was not courage, it was contempt. She had picked herself up and, with a sour mix of hope and hunger, determination and doubt, made her way to the busy, bawdy streets where the whores worked. She had stood there, clutching her dress about her and struggling to retain some sense of being Susanna Bardi – for never in her mind did she use Ludovico's name and call herself Susanna Rossi. But her determination had seeped away as an hour passed, then another, and no one approached her – not until the tall, odd-looking man, to whom she had said things, been prepared to do things, that could never have passed the lips, even entered the mind of Susanna Bardi. Two ideas had sustained her during the conversation: the knowledge that nothing she might have to do to, or with, him would be worse than what she had endured with Ludovico, and the groundless feeling that she could trust him because . . . Because cruelty had a scent as distinctive as the sea's, though very different – like metal heating in a forge or hair burning in too hot an iron – and no such scent emanated from him. And because in the comedy of his face she had seen no pity for hers.

He stopped before an inn. 'Here is where I lodge. Will you come in?'

'Why do you take this trouble for me?' Susanna asked.

He cocked his head to one side, as if listening for an echo. 'I do not know.'

Susanna believed him.

A lamp burned in the small court of the inn, and in a room to one side she saw several figures at a table. 'Some of my companions are still up,' he said.

Suddenly the scar, angry that hunger and despair had obscured it, called her fingers up to the veil.

'I will find you a bed with some of the women,' said Arlecchino.

'What women?'

'The women of our company,' he said. 'Of I Favolosi.' He spread his arms in a grand welcoming gesture, except that his fingers flapped like sticks.

'You must have a name besides Arlecchino,' she said. 'Or are you truly he?'

'Truly? There is a question for philosophers. Yes, certainly I am Arlecchino – eternally the comedic servant of some master – yet I was born miles from any stage-wagon, under another name, that of a man who is no one's servant and who still lives within me. When I wake up in the morning, I know I shall be Arlecchino before the day is out. And once one plays him, one never leaves him. One *becomes* him, playing his clever stupidity in whatever situations the scenarios dictate, improvising him each time. But does that mean I am truly he?' He looked at her kindly, as if they were together confronting an intriguing puzzle. 'And you, lady?' he said. 'Are you truly Anonima?'

From inside came a voice: 'Paolo! Why do you stand out in the street?'

'Paolo?' she said.

He inclined his head. 'Paolo Bertoldo. The man who

lives within Arlecchino and is therefore, presumably, his master.' He smiled down at her with a sweetness she would not have thought his odd features could express. The voice called him again. 'Will you enter with me?' he said.

Her hands went even colder, but she nodded. He smiled and took her into the room where three men sat. On their table were several bottles of wine and a platter with the remnants of some chicken. The smell of spicy, roasted flesh hit Susanna so strongly that she felt herself sinking even as Arlecchino said, 'Here is a lady who needs help. I have offered to find her a place to sleep for this night and – food, my friends!' he cried as she slumped on to a bench. 'Food!'

They thrust wine at her, and a chunk of coarse millet bread, and a chicken leg, and someone dashed out and came back with a pear. She turned away from them, pushed up her veil, and tried to keep the dizzying reality of the food from sabotaging the effort to eat and drink with decorum, as a wealthy Venetian woman must do. But halfway through the chicken, cold and stringy but redolent of sauce, she thought: *I have stood in the street of whores. Does it matter how I behave?* But the answer was yes, for one of Arlecchino's friends was the Male Lover. She lowered the veil and turned back to the men, who studied her with curiosity. The Lover raised an eyebrow. When she had seen him in the Piazza performance, hunger and panic had fallen away because he was quite beautiful: a fine, straight nose, full lips, dark eyes above strong cheekbones. Now at close range his face was so splendid that it hurt to see. Her scar, which the food had pushed from her awareness once again, reclaimed its place with a familiar sensation, igniting both cheeks until she feared their flaming would shine through the veil.

'These are my friends,' Paolo said. 'Here is Giulio, as his mother had him christened, but when we perform he is our Pantalone – Il Magnifico, the merchant from Venice. In some scenarios he is my master.'

The heavy but muscular man stood and bowed deeply. His face was oddly plump and bland; onstage the Pantalone always wore a mask with a hooked nose and pointed beard. Susanna nodded to him.

'And here,' Paolo said, 'is our Dottore, known as Umberto. A ridiculous fellow, with his Latin and legal phrases, but I am fond of him all the same.'

'Signora,' the man said, 'one must welcome you to this inn, now that you are within it. For it is not disputable, *mutatis mutandis*, that no one can be welcomed to a place until he has in fact arrived at that place. Therefore I bid you welcome, *loco citato*.' He picked a napkin from the table and flourished it as he bowed to her.

Susanna smiled and said, '*Gratias ago tibi, magister*.'

'Imbecile,' Pantalone said to him. 'You wave in her face a napkin stained with chicken grease?' He took a swipe at Il Dottore, who cowered. Arlecchino fluttered his fingers. 'Lady, I beg you to excuse these boorish persons with whom a cruel Fate forces me to deal.'

Umberto punched him in the arm. Paolo gave a soundless howl that showed all his teeth and half his gullet.

What strange persons they were, Susanna thought. She had never met anyone like them, except children – but these people's eyes were knowing and their faces rough, as if stubbled by experiences of a kind she could not imagine.

'Please, don't fight because of me,' she said. 'I am sorry to make you angry with one another.'

'Angry?' said Pantalone.

'Who is angry?' Il Dottore said.

'We do get angry sometimes,' Arlecchino explained. 'I have been so furious at Il Dottore that I wanted to pull off his ears – but now we only pretend to anger. We are players after all.' He made a fist and boxed Umberto's ear. Umberto smiled. The mock blow, Susanna realized, had expressed not only brotherhood but affection. 'We like one another well enough,' said Arlecchino. 'Otherwise it would be difficult to travel and work together.'

Did the theatre provide a special language of bodies and words in which to communicate – a language that was in itself a kind of mask?

'Finally,' Paolo said, 'here is our Innamorato, Luca the Lover. In some of our scenarios, he is the man Arlecchino serves.'

Lucky Arlecchino, Susanna thought. She said nothing, for he was looking at her with lively interest, as if he expected to be entertained or intrigued.

He said, 'May we know your name, Signora?'

'I cannot . . . I am Anon— ' She stopped and turned to Paolo.

'Anna?' said Luca. 'You are Anna?'

'Yes.'

'Welcome, Anna. We are somewhat mad, but only enough to make us more interesting.' He smiled. From the safety of the veil she stared not only at his beauty but at his indifference to it, which enhanced it – and which could be felt only by those who had never feared or experienced beauty's loss.

'If you have eaten sufficiently,' Paolo said to her, 'I shall take you to the ladies of our company and find you a place to sleep.'

'Thank you,' she said humbly. 'Many thanks to all of you.' She permitted herself to look again at Luca, who was regarding her speculatively. She thanked God silently for the protection of the veil.

Paolo took a lamp and led her up several flights of stairs. Hesitating before a door, he said softly, 'This is the room where our *corago* and his wife stay – Bruno, who plays the Captain, and his wife Isabella, our Female Lover.'

'I saw her in the Piazza,' Susanna said. 'She is beautiful.'

'Yes.' Arlecchino sighed, then moved on to another door and knocked. No answer. He knocked louder. 'Little redhead!' he called, his voice soft yet penetrating.

At length the door opened and, in the light of Arlecchino's lamp, a sleepy face appeared. 'Paolo? What do you want?'

'I have brought someone to you . . . a friend who needs a bed for the night.'

The eyes focussed, in an oval face with small, fine features. The hair that framed it, unkempt with sleep, was the hue of a pomegranate. 'Paolo,' said the woman, her voice low and exasperated, 'have you been to the Rialto? Have you brought one of those—'

'No, no,' he said hastily. 'This is Anna who was robbed on the streets and has no place to rest until morning. Anna, this is my redheaded friend Teresa, whom I know will help you. For my sake, Teresa, please.'

Teresa's glance moved to Susanna, not hard, not pitying, as neutral as if she were contemplating a purchase. 'Oh, very well,' she said.

'In the morning, see that she receives something to eat.'

Teresa regarded Susanna for another noncommittal moment. 'Come in.'

'You are in good hands,' Paolo told Susanna, as the door shut.

Teresa gestured to a narrow pallet. 'You will have to sleep with me.'

'In the same bed?'

'Do you prefer the floor?'

'No,' Susanna said faintly. 'Thank you.'

There were two other beds in the room, each with the hump of a female figure on it. 'Bianca, who plays the Older Woman,' Teresa said. 'And her daughter. They complain much of the day. At night they sleep like the dead.'

Suddenly the day's load of hunger, shame and fear slid from Susanna's flesh, leaving only numbness. She did not even try to slip off her dress, merely gathered it around her before falling gratefully on to the bed. Straw crackled somewhere beneath her, like a distant fire. She thought fleetingly of her linen sheets at home; she felt Teresa's weight depress the mattress beside her; she felt nothing.

In the morning, when a gondolier's cry awakened her, the two of them were wedged together, backsides tight against each other. Susanna moved away quickly, her body reacting to the shock of another's presence before she knew where she was or why, but the knowledge rushed up from the oblivion of sleep like logs freed from an anchor, crashing into one another as they surfaced. Winter would come before long, and she was a fugitive without money or resources, unable to earn her supper even in the street of whores, saved from hunger and humiliation by the charity of a player-clown and his friends, whose kindness made her feel even more alien because she was not used to the proximity of strangers, let alone kindness from them. A yearning for things familiar overcame her: the fireplace in her bedchamber that would warm her on a morning like this one; the stolid deferential servant who brought a drink of fruit juice and spices when she woke; the clothes in her chest and wardrobe, velvets and silks that carried the scent of her own perfume and body, and no one else's; her mother's face, loving and lovely, delicately painted . . . She put her head in her hands. The face of the male Lover, Luca, came into her mind – distant, glorious, cold. She could not make it recede; the inability made her feel panic, but the face made her feel flushed. The mattress gave around her with loud rustles.

Teresa stirred and said, 'What is wrong?'

'Nothing,' Susanna managed.

Teresa sat up and rubbed her eyes. 'If that were true, you would have your own bed and I would have slept better.'

'Yes. I am sorry.'

'It doesn't matter. Sleep is a waste of time. I must check my potions and elixirs this morning, to see what I need to prepare.' Teresa swung off the bed, pulled her hands through the bright tangle of her hair and stretched her arms high. In the morning light her skin was warm with colour. 'So,' she said, 'Anna – if Anna is truly your name, and if it is not, what matter – Anna, what does our Arlecchino want with you, eh?'

'Nothing. He was only being kind.'

'You are not a whore, then?'

Susanna stood. 'Why do you ask that?'

Teresa brought her arms down. 'He goes looking for one, sometimes. He thinks I do not know, but I understand his moods. Last night he was heading to the Casteletta, I am certain. Did you not meet him there?'

'Yes.'

'Why were you there, then, if you are not a whore?'

'I had . . . intended to be, but I failed.'

'Why do you wear a veil, even when you sleep?'

'I . . .'

'Are you afraid of letting me see your face?'

Susanna winced at the directness of it. 'Yes, but it is not only you.'

'Why? Are you hiding from someone? Are you a criminal?'

After a moment Susanna said, 'I am not a criminal.'

Teresa shrugged. 'Very well, it seems you don't care to discuss it. That is all right with me. I always ask what I want to know, but I don't insist on answers. Often I refuse to give them myself.'

A groan came from one of the other beds. 'Why can't you leave me to sleep? Why must you cackle at dawn like a rooster?'

'I shall be on my way now,' Susanna whispered quickly.

'Does Paolo know you are leaving?' Teresa asked.

'There is no need for him to know.'

'What shall I tell him, then?'

'Nothing. Only give him my thanks.'

'Where are you going?'

'To the one place left for me to go.' Susanna hesitated. 'May I ask you something?'

'Why not? If I feel like answering, I shall.'

'You spoke of elixirs and potions. Can you make poisons as well?'

'I can.'

'Have you ever . . .' Susanna hesitated.

'Poisoned anyone? No. But one day, perhaps I shall. Why do you ask?'

'I have my reasons,' Susanna said.

CHAPTER FOUR

Of Priests and Players

Holy Mother Church, we players know we offend thee!

Creatures of Satan. Lewd, lascivious, licentious. Thus have you described us since the long dark night that fell when Rome fell and did not lift for centuries. Even now, when princes have begun welcoming our improvised *commèdia* to their palaces . . . when some of your cardinals applaud us . . . still, in your sanctum sanctorum, you do not admit us. In your eyes we are flesh, and therefore Devil, our actions no more to be trusted than those of any man in the velvet grip of his pleasures.

Can flesh and spirit not live in peace? Must one always try to destroy the other?

On Bishop Palma's work table, which was covered with a fringed cloth, sat half a dozen handsomely bound books of theology, a writing stand and inkwell, and an hourglass, sand filling its bottom for the second time since the meeting had begun. 'Finally,' the bishop said, 'I shall of course want a complete accounting, month by month, of all the moneys spent on food for the poor.'

'Of course, Your Excellency,' said Fra Filippo, his clerk and chief assistant. Seated opposite the bishop, frowning in concentration, he took notes in an exquisite hand: plump *o*'s, and *a*'s of precise equality, *t*'s whose crossbars sailed like flags in a wind, *s*'s with trains a gown might envy. 'If only we could be certain how long you will stay in Rome.'

The bishop eased his back against the carved walnut chair. 'The Holy Father has ordered that each bishop visit Rome every three years. He has not indicated how long our presence is to last.'

Fra Filippo looked up from his notes. 'Do you expect to be given duties to perform in Rome?'

'I expect,' the bishop said dryly, 'to be queried about Venetian affairs, and lectured on the continuing insolence and independence of the Republic.'

'No one can dare to question your loyalty.'

'Do you mean my loyalty to the Holy Father? Or to Venice?'

'The former, Your Excellency, of course.'

The bishop smiled. 'Do not be distressed. I was merely making a small joke – small and not especially amusing, I see.'

'Forgive me, please, I did not mean—'

The bishop waved an elegant hand. 'I know. We approach matters in a different spirit. Has it not always been so?'

'Your Excellency's observation is correct, I believe.'

'Yet we work together well,' said the bishop, acknowledging the unspoken arrangement by which he moved among patrician merchant families and in the councils of government, while Fra Filippo stood earnest sentinel over the deeds of the individual souls in their keeping. To the bishop, Venice's position as one of the chief centres of book production in Christendom was part of her splendour; to the father, it was a constant worry, lest the works be heretical and therefore added to the *Index Liborum Prohibitorum*.

The father laid down his pen. 'If there is justice, you will return from Rome a cardinal.'

'What if there is only mercy? Forgive me, another levity. So, if the Holy Father does not choose to appoint me, you will accuse him of being unjust?'

'Your Excellency! I would never accuse His Holiness. I merely note that he views everyone in Venice, including we who serve him, with suspicion. Perhaps he has cause, from his seat in Rome, but if he were aware of Your Excellency's person and virtues, you surely would return as a cardinal.'

The bishop smiled broadly. 'My friend, if only you were in the Curia.'

'I? Never.' Fra Filippo's face and voice hardened briefly, in the way that was typical of him, as if he were periodically steeling himself for judgment.

The two men had come to the church by quite different paths. The father, born on a farm unable to feed all the mouths suckling at it, had been sent to a monastery, where he had disliked the life at first but gradually had grown to feel an almost physical ardour for the great struggle of man against the evil in his soul. The bishop, illegitimate son of a noble family that had never quite acknowledged him, had early felt the stirrings of ambition and of the intelligence to serve it and had yearned to enter his father's world. To his surprise, he found he could not resist the appeal of possessing moral authority also. Living in wealth might be splendid, but how much greater to live in rectitude as well?

At fifty Andrea Palma was dark and tall, his grey gaze roaming the worlds of church and state, screening his thoughts from their objects even while studying them; at thirty-five Filippo Bertoldo was pale, a bit plump, his eyes also grey but their gaze never easy, despite a seeming candour. Privately the bishop labelled him an eternally worried cherub. The father's private thoughts did not incline to images, except of a kind he forbade himself. He regarded the bishop only as the man he served, and had done for twelve years, ever since, for reasons Filippo did not understand but had never questioned, Palma had chosen a simple priest, newly sent from the Veneto, to be his clerk and chief assistant.

Yet despite the differences between the two there was also a likeness, buried as deep in their relationship as an anchor in the harbour. Neither raised it, neither always remembered it was there, yet neither felt safe without it.

The bishop lifted his hourglass and reversed it; sand ran from the top in a thin stream. 'Now, my friend,' he said, 'all other affairs are in order before I leave tomorrow, but a final one is not.'

'The matter of Signor Bardi's daughter?'

'Yes. I have promised her father and her husband that I will return her to them, and to fail before the Bardi is not acceptable.'

Fra Filippo nodded. The Bardi had long been members of the Signoria, and Antonio and the bishop had a close relationship, which the father did not fully understand; Antonio was hardly as devout as one might wish.

The bishop said, 'It is not merely a matter of personal honour to find the woman, you understand, but of demonstrating the power of the church.'

'She is not at any of the convents I have so far investigated.'

'How many remain?' the bishop asked.

'Only two. I will go to them tomorrow morning.'

'It must be done that way, with discreet visits. The family wishes the matter kept as quiet as possible, but I do not know how long their patience will last. If I cannot take them news of the woman before I leave, or better still take the woman herself . . .' The bishop shook his head. 'We do not want them to turn to the civil authorities. You must continue the search with all vigour.'

'Yes, Your Excellency. But if I am not able to find her?'

'Search until you do. When you succeed, you must make her understand, as I would do, that she must return to her husband.'

Filippo took up his pen, then laid it down again. 'Suppose she does not wish to return? Suppose she feels herself called to serve in God's house?'

'You must persuade her she will serve Him best in her husband's house.'

Filippo leaned forward and peered keenly at the bishop's face. 'We are certain of this?'

'We are certain.' In a moment the bishop added, 'Do you doubt me?' his voice as gentle as if he were describing the love of Christ for all mankind.

The father blinked twice, erasing some unbidden vision, then sat back. Reaffirming one of the mainstays of his life, he said, 'I do not doubt you.'

'Good.'

'But my powers of persuasion will never equal yours.'

'On this occasion they must. They will. Your voice carries authority with the woman – have you not heard her confession sometimes, in my absence?'

'Yes, I have.'

The bishop lifted two fingers and waved them as if blessing a crowd. 'Do not doubt yourself. You have done many things for me – for the glory of God. You will do this also. I am confident.'

Fra Filippo looked down at his elegant, almost voluptuously written notes. 'It is true,' he said. 'I have done many things for you.'

'And I for you.'

'I shall execute your orders as faithfully as my abilities allow.'

'I know,' said the bishop.

Paolo came down the stairs of the inn, sleepily

entertaining two pleasant thoughts: of Isabella's beauty and of breakfast. As he neared the room where he hoped to find both, the sight of someone leaving through the courtyard door pushed the heaviness of sleep from his eyes. He felt certain it was 'Anna' and nearly called after her, but something stayed his tongue. He ran back upstairs, to Teresa, who was laying out little sacks of dried herbs.

'Yes, she has gone,' Teresa said. 'Did you expect her to stay? Why?'

'Perhaps we could have helped her.'

'To do what?'

Paolo had no answer, but Teresa's practicality, which he usually found attractive, seemed cold and irrelevant beside the memory of Anna's hands, reaching to the veil that shielded her face. 'Where was she going?' he asked.

Teresa shrugged. 'She did not tell me.'

Paolo went back downstairs, trying to recapture the allure of breakfast in Isabella's presence. Instead he found himself running out of the door and along the *calle*, thinking that he was foolish, he was hungry, he should go back, but running anyway, the morning bells clanging in rhythms different from one another and from that of his feet; he seemed to be darting between the calls of clashing trumpets. The air was cold and thick with mist off the water; the stone faces of the buildings were wet. When he was sure he had lost her, he spotted her; he stopped, told himself to go back, and decided to follow from a distance.

Why? He could not say, except that Arlecchino had

made her laugh, and it might be pleasant to make her do so again.

She walked on, angling north and west, her pace a jerky mixture of reluctance and resolve. Mist clung to her feet and skirt, so that she seemed like a figurehead on the prow of a ship. Paolo imagined various destinations. Would she try to drown herself by leaping from the Fondamenta Nuove? Would he try to stop her? Would she seek shelter in the Ghetto? Finally she slowed and stopped before a church. When she entered, he followed and stood well behind her, watching her head lift to the wood-beamed ceiling and her shoulders rise and fall in heavy sighs. Then she lowered her head, as if in prayer. He walked to her, stood beside her, and whispered, 'Anonima.'

She swung to him; even through her veil, he could sense her amazement. 'Did you follow me?' she said.

'Yes.'

'Why?'

'I do not know. I suppose . . . I wanted to help you.'

'Why?' she repeated.

'Must there be a reason?' He waggled his fingers and grimaced. 'Arlecchino follows his nose.' Sensing no smile behind the veil, he said, 'My friend Teresa made you comfortable last night?'

'Yes.'

'She has a good heart, if a sharp tongue.' He shifted his weight from one leg to the other. 'What will you do? Where are you going?'

'To the convent,' she said.

'I thought you said you could never go there?'

'Yes. But the truth is that it will . . . suit me.' She clasped her hands together so tightly that her thumbs looked like shackles.

He was silent; who was he to know what needs or troubles might send a woman to a convent? For the first time in years he thought of the sister who had become a nun when he was a small boy and faded from his life, leaving little more trace of her presence than a crooked smile. Had she found peace? God knew she had not brought good fortune to the rest of family, which had remained bent over the fields.

'I have a sister in a convent,' he said.

'In what convent?'

'I do not know.' He had not tried to dissuade his sister; why should he try to dissuade this strange woman, this 'Anna'?

'I shall go now,' she said. 'If you will do me the final favour of accompanying me to the door, I know I shall be able to knock and request entry.'

'Why go to the convent if you do not wish to?'

'I beg you not to ask questions.' Her voice was as veiled as her face. 'Let us go quickly, if you are willing.'

Paolo offered his arm, but she declined, so he simply walked beside her.

When they were approaching the door, she pulled aside, as a frightened child might, because someone was just leaving: a priest.

Paolo and the priest regarded each other with the bland civility of passers-by; then the glance of one of them – afterwards Paolo could not say whose – caught on the other's, like silk on a thorn, and suddenly they looked at each other keenly, suspiciously. 'Excuse me,' said the priest, 'I beg your pardon, but you look . . . you seem to me . . . Do you come from the Veneto, by chance?'

'I do,' Paolo replied slowly.

'Near Asolo?'

'Yes.'

The priest blinked. 'Did you know a man there called Luigi Bertoldo?'

Paolo thought of denying it, of saying, 'I am Arlecchino, and no one else,' but the encounter was acquiring the heavy inevitability of a stone door swinging open against one's muscles and will. 'I know the man,' he said.

'He was my father, dead now these five years.' The priest hesitated. 'Can you be . . . Are you . . . Paolo?'

Paolo did not know what else to do; he gave a caper and a low comic bow.

'I am Filippo,' said the priest. His mouth, only slightly prominent – a child-shape of Paolo's own – broke into a wide smile. 'Praise God who has chosen to reunite us! Let me embrace you.'

Paolo found himself pressed against one of his elder brothers who had gone away when he himself was twelve and whom he had never seen again. His brother's body was soft and full beneath the cassock, and his embrace seemed that of a stranger, made all the more strange by the claim of familiarity in its pressure.

'My brother, my brother,' Filippo murmured, squeezing harder still.

'You are crushing me,' Paolo said, with as much of a laugh as his breath permitted.

'Forgive me.' Filippo pulled away and clasped his hands. 'Let me look at you. Paolo! I knew it was you. Still as thin as the pitchfork! Do you remember what Mamma called you? Little Paolo the Pitchfork. But so tall now . . .'

Paolo felt ridiculous, apprehensive and pleased all at once. He did not like contradictory feelings, especially if they touched his inner being; he preferred to look outward and to be as cheerful as the world's vagaries permitted. He tried to think of his present situation as one of the subjects on which I Favolosi improvised – the *scenario of The Twin Captains* – except that no one would take Filippo and him for twins. Nor had they been searching for each other. Perhaps it would be a new scenario, called *The Lost Brothers*. But what would the plot be, now that they had found each other? Awkwardness hung between them like a torn curtain, through which they peered hesitantly. What to say? Everything? Nothing?

'You look much the same,' Paolo said at last, although he did not know if it was true. Had Filippo been so pale, with a second chin swelling below the first and eyes moving cautiously even when the lips beneath them smiled?

'That we should meet at last,' Filippo said, 'in Venice! Do you live here? Have we lived in the same city for years and never found each other until now?'

'I am only a visitor. And you, Filippo? Is this your church, before which we stand?'

'No, no. I have the honour to serve God by acting as secretary to Bishop Andrea Palma, who sends me here on an errand.'

Paolo became suddenly aware of the woman, 'Anna', whose existence he had forgotten in the shock of finding his early life rise before him, wearing a cassock. She had been as quiet as the wall against which she stood, and she was making no motion now, but her stillness had grown so intense that it filled his awareness as if it held weight.

Filippo too glanced at her, for the first time, before turning back and asking, 'What do you do, then, brother? Where do you live?'

On the stage, for I am Arlecchino, who lives by his wit and his wits. No, he could not say that. 'Everywhere and nowhere,' he said.

'I do not understand.'

'I live wherever audiences gather to watch us. I am a travelling player. An actor.'

'An actor?' Filippo pursed his lips. 'And the lady as well? Is she one of those women who perform upon the stage?'

And who thus deny God? Paolo could hear the words as clearly as if Filippo had actually said them. 'No,' Paolo said, 'she is not a player. She . . . has business in the convent.'

Filippo glanced at her again and then peered at Paolo more closely. 'I hope both of you obey God and love Him?'

From behind Anna's veil came an odd voice, barely hers. 'Yes, Father.'

Paolo said, 'I do not think God will find fault with me.'

'He finds fault with all of us,' Filippo said sharply. 'Particularly those who make lewdness and licentiousness part of their trade.' Then he gave a little shake of his head and a forced smile. 'Has He reunited me with my youngest brother in order that I may help save his soul?'

'I have no sins on my soul.' Paolo felt anger spurt in his belly because Filippo had made him lie – he had indeed committed sins; had he not gone looking for a whore only the night before – and because a forgotten aspect of his childhood was rushing back: being ordered about day and night, not only by his parents but by his eleven siblings, all looking down at him, fetch this or do that, so that often he had had to lie in order to have a moment to himself.

'There are sins on every soul,' Filippo said. 'Do not be prideful, my brother, especially not at the door of God's house.'

Paolo's anger grew into a red, tailed figure with a fork that prodded him to temptation. He heard himself say, as haughtily as Il Dottore, 'And you, my brother, how does one know what brings you here? One hears that great wickedness takes place behind doors like these. One hears that priests abandon their vows of celibacy and force nuns to serve their newly liberated desires.'

He saw Filippo's face turn murky with shock and Anna's veil shiver with a gasp.

Filippo blinked rapidly. 'Ask forgiveness for your

blasphemy! At the bidding of His Excellency the bishop I am here to search for a woman who has run from her home and husband, so that I may return her to the duties God has chosen for her. I am here to do God's holy work. Do not dare to suggest otherwise.'

A retort danced on Paolo's tongue but was tripped to a halt: Anna's intense, listening stillness had turned to fear, which emanated from her in waves. He saw that Filippo was its cause, and, as if he had been thrown a cue on the stage, he immediately improvised an explanation.

Filippo too had gone silent. He inhaled deeply and clasped his hands.

'Brother, forgive me for allowing us to quarrel on the very day we are reunited. It was pride that responded to your words, not charity. I know you cannot mean what you say. You merely repeat the gossip of the street.'

Giving his reply no colour, so that the words were like boiled chicken without salt or spice, Paolo said, 'You are right, Filippo. I am in error.' But he could not stop adding, 'Perhaps I understand priests as little as you understand players.'

Filippo swallowed. 'Perhaps. We must come to know each other better now that God has reunited us. But first let us tend to our separate business within the convent. I shall be of service to you and the lady if the cause is just.' He turned to Anna. 'May I ask the nature of your business here?'

'Let me explain,' Paolo said. 'She . . .'

Anna, or whatever her true name was, cleared her

throat and said, still in the odd, choking voice, 'Father, I came to enquire after a friend. Your brother did me the service of escorting me here, but I am not feeling well. I must leave. No,' she said, when Paolo moved towards her, 'I need no help, beyond what you have given already.' She put her right arm across her breast like a shield, clutched her left shoulder, and walked off, disappearing into the thickening mist.

Filippo said, 'I think the lady did not wish to reveal her purpose to me.'

'She is not in good health, that is all,' Paolo said; once again Filippo had made him lie.

It had been raining heavily for several hours and gave no sign of stopping; there would be no performing that day. Instead, I Favolosi was discussing a new scenario. The whole company was gathered at a long wooden table in the inn's dining room, which, in mid-afternoon, was otherwise deserted. The players hunched inside their motley clothes, rubbing their hands or hugging their arms as if they were their own lovers. The fire on the hearth could barely lift its flames into the chill, damp air. Pedrolino struck occasional, morose chords on his guitar. Bruno, as *corago*, was at the head of the table with lists: all the episodes in the scenario, the persons in each, the properties and costumes required. He called off the players' names, to be sure each understood what to do.

Teresa, who would have only a small part but would do some acrobatics, laid her head on her arms. She felt Pedrolino staring at her in the melancholy way he sometimes had when he thought she was unaware, brown hair falling over eyes as moist as a dog's. She did not wish to be looked at that way, by him or any man, although he was rather sweet, in fact, and a fine guitar player. He always seemed to yearn for what was beyond his reach, whether it was her or greater skill as one of the *zanni*. He was not the equal of Paolo, whom he sometimes watched with the same yearning look on his face that was now directed at her. To know what one was, Teresa thought, and accept it – there was a desirable state of affairs. She herself was an arrow, aimed at finding the Man With the Ring.

Isabella and Luca were reciting the sequences of the Lovers' actions. 'After Pantalone leaves, I rave against Love and Fortune,' Isabella said in the elegant Tuscan inflections the Lovers used onstage. Peevishly she added, 'Today I rave against the rain.' The rain was keeping her from doing her hair. She spent hours at it: applying the ointment that kept it blonde, pulling it up through a crownless hat, and spreading it on the wide brim to dry in the sun. Teresa saw the darkness at its roots but felt no sympathy; it was foolish to spend so much time making oneself a blonde. Men might like blondes, as everyone said, but why listen to them? Besides, had not all men found her red-haired mother beautiful?

Umberto was next, fussing through his list of actions, forgetting which side of the stage he would enter from. One felt he never took a step without hesitating whether to go left or right. His wife had died in the plague. He mentioned her rarely, but when he did, it was to say, 'Catarina always knew what to do.' Luca, who would be his son in the new scenario, fed him the right answers.

Luca was quick to grasp anything new and eager for another challenge. 'Let us make the most of what we have!' he would say, when their coins were low and they were eating bread and soup. This was his first time in Venice, and he exclaimed over all he saw with such pleasure that one could only smile. White teeth gleaming, he would smile back, in the way that made women in the audience applaud and call out his name. One could not say he was vain; he simply enjoyed the face and body God had given him. Perhaps Isabella enjoyed them too. What did they get up to when they went off by themselves to find elegant phrases in her books?

'Someone wake Paolo,' Bruno said sharply. Paolo's head had fallen on to his arms and bubbles of snores escaped his fish-mouth. Pedrolino reached to shake him, but he only shifted and continued his gentle snore-song.

'Let him rest,' Teresa said. After dashing out that morning, he had returned before lunch, not loping in his usual comical manner but walking soberly, and had yawned through most of the meeting. 'He has already shown us,' Teresa added, 'that, as usual, he knows the scenario better than anyone.'

'Even so,' Bruno said, frowning, 'I wish to know what *lazzi* he may use.'

'Whatever they are,' Teresa said lazily, 'they will be good.'

'You always praise him,' Isabella said, still peevish.

'Have I said anything that is not true?'

Isabella gave an elegant little snort and smoothed her hair. She knew perfectly well it was true, Teresa thought; Paolo had a wonderful repertory of *lazzi*, the tricks and stage business that clown-players inserted into any scene, or between scenes. She herself would laugh, watching from offstage, no matter how many times she saw Paolo do them: the *lazzi* of weeping while laughing; of strutting all over the stage trying to catch a flea; of falling backwards and landing flat; of counting on his fingers and becoming certain he had lost two of them. The troupe's reputation owed much to Paolo and his *lazzi*. Also, to be fair, to Isabella's skill and beauty. And why not give some credit to her own ointments and potions and oils? Teresa thought. The crowds bought them in quantities because she had learned to prepare them almost as well as her mother had.

She closed her eyes, ignoring the talk. When they left Venice, she would gather more herbs, especially motherwort and yarrow . . . yarrow from churchyards. 'Where it tells the dead they might still be living if they had taken it daily,' as her mother used to say. Why did some scenes never lose their brightness? Why did they need only the smallest sidelong flick of memory to burst into living flame? The day the accusation of sorcery had been made against her mother; the day of Teresa's first visit to the cell, with Bruno, when she had pretended to be his daughter because her mother did not want the Tribunal to know she had a child; and of the last, when her mother had not seemed connected to her own body and said the things Teresa would never forget; the day a jailer at the gate had said, like a stone speaking, 'Prisoner Laurano has died.'

Died? Of what? Of what!

Shrug of shoulders massive as hillocks. Died of sickness that came on her.

What sickness?

Raising of eyebrows, like the shoulders. Sickness came at God's pleasure.

But God had not killed Ginevra Laurano. Some man had. *And one day I shall find him, and make him pay.* He had worn a mask and a lion's-head ring: the head made of rubies, a tiny gold ring through its nose. Her mother, in that hot delirium, her voice choking and twisted, had described it on Teresa's last visit; had told how she had felt it against her skin when the masked man forced his body into hers. She had not said the man's name. Perhaps she had not known it. When Teresa found him – because somewhere, most probably in Venice, there was a man wearing that ring – she would send him to join the dead in some churchyard, where neither yarrow nor God could help him.

'Good afternoon, lady,' she heard Umberto say, and Pedrolino struck a chord on his guitar.

Teresa opened her eyes. In the doorway, half in, half out, stood the woman Paolo had brought to share her bed the previous night. Her black dress and veil were rain-plastered to her body and face as tightly as paint.

'Do you seek us?' asked Giulio.

'I . . .' the woman said. 'I merely wondered if Paolo . . . ?'

Paolo's body shook. He sat up as if a trumpet had blown behind him and pushed stick-fingers into his temples. 'Anna? You are here?' He rose and went to her. 'I searched for you after you left, but – you came to find me?'

She nodded. The two of them spoke with their heads so close together that Teresa could not hear a word, even though her ears were straining, like everybody else's. No more rubbing of hands or arms against the chill, only all gazes settling on Paolo and the woman like darts to a board. I Favolosi was the audience, for once, but none of them could tell what scenario was being played.

Paolo turned to face them. 'My friends, it is good that we are all together because I have something to ask the whole troupe.'

'While we rehearse?' A hint of peevishness remained in Isabella's voice.

Paolo's face softened as usual when he looked at her. No one else seemed to notice, Teresa thought – except Isabella, who ran a languid hand over her hair. 'Isabella,' he said, 'I ask you for five minutes. I ask all of you.'

Luca, who had been chewing on an apple, set it down. 'My friend, you have us all waiting like cats at a kitchen door. What is it?'

Paolo frowned, then stood on one leg, leaned far to his left, and slapped his right ear, as if knocking water from his left. Bianca's daughter laughed, and Pedrolino drum-rolled on the guitar. The sounds seemed to reassure Paolo; he straightened. 'Last night some of you met this lady, my . . . my friend Anna.'

'The veiled lady who speaks Latin,' said Umberto. He bowed.

Paolo ignored him. 'She has had much recent misfortune and now has nowhere to go. She has come in desperation to ask that I – we – that I Favolosi take her in for a while.'

Isabella stared down her long, fine nose. 'How do you mean, take her in?'

'Let her work with us, travel with us. There are many things she could do – help with the properties and costumes, help Teresa with her elixirs—'

'I don't need help,' Teresa said, but not unkindly.

'We have enough extra hands,' Bruno said. 'Bianca's daughter and Giulio's wife and family.'

'Bruno,' Paolo said, 'I will pay for her keep out of my share.'

The woman gave a cry of surprise.

What on earth was Paolo up to? Teresa wondered. Why was he so determined to help the strange woman who needed to hide her face even when she slept? Perhaps she was merely one of his stray animals, like the dog that was sleeping nearby. He had found it by the roadside nearly dead, one leg severed by a cartwheel. He had implored Teresa to prepare ointments and potions for it, and when the dog survived to run about on three legs, he had been foolish in his pride. Was he about to be foolish again?

The men in the company began arguing among themselves. Another person in the troupe meant less room in the wagon, did it not? Why take in a woman who was not part of anyone's family and had no acting or behind-the-scenes skill? Things were fine as they were; why should they be changed? But Paolo was a major player, and – nudges and winks – if he wanted the woman . . .

'I do not want her for that!' Paolo cried, his face reddening in blotches and then, as he apparently realized how his words would sound to the woman herself, mottling to purple. 'I only wish to help her, for if we turn her away, she will starve on the streets of Venice.'

'Why does she not go to the Scuola di San Rocco or a convent?' Bruno said.

'Signor . . . all of you . . . please,' came the woman's voice. 'I am sorry to have troubled you. Permit me simply to thank Paolo for his generosity and then be on my way.'

'What generosity?' said Paolo.

'What way?' said Umberto.

Bruno said, 'Who is she? She speaks like a woman of education and good family. Why should she wish to join us? Why is she not with her husband?'

Paolo ignored him. 'My friends, are we really going to turn her away?' He looked to Isabella. 'I remember my plea to you, many years ago, when you stopped in my village and I chased after your wagon. You did not turn me away. You laughed, but you said "Come along, Paolo." '

'Because you showed us you were a clown,' Bruno said. 'A good clown. What can this lady show us?'

There were murmurs among the company – to her left, Teresa heard Bianca say, 'She would be good for nothing at all' – but they ceased when Isabella leaned forward.

'I should like to see this lady without her veil,' she said.

Silence descended again, thicker; the room was a cocoon wrapped in humming rain. They all looked at the woman, waiting.

She looked back at them through the fine, soft mist of the veil. *You are my last hope*, she thought – the words she had said aloud all the way to the inn, to numb the cold needles of rain, and her dread that she might have to reveal the scar to them. She had told herself that she could remain veiled until they were out of Venice and she left them and went off on her own. If she did not leave them, they would have to see the face eventually, all of them . . . Pedrolino and Bruno . . . Il Dottore and Pantalone . . . and Luca, who was looking at her intently, expectantly, twirling an apple core in his strong fingers. She felt light with hunger. For the apple, she thought. For the apple.

'You had better lift your veil, Anna,' Paolo said. 'Please.'

She had dared to come back, to ask his help, because he had not betrayed her to his priest-brother, even though he clearly realized she was the woman the priest sought.

'Does the lady refuse?' said Isabella, taunting softly. 'Is she afraid to have us know why she is veiled, lest we turn her away for that reason?'

The players disappeared; the Mantuans were watching Susanna march around a table. She saw the wart on the face of the bridegroom's father – brown, big, spongey. She closed her eyes, put her fingertips under the veil, and lifted it.

A female voice said, 'Mother of God.' Someone whistled in surprise.

When Susanna's eyes opened, the first face they saw was Luca's. He was staring, leaning forward. No doubt he was thinking, *Yes, ugly. I myself would not know what to do with such a face.* She refused to allow the pain to enter, as it had with the Mantuans. Since that day, she had learned to lock her heart against it as long as anyone was watching. She turned to Umberto. He opened his mouth, closed it, glanced to his left and right, then smiled at her. Teresa lifted her eyebrows, then shrugged.

Bruno spoke to the group. 'Now you see the wisdom of Isabella's request. How do we know this lady will not be a source of trouble? In what do we involve ourselves if she should come with us? We must know why she asks to join us.'

If she stayed now, Susanna thought, Paolo would have to tell the truth about her. Or else he would have to lie, which might be worse.

'We have a licence to play here for another two weeks,' Bruno went on, 'but it can be revoked at any moment, if the authorities wish. If anyone in power wishes. Our purpose is to avoid trouble, not take it into the company.'

'You are quite right, Signor,' Susanna said, glad that her voice, unlike the rest of her, was steady. 'I shall leave, ladies and gentlemen.' She lowered the veil and took one step, then another, in the rain-peppered quiet of the room.

'Can we not respect a woman's need to keep silent?' Paolo cried. 'Does any of us know or need to know all the others' secrets?'

The guitar player struck a burst of notes, like a patter of applause.

'Enough, Pedrolino!' Bruno said.

Susanna kept walking. Perhaps she would return to the Fondamenta Nuove, where she had gone after leaving the convent. There she was surrounded everywhere by water: not only the lagoon but the rain that raced and gurgled to join it and that had beat on her head and back, as if to push her closer to the edge. The drops had flung themselves into the lagoon: water drowning in itself, everywhere, a dozen times a minute, telling her it would be easy, for water was a friend she had lived with all her life . . . a mirror that would put an end to all mirrors . . .

'My friends,' said another voice, 'consider. The lady Anna speaks Latin. She is well educated, as you say, Bruno, and no doubt well read. I wager she could find new scenarios from the Roman authors and speeches from the poets.'

Susanna turned back to face the room.

Paulo struck his forehead as if spanking himself

then ran to Luca, grabbed him by both shoulders, and planted a loud kiss on each of his cheeks. 'O Lover, handsome and brilliant!'

Luca laughed. 'O clown, foolish and wise!'

They bowed to each other deeply and formally, like ambassadors.

'That is it, my friends!' Paolo cried. 'She shall help us find scenarios and speeches. She will not make trouble for us, I swear it to all of you. I guarantee it. What do you say? Shall we not do it, eh? Let us take a vote and say Yes.'

All of them turned to Bruno.

'Oh, very well,' he said. 'A vote.'

Up went Paolo's hand. Then Luca's. The guitar player's. Others followed slowly: Umberto's, Giulio's. His wife's. Susanna did not breathe. If not enough raised their hands, if she had to leave now, when Luca had seen the scar yet had come to her defence . . .

'Well, if Paolo wants it,' said Teresa, lifting her hand.

Isabella smiled enigmatically. 'Yes. Why not?' Her elegant hand rose partway, as if it were too much effort to lift further.

The older woman Bianca, her round, red face like an apple with a scowl carved on it, shifted in her seat, said, 'Yes', then poked her daughter, who did the same.

Bruno stroked his jaw, then shrugged. 'Very well. The woman may join us for a while.'

CHAPTER FIVE

Improvising

To take a scenario and play upon it – to loft it like the ball in the French game of court tennis: back and forth above the net, from one character to another, each responding to what the others say and how they say it, using whatever words come in that moment, before that audience . . .

It is much like life, you think?

Yes! But more demanding.

In life one may be a fool without effort, but to play a Fool on stage requires training. In life one may blind oneself to a lover's nature and take him anyway, but in *commèdia* the Lovers must know exactly what they do. One may get through life with no skills at all, but never through a scenario.

'You know who she is,' Teresa said matter-of-factly. 'I am certain of it.'

Paolo shrugged. They were ending another of Teresa's circuitous walks, heading back to the inn along the Zattere. The sun had just gone, taking all warmth with it like wind whipping off a cloak, leaving the water dark and slick. Passers-by were hurrying, faces intent on food and warmth.

'You do know, don't you?' Teresa said.

'Know what?' Paolo said.

'Do not play ignorance with me, my friend. I speak of Anna – who she is, whether she flees some danger, how she came to have her scar.'

'I know nothing of her scar.'

'But you know other things about her?'

'Arlecchino knows nothing.'

'Do not hide behind the mask. I Favolosi should know more about Anna than we do, and you are the best one to find out.'

'Do not hide behind I Favolosi. It is Teresa Laurano who wants to know. Why is it important to you?'

'If you do not know things, you court trouble.'

Above them, a window opened. They looked up and saw a courtesan standing there, resting a hand on a velvet cushion. Over a satin garment lined with fur, she wore a bodice cut low to reveal her nipples. She smiled out over the street, her gaze inviting yet exclusive.

'Is she expecting a lover,' Arlecchino murmured, 'or seeking to attract one?'

'Do you not think,' Teresa said, intense and low, 'that if my mother had known more about the men she . . .' The sentence hung unfinished.

Paolo looked at her in surprise; she had said almost nothing about her mother in years, especially of such a nature. 'The men she – what?' he asked.

'Nothing. There is no point in speaking of her.'

'Perhaps it would please you to remember.'

'I have not forgotten her,' Teresa said sharply. 'I think of her every day of my life.'

Uncertain what to do with this glimpse into her secret thoughts, Paolo juggled three invisible balls then said, 'She was so very beautiful.'

'Her beauty may be the reason she died.' Teresa looked at Paolo searchingly. 'Do you think it was?'

'I do not know, little redhead.'

'You are like Bruno and Isabella. I asked them every day for weeks why she died. They never had an answer, except that she was charged with sorcery and died in prison.'

'Perhaps there is no other answer.'

Teresa's eyes were almost gold with fire even though the dusk flattened all colours. 'Who put the accusation of sorcery into the lion's mouth?'

'No one can know. The accuser may remain anonymous – that is the purpose of such a method.'

'It is a disgusting purpose. To write out any charge one likes and slip it into a stone lion's head on a wall – to have those heads all around the city, with mouths that never answer, only swallow accusations—'

'Which must be examined carefully by the Council,' Paolo said.

'Do you defend what happened to my mother?'

'Certainly not! How can you imagine I would do that?'

After a moment Teresa said, 'Never mind. I do not want to speak any further of her. I merely say that no one *knows* enough about what happened to her.' She started walking again. 'It is always better to know, so one may try to avoid danger. And we *know* very little about Anna, except for you, who refuse to share your knowledge with us.'

'Ooh, ow, aaah!' Paolo said in his most piteous Arlecchino voice. 'You hurt me with such words, lady, please stop!'

'One day you will have to put aside Arlecchino and be Paolo, nobody else.'

'Why?' he said, so simply and sincerely that she had no answer. They walked on in silence, the night laying a chill cloak around them.

As they neared the inn, Teresa said, 'I shall find out, you know.'

'Why your mother was killed? Is that what you seek for on these walks? But whom do you expect to tell you?'

'I was not speaking of my mother,' Teresa said after a moment. 'I told you, I do not wish to discuss her any further. I was speaking of Anna.'

The servant looked down – far down, for the woman was bent low beneath a humped back. 'What is it, old mother? Do you want scraps from the kitchen?' His voice was pointedly arched with condescension; its sound was the shape of one of the dwelling's many windows.

'Please,' whispered the woman, 'may I see Ludis?'

'What?'

'Ludis,' the woman croaked.

'Who are you to wish to see a servant of the house of Bardi?'

'Please, Signor. I have something of importance to tell Ludis.'

'Tell me and I will pass it on to her.'

'I must see Ludis herself. She must come to this door.'

'Why should I call her to speak with a beggar? Either tell me what you have to say, or move on.'

The woman hesitated. 'I am not a beggar.' When the man snorted she added, still whispering, 'You are right, Signor, I am a beggar, but I must see Ludis. Please tell her. In God's name, sir, for all Venice knows the Bardi household is a devout one.'

The servant gave her a look as searching as a torch, then turned and went inside. The woman waited: three minutes, five minutes, rocking back and forth, her head angled towards the door as if she would catch whatever faint sounds came from behind it and absorb them into herself, like water into wool.

She was unaware that someone had been creeping closer and closer along the wall behind her, listening and watching.

She could not quite believe what she was doing: standing at the door of her parents' house disguised as an old crone.

It was all because of Paolo, she thought, with his admonition to improvise. And his dog.

She did not like the dog, although she could not really say why. It was old; it hobbled on three legs; it waited for table scraps with its long ears hanging – but none of these reasons was sufficient to cause her dislike, which she had to hide from Paolo. He was attached to the animal, which he called Buffa. It slept at his feet, pricked up its ears when he entered a room, and quivered with pleasure when he scratched it. He asked her to look after it during the day when the company was performing, and Susanna could not refuse the man who had done so much for her. So, dutifully, she called Buffa once or twice each day, patted it, and fed it the scraps Paolo left. Its rheumy eyes would fill with gratitude, and Susanna would think how her life had altered, that she no longer had servants but was herself servant to an old, crippled dog.

Although Susanna Bardi had wanted to leave her house as seldom as possible, 'Anna' felt trapped inside the inn and yearned to go out. She could not do so, of course, even veiled. The priest was searching for her, and no doubt Ludovico had servants doing the same. Perhaps her family did as well. She tried to keep busy by writing down comic plots she recalled from the Latin writers, or poems, especially those with lines that Luca and Isabella could use. When she handed Luca several pages, unable to speak, he had looked at them, smiled and said, 'These are good, Lady Anna.' He tucked them into his pocket. Later, she heard him tell Isabella there was new material to use. At night, in the bed beside Teresa, she would imagine how he might say them in performance, and improvise upon them. Forbidding herself such thoughts, she would recall instead her old room at her parents', where she had read all day and sometimes all night as well, by the light of the bronze oil lamp; where the books smelled of sweet leather and opened the treasures of their pages to her like slowly moving fans – Dante, and Gaspara Stampa, and Bembo's sonnets and his *History of the Republic*, and Petrarch . . . When the company left Venice in a week's time the world of the Bardi house, of its beauty and comfort, might well be lost to her forever. She might never see her mother again.

One night Teresa had turned over and said, 'Why do you do that? Sigh, sigh – as if something heavy is squatting on your chest.'

'I am sorry. Do I keep you awake?'

'Yes.' Teresa sat up. 'What troubles you?'

Susanna hesitated, tempted to confide in her. By morning their bodies had come to rest against each other, but something seemed to hold their spirits apart. Teresa's brown eyes were too watchful, like sparrows waiting for crumbs. Cautiously Susanna said, 'I grow weary of staying in all day.'

'Why do you not go out then?' Teresa asked. Susanna did not reply. 'Do you fear someone?' Teresa asked. Susanna remained silent. 'Or do you wish to see someone? If you tell me who,' Teresa added, 'perhaps I could help.'

'I – cannot say.'

'Very well.' Teresa slid back down beneath the spread. But in a few moments she said, 'Here, I have an idea. If you want to go out and see someone, then in the morning let us ask Paolo to make you a disguise, a complete one, so you can go where you like without fear of discovery. Are you willing?'

Susanna had stared into the dark, then whispered, 'Yes.'

Paolo's eyes had lit at the challenge. He led Susanna to one of the costume trunks and said, 'We must improvise. A courtesan? That is a possibility. We have nothing so elegant as a silk waistcoat, but we could—'

'No,' Susanna said firmly. 'I do not wish to be a courtesan. I would not be a good one.'

Paolo looked at her, then quickly away. He busied himself in the trunk and emerged with three objects: a cane, a large black shawl, and a wad of cloth sewn into a bag. 'Here we are – your hump,' he said, and tied it around Susanna's back with a cord. He draped the shawl over her so that it not only covered the hump but made a hood round her face and added its protection to that of the veil. Then he demonstrated how to walk: bent nearly double, moving at a crawl-pace, resting both hands on the cane whenever he stopped. 'You see?' he said. 'A crone, to whom no one will pay the smallest attention.'

'I do not think I can do that,' she said.

'If you think not, then you will not. You must think that you *can* – there lies the whole trick. Well, half the trick. The other half is practice.'

'You make it sound simple,' Susanna said.

'Because I am a simpleton!' He wiggled his eyebrows like two birds flying in separate directions. 'Let us see what you can do.' He got her to try it a few times, along the hall outside their rooms. He cocked his head and said, 'Not dreadful, but not good. You must practise. And do not merely imitate what I did. Improvise – add to it as you will, provided only you do not forget you are an old ragged woman, whose bones cannot move quickly. Now I leave you to yourself. If you wish to succeed and be able to go out into the streets, then you will. Otherwise . . .' He shrugged. 'Think of Buffa. If he had told himself, "No, I cannot run again, I am a three-legged stool that must stay in the corner," do you think he would be getting about as he does?'

Having the dog cited as an exemplar had been so infuriating that as soon as the company went off to perform, Susanna practised in earnest, up and down the hall many times until she felt, if not comfortable, at least not foolish. The first time she went outside, with people squeezing past her in the *calli* and a breeze ruffling the canals, robbed of its threat by a brilliant sun, her blood hardly knew which way to race – to her stomach in fear, or her temples in excitement. The latter won. She was free of herself, of being Susanna Bardi, who could not look into a glass or the mirror of a canal without loathing what she saw. She had breathed in the sweet, cold air and smiled – until she realised she had stood erect. The hump was sliding down her back. Her mood had imperilled the very thing that caused it. She hurried into a doorway, adjusted the disguise, and, chastened by forgetting to 'perform', returned to the inn, where she fed Buffa his scraps and, behind the veil, made a rueful face at him.

The next day she had gone out again, longer and

farther, and still more the next. On the third morning, as Luca came down the stairs for the company's breakfast of fruit and bread – singing, as he often did, 'la-la-la-la-la's that were bell-calls of high spirits – he had stopped and said, 'Today I shall use some of your lines, Lady Anna.' She told herself that danger would be too great in the Piazza, she forbade herself to go, but at midday she fed Buffa and set out. She hobbled among the stalls and carts and found a place at the edge of the crowd surrounding the platform where I Favolosi was playing *The Lady Who Was Believed Dead*: the scenario of a woman who conspires with her lover to avoid marrying the man her father has chosen by taking a potion that makes her seem dead. If only she had had such a potion to fool Ludovico, Susanna thought, looking up at the platform with her back bent and the shawl hooded around her. But neither did she have a lover with whom to conspire. She watched Arlecchino and the Captain come out and begin speaking at such comically cross purposes that the crowd shrieked in agonies of laughter and a man standing beside Susanna whooped and broke wind, in unison, shamelessly and frequently. Then Luca strode onstage and in his deep, rich voice began to speak of his love for the supposedly dead girl. His opening lines, from Gaspara Stampa, were those Susanna had written out: 'Who could recount my present state, the happiness I feel, the intense delight? One of the elect angels who reside in heaven? Perhaps a lover who experienced the same thing?' Improvising upon the lines, he had seemed as tall and golden as the winged lion on the Basilica. Susanna had forgotten to be afraid of Ludovico's spies in the crowd, or of Fra Filippo's. When the performance was finished, still in its spell, still exhilarated by her own ability to watch it undetected, she had felt she too could improvise, could even find a way to bid her mother goodbye . . .

She leaned on her cane, waiting and rocking. Ten minutes had gone by, and her determination was wavering, when the door finally opened and a handsome Circassian slave appeared.

'Ludis!' Susanna said. She pulled the Circassian down by the sleeve and began whispering in her ear.

The figure standing against the wall watched them both go into the house. Then she retied the scarf around her red hair and walked a distance away.

When Ludis brought her into the chamber, Susanna stood erect, pulled off the shawl and veil, and let the hump slide down however it would, like a bag of grief falling from her. Her mother seemed frozen, one hand to her lips, only her eyes moving, growing huge in disbelief. Then, like a statue breaking apart, she took a jerky step forward, told Ludis to guard the door, and held out her arms. The sleeves of her loose, fur-lined silk robe trembled.

'My dear child,' she said, when they were sitting on her bed, on the coverlet of yellow silk, embracing, 'have you come home to me?'

'Could I do so, Mother? Is it possible?'

For a time they rocked together quietly. 'No,' Signora Bardi said at length. 'It is not possible.'

'Is my father very angry?'

'Yes.'

'Are you, Mother?'

Signora Bardi sighed. 'They believe that I am.'

'Poor Mother. What a trial I have been to you, ever since the scar.'

'I do not complain. You are the one to whom God has given a terrible thing to bear.'

'Not so terrible, Mother, as being the wife of Ludovico.'

The Signora said nothing.

'Has he come here, Mother?'

'Yes. In a rage. Demanding your return. Everyone has pledged it. Even Bishop Palma. His people look for you while he is in Rome.'

'I will die rather than return to Ludovico.'

'A wife must accept many things, my daughter.'

'Have you had to do so, Mother?'

Signora Bardi's fingers, perfumed and soft, moved in circles on the silk coverlet. 'To be the wife of a noble house is to be . . . a possession. A valued one, like a marble figure, or a necklace of heavy pearls. One is meant to be admired, displayed, guarded. Envied by other families. And in so being, one must accept one's husband's freedom to do whatever he likes. To spend his time and take most of his pleasure elsewhere.'

Susanna pulled back to look at her mother's round, soft face, nearly as familiar as her own but suddenly different, as if a painter's brush had turned the known into the new with a few strokes: adding a glitter of directness to the brown eyes, an edge to the upper lip, a flare to the nostrils. For the first time, Susanna realized, her mother was looking at her, and speaking to her, as one woman to another, with nothing else between them – neither the fact of their blood bond nor the existence of the scar.

'Has Father made you very unhappy, then?' she said.

'What do you mean?' Her mother's tone was defensive yet pleading.

'I mean his going so often . . . I mean his courtesans.'

Her mother's fingers gripped the coverlet, then released it. 'If I tried to leave,' she said, her voice like wood creaking in a wind, 'or if anyone tried to take me away, he would be as angry as if one of his golden treasures had been stolen. He would swear vengeance. But I never wanted to be only a golden treasure. A possession.'

There was a movement at the door. Both women's heads swung in that direction. It was Ludis shifting position, her face impassive as usual, except for a slight upturn at one corner of her mouth.

'Is someone coming?' asked Signora Bardi.

Ludis shook her head.

When the two women turned back to each other, Susanna said, 'Do you love him, then?' amazed that she was putting such a question to her mother. For all these years, it seemed, passion had lain beneath the gentle manner and soft skin, like cargo buried at sea. Most amazing of all was that its object was her gruff and imperious father.

Her mother seemed about to answer, but she shook

her head several times and took both Susanna's hands in her own. 'My daughter, I am failing you. You came for help and comfort, not to hear of my life. Let us talk of you and what can be done for you.'

It was gone – the glimpse into her mother's life as a woman, as if the painter had covered it over with one broad stroke.

Susanna said, 'There is nothing you can do for me, Mother. I only wanted to see you once more before I leave Venice.'

'Leave? Where will you go? Not to your sister in Mantua, surely, for she would inform your father and—'

'I do not know where I shall go, Mother.'

'But . . . how will you travel if you do not know where you go?'

'I shall travel with some new friends I have found.'

'What friends? Who are they?'

Susanna hesitated. 'If I tell you, the knowledge will be a burden each time you speak to Father, or the rest of the family, or anyone from the church.'

'Not so great a burden as imagining you in company that neither God nor man would approve.' The Signora caught her breath. 'You have not joined with prostitutes, have you?'

'No, Mother.'

'But then . . . with whom? Beggars? Thieves? Oh, my dear child . . .' She put a hand on Susanna's cheek, touched the scar with one finger, and began to cry.

'Mother, please do not weep. Everything will be all

right. My new friends are players, about to leave the city for the north. They are good people.'

Her mother could not have been more astounded if she had said she was going to ship out on a galley. 'Players? Performers? Who set up in the Piazza?'

'Yes, Mother. Arlecchino and Il Dottore and Pantalone.'

'But why? You have no such skills.'

'True. Yet did not I get here by pretending to be an old beggar woman?'

Only when her mother sat back, frowned, and clasped her hands did Susanna admit to herself that she had been hoping to be praised.

'I don't know,' said her mother. 'Players . . . the bishop has spoken of their lewdness. Yet some of them have been invited to play at great houses, even for members of the Signoria. My child, I do not know what to say.'

Susanna kept her face from betraying what she had just realized. It must have been present in a thousand moments of the tapestry of her life in this house, but she had not known it – she had lived stitch by stitch, not seeing the whole scene until it hung on a wall and she could stand away from it: Her mother was weak. Kind, beautiful, elegant, loving, but also weak.

Was she herself as weak? Perhaps the quality was born into the blood. She looked down at her hands, her lap, her feet. Would she have thrown herself from the Fondamenta Nuove if it had not been for Paolo and I Favolosi? If Fra Filippo found her, if he were even now heading to the Bardi house, would she be able to survive? The hands she stared at began to shake.

'I must go, Mother,' she said. 'At once.'

'Shall I never see you again?'

'That will be God's disposition.'

'Will you not reconsider and return to Ludovico? It cannot be as bad—'

'No!' The shrillness of her voice fed Susanna's growing fear. She fastened the hump into position, put on the veil and shawl, speaking as quickly as her fingers worked. 'You will tell no one you have seen me, Mother.'

'Can you imagine I would?'

'And you will never reveal that I am with some players, or where we are heading. Do you swear it?'

'Susanna!' Her mother clung to her as she moved to the door. 'Wait, wait. Take some of my rings or pearls, so you will have some money.'

'They would be too difficult to explain. Mother, do not forget – I have not been here. If anyone asks, you saw an old woman to whose son you did a kindness and who begged to thank you in person.'

'My child, what will happen to you?' Her mother began to weep.

At the door Susanna said, 'Goodbye, Mother,' her voice muffled by more than the veil and hood. She turned to Ludis and embraced her. Ludis stiffened for an instant, then responded. 'Let us go back as we came. I am so grateful for your help, Ludis. My mother will reward you for it. Will you not, Mother?'

Signora Bardi nodded, but her face was buried in

her hands, so Susanna's last sight of her was the slope of her fingers and the crown of her golden hair.

Deep in thought, Fra Filippo walked along the *calli* at dusk, his hands folded before him like wings. People jostled him sometimes. On a bridge two boys, each with a loaf of round, fragrant bread, dashed past and bumped into his arm, so that he had to clutch the railing. Had they stolen the loaves? Filippo debated whether to give chase, knew he could not catch them, and asked God's forgiveness for not trying.

He did not truly regard his failure to chase the boys as a sin, but it was his habit to beg God's forgiveness, silently and regularly, for most of his actions. The soul of man was a sewer. One could vow to live by the commands of the Lord and His Holy Roman Catholic and Apostolic Church, but Satan could not bear the sight of souls given to the Lord and waited to entrap them with his powerful weapon: the flesh and all pleasures allied with it. Not even tonsure and cassock were sufficient protection. Had not one of the greatest of sinners, the heretic Luther, been a monk? Although his sin had been one of pride, not of indulgence. Even the most devout Christians were subject at all times to temptation, especially in Venice. To remain pure required eternal vigilance. So Filippo had acquired the habit of apologizing silently and constantly for whatever he might do to offend the Lord God. The search for purity had bred in him a chronic sense of inadequacy.

Wrapping his mantle more tightly, he continued

on his way to see his newfound brother. When they had parted at the convent door after their reunion, Filippo had asked Paolo to come the following day to hear him say Mass, then join him for a meal. Paolo had refused. 'Would you come to the Piazza the next day and see me perform?' he had said. 'I thought not. Let us meet halfway between Heaven and Hell – some ground that is neither church nor stage.' So they had supped in a dim taverna where neither had been before. The bread was dark and coarse, but the fish well seasoned. As Filippo peered across the table, trying to talk about their family and village while planning how to reclaim his brother for God, it occurred to him that God must be truly displeased with Paolo. Why else give him a face of such sharpness and foolishness, like something whittled to amuse a child?

'You stare at me,' Paolo had said suddenly. 'What do you see?'

'A face that . . . God loves.'

'Because it makes Him laugh?'

It had taken Filippo time to frame a proper reply. 'God created laughter, so it is natural for Him to be pleased by its sound.'

Paolo had waved his hand as if chasing flies and poured more wine.

Impious, Filippo had thought. Could his brother be, or become, heretical? At that moment the street door had opened. Cold air had guttered the lamps and chilled his flesh. An omen, he feared, of the difficulty of his task. In consequence, he had eaten too much chicken and imbibed too much wine, asking God's forgiveness as he did so. Too often he committed the sin of gluttony. No matter how many times he vowed to abjure it or how much penance he did, his flesh plumped and swelled around his soul more each year. He had left that meal dispirited. Paolo had not seemed happy, either. Still, they had agreed to meet in four days. But Paolo had not come, sending word he could not be there.

At first Filippo had done nothing about it – there were the parish affairs to see to, plus the search for Ludovico Rossi's missing wife. He had three young priests looking for her on the streets as well as in the convents. He himself could not go to the Piazza to find Paolo, for fear of witnessing the lewdness of a performance, but he had sent someone to enquire where the players were lodging. The information had simmered in him for several days. That morning a sense of urgency had gripped him. If he did not take some action soon, the players might leave Venice, and Paolo's soul might be lost forever.

Reaching a *campo* not far from their inn, he stopped to collect himself in front of a small, cavelike shop. Within, a leathery old man was hammering at a piece of metal with slow, hard blows that made sparks pop. He looked up and smiled, mouth full of blackened stumps. The smile seemed demonic; he was a shrivelled imp at Satan's forge. Filippo crossed himself and started off again, praying that at the inn he would find Paolo, and only Paolo, no other members of the players' troupe. In particular, no females.

Once inside, he looked about him in trepidation. Everything was ordinary: courtyard, dining room, stair to the sleeping chambers. He cleared his throat loudly. A man came from the rear, seemingly the landlord, wiping his hands on a filthy apron. 'Good evening, Father. How may we serve you?'

'I believe a troupe of players lodges here with you.'

'That is so.'

'I wish to speak with one of them – the man named Paolo Bertoldo.'

The innkeeper frowned for a moment. 'Ah, Arlecchino! I shall call him.'

So his brother was there. Filippo took it as an omen and settled on a bench in the inner court. Yet when Paolo's thin legs appeared at the head of the stairs, followed by the rest of his body and his sharp, foolish face, doubt rushed into Filippo's heart.

'So you have found me,' Paolo said, his voice offering no indication of how he felt about that fact.

Filippo rose and held out his hands. 'I had to search for you. Are you not my brother?'

'True.'

'Should we not rejoice in discovering each other and praise God for it?'

'No doubt you are right.'

'Then come, my brother, let us dine together – perhaps at this inn – and talk more of our family and our mutual love of God.'

'I fear,' Paolo said dryly, 'that your love is greater than mine.'

'What are you saying?'

'You have given your life to His service, whereas I have not.'

'True. I am a priest, where you are . . . not. But that is no reason for a gulf to lie between us. Is it?' Filippo heard his words and was bewildered. Why speak of gulfs? Some demon had seized control of his tongue and was twisting it to peculiar purposes.

'Filippo,' his brother replied, 'I have been busy with the affairs of the company. I still am. It is not possible for us to talk tonight. Perhaps tomorrow, or the next day.'

'When are you leaving Venice?' Filippo asked.

Paolo waved a hand – as he had at the taverna, chasing away flies.

'So you refuse to come to supper with me?' Filippo demanded.

'I do not refuse. I am unable to.'

'Are we not to see each other again?'

'Certainly,' Paolo said. 'I shall send word to you soon, and we shall have another evening to continue our reunion' – Paolo's eyes widened – 'our blessed reunion. Excuse me, brother, please excuse me for a moment.' He rose. 'Be off with you!' he said sharply. 'We want no beggars here.'

Filippo turned and saw that someone had entered the court: an old woman, bent, leaning on a stick, swathed in shawls. 'Go away!' Paolo called, but the woman did not move, only stood as if frozen by his voice.

Filippo rose. 'Brother, brother,' he chided. 'Are we not all God's children?'

'Yes . . . yes, you are right,' Paolo said. 'I shall give this poor creature a coin to help her on her way.'

Someone else entered the court. The old woman shifted.

The next thing Filippo knew, he was sitting on the bench again and Paolo was holding a glass of spirits to his lips.

'What is it?' Paolo said. 'You turned as white as a miller's cap and fell to the ground.'

'It was indigestion,' Filippo said. 'My stomach is not strong.' But he was not speaking the truth, for which he silently asked God's forgiveness. His stomach was fine; it was his heart which had given a great thunderclap when he saw who the woman was. He looked around, but she was gone. No one else was in the court but his brother.

'I must help you home,' Paolo said.

'Yes. Thank you, brother.' Filippo got slowly to his feet which seemed unable to support his weight.

Leaning on Paolo, he left the inn. They went in silence, darkness thick around them, the moon veiled with clouds, until Filippo said, 'Who was that woman?'

'How do I know? An old beggar. She took her coin and went off quickly enough.'

The two of them walked on, crossed a bridge. Filippo said, 'And the other woman?'

'What other?'

'She came into the court just as I . . . fell.'

Paolo shrugged. 'People come and go all day. What did she look like?'

'She— It does not matter,' Filippo said.

* * *

But it did matter, profoundly. An hour later Filippo was at his desk, composing a long letter to Bishop Palma in Rome, the *o*'s and *a*'s not so plumply equal as usual, the trains of the *s*'s quite short, even jagged, as he wrote of the woman in the court, the beautiful woman with the hair as red as no other head of hair on earth, the woman who was supposed to be dead. *Had* to be dead.

CHAPTER SIX

The Lovers

We are naked. Nothing hides our faces – no leather masks, false eyebrows or beards.

Yet, being naked, we are still masked.

Our nakedness is not like a babe's, which can only sleep or suck, its face as smooth as a pudding, or lie squalling, as wrinkled as a dried plum. We can clothe our faces in as many expressions as God, and our skill, permits them to assume. We can make our voices sound like lutes or viols. We can keep our supple bodies dressed as splendidly as our monies allow.

We can make the crowds believe we are young and glorious – even when we are not.

What is our mask? Its name is Beauty, which draws all eyes and can change the course of an action.

The company left Venice on a cold, bright morning, after three days of fog that had swaddled the lagoon and the foundations of the buildings like rags on beggars' feet. Suddenly the sun pushed aside all things grey. The waters glittered blue-green again, the richness of mosaic and marble reappeared, and the paintings on the façades of the *palazzi*, where artists displayed their talents in the hope of attracting commissions, bloomed again in full hue.

'How I hate to leave,' said Isabella, as the spires and domes shrank slowly behind the company. A boat was carrying them to the mainland where they had left their travelling wagon.

Luca, who stood beside her, his gaze also directed back at the city, lifted his arms as if to embrace what he saw. 'Farewell, glorious city,' he said. 'We shall see you soon again.'

'I do not think so,' said Bruno, on Isabella's other side. 'Venice is both costly and capricious. She once banished all players. She may do so again.'

Isabella sighed. 'If only we had the protection of a patron—'

'But we did not find one,' Bruno said curtly.

'We might have tried harder.'

'Do you mean that *I* might have?'

Isabella did not reply, merely shrugged and adjusted her wool cloak as a fine spray flew up towards her.

Behind them on the damp deck was the rest of the company, with their bundles of personal belongings, trunks of stage materials, and rolled-up backdrops. Their bodies rocked with the motion of the water. Pedrolino plucked his guitar tunelessly. Giulio and his wife dozed on a trunk, heads together.

Teresa clutched a basket full of her packets of dried herbs, thinking that Venice had failed her. Despite her walks and vigils, she had never seen the ring her mother described. And if she did not find it in Venice, was she likely to see it anywhere else? Four days earlier she had awakened in excitement, for she had dreamt of sitting at a long table splitting chestnuts; in the lexicon of dream interpretations her mother had taught her, splitting chestnuts meant that a mystery would be solved. She had gone out that day alone, spirit singing with the certainty of seeing the ring. But she had not.

Instead she had seen Anna in her old-crone disguise. It had been wise to encourage her to go out, so she could follow and learn whom Anna saw, but the mystery was deepened, not solved. Why had Anna gone to one of the great houses, been admitted, and stayed a quarter of an hour? Teresa had found that the house belonged to the Bardi family, of whom her mother had spoken; she had often said that within great houses lived the lowest creatures. Why had Anna been almost ill when she returned to the inn? Teresa looked at Paolo, wondering why he would not share what he knew, wishing she had a spell for making people tell things. If there was such a spell, her mother had not taught it to her.

Paolo stood with arms folded across his chest, his gaze on Isabella's back and, beyond her, on the pastel façades of the buildings fading away. But his thoughts were on his brother, who kept worming into his mind. Paolo had managed to avoid seeing him again, but Filippo had sent several messages. Perhaps it was wrong not to see one's own brother. Perhaps God would punish him for what he had done. So be it, Paolo thought; he was Arlecchino, and he would not let anyone preach at him that being Arlecchino was wrong . . . especially someone who let chicken grease run down his chin while the rest of his plump face pinched itself into piety, someone who would have taken Anna from the inn if he had known she was upstairs. *Out of my thoughts!* Paolo ordered his brother. He looked around for Anna, who had been even more quiet than usual for several days. 'Are you sad to be leaving Venice?' he had asked. All she had said was, 'No,' so softly but firmly that he had not even tried a caper to make her laugh. He reached down to pat Buffa, who snuffled gratefully.

Susanna sat in the stern, as far back as possible. When Paolo craned his head at her and smiled, she lifted a hand instead of smiling in return, for she was wearing her veil. Paolo had saved her again. Somehow he had got rid of Fra Filippo.

She looked through the mist of her veil. Venice had almost melted into the water, leaving her alone with I Favolosi and the future. She saw Luca speak to Isabella, his profile against the canvas of the sky. When he turned away, she saw only the back of his head, his hair smooth and golden in the sun.

He began to sing a tune popular in the streets. His voice made her think of cinnamon bark.

The sun was low by the time they reached land and made their way to a farm where their wagon was stored. 'Eccolo!' Paolo cried. 'The house of I Favolosi!' He raised his arms, did a cartwheel, landed in front of the wagon, and planted an elaborate kiss on the wood. Buffa barked hoarsely.

The company moved to the wagon and inspected it as if it were a horse, touching the frame, the shafts, the canvas. There was a large platform on one side, to be used as a stage; Bruno undid the ropes that held it up, lowered it, studied it and raised it again. Umberto and Giulio hoisted up the trunks.

Susanna hung back, partly because she always did so and partly because she could not take in what she saw. The wagon. When they spoke of it, she had imagined something large and handsome, a galley of the land. But this narrow conveyance, mud caked on its painted wheels and patches sewn on its canvas . . .

'So, Lady Anna, what think you of it?'

Luca stood beside her, although she had not heard him approach – had not, for once, been aware of him at all. Safe behind the veil, she turned to him.

'I think you are surprised,' he said, 'and somewhat dismayed.'

'Why should you imagine that?'

'Every line of your body tells it to me.'

Susanna did not know which was more difficult to believe: that someone could read one's thoughts merely by looking at one's body, or that he had looked at hers. She pulled her shawl tighter.

'Have you been much in the countryside?' he said.

'Seldom.'

'You will be able to breathe, and see into the distance, and feel the earth alive beneath your feet.' She said nothing.

He cocked his head at her. 'Do you prefer not to speak?'

'No. I am . . . How is there room for everyone in the wagon?'

'We are used to close quarters.'

'Do we . . . do you . . . where does everyone sleep?'

'In the arms of Nature – which is to say, a field. Or a barn if we are in luck. Or an inn, if there is one and we have the coins. Or under the wagon, when there is no other choice and God sends bad weather. And now your shoulders tell me you are terrified by the thought, for they have given a great shiver.'

'I did not realize—' she said faintly.

'Perhaps, Lady Anna, you will regret you asked to come with us.'

'No.'

'But perhaps you will miss Venice, as I shall. What a city! The gold, the velvet, the silk. Yesterday I saw a house where the women put the eggs of silkworms in their bodices, in little bags, to keep them warm until they hatch. "Ladies," I said, "foster-mothers to a precious thread, I never believed I could envy a worm!" Then I wanted to see a painting by the Tiziano of whom everyone speaks. I was directed to Santa Maria Gloriosa dei Frari, and I now know why everyone speaks of him. I stood for an hour. The robes of the Virgin – the crimson hue makes your mouth hang in awe. Have you seen it?' She nodded.

Paolo called, 'Luca! Come help put this trunk in position.'

'Very well!' Luca said. He smiled at Susanna. 'The

Lover must lift his share of the load. *Addio.*' He walked off.

Why had he spoken to her? Why had he smiled? Had she answered so foolishly that he would never again start a conversation? Had he divined her feelings for him? Did he enjoy inducing them? The questions flew at her like gulls. Had he – most tormenting of all – spoken and smiled out of pity? Her hands gripped each other as if wringing out linens. Better to be sold as a slave, like Ludis, than to travel with these strange people, the object of their frank looks and their pity. Pity was a dark feeling, born of superiority to its object. One felt pity for those one held at a distance: for a slave, or a dog, being whipped; or a man suspended for days in a cage from the Bell Tower because he was guilty of sodomy. She knew, because she had felt pity for such creatures. To be the *object* of pity was to realize one could elicit no other feelings: not admiration, and certainly not love. Never love. She watched Luca help Paolo and Umberto hoist trunks into the wagon. The muscles of his thighs and back swelled beneath his clothing, and his gold hair was darkening with sweat. She would rather have his hatred than his pity. At least, then, they would be united in something – in loathing what her brother's sword had made of her.

'Come along, Anna.' It was Teresa. 'Do not stand there doing nothing!'

Teresa felt no pity for her. Teresa treated her as an equal, complaining to her and about her. Susanna had seen the brown eyes darken with suspicion, more than anyone else's. Yet Teresa, like Paolo, accepted her fully.

'We must find a place for your bundle,' Teresa said impatiently. 'Come.'

Susanna followed her to the wagon and stepped up into it, a step as high as a leap. Inside, it seemed like a *sottoportego*, one of the arched passages under Venice's private buildings, except that it smelled of bodies, both human and equine. And of dried fish, sausage, and garlic, which hung in strings from the top supports. Along the sides, cooking pots and utensils were tucked into the boards. Trunks sat below them, along with the players' bundles and the backdrops. Straw mats covered the floorboards. 'Here,' said Teresa, pointing to a corner where her possessions, including baskets of herbs and oils, were stacked. 'Put your things beside mine.'

Susanna's 'things' had all come from the players: the old crone's shawl, a plate and spoon Paolo had given her the day before, a washing pot and cloth from Teresa, and the pen, ink and paper she needed to reconstruct plots and poetry. 'Tonight we sleep here in the barn,' Teresa said. 'You will need a blanket. I shall get one from the farmer's wife.'

'How?'

'By giving her a potion. She is always looking for ways to keep from conceiving.'

'How do you know about such matters?'

For a moment Teresa silently arranged objects in her baskets. 'My mother taught me.' When Susanna said nothing, she added. 'My mother died years ago.'

'In the plague?'

'In prison. Accused of sorcery.'

'Oh,' said Susanna faintly. 'I am sorry.'

'Paolo says one must accept what happens.'

'Do you think he is right?'

'Certainly. Would you not find life easier if you could accept your scar?'

Susanna bit her lip. 'Have you accepted what happened to your mother?'

'God leaves me no choice.' Teresa looked at her searchingly. 'Are you not going to ask whether she was indeed a witch?'

'Do you care to tell me?'

'Perhaps. Some day.' Teresa took a packet of dried leaves from her basket. 'What of your mother – is she living?'

'Yes.'

'And your father?'

'Yes,' said Susanna cautiously.

'They are Venetian? Nobles, I imagine?'

Susanna did not reply.

'Why do you never speak of them?'

'Until this moment, you have not spoken of your family either.'

Teresa put the packet of herbs to her nose and regarded Susanna above it. In the dimness of the wagon, her brown eyes were black holes. 'I do not know who my father is. My mother never spoke of him. Therefore I cannot either.'

Susanna was silent.

Softly Teresa said, 'Would it not be easier to speak

of those you are leaving behind? I feel you wish to tell me about them.'

Sparrow, Susanna thought, *you are too eager for crumbs*. She was relieved to see Giulio clamber into the wagon, muttering that he did not know where his mask had been packed. In the next moment, Bruno lifted one of the flaps and announced that the farmer's wife had their supper ready.

That night Teresa put her own blanket close to the one she had procured for Susanna and whispered, 'What were you going to say before, about your family?'

'Nothing,' Susanna said. She clutched the blanket around her and burrowed her face into the hay, which poked inquisitive spears through her veil.

In the countryside, the company stopped at every town, announcing its arrival by parading the streets, drumming and singing, Arlecchino loping and clowning in front. Then they set up the stage and a backdrop, hawked Teresa's potions and other wares, and played the scenarios Bruno had chosen. If there were no towns for many miles, they waited at a crossroads until enough passers-by collected. When they had cajoled every possible coin from the crowds, or every loaf of bread or piece of poultry or game, they packed and set off again, on foot, forming a ragged train around the wagon, which was pulled by two horses so old they could not be made to carry human cargo as well, except in an emergency.

Susanna had not realized they would be walking everywhere. Her feet ached constantly, feeling every bump in the cold, rutted soil of the paths, even through the soles of the boots Paolo had found for her. She would have begged to ride in the wagon, but the sight of Buffa hobbling along on three legs made her bite her lip and go on. Gradually her feet toughened and ceased to dominate her attention, and she could look about at the land that sloped around her, the clouds resting on its peaks, the streams like ribbons dropped on the earth, the vineyards rising in green stairs, the occasional cattle that watched the company's passage with eyes as weary and patient as saints'.

Susanna set out each morning by herself, in the rear, but sometimes either Paolo or Teresa would join her. Each was trying to pull her into the society of the troupe; each, she sensed, had a different reason for doing so. Neither had been very successful. Bruno and Isabella tolerated her. Umberto asked about Latin passages and smiled at her, but only occasionally. Giulio and Pedrolino stayed at a distance: and so did the other women, almost as if the scar were a threat to their existence – *how can a woman be a woman with such a face?*

'Why do you always walk by yourself, Lady Anna?'

She had been looking at the foothills, thinking that, in her other life, she would have travelled in a carriage, to Milano or Mantua or a villa near the sea. She had not realized that the figure walking back to join her was not Paolo but Luca. She could not answer him; her tongue had frozen.

'I ask, Lady Anna, why you prefer to walk alone each day.'

'I . . . do not know.'

'Perhaps you feel you are not a part of us yet?'

She nodded gratefully. 'I must think of leaving. You recall that I asked to join you only in order to leave Venice.'

'Do you wish to leave us?' She said nothing. 'Where would you go?'

'I . . . do not know.'

'Then why consider it?'

She said nothing.

After a while Luca drifted ahead. He turned back and said, 'In the scenario of *The Trick*, the lines that Isabella and I use to open and close our first scene seem poor to me. Could you suggest something better?'

'I shall try.'

'Good. Everything you provide is excellent. I have said so to Bruno.'

'Thank you.'

He patted her arm, smiled, and walked away.

They were several leagues from the next town when they stopped for the night, to roast chicken and rabbit over an open fire and then to camp in an abandoned tower near a rank of poplar trees. The air was cold enough to hold their breaths for a few moments, but Susanna was growing used to it and seldom thought of the furs and brocades that once embraced her.

She sat alone at the edge of the fire, watching and listening. Sometimes the troupe talked business, sometimes they laughed and joked, sometimes they told stories – not the kind they performed for the public, but tales they had read or heard.

'If I were rich,' said Luca into a sudden quiet, 'I would take a sea voyage like the English knight did – to the kingdom of the pygmies, and the land of dog-headed men, and the island of those who eat serpents and speak in hisses, not in words.' His head moved from side to side, then forward, and he said, 'Sssssssss.'

Isabella hissed too. Everyone laughed, except Bruno, who sat beside her, a bottle of wine to his mouth. 'Tell us about these places,' she said.

'Such places! On an island in the Atlantic Ocean, a huge island, all the inhabitants have the heads of dogs and worship the ox. They love war and carry shields as large as their bodies. Their king wears a gigantic ruby, five fingers wide, around his neck and prays three hundred times to his god before each meal.' Luca leaned forward. 'In the Indian Ocean, very difficult to reach, is the fabled island of Pentixore, where the emperor's palace has windows of crystal, tables of amethyst and gold, and a throne with steps and sides of emeralds. But the island's greatest wonder is the Sea of Gravel, which is dry yet filled with fish. Three times a week a river of precious stones flows into it.' The image glittered in the air, painted by his voice. 'On a river in India itself is the land of the pygmies, who are only three spans high' – his hands conjured such a person – 'who work gold and silver, and cotton and silk, more beautifully than anyone else in the world, and who live to be only six or seven years old.'

Sighs escaped into the silence around the fire, as if everyone contemplated riches and mortality: the impossibility of one, the inevitability of the other.

'What of the people who eat serpents?' asked Bianca's daughter, Fiorenza.

'They live in caves, on an island in the Pacific Ocean, I believe. Serpents crawl about on the sands and into the caves, where people pick them up, strip off their skins, and devour their flesh. The people have no words. Everything that needs to be said, they say in hisses.' Luca lifted his head, so the fire lit only his mouth and cheekbones, and a series of ssssss's, each different – loud, soft, sharp, angry, languorous – slid from his lips. 'I do not recall the name of the island,' he said, 'but perhaps Lady Anna does. I am certain she has read the book that tells of these voyages.'

Everyone turned to Susanna. She cleared her throat. 'Yes, I have. *The Voyages of Sir John Mandeville, Knight*. I think the island you speak of is called Tracoda.' Though many educated persons now declared the entire book to be an invention, for her the places in it were real, they existed, throbbing with life. Luca's voice and being had made her believe.

Later that night, when everyone had settled into the shelter of the abandoned tower, she allowed questions to come. Why had Luca tried to draw her into the circle? Why had he spoken to her that morning and encouraged her to remain with the company? Only one answer could be true. He needed her help with lines. But she could not crush hope; it kept hissing softly in her mind.

The next day, on the road, Paolo came to her and said, 'Look here, you could learn some acrobatics.'

'I?'

'Why not? You are young, you are strong enough, your body is slender. If you were skilful, Bruno might use you in the performances. Then you could stop thinking of leaving I Favolosi, for you would be truly part of us.'

'Do you think everyone would accept me?'

'I think Bruno would be willing, and he is the only one who matters. He is not unhappy with the language and the scenes you have given us. If, in addition, you were able to perform . . .'

'I would not be skilful. In any case, how could I do somersaults and handstands while wearing a veil?'

'True. It would be in the way. Therefore,' Paolo said with half a dozen stiff-legged Arlecchino steps, 'you would remove it.'

'No. No. I cannot! Do not ask it.' She spoke so sharply that Umberto, who was not far ahead, turned to stare.

'Very well,' Paolo said. 'You could wear a mask. Then you could do acrobatics easily.'

'I doubt that.'

'I do not! I taught Teresa, and you see how excellent she is. We shall begin work at the next stop.' Before she could protest, he had loped ahead to talk to someone else.

That evening after supper, he took her out of reach of the others' hearing but not of the fire's warmth and light. 'Here, put on the mask,' he said.

'Arlecchino's?'

'Do I control any other? In truth, I do not even

control Arlecchino. He controls me.'

'How?'

'Look at the mask – how long and sharp the nose is, how the eyebrows spring up and out. When you put it on, your own face will disappear. *This* will be your face. It will guide you. You will see. Lift off your veil – do not worry, no one is watching – and put on the mask. Tie the bands behind your head, so the fit is tight.'

She did not know how to refuse him, so she did as he said. The leather face lay on her forehead and cheeks and sloped around her mouth. The mask was light in weight and rougher in texture than those she had worn for Carnevale, and it smelled of sweat. 'Now sit,' Paolo said, 'and see what happens.'

She looked at him. The eyeholes of the mask were like fingers curled into telescopes; through them his face seemed even thinner and sharper. She turned towards the fire and saw Luca talking to Isabella. The familiar feelings, which she normally stifled, rose inside her. Why hide them when she was someone with a nose like a curved knife and eyebrows like tufts of hay? She felt her mouth curling down in a mockery of pain, a mockery that was also real. 'Oh!' she said in surprise. Paolo laughed.

'Walk,' he commanded. 'Just here, back and forth.'

She did, although she felt foolish. Without her willing it, the foolishness became part of the walk, seeping into it like spices into sauce, and her steps became a wooden strut.

'Hop,' Paolo said. 'Jump!'

She was going to say she couldn't, but her legs lifted from the ground of their own will. Her body no longer seemed connected to a face, either her own or the one made of leather, yet her eyes saw piercingly. She skipped in a wide circle, hands moving the skirt of her dress back and forth in front of her. 'See the scar!' she said in a voice quite unlike her own. 'The witch's scar. See it run. Rrrrrrun awaaaaay!'

Buffa, lying near Paolo, sat up and barked. The sound was a trumpet calling her back to herself, making her see what she was doing. Abruptly she stopped, looked at Paolo, then sat beside him and untied the mask. Holding it, she stared at the leather features as if she had never seen them before.

'I . . . I already have a mask,' she said.

'What do you mean?'

She had never confessed it to anyone before. 'When the scar happened, it was as if someone had come in the night and put a mask over my face, which I could never take off.'

Paolo frowned and looked down at his hands.

'Do I make you uneasy?' she asked.

'I do not know how to answer you,' he said, with his characteristic simplicity.

'I am sorry. I should not have mentioned it.'

After a silence he said briskly, 'Look here, you will do very well. You must have your own mask, however – something gentler, with a round nose, I think, and no eyebrows. There used to be such a one in the trunks. Or perhaps we will make you one for your own.'

'Why do you take this trouble with me?'

'Perhaps I do not regard it as trouble.' He lifted his hand as if to touch her face, but instead he gestured as if dozens of flies hovered before his eyes. 'We shall begin work tomorrow,' he said. 'Come, Buffa! Back to the fire!'

The winter passed, chilly nights and occasional dustings of frost giving way to the bursting vigour of green and the higher, longer light of the sun – a giant gold coin melting over the fields and hills and roofs. Laurel and poplar leaves glistened as if with oil, and the clumps of cypresses put out tips of pale, newborn colour.

The company was rejuvenated, too. Umberto and Pedrolino painted the wheels of the wagon crimson and green. Luca and Paolo redid the main backdrop curtain so the façades of its buildings were freshly yellow and red and the sky behind them nearly blinding in its blueness. Giulio's wife and daughter mended the costumes and scrubbed them on white stones beside a clear stream. Teresa went off to gather herbs and returned with a look in her eyes as if she had been to places as distant and magical as those Luca described by the firelight. Isabella restored her hair to new gold. With a sponge attached to a stick, she applied the bleach Teresa concocted for her – the ashes of vines boiled in water and white wine, with barley spears, twig-bark, and a lime – and sat in the sun for hours.

The performances took on new life. Umberto doddered and drooled such Latin nonsense that

Susanna had to laugh aloud behind the curtain. Luca and Isabella kept a Lovers' argument flying back and forth as if it were winged. Arlecchino improvised with the impetuosity of madness. After serving dinner to his master Pantalone, he wiped the plates on the seat of his pants. He stole Pedrolino's soup, tried to eat it with his fingers, and beat himself soundly with his *batte*. He got his arms stuck in the legs of a stool and hopped about the stage howling that a devil had turned him into a tree. He stood for a long time with one elbow resting on nothing but air, turned to look at it, and collapsed in a heap. He hid beneath a table where Teresa sat, poked his head under the hem of her skirt, and twitched his body so long and so suggestively that the crowd's laughter would not stop and the village priest, who was present, left the square and threatened his flock with hellfire if they attended more performances. Bruno counted the coins, smiled, treated himself to an extra bottle of wine, and blessed the day Paolo had run after the wagon and begged to join them.

Practising under Paolo's guidance, Susanna grew steadily more adept at cartwheels but was not yet quite good enough to show Bruno what she could do and ask to perform. She and Paolo went into the fields to practise or found a screen of trees, but Umberto saw them, and then Bianca's daughter, and within a day the whole troupe knew. Teresa said to Paolo, 'You are teaching her as you taught me. Do you wish her to stay with us, then?'

'Why not?' he said.

'Better to ask why?'

'*Sais pas*,' he said, and pretended to be an idiot.

Teresa shook her head in exasperation. 'Are you learning something about her?' He shrugged. 'How she got her scar? Who she is? Why she is escaping?'

'Why not ask her yourself?' he said.

'I have tried a dozen times! I tell you, we need to know about her!'

Susanna had grown comfortable with the mask Paolo had produced for her: an old one from the trunks, the leather of which he softened and reshaped so that the mask looked neither male nor female but could be either, the brows two eternally surprised lines above the eyeholes, and the mouth a perfect circle. The mask had no personality to grip her as Arlecchino's had, but its relative blandness had an even stranger power, for it left her imagination free to cast herself in many different roles – even to be the nine-year-old Susanna, on the day before the falcon had flown too low into the Bardi courtyard. Or, if she was quite alone, an adult Susanna into whose life the falcon had never swooped at all, who would never hesitate to make herself as desirable as possible.

One night she said to Teresa, 'Can you make me a bleach like Isabella's?'

'Why? Your hair is a fine, dark colour.'

'I would prefer it to be gold.'

'No,' Teresa said. 'You cannot have hair like Isabella's. That would anger her.' Later, however, Teresa turned over in the bed at the small inn where they were sleeping and said, 'Take the dregs of white wine, dry them, chop them in olive oil, and comb the mixture through your hair while you sit in the sun.'

It was a week before Susanna found the courage and opportunity to do so, on an afternoon when I Favolosi, after playing successfully for five days in one town, was walking to the next. They stopped early, and while the others were lying about near the wagon, talking idly and stretching, Susanna slipped away to a dense stand of cypresses with a stream nearby. She took the mask with her, to practise a bit – for she had made the peculiar discovery that without it her body was a dozen times more awkward and slow – but when she took off the veil, the sun was so warmly inviting that she sat at the foot of a large tree, slipped her dress down to her waist, and began combing the mixture of wine dregs and oil through her hair. She felt the sun pour over her naked face, imagined it consuming the scar. She dozed, dreamed, pictured herself as the Female Lover. She would enter the stage to deliver a soliloquy on the power of Cupid to dip his arrows in fire and ignite the flesh they found. Luca would enter from the opposite side. They would see each other, move to each other, begin improvising the kind of short, rapid bursts of dialogue she had by now heard dozens of times:

> He says a word, She retorts with its mate; He another, She another, the words flying as fast as the ear can follow, weaving into a tapestry on the loom of the scenario.
> He:Ropes . . .

She: Chains . . .
He: . . . of desire . . :
She: . . . of fire . . .
. . . that bind my soul . . .
. . . that anchor my heart . . .
. . . will pull asunder . . .
. . . will twist apart . . .
. . . if you do not swear . . .
. . . or care . . .
. . . to love forever . . .
. . . without cease . . .

'How much more handsome you would be without those clothes.'

'Is that a command?'

'One you have taken before, without protest.'

'And which is now being issued again?'

'If it is, will you obey?'

'Do you offer me a choice?'

Someone laughed softly. 'Choose to kiss either my foot or my breast.'

Susanna opened her eyes and clutched her dress to her nakedness. The man's voice was indeed Luca's, pulled from her dream into the reality of the lengthening sun, but her own voice had been usurped by Isabella's. Both came from behind her, on the other side of the trees. She listened with the horrid fascination of hearing someone's confession, except that the sins were actually being committed, not confessed. She heard – or did she merely imagine? God, let them be imaginary – the sounds of lips on flesh, of clothing sliding away. Each sound drilled into her like a nail, painting pictures in her mind she could neither bear nor ignore. She closed her eyes again, feeling frozen in time, like a figure on a tomb. Yet her cheeks burned, more with each moment, as the action taking place behind the trees grew inescapably real and clear. Moans, laughter, sucking, groans.

She felt another presence. Her eyes unlocked, and she saw Paolo standing before her. She put a finger to her lips, but it was clear he had been there for a time and was already silenced by what he heard. She saw her own feelings twist across his face. *He loves Isabella*, she thought, and wondered how she could have failed to know it until that moment. Slowly he sank to his haunches. She saw her comb lying in the grass, took it up, and began pulling it through her hair mechanically. It was the only motion either of them seemed able to make. They were in a cell made by the sounds coming from behind them, which grew more insistent and painted images even more cunningly real than Tiziano's.

Finally there was silence from behind the trees. Birds began to fill it with flute-songs. A breeze rustled; so did clothing.

Luca's voice said, 'We must go back.'

'I don't see why.' Isabella's voice was languid as the stretching of naked arms. 'Bruno will be busy with his bottle of wine.'

'I am going back. We have sufficiently discussed the new scenario.'

Isabella laughed. A moment later she said peevishly, 'Oh, very well.'

More rustling, then the sounds of leaving. Gradually the birds and the wind reclaimed the afternoon.

'I hate my face,' Susanna whispered.

'Yes,' Paolo said.

She turned to him. 'You love her?'

He nodded. 'You love him?'

Susanna wiped her eyes. 'Today is not the first time they have been together,' she said, accepting that only her disinclination to know it had kept her from doing so.

'No, it is not,' Paolo said. She saw that he had not known either, probably for the same reason.

They stared at each other like survivors of a shipwreck. Then the realization of what they had confessed began to surface in their eyes.

'I must wash my hair,' Susanna said awkwardly.

Paolo said nothing, but all the way to the stream, all the time she was rinsing out the oil mixture and drying her hair with a rough towel, she felt that he was watching her. For the first time in many, many weeks, she recalled that they had met on the street of whores.

When she walked back to where he still sat beneath the trees, he said, 'You have made your hair gold. Redder than Isabella's, but gold.'

'I . . . thought it would help.'

After a long silence he said, 'I am a foolish-looking fellow, you know.'

'Yes.' No other answer was possible. 'But you are a wonderful Arlecchino.'

'Arlecchino is a foolish-looking fellow. I say that the mask controls me, but in truth I chose him, did I not?'

'Yes,' she repeated.

'If I chose, I could walk as elegantly as any Lover. I could recite poetry as beautifully. I could improvise scenes that would . . .' He looked up at her and said in the voice of a dreamer, 'The sun is going, but your hair is gold. As beautiful as hers.' He picked up the comb and held it out. 'If the beautiful hair fell on one side of your face, if you combed it so that it did so . . .'

His voice seemed to be drugging her. She took the comb and pulled it through her hair, slowly, each time letting more and more strands hang over her twisted eye.

'The scar is gone now,' he said. 'You can be anyone. Anyone it suits your pleasure to be.' He smiled, fish-lips wide. Then he took up her mask from where it lay in the grass and tied it over his own face. 'Arlecchino exists no longer,' he said. 'Paolo exists no longer.' In the bland mask-face, he cocked his head and began to sing, in a surprisingly clear, sweet voice, one of the songs Luca sometimes used in performances. 'O lady, your neck is a swan's, your arms two white waves on the lake, your eyes two sapphires on a cloth of velvet . . .' She stood above him, listening, one hand anchoring the red-gold mask of hair, and then she was standing still no longer, for some power within her, though not known to her, was making her move, bending her body to the sweetness of the song, freeing it to sway and circle as if she were a great beauty, to show off the treasures of her flesh, the slenderness of her waist, the gracefulness of the hand she waved as slowly as silk, in a faint breeze, the roundness of her breasts as she moved her arm to pull her dress tight and reveal them . . .

'Lady,' said the voice behind the mask.

'Sir,' she said, watching him get to his feet.

'No ruby . . .'

'No pearl . . .'

'. . . no spice . . .'

'. . . no silk . . .'

'. . . is more rare . . .'

'. . . a treasure . . .'

'. . . than love . . .'

'. . . than being loved . . .'

'. . . by her . . .'

'. . . by him . . .'

'. . . whose beauty . . .'

'. . . whose beauty . . .'

'. . . I revere . . .'

'. . . I revere . . .'

They moved together, woven into the same trance by the sound of their voices and by the faces that their two masks, one of red-gold hair and one of bland leather, allowed them to imagine.

On the road the next day the company was overtaken by a stranger on horseback who asked if they were the troupe called I Favolosi.

'Yes!' Bruno said with a flourish.

'At last,' said the man. 'I have been searching every town in the Veneto, Lombardy, and Emilia-Romagna. I have a letter for you from Venice.'

Bruno opened it, read it, gaped, read it again.

'What is it?' Isabella cried.

'A miracle,' he said, his eyes round as goblets. 'We are bidden to return to Venice at once, to play under the patronage of one of the great houses, the Polani!'

CHAPTER SEVEN

The Mask

Only four wear The Mask: two *vecchi*, older men, and two *zanni*, clowns. Only we know the sweet communion between man and leather, in which we surrender our faces but receive a new being, who lived in us but whose existence we did not know until The Mask revealed him to us.

Flowing into our bones and blood, The Mask tells us how to act, speak, sing; allows us to feel and know things never felt or known before; controls us yet leaves us entirely free.

Are not those with naked faces jealous?

Why? wondered Signora Bardi.

Wherever her gaze fell in the room in which they dined, it found things to question. Why did the slaves look as impassive as statues when they served the meal – what were they thinking? Why did the wife of her son Matteo glance surreptitiously at her image in the silver tureen, the gold trays, and every other shining surface? Why did Ludovico Rossi dine with them so frequently? Often there were no answers to the Signora's questions, but they formed a busy inner stream that both expressed and relieved her disaffection with the way her life was arranged and lived: a roiling underground counterpart to her public smile.

She directed that smile at Matteo's wife, whom she did not much like, and reached up to touch her hair. Why did one's hair fall obediently into a smooth braid one day and, the next, resist and look as rutted as a country road? Why did one endure a *gamurrina*, letting the metal rods sewn inside its rich fabric squeeze one's flesh into a painful thinness? Why did Antonio smile to himself? Was he planning a late visit to the woman who had eyes like almonds and lived near the Campo Santo Stefano? If he thought that she, Veronica Bardi, did not know about Almond-Eyes, he did not know the woman he had married. Why had he married her instead of some other beauty of some other noble family?

Smiling at him, the Signora let her hand fall to the collar of pearls around her neck. She had a dozen such collars, of pearls in every size from rice grains to grapes. Courtesans were prohibited by law from wearing pearls.

Antonio looked back at her with the dark impersonality that was his public face. Their son Matteo called to him. Why had Matteo's birth been so painful? Because his father conceived him without love?

'Father,' said Matteo, 'have you heard that Bishop Palma will soon be returning to us?'

'Yes,' Antonio said. 'Whatever else he achieved in Rome, I understand it does not include a cardinal's hat.'

Ludovico looked around the table pugnaciously. 'Perhaps the Holy Father has learned that the bishop does not always fulfil his promises, especially the one he made here. In this very room.'

'What promise?' said Matteo's wife, pouting her lips and angling her head to see herself reflected in a golden bowl.

'The restoration of my wife to me!' Ludovico said.

'Oh. Yes, of course,' said Matteo's wife, eyes still on her reflection. Why, the Signora wondered, could the woman never attend to a conversation? Why had the devout Matteo wanted a wife who spent her days studying the dolls that modelled the latest French fashions?

'Fra Filippo strives to fulfil the promise,' Matteo said. 'And when the bishop returns, his efforts will no doubt acquire greater force.'

The Signora said, 'It will be pleasant to have the bishop's presence and his conversation enlivening our table again.'

Ludovico snorted and took another wing of partridge. His teeth sank into it like ivory daggers, for an instant its flesh was Susanna's..

The Signora blinked and cleared her vision. Why must they have Ludovico in the house so frequently? Once his initial fury at Susanna's leaving had passed, he had attached himself to them. 'Damn it,' Antonio had said when the Signora objected, 'he was wronged by our daughter, we must show that we reject her action.' But why must they? To that question, of course, the Signora did know the answer: so that all Venice would not think the Bardi countenanced Susanna's behaviour.

She sighed, recalling Susanna's secret visit. Why had she not found some way to detain her? Where was Susanna now, the beloved daughter whose scar cut as heavily into the mother's heart as into the child's face? Why had the saints not answered her prayers at the time and taken her own beauty in exchange for curing the child's disfigurement? Was it because she had also appealed to a servant of the Devil – a courtesan too old for anything but sorcery – and paid her to cast spells to try to help Susanna? That was in the days when the Signora had still thought such things could be helpful, when she had consulted diviners to learn whether Antonio would come to love her. Holding her breath, she had watched them cast the rope to see where the knots fell, or cast pairs of beans marked as male and female. If the two fell together, it would signify that he would grow to love her. In those days the pockets of her silk and taffeta gowns had held magic love spells written on *cartavergine*.

But if the saints had done as she asked, if they had saved Susanna at the expense of her own face – what would Veronica Bardi be without her beauty?

Ludovico laughed at something Antonio said. His face was flushed and sweat beaded in his eyebrows like fog droplets in grass. Why was Antonio so tolerant of him? What were they discussing?

As if to check on the serving, the Signora rose and moved slowly along the table. Bits of conversation floated up like the scents of the dishes: the preparations being made for Ascension Day and the upcoming ceremony of the Marriage with the Sea, the progress of Tintoretto's paintings at the Scuola di San Rocco, the ruin of a velvet dress soiled by the filth in the street. As she neared Antonio and Ludovico, she heard the words.

'Have I not fulfilled my part of our pact?'

'And did I not fulfil mine?'

'That was long ago. What do I have now, except a cold bed?'

'But you . . .'

The rest was lost for Ludovico looked up, saw her, and said, 'My dear mother' – why must he call her that, his voice like oil rolling in a pan – 'how beautiful you are this evening.'

'Thank you,' she said.

'To share your presence is to be compensated, in part, for your daughter's continued absence.'

'Thank you,' she repeated.

'The church has failed me, but I never cease to search for her.'

'I did not realize you loved her so deeply,' said the Signora.

'She is my most cherished possession,' Ludovico replied.

The Signora moved away from him. What had he meant by a pact? The marriage? Why refer to it in that way? He must mean something else, but what? Why did Antonio refuse to discourage the man's presence?

Regaining her place at the foot of the table, she resumed her public smile.

'Do you wish to return to Venice?' Bruno said.

'Venice?' echoed Susanna.

'That is my question,' he replied. 'Do you ask to return with I Favolosi? Or do you leave us to go your own way, as you once said was your intention? If the latter, then this is the best place for our paths to separate, for we must now head due east.'

'I . . . I believe that I . . .' To Susanna, her voice seemed to come not from behind her veil but from the ceiling of the inn where the company was stopping. She had tried to stay apart in the three days since the news of the good fortune that was recalling the players to the Most Serene Republic, but after supper Bruno had taken her aside, saying, 'Look here, Anna, I must speak to you.'

'Look here,' he said again, 'you came with us in order to leave Venice, so I make the assumption you do not wish to return.' In performance as the Captain he was imposing, delivering his boasting harangues in a loud, dark voice, flourishing his sword so that it sang, displaying his muscled arms as if they were hams on golden platters. Offstage his presence shrank and hardened, and he seemed as wiry as a long-cured sausage. He never wore a mask, but much of his ruddy, handsome face lay behind a dark beard, thick brows, and a moustache with curling wings. 'Well?' he said. 'Do you take leave of us here?'

'Do you wish me to do so?'

'Damnation!' he said after a moment. 'How can one hold a discussion with a veil?'

'Do you wish me to lift it?'

He scowled. 'No.'

Behind the veil, Susanna's good eye was calm, but beneath the other a muscle began twitching, as if the scar were struggling to be free of itself. She did not want to make a decision; she wanted God to send her a sign. But there was no sign, only Bruno's impatient scowl. She thought of Dante's words on the freedom of the will – 'with which all creatures of intelligence are endowed, they alone' – which had often seemed inspiring, but they did not inspire her now. She did not want freedom of the will, which would make her choose between Venice, where every *calle* could hold someone searching for her, ready to return her to Ludovico, and the countryside, where she would be without resources or companions. Without a certain face her gaze needed to rest upon, for did not all eyes need to contemplate beauty? No matter that it was unattainable.

'Why do you not answer me?' Bruno said.

'I find it difficult to know the best answer.'

'Damnation!' Bruno rolled his eyes and tugged on his beard. Susanna saw that he did not wish to make a decision either; he had been hoping she would relieve him of the need by announcing that she was leaving the troupe. She thought of reciting the Dante to him; the idea made her smile.

'Are you laughing behind that veil of yours?' he said.

'No, I assure you.'

Bruno shifted his weight. 'Look here, it is my belief that you are not worth the trouble of taking with us.'

'I cannot blame you for that opinion.'

'However, others speak strongly on your behalf. Luca – although I do not much heed what he says, my wife values his opinion. And it is true he makes her a fine partner. Then of course there is Paolo. We must keep him happy. That is understood.' He stared at her keenly, as if he could see through the veil. Then his gaze escaped. 'Paolo!' he called across the room, where Paolo sat with Giulio and his wife. 'Come here!'

Paolo hesitated, then rose and came to them, face tight with the effort to appear at ease. Paolo and she had not spoken since their afternoon in the cypress grove and the coupling that could neither be dismissed nor understood. As he approached, the space between them seemed to become a large balloon that pressed against her in the shape of his sharp, thin body, pushing the air from her own and squeezing the blood up into her cheeks.

Without preamble Bruno said, 'We speak of whether Anna shall leave us here or return with us to Venice. She does not, or cannot, give an answer. You are her advocate, you pay her share of expenses, so I ask what is your wish?'

'My wish?' Paolo repeated stiffly. He looked around the room, except at Susanna. His thin face twisted, as if he were in a trap. In fact he was transforming himself into Arlecchino, who banged on one side of his head – 'No wishes in here' – and then on the other – 'None here, either. No, Master, there are no wishes hidden on my person, I swear it by the cheese I ate for supper. And the bread, and the soup, and the wine—'

'Enough,' Bruno said. 'Enough! If you have no wish for her, why did you plead for her to join us? Why do you train her in acrobatics, so that she may become a member of the company? Why have you made me promise that when you deem her to be ready, I will allow her to show how well she can do? Ah, there you are stopped, my friend. So I ask again, are you of a mind to leave her here, or take her with us to Venice?'

Paolo looked at the ceiling. 'I wish Anna . . . to do what she wishes.'

It was not fair, Susanna thought, to make that poor face and body strain with the effort of revealing nothing – perhaps of feeling nothing. She opened her mouth to tell them she had decided: she would leave the company. But to her annoyance, she started crying instead.

Bruno swore. Paolo looked at her for the first time. His face reddened, his eyes leapt away like fingers held to fire.

'By heaven,' Bruno said, 'there is not one sensible tongue between the two of you. *I* shall decide what to do. Paolo, I promised you I would give Anna a chance. She shall have it tomorrow. We reach a village and she will lead our parade, demonstrating her abilities as an acrobat. If she does well, she may remain with us. If not, she must leave.'

'But she is not ready yet!' Paolo cried.

Bruno smiled.

* * *

'Back to Venice!' said Luca. 'Is it not splendid that we will return?'

Isabella nodded. On the way to the next town, when the company stopped for a rest, Luca had found a large smooth boulder to sit on. She had sauntered over to join him.

'But the Polani family,' she said. 'Why have they asked for us? Why do they wish to be our patrons?'

The troupe speculated constantly without finding an answer; they raised the question like an incantation, a way of both rejoicing in their fortune and protecting it. 'We must show the Polani only our finest performances and best scenarios. Therefore, I do not think we should play *The Two Notaries*.'

'Why not?'

'Teresa has too large a role.'

'As large as yours, you mean?' Luca said equably.

'I mean her performance is not strong enough.'

'Teresa herself would probably agree.' Luca spread his legs, picked a blade of grass, and began to chew it. 'She has never claimed to be a great player.'

'Do you think she is a great beauty?' Isabella asked.

'She is beautiful. But she may as well not be, for as best I can see, she finds little use for that beauty and takes small pleasure in possessing it.'

'So you have noticed.'

'I have eyes.'

'Indeed.' Isabella lowered her voice. 'Eyes of the most exquisite brown, such as would match a powder of cloves or a dark velvet from the East.'

Luca took the blade of grass from his mouth and

inspected the pale squares his teeth had left in its green. 'Are you preparing lines for a scenario?'

'Is that what you wish to believe?' When Luca did not reply, Isabella pursed her lips and sat back. No matter how she used her small, fine mouth, it seemed incapable of falling into any but beautiful lines.

Luca said, 'I have heard that Teresa resembles her mother.'

'Yes. If you had been with us when Ginevra Laurano was, you would have hovered about her like a bee to honey.'

'Indeed? Why?'

'Because you are a man, and that is what all men did.'

'Then as a lover of honey, I regret not having known her.'

Isabella sniffed daintily and patted her hair, which was freshly golden and shaped into a crown on top of her head.

'Was Bruno one of those who hovered about her?' Luca asked.

'He is a man, is he not? At least he was then. And even though she had left us and set herself up in a house she had bewitched some men into providing, even though she had not worked with us for more than four years, Bruno still ran when she called and promised her to look after her child.'

'With what was she charged?' Luca asked.

'Casting spells and uttering incantations.'

'Was she guilty in truth?'

Isabella drew circles on her round chin with one

finger. 'Ginevra Laurano knew every magic that herbs and oils can produce, and some others as well.'

'Did she use them in God's name and for His glory?'

'I do not know to what purpose she put her skills after she left us. Perhaps she used spells and love magic to draw men to her. Many courtesans do so.'

'Do not let the sound of jealousy sour your voice.'

'Do you think I need spells to draw a man to me?' Isabella picked up a twig and ran it along the inside of Luca's thigh, where his pale tights covered flesh that was soft.

'You grow incautious,' he said calmly.

'Danger excites me. As do you.'

They looked at each other. On stage they spoke of nothing but love; offstage they never mentioned the word.

Luca said, 'I do not care to become a spectacle for others.'

'Strange words from a player of *commèdia.*'

'You well know what I mean.'

'I well know it is days since we were together.'

'Suppose it should be many days more?'

'Why should I suppose that?'

'Caution, Isabella. Eyes are upon us.'

'Bruno's?'

'The Lady Anna's.'

'How can you know? She hides behind her veil, as always.'

Luca tossed his blade of grass aside and picked another. 'I know by watching her body.'

Isabella turned to look at Susanna, who sat at a

distance from them and from everyone else. 'What does it matter if she watches us? Ah! You think she may say something to Bruno about us, to secure her position in the company if she fails to please him tomorrow – as she is almost certain to do. You may be reasoning correctly.' Isabella shrugged. 'It does not matter what Anna says to him. I can take care of Bruno.'

'Perhaps Anna will surprise us tomorrow. Paolo is guiding her to become an acceptable acrobat.'

'But he cannot make her face acceptable.'

'Do not be cruel, Isabella.'

'I? Cruel? When Anna tried to make her hair the colour of mine, I did not chide her. I pitied her. I have a good heart, Luca. You know it well.'

'As well as I know that smile, which is one of your most renowned.'

The smile disappeared. 'What do you think Anna can have done, that God cursed her in such a way?'

'To reason thus is dangerous, Isabella, for then we shall have to ask what great virtues we possess that He should bless us with the faces we have.'

She looked at him in surprise. The golden splendour that defined their roles in the company and formed the bond between them was too deeply ingrained in each of their lives to be questioned. Isabella crossed herself. Then her fingers returned to her hair, stroking it as if it were velvet.

'Yet here is an interesting thing,' Luca said. 'If one does not look at Anna's eye and the scar that pulls it askew, one might call the rest of her face beautiful.'

'Do you think of nothing but beauty, that you imagine it even in such a woman?'

'What else do you think of day and night?'

Isabella leaned closer and said, 'You.'

'I think of all the fascinating sights and sounds and creatures God has placed upon the earth,' Luca said. 'Do you ever wonder what it would be like to have beauty stained by a blemish that, however small in size, eclipses all else?'

'Never,' Isabella said. 'Why should I? Why should anyone, except someone like Anna?'

'But she has no need to wonder. She knows what it is like.'

'Why do we speak of her, then?'

Luca stood, shoved his hands into the pockets of his knee-length jacket, and said, 'I need to speak with Paolo. Farewell for now, incautious one.'

Isabella started to protest, closed her mouth, and watched him stride off towards the others.

'Back to Venice!' Teresa said, tugging upward on the tights Susanna would wear for her acrobatics trial. 'And to perform on Ascension Day! Do you not love to see all the flowers, and the Doge in the golden boat?'

Susanna grunted at the tugging but said nothing.

'If you do well today, you will return with us,' Teresa said. 'Keep that thought in your mind.'

Susanna was silent.

'I shall tie these tights to hold them up.' Teresa reached into the costume trunk that was open in a corner of the travelling wagon and found a piece of rope. 'Would you like a charm, to ensure that your cartwheels are successful? A handful of herbs, over which I will say certain powerful words, and you can tuck the bundle on your person.'

'No, thank you, Teresa.'

'No? Perhaps you do not truly wish to return to Venice?' Teresa tied the rope belt and surveyed the costume. Along with the tights, yellow with blue stars sewn upon them, Susanna wore a white shirt, a sleeveless green tunic with a drawstring at the waist, and black slippers. 'Your hair is not bound tightly enough.' Teresa said. 'The worst thing in cartwheels is for hair to come loose. I shall do it for you.' She began braiding and twisting the red-gold mass. 'There must be someone or something in Venice that you fear, or else you would not have needed to escape with us last winter. Or do you believe the danger to you has now passed?' Susanna was still silent. 'Whether you remain with us or not,' Teresa said, 'perhaps you will want another kind of charm, one to protect you from danger. The best day for preparing it would be a Thursday, but still, I could do it before we reach Venice. You are not bleeding, are you?'

'No.'

'Too bad. Some drops of monthly blood would add power to the charm. But no matter. All I truly need is to know what or whom you fear.'

'Teresa, I do not want a charm of any kind.'

'Very well. But if Bruno does not like your acrobatics – my charms have done wonderful things.'

'Did you learn them from your mother?'

'Yes. She was powerfully skilled in such matters.'

'What a pity she could not make a charm to safeguard her own life.'

Teresa let go of a half-finished braid; it slapped on Susanna's neck. 'Do you criticize her? Do not dare! The evil of some men is too strong for any charm. Even the saints could not withstand it!'

The vehemence was as unexpected to Susanna as a knock in the dead of night.

'I mean no offence to your mother's memory,' she said.

Teresa bit her lip. Then she gave a shrug, like tossing salt over her shoulder. 'Let us forget what has just been said.' She took up the braid again. 'Do you know this Polani family that is to be our patron?'

'I have heard of them.'

'Well, of course. Who has not? Wealthy merchants, with a splendid house on the Canal. Do you think we may be invited to live in that house?'

'Oh dear,' Susanna said.

'What is wrong?'

'Nothing.'

'If you did know the Polani, would you share your knowledge with us?'

Susanna hesitated. 'I have no knowledge of the Polani that would be of use to the company.'

'Ah. But you do know them.'

'I have not said that.'

'True. In fact you have said nothing.' Teresa braided three more strands. 'There are so many splendid houses on the Canal. I have walked outside them sometimes, trying to imagine the life within. The Polani, the Pesari, the Ruzzini, the Bardi— Ah! Why do you jerk from my hands? You nearly ruined the braiding.'

'You hurt me.'

'Did I? When my thoughts are elsewhere, my fingers forget what they are doing.' Teresa worked for a moment. 'Your lack of knowledge of the noble families surprises me. A well-born Venetian woman, as you seem to be—'

'I have never said who I am or where I was born.'

'Oho! As if I have not noticed that.'

'Then do you not conclude that there are matters I need and wish to keep to myself?'

'Do *you* not conclude that your need for secrets worries the rest of us and makes us afraid?'

In silence each of them contemplated the tone of the conversation: light, pleasant, yet within it something was growing angry, like a wasp inside a veil of gauze. Whoever spoke next would either quiet the creature or inflame it.

'Perhaps it will be best for everyone if I fail the test today,' Susanna said softly.

'Perhaps.' Teresa spoke softly too. She finished the braid and pinned it in place.

'Why do you help me,' Susanna said, 'if you do not like me?'

'I do not know enough about you to like or dislike you. But I do not trust you.'

'Then I repeat – why help me?'

'In the hope of learning more about you.'

'At least you are honest.'

'I see little advantage in lies.'

The two looked at each other. The wasp buzzed, then alighted.

Teresa put her hands into the bright tangle of her hair. 'Also,' she said, 'I help you because Paolo asked me.'

'When? Today?'

'When you first appeared. Many times.'

Bruno's head appeared through the canvas. 'Are you ready? It is time to start.'

'In one moment,' Susanna said. 'I must put on the mask.'

She took it up and looked at the sexless leather face, fixed in eternal surprise. A picture lunged at her: Paolo donning the mask, her own hair falling over the scar, the two of them moving into a dance . . . She thrust the memory away, took up the mask, and tied it on. As it settled over her face and eased with the warmth of her skin, the familiar disembodiment began, the sense of being Not-Susanna but someone created and guided by the motions of her limbs and the voices of her mind. Through the eyeholes, Teresa receded, no longer a potential adversary but only a bright figure saying, 'We must go.'

In ten minutes they were all on the way to the village, clustered around the wagon. Paolo, dressed as Arlecchino, trotted with Giulio. Pedrolino pranced like a colt, holding his guitar. Bianca, who always looked as if her skin were too tight for her nature, beat on a drum as if she were angry at it, and her daughter Fiorenza, tall and bony, played a whistle flute with more zest than musicality. When they could see the roofs of the village across the fields, Bruno said, '*Avanti!* Let us make a good crowd for I Favolosi.'

The drum throbbed, the guitar sang. Susanna took a breath so deep it swelled her neck. What irony that the price of returning to Venice was to exhibit herself in public, the thing she had always feared most. She would do her best, even though it would not be good enough, even though to fail might be best. She stretched her arms, flexed her hands, bounced on the balls of her feet, tried to recall everything Paolo had taught her, recalled nothing, knew nothing but terror.

'Lady Anna,' said a rich voice, 'I wish you luck, so you may remain a part of us.' She swung around and saw him smiling at her broadly. Vitality streamed from him like warmth from the sun; he was a splendid animal enjoying its existence, unaware of its splendour.

'Go!' said Bruno. His voice dug its heels into her and she was off, running over the field, trailing the drum- and flute-sounds behind her like ribbons, gathering the speed that would let her fling her body into a series of wheels; she was Not-Susanna, for Susanna Bardi was born to water but she must now be a creature of land, planting her hands into it and using its power to launch all of her into the air – into circles that brought the sky down to earth and sent the land flying up, over and over and over, one circle, two circles, three circles and more, with a prayer every time that she would find the land beneath her yet again.

Back to Venice, thought Bishop Andrea Palma. And added, for at least the dozenth time since his journey had begun, *back without the prize.*

As if to punctuate his thought, the wheels of his carriage thudded into a hole, and the motion travelled back up along his spine and forced him to cling to the hand-bar on the door. Support, he thought; every goal in life required support, and he did not have enough. Not yet. He had conducted himself well in the world of the Curia, where humanist erudition, fiscal chicanery, and power struggles seemed to hold equal sway. He had done nothing to suggest that, as a Venetian, he resisted or resented the supremacy of Rome. He had spoken vociferously against the pernicious threat of the Reformation – to which, in Venice, it was sometimes prudent to seem sympathetic. He had engaged in lengthy discussions on subjects from the theses of Pico della Mirandola to the nature of the musical proportions discussed in the *Practica Musice*. He had dined at the grand houses of a number of Roman cardinals. And what houses they were, with staffs of a hundred or more, stables, and elaborate gardens. A scholar in one household had confided that his cardinal drew cash from his banker of more than three thousand ducats per annum.

He had learned many things in Rome, Palma thought, but perhaps the chief one was the depth of his desire to rise in the hierarchy of the church. For the glory of God. From his earthly father he had acquired a connection to the patriciate, albeit an illegitimate one, which was necessary for a red hat; from his other Father would come the requisite skill and perseverance.

More – that was what he needed. More influence, more benefices to swell his income, more patrons to advance his cause. Therefore, back to Venice, where he would have to acquire more.

And where no threat to that acquisition must be permitted. Fra Filippo's first letter, in the winter, had been shocking, and pathetic as well, for fear had not only imbued the words but spilled into the penmanship. From Rome, the bishop had found it difficult to arrange for the troupe of players to be located and returned to Venice, to a situation that would make them easy to observe and deal with. But it had been necessary.

The woman could not have come back to life, as Filippo feared. Nor could God have sent someone in her image, for some purpose of His own.

There was, there must be, an earthly explanation.

In any case, the woman must be dealt with.

He would do so, Palma thought. With God's help. His carriage wheels groaned and sank into another rut. Three more days to Venice – to the solidity of the sea and the sweet, pervasive smell of it, which was almost as sweet as the scent of a woman.

CHAPTER EIGHT

Patrons

We pray to find you: men of wealth and power, who shield us from the authorities and serve audiences to us like birds on platters.

But in return we do your bidding and exist at your pleasure.

Be not, we pray, like the Duke of Mantua, who requested a ridiculous play; was much amused by the creation, in which all were hunchbacks; asked for the author; and when the clown, the Dottore, and Pantalone all said 'Me!' had them arrested and sent to the gallows. The troupe's ladies contrived to supply the ropes, and made them so frail that the actors fell to the ground alive. But the Duke had them returned to their cells and tortured.

Lord, send us patrons! Make them generous and not cruel!

It was the height of the day, yet the sun seemed to be setting, crimson and gold, floating on the sea, on a carpet of flowers. But it was not the sun; it was the *bucintoro*, the huge barge of state, sailing towards the Lido for the Marriage of the Sea. All its surfaces were gilded, including the oars that protruded from the hold and stroked the lagoon. The roof of its superstructure, where the Doge and several dozen dignitaries rode, was an expanse of heavy red silk. Behind the *bucintoro*, also gilded, sailed the gondolas of the Council of Ten, the Signoria, other patricians, and ambassadors. Spectators hung from windows like flags and crowded along the *fondamente*. There were not only Venetians but thousands of visitors, who came for the May trading fair and for the Marriage, because it was the most splendid display in the world: a mixture of Christian piety, pagan belief, and Oriental splendour – like Venice herself.

At the ceremony at the church of San Nicolò on the Lido prayers would be offered ('Keep safe from stormy weather, O Lord, all your faithful mariners'), and the Doge would cast the ritual golden ring into the sea, witnessed by all in Venice who possessed power and who, on their return to the city, would begin celebrating. At the Polani palace sixty guests would attend a banquet, featuring a performance by I Favolosi.

The company had arrived the day before and gone to the same inn as on the previous visit. After a rehearsal they dispersed to watch the Marriage pageantry. Paolo had set out with Pedrolino and Giulio but lost them in crossing the Piazza, which was filled with pavilions for the trading fair. The crowd in the Piazzetta was so dense that none could move as individuals and all must pull together like galley slaves. Over heads, Paolo could glimpse the massed choirs that had sung to start the *bucintoro* on its way and would welcome it back. In robes of red and gold, the singers were one huge body with hundreds of small faces, from which chants ricocheted like bell-calls. A man could dream every night of his life, Paolo thought, and never imagine such a spectacle. A man could forget all else, while his eyes and ears feasted and his body was squeezed into odd new shapes by the press of other bodies. They were all like grapes; nothing would be left of them by the end of the day but a vat of wine. He laughed at his thought, and watched and listened and swayed with the crowd, drowning in the day's glorious assault on his senses.

Then, from behind, a young woman squeezed tight against him. He felt the globes of her breasts flatten on his back and sensed her legs and the valley between them. His face went as crimson as the robes of the choirs, not because of the young woman but because of the memory that leaped into his mind, of the mad, golden afternoon with Anna. What had possessed him? Satan? Perhaps Filippo was right, for to allow oneself to lie with one woman by pretending she was another . . . surely only an actor could be tempted to such wickedness? No, it was not Satan. It was Isabella, and the knowledge of what she had been doing on the other side of the cypresses. He had wanted to kill her and, at the same time, to tear her body away from Luca's and force his own upon it. Instead he had—Madness! Wickedness! In the execution of which he had desecrated Isabella as well as Anna, had he not? Still, he had first met Anna in the street of prostitutes, where she had been willing to . . . Why must he suffer such a seasick churning of thoughts and memories, which surely must upset the balance of the humours in his body? He wanted to dig his hands into his temples, but the crowd imprisoned them at his sides. So he shook his head, violently. Ever since the cypress afternoon, he had tried not to recall what happened, but it would suddenly appear in his mind, even if Anna was nowhere in sight. And especially if she was. The odd, almost frightening part of the memory was that he could not remember what should have been most important – whether he had truly pleasured himself, or Anna. At the heart of his memory lay a void. Perhaps that was why it kept cartwheeling into his mind. Why had his peace of mind left him? Why could he not be purged of the turmoil in his breast? *I am Arlecchino*, he thought, but he could not move to caper; the crowd pressed too tightly. Of a sudden he had the notion that everything would be squeezed from him, there in the Piazzetta on Ascension Day – not only the disturbing thoughts but all of him, including his ability to improvise and clown and make people laugh at his will. In punishment for that lustful afternoon, all would be squeezed from him, like juice from a grape.

'Paolo! Paolo!' From afar he heard his name, and when he turned as best he could, he saw Bruno and Isabella at a distance behind him in the Piazza, where people seemed better able to move. He shoved and wriggled through the crowd, like a swimmer against strong currents, and made his way to them.

'Paolo, my dear!' said Isabella.

With her greeting, all his feelings of only moments earlier were banished, and his spirit warmed as if at a hearth on a cold night. 'Am I thinner than I was this morning?' he asked cheerfully.

'No. Why do you ask such a question?'

'The crowd has so crushed me that I must emerge from the Piazzetta even thinner than I entered it.'

Isabella laughed. Paolo grinned at her.

'Look here,' Bruno said, 'you must return at once. Signora Polani sent word that you and Pedrolino are to entertain during the banquet. We found him a quarter of an hour ago and sent him to the inn. And we may have to do *The Two Notaries* after all, for Umberto has a great ache in his belly and can do very little tonight. Giulio's wife is at work on the costumes, and we must all help to prepare. Curse Umberto for eating a pig's portion of lamb last night!'

'Here is an idea,' Paolo said, feeling that his powers of invention were intact. 'Let us arrange that I appear at the banquet lying on my stomach on a plank with an apple in my mouth, as if I were being served on a platter.'

Isabella laughed and clapped. 'Excellent,' Bruno said. 'And to introduce the platter, Teresa can do rounds of cartwheels. This is going to be a good time for us, I am sure of it. Look!' He pointed to a platform where some mountebanks from Padua were attempting to draw spectators. 'We would be up there, doing as they are, if it were not for the Polani. We must show them we are worthy of their patronage. Come, let us hurry.'

Paolo followed them happily through the Piazza crowds and out past the bell-tower, his eyes on Isabella's back and her golden hair, telling himself that she was not to blame for what happened in the cypress grove; that Luca had forced himself upon her.

When they reached the inn and the courtyard, Bruno said, 'You, Anna! You can work with Teresa doing cartwheels at the banquet tonight.'

She got to her feet at once. 'But I . . . I . . .'

'Make no excuses,' Bruno said.

She put a hand to her veil and Paolo hurried past her and up the stairs, his thoughts churning again. For he could not forget that before her test, God help him, part of him had wanted her to fail and be forced to leave the company. He had expected it to happen. But she had executed a series of cartwheels so long and perfect that Bruno, like all of them, had been quite astonished and Paolo himself, the good part of him, which had helped and taught her, had stood and cheered.

Along the Grand Canal, the great houses were filled with chatter and laughter and music. Light streamed from the arched and pointed windows, casting their shapes on to the water, where they rocked and swayed in the wake of gondolas bringing more guests. On the balconies men in sombre finery and women whose flesh and gowns were equally heavy with jewels talked of the splendour of the day and of the pleasures, still to come, of the night. Inside the houses tables were laid with platters of trout, lampreys, boar, ducks, geese, quail, pigeons, thrushes, peacock. There were truffles, fried figs, silvered vegetable cakes, and fresh almonds; and the passage of all down the diners' throats was eased by Lacrima Christi, claret, liqueurs, and cinnamon water.

Andrea Palma had been invited to several houses. He spent time at two of them, first the Bardis', where he talked of his sojourn in Rome, endured a tirade from Ludovico Rossi, and reassured the man, as well as Antonio and Veronica Bardi, that he would redouble efforts to find the missing wife and daughter. At another party he spoke with several Procurators. those patricians responsible for maintenance of the church and administration of its revenues, but his true destination was the Polani house, where he arrived in time to slip into a seat at the banquet and dip his fingers into bowls of rosewater being proffered after the first course. The food seemed particularly exquisite to him this night – perhaps because he was back in Venice. The centrepiece of roasted peacock was a work of art, the meat framed by fans of blue-green feathers waving in the breeze of people's coming and going and regarding all that happened with unblinking golden eyes.

'Did you know,' said the lady to his left, keeping a huge sleeve away from her plate with one hand while the other aimed a silver fork at its contents like an arrow, 'that after the banquet there will be a performance by a troupe of players that Signor Polani has engaged to his service?'

'So I have been told,' Palma replied.

'One hears they are very good, especially the *zanno* Arlecchino.'

'Let us hope that one has been correctly informed.' Palma smiled, but he meant the words in all sincerity, for when he had written to ask Alvise Polani to engage the players – suggesting but never precisely stating that some church interest would be served in the process – he had declared them to be excellent. But he had only Filippo's word for it, and what did Filippo know of players?

As the feast was concluding with an assortment of sweets – *tagliatelle* with caramellized oranges and toasted chopped almonds was extraordinary, the bishop thought – there was suddenly a banging of drum and blowing of whistle-flute, and two acrobats in caps and tights appeared, clapping for attention. One wore a mask, and the other's face was painted white. They struck a pose, cartwheeled in separate directions around the edges of the banqueting room, then met and struck another pose, pointing at two men who carried in a huge platter. On it another man, in the tight-fitting, patch-strewn costume of Arlecchino, was spread out like a roast pig. When the platter was set down, he reared up, astonishment in every line of his body, and tried to pull the apple from his mouth; it refused to come. He leaped off the platter to struggle with it, contorting himself into ridiculous positions. Finally he pulled out the apple and ran from one guest to another, crying that he was too thin to be a good meal, uttering pig-squeals, complaining that in the kitchens they had put spices in his hair and tried to oil his shanks, and altogether behaving in so antic a manner that the whole room was convulsed. This, the bishop thought, must be Filippo's brother – a relationship Filippo had revealed only the day before. 'Your brother?' the bishop had cried. 'Why did you not ask him who the red-haired woman was?' Filippo had cast down his eyes and said, 'Your Excellency, forgive me, I did make an attempt, but I was so overcome by the sight of her that I scarcely knew what I said. And Your Excellency will understand that I did not want my brother to realize I knew the woman.' The bishop had managed to control his impatience.

The two acrobats approached Arlecchino, coaxing him back to the platter. The bishop's gaze moved over them, then back to the clown, trying to search for some similarities of feature between his clerk and the man before him, but the *zanno*'s mask prevented him. Certainly the two bodies could not be more different: Filippo as round and soft as a new loaf, Arlecchino sharp and thin, like the knife that would cut it. He and the acrobats began leaving, capering out of the door as the diners applauded.

The woman on the bishop's left started talking about what they had seen. He did his best to be attentive, for she was the wife of an important *nobilomo*, but the golden eyes on the peacock's train seemed to be staring deep into him; his heart was drumming with impatience, waiting for the performance that would begin when the dishes were cleared.

At length a platform was trundled in, up went a

painted backdrop of streets and buildings and windows, and out came a figure costumed as a Captain, who bowed obsequiously and then announced: 'We are the players known far and wide as I Favolosi! We are here to please our gracious masters, Signor Polani and his family, and their honoured guests! On this night of the glorious celebration of the Marriage of the Sea, we present for your amusement a tale of love and trickery that will culminate in a wedding! – the play of *The Two Faithful Notaries*. Our scene is the city of Bologna!'

The Captain bowed himself out, a player in the black gown and hat of Pantalone strode in and gave a comic Prologue, and then the action began: Two women entered with Pedrolino, to whom they had given a sleeping potion, so that he would not see . . .

The bishop listened no further, for one of the two women was blonde and quite beautiful, but the other . . . He leaned forward, his senses as keen as if they had been pulled to attention on strings. She had the same unforgettable hair, but the face, a perfect oval with ivory skin and straight nose and small mouth, was not, God be thanked, identical. Yet the face was so similar in feature and colouring, with only a few lines subtly rearranged, that he blinked several times, certain that he would see Ginevra Laurano. What was so singular was the combination of face and hair, the face virtually a definition of the beauty sought by painters, the hair a defiance of it, not a soft, pale blonde but a sharp, sweet red, like the hue of the caramellized oranges. He watched her move jauntily about the stage, but his thoughts were in another time and place, and the laughter of his fellow guests was transmuted into pleading and whimpers. Blood thumped in his ears. He should laugh, he thought; if he sat watching a comedy without laughing, people would find it strange, or would think, perhaps, that he was signalling the disapproval of the church. So he forced himself to join in whatever the others did, and sat smiling and uttering barks of laughter while staring at memories in which there was nothing amusing.

By the time the bishop arrived at his home, after Signor Polani had taken him aside and thanked him for recommending such excellent players, he was composed. However, Fra Filippo was not.

The priest had waited up for him; the room held echoes of his pacing and the heavy scent of anxiety. He must have been repeatedly running his hands through his hair, for it clumped around his tonsure like black weed left behind by the tide. A thick red candle on the table had burned more than halfway down, the wax forming knobs and spires all along its sides. 'You have returned,' Filippo cried. 'Did you see her? I have been praying since sundown that there is no substance to my fear. Is she . . . Has she come back to . . . to . . . ?'

'God,' the bishop said firmly, 'has not restored her to life.'

Filippo crossed himself. Then his eyes widened. 'Has the Dark One sent her, then? Is she a creature of

Satan, whom the woman served in life?'

The bishop hesitated. 'One can never be certain of the forms that evil can take, but I do not believe her to come from Satan.'

Filippo fell on to a carved chair. 'Who is she, then?'

'I believe her to be a member of Ginevra Laurano's family. Was evidence not given at that time that the woman had had a child?'

Filippo sat erect. 'But she swore the child had died.'

'Clearly she was lying to us. The child must have survived.'

Filippo clasped his hands. 'Then God has not sent us a sign of His wrath, nor is Satan trying to tempt us! Your Excellency, I am greatly relieved, for I confess I had been very anxious. In fact, my concern over this affair has distracted me from others, like the matter of the Bardi daughter.' He wiped his brow. 'I ask your forgiveness for I see now that I have needlessly worried Your Excellency and caused you to take much trouble in having the troupe of actors returned here.'

'Needlessly?' asked the bishop.

Filippo seemed not to have heard. His fingers dug at his temples. 'I have been the instrument of bringing back the players, whose lewdness and licentiousness is an offence to God, and of causing Your Excellency to spend an evening needlessly in their company!' He rose from his chair, went to Palma, and knelt. 'I have committed a grievous error and must do penance.' He bowed his head.

The bishop looked down at the figure that was foreshortened into three widening circles: tonsure, belly, and the cassock pooling at its feet. He put a hand on Filippo's shoulder and repeated, 'Needlessly?'

Filippo lifted his head, his grey eyes puzzled.

'You did well to advise me at once,' the bishop said.

Filippo smiled uncertainly.

'And I did well to arrange for the players to be found and brought back. For if the young red-haired woman were ghost or demon, she would threaten one's mortal soul. But as the daughter of the woman Ginevra Laurano, may she not threaten one's mortal life?'

Filippo took a deep breath which escaped through his open mouth. 'Your Excellency is wise,' he said at last.

'Let us hear whether you are wise as well.'

Filippo climbed heavily to his feet and began pacing the small room. 'A mother often confides in her daughter, especially if that mother is dying.'

'Most especially,' said the bishop quietly, 'if she wishes to be avenged after her death.'

'So,' Filippo said, 'when the woman Ginevra Laurano was charged with sorcery and imprisoned, she might well have told her daughter of certain events . . .' He stopped at the small table that held the candle. A new gout of wax welled over its edge and ran down its side, red and slow.

'Certain events,' said the bishop.

'Yes.' Filippo crossed himself.

'Events that, if made known by this daughter, could spell danger to all who had participated in them.'

'Yes.'

The two men looked at each other. The anchor

buried deep in their relationship shifted in its sand.

'You have done many things for me,' the bishop said. 'And I for you.'

'Yes.' It was more sigh than word.

'Together we must continue doing God's work.'

Filippo nodded, as if the previous exchange had been a model of logic.

'Therefore,' the bishop added, 'in His name and for His glory, I bid you eliminate this threat that looms before us.'

'Eliminate?' Filippo's hands made circles on the cloth over his belly.

'Elim—' His voice faded, then returned as shrilly as if he had been stuck. 'Your Excellency! Do you mean me to kill the woman?'

'Kill? Do you suggest that I – I, God's devoted servant – would call for the commission of a murder?'

'No, Your Excellency. No.' Sweat beaded on the father's upper lip.

'Such a thought demeans both its object and he who utters it.'

'Your Excellency, you are right. Of course. I abase myself before you.'

'There is no need for that. Get up, Filippo. The one and only need is to make certain that this woman does not threaten us. I charge you to find a just and merciful way of doing so – not only for the preservation of our work for the glory of Our Lord but also for your own safety.'

The father put a hand on the table to steady himself. The candle rocked, and bled afresh. 'But I may fail,' he whispered. 'Just as I have failed in the charge you laid upon me before going to Rome, to find the Bardi woman. And I do not know how to – remove the threat of which we speak.'

'Pray,' said the bishop gently. 'You must pray for guidance to do whatever is necessary.'

But what was it that was necessary? Filippo thought, back in his own room, kneeling before the crucifix. He had stripped off his cassock and simple undergarment so that the cold of the hours of darkness could sink into his bones and the rough floor dig into his flesh. How might one be certain of removing a threat without silencing the lips that could utter it?

As he had done many times since leaving the bishop, he begged God's forgiveness for being unworthy, for having lived in such a way that he now had to pray for guidance on silencing the daughter of Ginevra Laurano. Ginevra Laurano had had a child who lived . . . a child . . . the consequence of lying with a man . . .

He groaned, as the memory of lust came over him and he struggled to keep it only a memory, not an actuality that would stir his flesh. The very act of the struggle made a heavy warmth swell into his loins, and he rocked back and forth, on the precipice of surrendering to it, letting it grow and flood through him. He forced it back, biting his lip deeply, and shivered with relief. God was helping him to remain virtuous, as he had steadfastly fought to be in the years since the woman Ginevra Laurano had tempted him.

He had taken the early desert fathers as his inspiration – holy men like Saint Jerome, who lived in sackcloth, in scorching heat, among scorpions and wild beasts, until he was misshapen and emaciated but who even then imagined himself surrounded by dancing maidens. 'The fires of lust,' he had written, 'flared up from my flesh that was as that of a corpse.' Such had happened to him, Filippo thought, when he saw Ginevra Laurano.

The bishop had said she was a sorceress, and the moment Filippo's gaze fell upon her, he knew it to be true, because from her there had emanated not a scent, not an aura, but something that could only be called a spell, for it drew a man's eyes, against his will, to the fullness of her breasts beneath their cloth and to the soft separation where her legs joined . . . The spell had enmeshed him, sending her image to rise before him even when he was at his prayers, and especially when he was on his bed. Many nights he had lain with hands clenched at his sides and recited to himself from Saint John Chrysostom – the *Letters to Theodore*, which made clear how loathsome was the beauty of a woman, for its groundwork is 'nothing else but phlegm and blood and humour and bile, and the fluid of masticated food' . . . Many nights he had thought of the Irish holy man named Scuthin, who slept with two beautiful virgins in his bed so that his desire would be more fully aroused and his triumph over it thus won at a more agonizing cost to the spirit. Many times when Filippo had had such thoughts, they had broken the woman's spell. Many times, but not always.

As he knelt before his crucifix and recalled the struggles of years before, he felt his flesh stirring again, hardening. Evil! he thought desperately. His lust was evil! And the woman who could call it forth even in memory was evil.

With a mixture of loathing, anguish, and excitement he looked down at his swelling organ. He got to his feet, staggered to the candle on a small table, hesitated, and put his left forefinger close to the flame. Then he pulled it back, praying to God to forgive his sin of pride, for he did not want to use his right hand because it was the hand with which he wrote and he was proud of the beauty of his penmanship. He breathed deeply and put his right forefinger into the flame, which parted to accept it, like a woman's flesh. For an instant he felt nothing; then pain began and grew and consumed him all at one time, draining his tumescence, focusing his entire being on the throbbing ball of his finger. He would endure it; he forced himself to endure it; he smelled the charring of his flesh and whispered to it, 'Endure! Endure!'

He feared he would scream aloud, and pulled his finger free.

He stared at it, feeling the pain thump in the same metre as his heart, waiting for it to subside. But it did not. Holding the blackened finger with his other hand, he went slowly to a chest in one corner of his small, spare room. At the back of one drawer was a small box; within that box was a smaller one. He took a ring from it. Yes, he thought, the accusation of sorcery had been justified completely. All that had happened to the woman was proper, in accordance with God's holy will. He held the ring for a long time, praying, waiting for guidance on how to silence the woman's daughter without killing her; for whatever his sins, he could not, would not, kill. Not even for the bishop.

CHAPTER NINE

The Scenario

Beneath us, our tightrope, is the outline of whatever story our chief tells us to play. Perhaps *The Old Twins*, in which two rich brothers are captured and sold for slaves and their sons search for them. Or *The Disguised Servants*, in which a girl disguised as a boy becomes a servant to the man she loves. Or *The Jealous Old Man* or *The Fake Blind Man* . . . or anything else we can steal or invent.

On this tightrope, we keep aloft our ball of improvised words and wit. Who drops it will suffer the scorn of all. For in theatre, even more than in life, to betray is unforgivable.

In the dining room of the inn, I Favolosi was celebrating.

The troupe had left the Polani palace to its further merrymaking – a ball, more wines, and whatever pleasures of the bedchamber the dancing and drinking might lead to as guests regained their own homes. The players had returned to their inn, where the landlord put out cold meats, cheeses, and drink. It was impossible to retire directly after a performance, for the demands of keeping their feet on a new scenario while improvising spins and turns stirred the blood to a ferment like a high tide, needing time to recede. It was stirred even higher than usual after a performance so critical to their future.

'Signor Polani told me we had not only fulfilled his expectations but exceeded them,' said Bruno for at least the tenth time. 'Exceeded them! And the Signora stood beside him, nodding and clapping!' Each repetition required a generous swig from the wine in Bruno's glass. No one paid much attention to him, so busy were they all in reliving the performance – praising one another, re-enacting choice moments, saying they were 'fabulous ones' indeed, speculating on their future.

'We shall be in demand everywhere,' said Luca, who then sang up and down a scale: 'Toast of all skies, admired by all eyes, lalalaLAlalala!'

'Perhaps we shall go to Paris,' said Bianca, her round face, usually fixed in displeasure, struggling with its opposite.

'*Oui! Belle Paris!*' cried Pedrolino. He pushed his hair from his eyes and did a mad little dance, which made the hair hang down again.

'Or Germany!' Umberto cried. '*Ich bin eine keine Herr Dottore, mitt beschriften und grossen Spaetzle und diesen Pfeffern . . .*'

'We shall be wealthy,' Giulio said. 'We shall travel to the islands Luca told of – with the emerald throne and the pygmies and the dog-headed men!'

'They will bark gold coins at us,' Pedrolino said.

Paolo draped Buffa around his neck, stood, and made barking sounds.

Isabella reached for a piece of cheese and said, 'The only word for Paolo's performance tonight as a roast pig is . . . succulent!'

Paolo turned red. He put down the dog and hid his face by bowing so low to Isabella that his hair scraped the floor.

'Exceeded their expectations!' Bruno said, and drank.

Pedrolino, who had had too much wine, took Bruno's glass and lofted it. 'Here's to Teresa, who played a new part this evening with great skill!'

Teresa shrugged. 'Let us say that I managed to get from beginning to end without mishap.'

'We were all there to cover for you if you stumbled, my dear.' Isabella's smile stretched brilliant and wide.

'Hey!' Bruno said. 'My glass . . .'

Luca had been tapping his fingers on his thigh; he leaned forward. 'I say Teresa was excellent, especially when she came out to announce that her mistress was struck dumb. And Isabella, pretending to be unable to speak . . . my friends, did we believe it possible – a silent Isabella? Yet she was splendid, although muffled. Perhaps *because* she was muffled?'

Bruno laughed. The rest looked at one another, then joined in.

Isabella took a piece of her cheese. Shifting her gaze between her husband and Luca, she rolled it into a ball, lifted it, and threw it at Luca. The company watched in silence.

Luca caught the ball of cheese, sniffed it as if it were a rose and tossed it to Buffa. 'Now let us applaud Anna,' he said, 'whose acrobatics added much to the entrance of our Roast of Paolo.' He began clapping, looking at the others until they did the same.

Susanna, at the far end of the table, felt herself colouring beneath the mask. She wore the mask instead of her veil because . . . she did not know why. She had worn the mask all evening, of necessity, not only to perform but also to ensure that no one at the Polani house, guest or servant, could identify her. When the company made its happy way back to the inn, she had not wanted to remove her costume or replace the mask with the veil because . . . because, she had thought, the mask made her feel safe. Now, seeing Luca smile at her – surely with admiration, this once – seeing the whole company looking at her and applauding, if not warmly at least with acceptance, she knew that the mask made her more than safe: it made her feel she belonged. The players accepted her in the mask because they understood, some of them firsthand, what it was to be freed of one's face. Not Luca, of course, who needed no such freedom. Who was still smiling at her although the clapping had stopped.

'Indeed,' said Isabella, 'congratulations to Anna-With-No-Other-Name.' In a voice as golden as her hair, she added, 'Will Anna not remove the mask so we may offer congratulations to her face?' There was only the faintest emphasis on the last word, but given her skill as a player, no more was needed.

Once Paolo would have tried to intervene, Susanna thought, but he sat silent, looking away. The others stared at her curiously, except for Bruno, who turned to his wife, smiled, and said, 'Generous Isabella!'

'Magnanimous lady,' Luca said, but his delivery contradicted the words.

Susanna breathed deeply to quiet her fear, and with the breath came a realization so strange she did not trust it. She was not afraid.

Yes, she would trust it, for she had felt its opposite so often – including that very evening, earlier, when she saw that among the guests at the banquet were people she knew, especially Bishop Palma who dined frequently with her parents. She had been cold with fright before the time came to begin the acrobatics – certain she could not move, except to shiver. When Teresa said, 'Here we go, then!' the mask had spun her into the sequence they had hastily practised, and she had whirled around the banquet room with no thought save for her balance and accuracy, not even when she was close enough to the bishop to reach out and touch his robes. It had been the same way when she had had her trial for Bruno. There had been terror, but when he said, 'Go!' the mask had taken over and swept her with it. Or had it been Luca who had given her the courage, with his wish that she remain with them? Sometimes she found it difficult to separate Luca and the mask; both had become necessary to her.

Perhaps it was Luca who was now giving her the courage to stand and calmly untie the strings of the mask.

When it was off, she swung her head and said, 'Thank you, Isabella, for your good wishes, which I accept with pleasure.'

Isabella lifted her chin but smiled blandly. The others rustled and murmured in relief. Susanna recalled the day, in this same inn, when she had revealed her face to them for the first time. Then, too, it had been at Isabella's behest – why should someone so beautiful need to make someone else reveal ugliness? – but, that time, the company had been shocked by the scar. Now, except for Paolo, they merely looked at her, then returned to their wine and merriment, recalling the performance: 'When Arlecchino said Il Dottore's breath stank, then clutched his throat and went gasping and choking around the stage—'

Susanna sat down again. It was, she thought, the most memorable Ascension Day of her life, the first whose scarlet and gold splendour she had not watched from the windows of the Bardi *palazzo*; the first in many years on which she had attended a banquet – a banquet where, for the first time, she had been not a guest but a servant. She recalled her childhood dream of marriage as a ceremony like that on Ascension Day, with the pretty little blonde boy from Mantua throwing a golden ring into the water and taking her to live in a great house. But it was her sister who had gone to live in that house, and the little boy, who should have become someone like Luca, had grown into a not particularly handsome man. How strange were the workings of fate. Could one truly have freedom of the will, as Dante said?

Slowly, without thinking, she started to lift the mask back to her face. But she stopped, put it aside, and sat feeling naked – and amazed, because she did not fear being naked. At least not for the moment; and the moment was enough because Luca lifted his glass to her before emptying it. She reached for her own glass but put it back, beside the mask; she did not care to drink, lest she wash away the taste already in her mouth – pride. She sat listening to the voices around her, looking at Luca when he was not aware, leaving her face open to these people who had come to be her life and whose calling to make others laugh and sometimes cry – by means of the power of their observations of human nature – seemed as great an exercise of the imagination as anything between the covers of books. Occasionally one of the players would glance at her and smile or nod or say a few words. All of them except Paolo.

She watched him talking with Giulio, face flushed with wine, stick-fingers flying. This estrangement – which allowed them to be at ease with each other only when performing – could not continue. She would speak with him, she decided. She would go to him in his room – not this night, lest it appear she was thinking of going to his bed – but in the morning, in the sun, when she would speak frankly. *Look here* – as Bruno might say – *if I am now to be a true member of this company, we must forget what happened in the cypress glade*. She vowed to do it, taking courage from the events of this amazing Ascension Day.

* * *

After saying morning prayers and fulfilling other essential duties, Fra Filippo left the church, closed its ancient rear doors firmly behind him in a kind of Amen to his resolve, and set off for the inn where he had learned his brother and the players were again staying. It was a glorious May morning: green water pearly with sunlight, gondolas sailing it like swift black birds, air filled with pious bells. But the father had not formed a plan until nearly dawn; his eyes, hot with lack of sleep, cringed beneath the blows of the sun, and the bells, God forgive him, threatened to make his head ache. He walked carefully, hands folded before him as always, going over and over what he must do.

The inn seemed deserted. Once again he stood in the courtyard where he had seen the apparition of Ginevra Laurano and fallen to the ground in a swoon. No such thing would happen to him on this day. He waited several minutes and when no one appeared walked to the kitchen. A sleepy boy was half-heartedly trying to start the fire on the hearth. He blinked at the sight of Filippo's cassock and repeated 'Paolo Bertoldo?' as if the name had been said in a foreign tongue.

'Arlecchino, then.'

The boy laughed. 'Oh, yes! Arlecchino.'

Filippo clenched his teeth. Such a hold did the theatre have over his brother that he was not even known by his Christian name. But that hold would be broken; Paolo's soul would be saved. 'Take me to his room,' Filippo said, 'I wish to speak with him at once.'

The boy let go of the bellows and started to lead him up the stairs.

'A moment,' Filippo said. 'Is there a – does a red-haired woman stay here also?'

'Do you mean Teresa?'

'Ah,' Filippo said. 'Teresa? Yes.'

'She is here. Do you want to see her too?'

'No, no,' Filippo said. 'Take me to Signor Bertoldo.'

Some sharp knocking was needed before Paolo came to the door, hair awry and eyelids bulging with sleep. 'Filippo?' he said thickly.

'This time I will speak with you. I will not be put off.'

'Go downstairs, then. I will join you when—'

'No. I fear I cannot trust you. Let me in.' Filippo felt that Paolo would have resisted if he had been fully awake, but his brother merely looked at him for a moment, then admitted him.

The small room held two beds. A dog was curled at the foot of one; the other was empty. The shutter was open on the single window. 'Are you alone?' Filippo asked.

'Do you not see my esteemed colleague, Buffa?' Paolo gestured grandly towards the dog.

He would not grow angry, Filippo told himself; he would be calm but firm, and God would aid him. 'I ask again, brother. Are you alone?'

'As you see. Pedrolino, who shares this room, must have risen early.' Paolo rubbed both hands over his hair, sending it askew in new directions.

'No one else sleeps here with you?'

'We do not need to crowd three or four to a room, for we have patrons now.'

'So I have heard.' Filippo suppressed his desire to add, *Do you know who convinced the Polani to hire you? My bishop*. Instead he said, 'We must speak on a grave matter and should not be interrupted.'

Paolo splashed his face with water from a bowl, shook his head like a dog in a pond, ran his hands along his tights. Then he pulled on a shirt. 'What could be more grave than going downstairs and giving the belly something to sustain it?'

'This,' said Filippo, attempting without realizing to mimic the voice and manner of Andrea Palma. 'I come, in God's name, to warn you that your troupe of players must leave Venice.'

Paolo's brows rose into peaks. 'We have just returned, under the protection of the Polani.'

'True, but if you do not leave freely, your permission will be revoked.'

'How do you know such a thing?'

'I have been charged with the doing of it.' Filippo knew he was telling a lie, but he need not beg God's forgiveness, for he was doing it in God's cause.

Paolo sank to the bed and put a hand on the sleeping dog. 'Who has charged you?'

'I cannot say.'

The dog stretched beneath Paolo's hand, and Filippo saw it had only three legs. 'Why do you keep such an animal?' he demanded.

'Pity made me take him, admiration makes me keep him.'

'But he is malformed. He might be a creature of Satan.'

Paolo laughed, and the clear, happy sound made Filippo know once again that he faced a considerable challenge. He sat beside Paolo on the narrow bed, the straw of the mattress crunching beneath him. 'If you persuade your company of actors to leave Venice, all trouble may be avoided.'

'They are not *my* company.'

'You know very well what I mean. As one of their chief players you surely have much influence on their decisions.' Filippo heard his voice cracking for here was the heart of his plan, and if it failed, if Paolo did not agree, then he would have to find some other means of ridding the world of Ginevra Laurano's daughter. And he had no other means, save those he did not dare consider.

Paolo's dark eyes were as unreadable as the language of Englishmen. 'For what cause,' he said, 'would our permission be revoked?'

'For lewdness and licentiousness.'

'Is this your doing, Filippo?'

'It is the will of God.'

'I believe it is the will of Filippo, who, since our reunion, has resolved to separate me from the craft I practise and to which I am devoted.'

'I swear to you, my brother, that I am trying to help you. To save you – yes, to save your mortal being and then your immortal soul! God has sent me to save you.'

As he spoke, Filippo felt his blood surge and his head grow so light that the room blurred; it was the blessed sign. He received it only rarely, the sign that his actions were righteous and pleasing to God. If he saved his brother's soul – the realization burst on him with the certitude and blindness of holy light – in doing so, he would help save his own. God was offering this chance to cleanse himself, to rise from the sewer of his lust-filled thoughts and grievous actions. He would convince Paolo to take the players – and thus the Laurano woman – from Venice. Then he would follow them, and he would not return until he had brought his brother's soul to the altar of God.

When he opened his eyes, they met Paolo's dark, sharp gaze. 'From what,' Paolo said, 'does God tell you I need saving?'

'You ask in jest, brother, but I answer in earnest. First, from the danger of remaining here. You must convince your friends to leave Venice, and then—'

'Even if I tried to persuade them, I doubt they would go. The Polani are powerful, and we are all revelling in the chance to earn a purse of gold.'

'I have considered that,' Filippo said. He dug into the pocket of his cassock. 'Look at this. Is it not beautiful?' He put it on the index finger of his left hand. 'The lion's head is made of rubies. It is worth a great deal of gold. I will give it to your company, in compensation for their leaving.' Paolo was silent. 'I understand,' Filippo said. 'You wonder how I came to have a thing of such richness.'

'In truth, I was wondering how you had burned the

finger of your other hand so badly.'

Filippo stared at it too, the magnitude of his unworthiness filling his throat, subsiding only when he reminded himself that he was doing God's will. 'A mishap with a candle,' he finally said.

Before Paolo could reply, a knock came at the door. 'Who is there?' Paolo said.

'It is Anna. I must speak with you.'

Paolo shot to his feet. 'No. No.'

'Please do not refuse me.'

Paolo ran to the door. 'I cannot speak with you now.'

'Please!'

Filippo shifted on the bed, wondering what sort of woman would importune his brother in such a way.

'No,' Paolo said.

'Then,' replied the voice, 'you make me fear for my future with I Favolosi.' So she was one of the players, Filippo thought; she defiled womanhood by exhibiting herself on the stage. 'I ask you one final time,' the voice said, 'please open the door.'

Paolo did, but only a little. A thought struck Filippo. Might the woman be the red-haired one? Teresa, the boy had said. Filippo's mouth formed the syllables of the name in silence. He got to his feet and crept closer to Paolo, who was whispering urgently. From behind Paolo's head and shoulders he managed to get a glimpse of the woman.

Paolo closed the door and turned around, clearly collecting himself to make some explanation. But Filippo gave him no chance. 'That woman is Susanna Bardi,' he said serenely. He had urged the bishop to return the players to Venice because of Ginevra Laurano, and now, in their midst, he had found the woman who was missing. What could it be but another sign that God approved the plan he had conceived while dawn paled the sky and pain beat in his finger?

'What do you mean?' Paolo said. For once words did not tumble from his mouth, mocking and arguing. He looked quite ridiculous, tights sagging on his shanks, face creased equally with sleep and worry.

'I mean that she is Susanna Bardi, the missing daughter of the Bardi family, the missing wife of Ludovico Rossi.'

'No. You are mistaken.' Paolo sounded almost as if he were dim-witted.

'Do you think I do not know that face, with the twisted scar that pulls the eye? Do you think I do not recognize someone whose confessions I have heard? It can be no other woman.'

Paolo attempted a shrug. 'What does it matter who she is?'

Filippo laughed. How long it had been since he had laughed! 'Here is what matters – my bishop charged me to find her. I have searched for months. Now I have found her, and must report to him accordingly.'

Paolo rubbed his hands on his hair. 'You cannot do that.'

'I can, and I must.'

'In the name of God, I beg you not to do it.'

'Ah. Now you call on God. But why should I not return her?'

'For the reason that . . . that . . . she does not wish to go.'

'She has a duty to perform.'

'Filippo, please, forget that you saw her.'

'Why do you plead on her behalf? What is she to you?'

Paolo coloured.

'Ah!' Filippo cried. 'Do you lust after another man's wife?'

Paolo's face turned scarlet. He went to the window and looked down, then faced Filippo again, his colour normal but his voice high with feeling. 'I cannot be the means of sending the lady back to a life she chose to leave.'

'But you are.'

'Filippo, please. I beg you.'

The brothers looked at each other. 'Please,' Paolo whispered. He cleared his throat. 'If you keep silent, I shall . . . try to get the company to leave Venice.'

What did God wish him to do? Filippo thought. The bishop had commanded him to do two things: remove the threat of Ginevra Laurano's daughter, and return the Bardi woman. But could he do both? Driving the players from the city for lewd and licentious behaviour was possible, but not so simple as he had indicated to Paolo. If he achieved it, would Paolo ever speak to him again, so that he might save Paolo's soul, as God wished him to do, as he needed to do, to cleanse himself? It would be much better if Paolo got the troupe to go willingly. Then, when Filippo followed them and brought his brother's soul to God's altar, he could convince Susanna Bardi to return to her husband and family. He could pray with her and make her understand her duty. Was that the way God wanted him to fulfil the bishop's commands?

'Very well,' he said to Paolo slowly. 'If you make certain the players leave Venice and never return, I shall not tell the bishop of Susanna Bardi.'

Paolo put his face in his hands. His fingers writhed as if they had no bones. Filippo suddenly recalled a hot summer day in the Veneto and his young brother capering in a field like a scarecrow come to life, ready to chase birds away with laughter, not fear. 'You will need the ring,' Filippo said, pulling it from his finger and holding it out. 'Take it.'

In the courtyard of the inn Teresa sucked the juice from a large, sweet pear and let it trickle down her throat. The day was going to be fine – sunny and warm – and if the previous night was an indication, performing for the Polani would be a success. I Favolosi's stay in Venice should be not only pleasant, Teresa thought, but long enough to achieve her goal. In fact, since the company was not meeting until after noon, to review scenarios for its next several performances, she could be on the streets immediately. First, she must attend to something, so she sat on the bench and waited, sucking on the pear, dreaming of finding the man she had sought for so long, stretching her legs out in front of her.

Buffa's barking invaded her reverie. She opened her eyes to see the animal trotting down the stairs awkwardly. Her mother had kept a cat, which she would often put on her lap and stroke while talking. Its long, black-haired coat shining in the light, the cat would stretch and purr beneath her hand. *It seeks pleasure and keeps its own counsel,* her mother had said. *Is that not a proper motto for all of us?*

Behind Buffa came the spare figure of Paolo. Teresa sat up, licked the pear juice from her chin, and wiped her fingers. 'Hello,' she said brightly. 'You need not go to the kitchen,' she added. 'See, there is fruit for you here, and bread. Sit with me. I wish to speak with you.'

Paolo clutched his head. 'After last night, it is too early for speaking.'

'But you have already had visitors this morning, have you not?'

'Do you spy on me, little redhead?'

'I do not spy. If I wish to see something, I stand in the open and see it.'

Paolo smiled. 'That is true.' He sat down and took a plum from the plate of fruit beside her.

She waited until he had taken several bites. 'Earlier,' she said, 'when I was on my way down, I saw Anna at the door of your room, talking with you, agitated. I was puzzled, because I notice that you and Anna have barely spoken to each other lately, almost as if you have quarrelled.'

Paolo finished the plum and reached for another.

'Moments later I see Anna leave your door and run past me to our room, refusing to stop, with no colour in her face and tears starting in her eyes.'

'What a good deal you see so early in the morning,' Paolo said mildly.

'There is more. As I stand in the hall, wondering whether to follow Anna and learn what is wrong with her, I see a man come from your room and hurry to the stairs. The man is a priest.'

Paolo broke some bread from a small round loaf and gave a piece to Buffa.

'Paolo! We are such good friends. Do you have nothing to say?'

'What need is there, when you say so much?'

Teresa threw up her hands in exasperation. 'Have you quarrelled with Anna?'

Paolo bit into the bread. 'No.'

'I was thinking you might have pressed for information about her and made her angry. But that explanation would not account for the priest, would it? So the question remains to be answered. Why did Anna leave your room in agitation, followed soon by a priest?' Paolo chewed and said nothing. 'You wish me to work hard, to create my own scenario?' Teresa said. 'So be it. Let me see – you were so displeased with Anna's acrobatics last night that you called her to your room, where you had also summoned a priest to help you reprimand her.'

Paolo smiled. 'Anna did well last night, as we all know.'

'True. Ah! Now I have it! You called her to your room to demand payment for teaching her so well, and brought the priest to ensure that she complied.'

Paolo laughed. 'Not good enough. Say that she

brought the priest to intercede for her, but I was merciless in my demands.'

Teresa cocked her head at him. 'Very well, my friend. What of this scenario? You and Anna are lovers. The priest came to join you in marriage, but at the last moment Anna revealed she already has a husband and—'

She stopped because Paolo had leaped to his feet. 'We are not lovers!' he said. 'How can you utter such a stupidity?'

They stared, faces newly strange to each other. For years, made up of countless hours of performing together, they had scrutinized and learned each other's physical beings and expressive capacities. Now the hundred strands of familiarity that lay between them shifted and loosened, like a spider's web jarred by someone's passing.

At length Teresa said, 'You have never been angry with me before.'

'You have never said anything so foolish.'

'I was only trying to bait you, in hopes I could trick you into telling me what happened.'

'Hah! Arlecchino knows more of trickery than you can begin to imagine.'

'That is true,' Teresa said, making her voice as cold as his. 'But I am not stupid, and I believe I have tricked him after all. From the way he is behaving, I think I have struck upon the truth. I think Arlecchino and Anna are indeed lovers – lovers who have quarrelled.'

'And who therefore summon a priest to marry them?

The worst players in all of Italy would not use such a scenario.'

'Say what you like, but I believe I have named the truth – at least enough so that I can learn the rest from Anna. I shall find out what has occurred between the two of you and what part a priest plays in it—'

'No!'

'And if Anna does not tell me willingly, I shall mix a potion that will loosen her tongue. I have been thinking of it for some time.'

'Do not do it!' Paolo glared at Teresa. 'Arlecchino forbids you!'

'If he wishes to prevent me, let him tell me himself what happened in his room this morning.'

They glared at each other again. Finally Paolo looked away – at the piece of bread still in his hand. He hurled it to the brick floor, where it skittered mockingly, so that Buffa yipped and chased it.

Paolo sat down, a balloon collapsing. 'What happened has nothing to do with lovers,' he said. 'Nothing. The priest is my . . . The priest visited me because we are from the same village in the Veneto. Anna came to my door on some trivial matter. The priest recognized her. She is a Venetian noblewoman who ran away from her home and for whom he has been searching. Now he threatens to reveal her whereabouts to her family.'

Teresa let out her breath and sat down too.

'Perhaps it is as well that you know,' Paolo said. 'It has been difficult keeping the secret to myself. But I do not forgive the way in which you forced me to tell you, or the curiosity you have not set aside for a moment since Anna came. Why could you not leave her alone? Why did you endlessly try to coax me to tell what I knew?'

'I . . . I am afraid of danger to I Favolosi.'

'Hah! When were you appointed guardian of the troupe?'

'But if anything happens to them – I am afraid . . .'

'Of what?'

Teresa looked down at her folded hands. 'I do not know. Of what happened to my mother.'

When Paolo spoke, his voice was less harsh. 'A man does not like to be coaxed and spied upon.'

'I did not spy, Paolo, never. You know I would never do anything to cause you unhappiness!'

'Then how is it you have done so?'

Teresa swallowed with difficulty. 'Let me make up for it, then. Tell me what I can do to make you forgive me. I will do anything.'

Paolo looked at her searchingly. 'Help me save Anna.'

'But why is she so important to you? Do you indeed love her?'

'No! No! Why do you offer to do anything I ask, and instead pummel me with more questions?'

'I am sorry.'

'Indeed.'

'I am, Paolo. Truly.'

He shrugged. 'I do not know if I believe you. But it does not matter.' He stood. 'I am going out now. Buffa! Come! Let us see how the streets of Venice look on the day after the Marriage of the Sea.'

Teresa watched him go, the dog trotting behind him. She no longer felt like going out herself. As she walked up the stairs to her room, it was as if she bore the weight of a great yoke on her shoulders.

CHAPTER TEN

Lazzi

> Laugh! you out there watching, for laughter is air and blood to us. Without it we *zanni* cannot function, or live. So we need a hundred ways to make your bellies roll, your eyes water, and wind break from both ends of you. We take any simple object – a pie or a rope or simply a word or a name – and devise ways to say or use it ridiculously, which we insert into any scene, or between scenes, to no purpose but to keep you laughing. Laugh! Is not laughter man's answer to the life God gave him?

The waters rocked and slapped against the pilings before the Bardi *palazzo*, where part of a galley's cargo was being unloaded from a barge. Ludovico Rossi's gondola manoeuvred around it and deposited him. He stepped out with more agility than his stocky frame should have allowed and entered through the water door, sidestepping men with bags slung over their shoulders: nutmegs, to judge by the aroma that seeped from the heavy fibres. The ground-floor hall was noisy with shouts, jokes, and the voices of clerks calling out numbers. A cargo's arrival brought an air of triumph with it, for it meant not only that gold would pour into the trading house but that the crew had survived the journey to the Levant and back – the turbulence of the Mediterranean, the spectre of illness, the constant menace of pirates.

'Hey! Out of the way!' yelled a burly man in ragged garments.

'I am a member of this household,' Ludovico shouted, and watched caution drop over the man's face like a veil. Could the fool not see from his crushed satin cloak and linen shirt that he was a wealthy member of the merchant class? However, Ludovico thought, not as wealthy as he planned to be. He smiled as he made his way up the stairs to the mezzanine and Antonio Bardi's offices.

In a room whose walls were lined with many shelves, filled with boxes and small chests of woollens and silks, corals and ambers, and spices of all kinds, sat Bardi seemingly unaware of the noise and bustle outside. His heavy brows, and his moustache and full beard, which he groomed so that the hairs resembled silk threads, obscured much of his face and focused attention to his high, broad cheekbones and dark eyes, which at the moment were tight with concentration on bills of lading. 'Antonio,' Ludovico finally said. Bardi looked up. His brows joined together in a frown. 'Rossi?' he said. 'What the devil are you doing here?'

'I came to offer congratulations on the safe arrival of your ships, which I hear have returned with lucrative quantities of spices and pepper.'

'There was no need to come.' Antonio's voice turned

the simple words into an accusation.

'But there was. Should a man not share in the good fortune of his father-in-law?'

'Should a man of your age not stop posturing as a bridegroom?'

'It is no posture. I am a bridegroom in every sense but the most critical one, which lies beyond my control – that is, the presence of my bride.'

Antonio laid down the paper he had been studying. 'What is it you want?'

'As I said – to offer congratulations.'

'I accept them. Now I must return to—'

'I thought you might want me to share your good fortune in more than a spiritual sense.'

'Damnation, Rossi! Say whatever it is you mean. I have no time to waste in pleasantries and guessing games.'

Ludovico ran his hands down the front of his shirt, over the hill of his belly. 'I have not received my proper share of our bargain. Since you remain unable to restore your daughter to me, surely it would be seemly on your part to make some recompense in gold?'

Bardi regarded him with a lack of expression that might have unnerved anyone less determined. But instead of displaying the choleric humour for which he was famous among his fellow merchants, Bardi sat back, let the red lips between beard and moustache form a smile, and said, 'There is one thing I have never understood, Ludovico. I know why you agreed to marry Susanna, but why did you consent with pleasure? Why do you behave as if her return would be a cause for celebration in your life?'

Ludovico blinked. 'She is my wife.'

'Is a man then obliged to find joy in his spouse?'

'Is he forbidden?'

'With a wife like my daughter, I should think a man's own nature would forbid it.'

Ludovico did not answer. He could not. There were things he could not explain, even to himself, and, if he could, would certainly not have shared with Susanna's father. They had an arrangement about Susanna that suited them both and that Ludovico would exploit as fully and as often as he could. The fact, unexpected and amazing to him, was that he needed and desired Susanna. He had had a suspicion when he first saw her, aged eleven. Everyone, including Bardi, had warned him of the scar, and he had expected to feel a revulsion he would have to suppress in order to bring about the necessary result of the betrothal, but he had not felt it. During the years he had had to wait for the marriage, while Bardi put him off with various excuses, a warmth had grown in him for the young woman, a fluttering in his loins like the wings of a bird that he could not be sure would ever fly. When they finally did marry . . . how to explain to anyone the blessedness of his restored potency, of finding that what had been taken – stolen – from him had returned miraculously? He would have her back; he must have her back. Let Bardi think it was only to forestall the chatter and laughter of society; let Bardi pay for her absence with every meal and ducat of apology that Ludovico could squeeze from him; but above all, let her return so that his manhood could rise again.

'You do not answer my question,' Antonio Bardi said.

'Perhaps I cannot,' Ludovico said. 'Or perhaps I will not.'

Bardi had pulled a ducat from somewhere. It twisted in and around his fingers like a child playing at hiding. His teeth chewed his lower lip.

'You would not be thinking,' Ludovico said, 'of tossing me a single ducat and telling me to be on my way?'

'Can you think of any reason I should not profoundly wish to do so?'

'I can think only of the reason you cannot.'

Bardi laughed harshly, then stood. 'Very well. Ten *colli* each of cinnamon and ginger will be sent to you.'

'Ten?'

'Ten! Now leave me to attend to my work. I see your ugly face too often of late. By God, the bishop had better find Susanna, so I can rid me of you.'

'You know that we can never be rid of each other,' Ludovico said. 'So – ten *colli*. Cinnamon and ginger. I await their arrival. Good day, esteemed father of my bride.' He went off smiling. Bardi's growling faded behind him.

Hubris the Greeks had named it, and had known its dangers, thought Susanna. If she had remembered the lesson of their writing, if she had not permitted herself to swell with pride merely because she had sat celebrating with the troupe without veil or mask or fear, then Fate would not have reprimanded her. She would not have gone to Paolo's door in the confident assumption of easing the strains between them, her face naked in sign of that confidence, and seen Fra Filippo . . .

And Teresa would not have returned to their room as she had, her manner as muted as if someone had placed glass before her face. 'I do not like to say this, but for the safety of all – you as well as I Favolosi – should you consider leaving? Perhaps you could return to your family.'

Susanna had needed to get away from the shocks of the morning, yet had not dared to venture far. She sat in a *campo* near the inn, disguised by the veil and her old black dress, grappling with the idea of going to her mother once more. But suppose her mother was the one who had betrayed her whereabouts before? Even if she had not, what could she do except deliver Susanna to her father, whose face would swell with rage, or to Ludovico?

Imagining it, Susanna shivered in the sun.

'Is all well with you?' said a familiar voice.

She looked up and saw Giulio passing.

'Oh, yes,' she lied.

'We meet soon for rehearsal, you know.'

'I shall be there.' But would she?

She watched Giulio move off in his Pantalone stride. Sometimes they all seemed taken over by the characters they played – Giulio fed by the confidence of Pantalone, merchant of Venice, who strode commandingly onstage in a round black hat and long black gown over red breeches. But Pantalone was also foolish: a cuckolded husband, or a father whose daughter refused to obey. Once, when Susanna's father watched some players at a banquet, he had scowled as much as laughed at their Pantalone. 'No Venetian merchant would be so foolish!' Later she heard him tell her mother, 'Yet Pantalone speaks truth. A man's daughters can be his undoing.' If she went home now, how would he punish her? She did not know – the man who had given life to her was a virtual stranger, cloaked in black, his intentions buried in brows and beard – but that he would punish her was as certain as the movement of the heavenly bodies around the earth.

'You are a Bardi,' Teresa had said. 'I have had my suspicions for many months. Now I know it. I also know that you ran away from your family.'

Susanna had not corrected her.

'Paolo says the priest knows who you are. Therefore, you endanger not only yourself but all of us by staying. Is it not best, then, to leave and find somewhere else to go?'

Before Susanna could answer, Teresa had leaned forward, her directness returning. 'I think you love someone in this company. Ah – your cheeks turn red. I am correct. Do you not wish to keep the man you love from danger?'

Susanna put her head in her hands. Had Teresa guessed her feelings for Luca? Had they all guessed – even Luca himself? She rose, walked hurriedly out of the *campo* and on to a wooden bridge over a little canal, where she leaned on the railing and looked down. The sun shone in the water, the bricks and stones of the buildings waved in it, her own veiled face shivered as a breeze passed over the surface. One rainy morning she had stood on the Fondamenta Nuove and contemplated a private, eternal Marriage of the Sea. Could she consider such a solution now? Impossible. Staring into the sun-dappled canal, she realized how much she had changed in the months since that day. But what was the changed Susanna to do? Crawl back to a family into which she would at best no longer fit and at worst would not be allowed? Keep her situation hidden from I Favolosi by somehow persuading or cajoling Teresa and Paolo not to reveal it to them? Leave the troupe at once and search for another to join?

'Why such a heavy sigh, Lady Anna, on such a beautiful day?'

He was in the water below her, a bulk of gold. For a moment she could look only downward, where his face and hers blurred and rocked together. She straightened and turned to him. 'I am thinking of what is to come.'

'How can you think of that which you cannot know?'

'Do you not believe we affect our destinies?'

'What a question! Surely it would take one's whole life to answer.'

'Perhaps. But surely one needs the answer in order to live one's life.'

He laughed. 'Lady Anna, you put matters in a way that stirs the mind. Very well. What do I believe? I believe we make efforts to affect our destinies, but I cannot tell whether God rewards or ignores them.'

'What is the greatest effort . . .'

'Do not stop. What is it you wish to ask?'

'What is the greatest effort you have made?'

He shrugged. 'I have not made any great effort, unless one counts the time when the wagon stuck in mud halfway up the wheels and Bruno and I pushed until our eyes bulged so far they nearly fell into the mud themselves.' He looked at her as if he could see through the veil and added, 'But I believe you ask me in seriousness.'

'I . . . believe I do.'

'Then I must answer in kind. Shall we start back to the inn? It is nearly time for rehearsal.'

Without thinking, she nodded. She stared at the motion of their feet on the wooden slope of the bridge and then down on to the stones.

'I made no great effort,' he said. 'I had six older brothers and sisters, and Mother said I was the only one whose birth came easily, like a cat's. We travelled from fair to fair selling songbooks, tales of the saints' lives, and almanacs. I sold a great many. I wore a blue smock and held out books and smiled and sang. Women, and some of the men too, patted me on the head and called me *cherubino* and parted with their *soldi*. When I was older, all I had to do was smile. One day the lady of a fine house took a liking to me and asked me to live with them. I stayed nearly a year, learning my letters and eating splendid foods. But the lady's husband feared her liking for me was too strong

– what a clever fellow – so I left. I went into France and Spain, travelled a dozen roads, and on every one of them were people to talk with, drink with, make love with.' He spoke with ease, as if merely recounting a scenario. 'I met a man who gave me work on one of his ships and another who offered to teach me the baker's craft. But I wanted to roam as much of the world as I could – to see things that would make me laugh or weep or stand in wonder. I met some mountebanks, and I thought, what a sweet feeling to be up there making people laugh and applaud. And to be free. It is in my nature to be free. So I joined them. I was learning their tricks when Isabella saw me and urged me to come with her and Bruno.'

Luca stepped aside as an old woman laden with brooms approached them on the narrow path of stones beside the canal. 'Hello, old mother,' he said. 'Is it not a bright day for sweeping?' She lifted her head and grinned, showing off her remaining teeth. When she passed, he said, 'Perhaps one day I too shall be old and ugly, and then my great effort will be to forget it.' He started to laugh but stopped as if hearing the import of his last words.

'What is wrong?' Susanna asked.

'Nothing.' He looked at her. 'I wonder why you wear your veil today when you did not do so last night.'

'I . . . have a reason.'

'Would you not like to feel the sun on your face?' He lifted his head to the sky; his jaw and cheekbones and nose made sharp angles against the blue and his hair was falling gold. Then he looked down again and, in a motion so startling that she could make none herself, lifted the veil and laid it back over her hair. 'Do you know, Lady Anna,' he said, 'I often wonder what your life is like and what thoughts dwell in your head?'

She felt blood beating in her neck. 'Do you mean . . . how I bear this terrible face I have?'

'I forbid you to call it terrible,' he said. 'I do not call it so. But I admit I wonder what it is like, what effort you must make, and how you are able to conduct yourself with a grace and courage that all must admire.'

'Grace?' It was the only word she could manage.

He laid a finger on the scar. She could not stop her intake of breath.

'Do I distress you?' he asked.

She could not tell him that for an instant Ludovico's face and the dreadful, hungry way he used to look at the scar had swooped into her mind like a falcon. In Luca's gaze there was nothing of Ludovico – only gentleness and a curiosity devoid of either pity or judgment – a curiosity like a child's, which was also a man's. 'You have never distressed me,' she said, allowing her eyes to find his. 'But I do not think I can explain my thoughts, even to you.' He raised a brow. 'I mean,' she said hastily, 'even to someone as kind as you.'

He smiled, took away his hand, and said, 'Let us get to the inn.'

She nodded and they walked on in silence, the sun beating on her face. Or perhaps it was the remembered warmth of his hand.

* * *

The troupe was gathered in the inn's dining room, waiting for Bruno to arrive and begin the rehearsal. There was an off-balance feeling among them, as of a wheel that had been taken apart and put back with some of its spokes in the wrong holes, for Paolo, instead of behaving in his usual merry way, sat silent in a corner with Buffa, frowning deeply at nothing. When Teresa came in, they did not look at each other. She went at once to the opposite corner, folded her arms, and sat frowning also.

When Susanna and Luca entered together, silently, everyone looked at them as if they had walked into the wrong action in a scenario.

'Luca!' Isabella said, and lifted her chin in a manner that said, 'Sit here by me.' When he did not move, she said it aloud. He shrugged and walked to her. Susanna stood at one side of the room, started to pull down the veil, then stopped and let her hands fall to her sides.

Bruno came in with a pile of papers. He seated himself at the head of a long table and looked around the room; for a moment the wings of his moustache quivered as if he too sensed the strangeness in the air. 'We perform tomorrow night,' he said, 'at a much smaller banquet than the one that established our success. This time our scenario will definitely be *The Jealous Old Man*. Umberto, I charge you to eat sparingly tonight – perhaps bread and water. I cannot permit your stomach to disrupt our plans a second time.' No one laughed, although Umberto lifted his hands and swung his head from one shoulder to the other. 'In two days' time,' Bruno continued, 'we perform again at an all-day celebration for the birthday of the youngest Polani daughter. Songs and acrobatics and *lazzi*, and a scenario I shall decide tomorrow, into which we will insert scenes of a young girl and her dog. The child dotes on a pet, it seems. Now, to the immediate matter of *The Jealous Old Man*. I shall remind us of the order of scenes, and then we— Yes, Paolo? What is it?'

Paolo had stood. Rubbing his hands together like sticks that would start a fire, he said, 'I should like to ask the company – are we all certain—'

'Certain of what? Speak up, man. If Arlecchino is at a loss for words, we are all doomed.' No one laughed.

'I . . . It is nothing.' Buffa barked, and Paolo sat down again.

Bruno, and everyone else, looked at him in surprise. 'Let us continue,' Bruno said and began reading out the order of scenes and the names of the players in each. When he was halfway through, Paolo again got to his feet but said nothing, only looked at Teresa and, quickly as a dragonfly skimming water, at Susanna. Bruno frowned. 'Look here, Paolo, have you something to say or not?'

'I do.'

'Well?'

'I wish to suggest to the company . . . no, to ask the company . . . whether we truly should remain in Venice.'

Stares. Cries of '*What?*'

'I have been told . . . There is reason to believe . . . we may be in danger.'

More astounded stares. Louder cries of 'What?'

'Danger?' Bruno's voice cut through the others' like an axe. 'How can we be in danger when a noble family has brought us here?'

'We may be charged with . . . licentiousness.'

'Ridiculous!' Bruno said.

But no one laughed.

A voice ended the uneasy silence. 'Paolo has protected me long enough. Let me speak the truth. There is danger to I Favolosi, and it comes from me.'

People did not recognize the voice; they looked about as if someone were speaking from behind a backdrop. Paolo closed his eyes.

'As some of you feared from the beginning, I, Anna, am dangerous to you.'

They turned to her. Some were seeing her in daylight without mask or veil for the first time. Her colour was high; on it, the scar lay like a thin piece of white rope, pulling downward. They had always perceived her voice as soft, but it had a sharp new edge.

'I ask your help. But this time I shall hide neither the dangers nor my identity.' She ran her hands over her red-gold hair and then clasped them beneath her chin. 'I am not Anna. I am Susanna, daughter of the house of Bardi. I am also wife to Ludovico Rossi, from whose house and bed I was escaping when I first came to you, many months ago. He and my family have been searching for me ever since, with the help of Bishop Andrea Palma. If they find me, they will force me back to Rossi's house. But I cannot go back. If they knew you were hiding me, things would not go well with you. I endanger you, for which I am deeply sorry. Yet, even recognizing that I have no more right to ask than you have reason to agree, I nevertheless do ask you . . . I beg you . . . to let me stay with you because . . . because being one of you has been the happiest time of my life.'

Her palms were damp, and ribbons of perspiration ran down her neck. It was a great effort, she thought, not to hide, not simply to pack up her few belongings and leave silently – but to show them her face and, in asking to stay with them, her soul as well. She had not known she was going to do it until she began speaking. Or perhaps she had known. Perhaps the decision had come in the moment when Luca had touched her.

She looked at him. He was frowning, but not with anger. Paolo, she saw, had opened his eyes. Why was he trying to persuade the troupe to leave? It must be the result of Fra Filippo's visit, but was it for her sake? Why would he do that, when he had barely been able to look at her since the cypress afternoon. He was looking at her now, steadily, his gaze solemn, as if his reason were groping to understand her action. She wanted to smile at him, but too much was still unspoken between them.

The others, like a single body with one means of

sight, had been regarding her. Slowly they began to resume their separate natures. 'Look here, Paolo!' Bruno said. 'Did you know of all these matters?'

'I never knew Anna's true name.'

'But the rest of it – that she was fleeing an important family and a wealthy husband?' Before Paolo could answer, Bruno turned abruptly to Susanna. 'Is your family friendly with the Polani?' When she nodded, he groaned.

'I did not know her situation,' Paolo said, 'but I suspected it.'

Bruno groaned again. Giulio rolled his eyes. Umberto's gaze went left, then right, before he said, 'Will the Polani be angry?' No one answered him.

Isabella leaned forward, her pale green eyes wide, her honey-voice a plaintive thread. 'Why did you do this, Paolo? Why did you place us in jeopardy? Have we ever been anything but kind to you?'

Paolo swallowed twice. Do not love her so much, Susanna wanted to say, watching his cheeks pale and his fish-lips tremble. But what was the use of telling people not to love what they loved?

'I . . . I . . .'

'Arlecchino stammers?' said Isabella, still honey-slow.

'You are my . . . family,' he said. 'I thought – I was certain we would all be safe because Anna – excuse me, I must say Susanna – always wears her veil and performs in the mask. And we have indeed been safe, have we not?'

'Until now,' Bruno snapped.

'She is not wearing veil or mask now,' said Bianca, each word a little bite.

'I swear to remain covered at all times,' Susanna said. Now that she finally was able to face them openly, without shame colouring her cheeks, she had to promise not to do so.

As if she had not spoken, Isabella said, 'One wonders, Paolo, why you have taken such risks for this woman. What is the reason?'

Buffa wagged his tail violently, as if to make everyone ignore his master and look at him instead. Susanna wanted to pat his head. She did not move.

'I felt pity for her,' Paolo said, 'and wished to help her.'

'No more than that?'

Paolo clenched his hands. 'No.' He bent over, picked up the dog and held it in his arms, staring down at its fur.

Silence. 'Surely,' Luca said, 'any of us would have done as Paolo did?'

'Paolo does not speak the truth!' Everyone turned to Bianca's daughter, Fiorenza, who swung her head, pale brown hair flapping beside her reddening cheeks. 'I saw them, Paolo and her, one afternoon when we were on the road. They were rolling on top of each other in a cypress grove.'

A noise like a high wind filled Susanna's ears. She forbade herself to look at Luca, prayed for silence, hoped for disbelief.

Instead, there was laughter: Isabella's. On and on and on, like bells.

Finally it stopped, abruptly. 'Is that true, Paolo?' she asked.

He did not answer. Susanna could feel his paralysis.

'So,' Bruno said, 'what we suspected at the first was true. You brought this woman into our midst to serve your pleasure.'

Giulio laughed. So did Bianca. Teresa shifted her position.

One of them must speak, Susanna thought. If Paolo could not, then it had to be she. She gazed into the middle distance, above all their heads. 'I did not come to serve Paolo's pleasure, nor did he bring me for that purpose.'

'But I saw you!' Fiorenza said.

'I do not know what you saw, or believe you saw. I am telling the truth.'

'Yes, it is the truth.' Paolo's voice was a croak. He shook his head several times. 'Anna – Susanna – speaks the truth.'

'Look here,' Bruno said, 'it does not matter what is true. The question is, what are we going to do about her?'

'If we all leave Venice,' Paolo said, 'she will be safe. And we will all be safe from the threat of banishment.'

Bruno scowled. 'You sound like Il Dottore. We should leave, in order to avoid being made to leave? Ridiculous.' Umberto laughed nervously.

'But I have told you,' Paolo said, 'there is a threat to banish us for licentiousness.'

'How do you know of this threat?' Giulio asked, with Pantalone's bluster.

Paolo put down Buffa, wiped his face on his sleeve, and said, 'A priest of my acquaintance came this morning to warn me.'

Giulio muttered to his wife. Others shifted in their seats. 'I do not like this,' Umberto said. 'I do not like having to make such decisions. Catarina—' He seemed about to invoke his dead wife, but stopped.

'Teresa,' Bruno said, 'what have you to say?'

'Yes!' Pedrolino said. 'Let us hear Teresa.' He fixed his gaze on her, smiling as if he had solved the problem.

She stood by the fireplace, arms still crossed. 'I have nothing to say. Yet.'

Isabella laid her middle finger against her lips, then said blandly, 'I have a solution. If we see that Anna returns to her husband's house, that should please all parties.'

'I cannot return,' Susanna said, without intending to do so. A voice not yet born, or even begotten, seemed to command her words. 'Please do not ask why – not because I refuse to explain but because my resolve on the subject cannot be changed.'

Isabella ignored her. 'If she returns, and we are known to be responsible for that return, we should have no difficulty with the authorities. Do you not agree, Luca?'

Susanna finally looked at him.

'Possibly you are right,' he said. 'But I find it cruel to return a woman to a man against her will. I should not like to be party to such an action.' He gave Isabella a smile so guileless it could not be free from guile. 'I am certain the goodness in your nature will make you reconsider such a proposal and reject it as well.'

'Of course it will!' cried Paolo. 'Luca is right! No one can dispute Isabella's goodness.'

If so much had not been at stake, the look on Isabella's face would have been comic. Her mouth opened, then regained its perfect shape. 'There is much kindness in my heart,' she said curtly.

Giulio's wife stood, wrapped her arms around her heavy breasts, and said, 'If Anna, or whatever her name is, stays with us, does she not put at risk our dealings with our patron and the gold we are to receive?'

Paolo waved both his hands wildly. 'We will not lose any gold! The priest who warned me wished to help us leave Venice. He gave me something worth many ducats – look.' He put a hand into his jacket, pulled out a ring, and held it up so that light seemed to flash from its lion's-head eyes. 'Here! See?'

In a moment the ring was gone, clutched in Teresa's hand.

'Where did you get this?' she cried. 'Where? You must tell me!'

Paolo stared at her.

'Tell me!'

Her voice was such a whip of demand that Paolo's head sank like a cowed animal's and he said, 'From the priest.'

'The priest who came to see you this morning?'

'Yes.'

'Tell me his name. Tell me!'

Paolo's lips worked but produced no sounds.

'He is Fra Filippo,' Susanna said. 'He assists Bishop Palma, who searches for me.'

'Ah!' Teresa cried, her eyes shining. The others stared at her, as motionless as marionettes. She looked at the ring for a long time, then closed her hand over it and turned to Paolo. 'Do not worry. I shall see that Anna does not have to leave.'

'What do you mean?' Paolo asked.

Her gaze moved over the rest of the troupe. 'I shall remove the threat that Anna poses to us. Leave everything to me.'

Isabella shook her head as if returning to sentience. 'Explain yourself, Teresa. We must know what you mean.'

She smiled. 'You shall know soon. Very soon.'

CHAPTER ELEVEN

Conjuration

> Throw three grains of salt on the floor and three outside the door while saying these words: 'There, devil, I am paying you. Bring him here to me at once!'

The church was cold, Andrea Palma thought as he walked along its nave. The air within its thick stone walls held the chill of a crypt no matter how many candle flames pierced it or how brilliantly the May sunlight fell through the tracery of its windows. Perhaps God wanted man to shiver in His presence, to feel no warmth but His own.

As if responding to his thought, an old man who was muttering in prayer began shaking, like someone with fever. Palma stopped and touched his shoulder. 'Are you unwell, my son?'

The man's eyes opened, squinted, widened. 'Your Excellency,' he whispered. 'I am a grievous sinner.'

'We all are,' Palma said. 'But God forgives us if we repent sincerely. If you are sincere and make a good confession, the weight will lift from your soul and you will find peace.' He held out his hand so that the old man might kiss his ring, with lips that were thick and dark, almost black in the dimness. 'Your shivering will stop soon,' Palma said softly but firmly.

The man's rheumy eyes filled with fervour, and he pulled a rough hand down his cheek; it rasped on his beard.

Palma walked on, to the place where the Tintoretto hung, its colours glowing with their own light, its composition alive with movement. The painting added beauty to the church and thence to the glory of God. In fifty years' time, which name would be remembered: that of the artist or that of the bishop who had admired him, gone to his workshop, discussed the motto on his wall that one must follow 'Michelangelo's design and Tiziano's colour' – although it was arguable whether he had in fact done so – and commissioned the work from him? Art was surely the more secure path to immortality, if not to Heaven – unless one were Cardinal. Or, dare it be thought, even greater than Cardinal . . .

Palma sighed and moved towards the entrance. He had just passed the bank of votive candles, each little flame blurring into the next, when it came upon him: the desire to pray, so strong it made him shiver like the old man he had comforted. He fell to his knees where he was, because he could not do otherwise, the hardness of the flagstones bruising his flesh through the cloth of his robes. It was a paradox of his nature, which he did not understand and could only accept, that often when he prayed, be it in the privacy of his study or at the altar before hundreds of parishioners, he felt virtually nothing.

The words came mechanically. Although he could hear his voice uttering them with both resonance and feeling, only the resonance was real. Occasionally, at times he could neither predict nor alter – except that they seldom coincided with his designated hours for prayer – he would feel himself crushed, pushed to his knees as if by a giant hand, by a need for forgiveness.

'Almighty Lord God,' he whispered, clasping his long fingers, 'Thy servant begs forgiveness for any sins he may have committed in word or deed, for the pride that can surge beyond his control, for any actions of the past in which Thy servant betrayed, may have betrayed, the sacredness of his calling and surrendered . . . may have surrendered . . . to the powers of Darkness that threaten Thy rule on the face of this, the earth Thou has bequeathed to us in Thy magnanimity.' Two hot, wet paths formed on Palma's cheeks. He unclasped his hands and let his face sink into their cradle, waiting for the sense of forgiveness he knew would come; had to come. He felt only the bony cold of the floor, and the inability to rise to his feet. The face of Antonio Bardi came before him – not careful and controlled, as he had seen it for years at private and official banquets, but crafty – the trader's face, asking and promising in the same gaze.

'Thou knowest,' Palma whispered, 'that Thy servant loves Thee and ever has acted to be more able to honour and serve Thee better. Thou knowest that all is done, has been done, solely for Thy glory . . .'

The crushing sensation began to dissipate at last.

Palma saw that several parishioners were standing nearby, regarding him with reverence and confusion. One of them, a burly young man, spoke hesitantly. 'May I help Your Excellency?'

'Assist me to stand.'

The young man came forward; leaning on his arm, Palma regained his feet.

'Is Your Excellency ill?'

'No, my son. God in His wisdom seized me with the need to speak to Him.'

The young man's eyes widened, but before he could reply, if indeed he had words with which to do so, Fra Filippo was there, saying shrilly, 'Your Excellency! Your Excellency! Are you ill?'

'Not at all,' Palma said; his normal sense of himself was returning and dispelling his weakness. He turned to the young man. 'Go in peace, secure in the knowledge that the Lord God loves you.'

The young man reddened, bowed, and backed a few feet away.

'What happened?' Filippo said. 'I came in search of you, and saw you being helped to your feet.'

'Let us step out into the *campo*,' Palma said, aware of eyes upon him.

'Would Your Excellency wish to lean upon me?'

'No.' Palma spoke with asperity. 'I am entirely well.' He walked to the door and out into sunshine that made his eyes water. Filippo would have to have an explanation, he knew. 'I was driven to my knees by a vision,' he said.

Filippo's hands met in a steeple before his lips. 'May

I . . . Will you describe it, so that I may find comfort in its reflection?'

'I can describe it only as a sensation of light and of God's blessing upon that which we are undertaking.'

'We . . . undertake?'

'Are you not engaged in removing the present threat to us – to our work for the glory of God?'

Filippo let out a sound of wonderment. 'Then truly God sees and knows all, for here is the reason I was searching for Your Excellency.' He dug into the pocket of his robe. 'Here is a message, delivered to me only just now, from my brother, promising to do as I requested – to remove the players from the city forever – if I will meet with him this evening.'

'To remove the players forever? How can one be certain of "forever"? How can one be certain the woman will not leave them and return on her own to Venice?' Palma hesitated, wondering whether to press for details of whatever Filippo was planning or offer suggestions, but he did not wish to become involved too directly.

The priest moistened his dry lips. 'Your Excellency has commanded me to find a way to remove the threat of the Laurano woman, and I have sworn to do so. Does Your Excellency not trust me to execute that command?' Palma was silent. 'Did I not faithfully execute all commands in regard to the woman's mother?' Palma nodded slowly. 'And now, today, Your Excellency's vision of God's blessing our efforts – surely it is a sign that He approves what I am planning?'

'You are right,' Palma said. There was nothing else he could say.

The sun was setting in streaks across the bowl of the sky, casting nets of orange on the lagoon and reddening the tops of buildings that rose from their own shadows. The light was never quite the same, changing with each lap of the water and every inch of the sun's lowering. Paolo stood on the Molo and watched in silence, his thoughts shifting with the light and the water. But the sky was heading into darkness; and his thoughts were going nowhere. Since Filippo's visit, everything had changed. Teresa was a stranger, whose intentions he could no longer decipher. Isabella looked at him with a smile that was either pitying or amused, he could not decide which – or which would be worse. The rest of the company shot glances at him behind his back, which he felt through the cloth of his jacket like darts. And if it had been difficult to be with Susanna before, it was impossible now. She had tried to talk with him – 'We must speak, Paolo, we must talk about what has occurred between us, I must know why you were trying to persuade the troupe to leave – was it for my sake?'

He had shaken his head and walked away with an Arlecchino strut, for how could he explain what he did not understand himself? When Filippo had revealed her identity and threatened to return her to her husband, Paolo had known he could not allow it. But that was all he knew. Teresa had appeared to believe he acted out of desire for Susanna: now the whole company appeared to think it, thanks to the prying Fiorenza. Perhaps Susanna herself believed it. God forbid such a thing, for how could one look a woman in the eyes and say that one did not love or desire her? Especially a woman with whom one had . . . Paolo put his hands into his hair. Why *had* he decided to try to save her – from the first night, in the street of whores? Why, if he did not love nor desire her?

He turned back towards the Piazza, where the magnificence of gold and mosaic was surrendering to the softness of light that was neither blue nor grey yet was both.

Teresa had taken them aside after breakfast, a firm grip on each of them, so they had no choice but to go with her. 'After the performance this afternoon,' she had said, 'do not return to the inn until well after dusk. Neither you nor Susanna. Everything will be settled this night,' she had said, but refused to answer questions.

She had been refusing ever since the rehearsal at which she had announced she would solve all their problems. The company had muttered and grumbled and tried to get explanations, but she said only, 'Wait. You will see.' When Paolo had asked about the ring she said, 'I shall return it soon. You must trust me,' in a manner that precluded argument. There was something about her, something new, that prevented even Isabella and Bruno from ordering or threatening her. A hard, bright fire seemed to burn within her, its heat holding them all at bay. Pedrolino, who always tried to sit near her, hoping for a smile as Buffa hoped for a bone, had been staying away, puzzled and unhappy. If Paolo tried to call her 'little redhead', the name died in his throat.

'Remember, do not return until well past dusk,' she had told him and Susanna, and then added, 'Perhaps you could stay somewhere together until it grows dark.' Paolo could not recall what he had mumbled before walking away, not looking at Susanna.

He did not know whether she too was staying away from the inn, which she had barely left since the troupe heard who she was. Where would she go? But why think of her, when he had no answers and the questions sent his mind in a circle? He gave an Arlecchino skip. If he had the mask with him, he thought, he would put it on. He imagined sliding it over his face, breathing its leathery familiarity, surrendering his person to it, moving as it dictated. No one could understand who did not perform as a Mask. Even Isabella could not. It was her one failing. Yet if she wore a Mask, no one would see her beauty, so how could not wearing one be a failing? A riddle, he thought: What would make Isabella more perfect if she wore it, yet would diminish her perfection by covering it?

Beginning to be cheered, he strode into the throngs that still filled the Piazza. It would not be long now till dark, and then he could return to the inn to find everything settled. Teresa had promised.

Orange lay in fading bands in the sky above the

campiello, and the shadows of the buildings and the passers-by grew longer and bluer. A young man paced the stones, planting a booted foot in the centre of each, looking around frequently to check the *calli* that fed into the open expanse from half a dozen directions. He wore a knee-length jacket of stout monk's cloth and a cap that covered all his hair and shaded his face. When a lamp was lit in a barred window above him, his head jerked towards it and his beard pointed to the sky.

He had been waiting for a quarter of an hour when a plump figure in cleric's robes emerged at the opposite end of the *campiello* and stood for several moments breathing heavily and looking about. 'Yes,' muttered the young man to himself. He went towards the priest and said, 'Are you Fra Filippo?'

The priest drew back a little, but nodded.

'Paolo is not able to come to this place. He sent me to meet you and to take you to him.'

'Where is he?' Filippo's voice was still breathy.

'In a room nearby.'

'Why did he ask me to meet him here, then?'

'I cannot say,' replied the young man. 'I know only that he asked me to take you to him.'

Filippo peered through the dusk. 'Who are you? One of the players?'

'I am a friend. You may call me Lorenzo. Shall we go?'

Filippo took one step and then said, 'Paolo is not ill, is he?'

'So far as I know he is not.'

'It is very peculiar. His message clearly instructed me to meet him here.'

'I regret that although I am Paolo's friend, I do not understand all his actions. Please, Father, will you follow me?'

'It is very peculiar,' Filippo repeated, but he set off after the young man, whose brisk pace made his breathing labour again. However, they were soon at the destination: a small house in a *calletta* so narrow that only one of them could pass at a time. 'What on earth is Paolo doing here?' Filippo asked.

'Enter and discover.'

Leaving the dusk behind, they went up a flight of stairs and into a small, square room with one high window; its bars sliced the sky into strips of deepening blue. In the centre of the room were two stools and a table, which held two glasses and a small oil lamp that Lorenzo lit.

Filippo's gaze flicked about the room. 'Paolo is not here,' he said, almost petulantly.

'I shall fetch him,' said Lorenzo. 'Please be seated, Father. Paolo has ordered wine and some food. I shall bring them.'

The young man was gone before Filippo could protest or agree. He rubbed his hands on his cassock, sighed, and looked more carefully around the room. Along one wall was a trestle bed with a striped mattress; along another, a low, plain chest. It was the dwelling of someone with little wealth or position. 'What on earth . . .' Filippo muttered, then sank on to a stool. The wick of the lamp was low; he adjusted it and, in the brighter light, examined the swollen, blistered index finger of his right hand. With his teeth he worked loose a sliver of hard, curled skin and placed it carefully on the table. Then he bowed his head in prayer.

The door opened. His head jerked up. 'Paolo, why have you . . .' His voice trailed off, then resumed several tones higher. 'Where is Paolo? Who are you?'

'My name is not Lorenzo.' The young man's voice, too, was higher, and although he still wore the cap, his beard and thick eyebrows were gone. He put wine and a plate of chicken and fruit on the table and took the other stool; in the lamplight his features were clear.

'You are – you are a woman,' Filippo said, as if trying to deny the fact.

'I am.' Off came the cap; red hair sprang free.

Filippo said, 'Oh!' as if someone had hit him on the back. 'You are she.'

'Of whom do you speak?'

'The daughter . . . She who . . . Why did Paolo send you?'

'Tell me whose daughter I am, and I will tell you why I am here.'

They stared, each silenced by the other. The lamp flame wavered, reduced to tiny yellow flickers in their eyes. Finally Teresa said, 'Are you afraid, Father, to say whose daughter you think me to be?'

Filippo's tongue circled his mouth. 'Your name is Teresa Laurano.'

'How do you know it?'

'The kitchen boy at the inn told me.'

'He would not know the name of Laurano. None of them do at the inn. I am only Teresa.' When Filippo did not reply, Teresa's voice assumed an edge of broken glass. 'Whose daughter am I?'

Filippo crossed himself. 'Perhaps I am mistaken. Perhaps what they said was true – that the daughter of Ginevra Laurano died.'

'It was not true.' Teresa smiled, with a pleasure so strange and slow that Filippo put the knuckles of one hand to his mouth. 'I am indeed her daughter. How do you know of her existence?'

Filippo leaned forward. 'Why did Paolo send you?'

'You need not raise your voice, Father. I shall tell you. Please, share some of this supper with me.' Teresa lifted the wine, filled the two glasses, and took a piece of chicken, which, although cold, was coated with a dark, pungent sauce. She took a bite and said, 'Paolo tells me you wish I Favolosi to leave Venice and never return.'

'I do.'

'Why?' Filippo wiped a hand across his brow but said nothing. 'Why?' she repeated.

'Because your behaviour is offensive to God.'

'Do you speak of our performances?'

'Yes. They are filled with bawdy comments, lewd gestures, and suggestions of great licentiousness, such as all good Christians should strive not to see or to hear.'

Teresa nodded. 'Paolo told us you had said so.'

'The women desecrate the purity of their sex by

exhibiting their bodies or deny its nature by donning the clothing of men.'

'Such as I am now wearing?'

Filippo blinked. 'Yes.' As if he did not realize what it was doing, his hand went to the plate and lifted a piece of chicken to his mouth. The odours of cinnamon and cloves escaped in little bursts with each of his bites.

Teresa watched until he had finished, then reached into the pocket of her jacket. 'Paolo said you gave him this ring to compensate us if we agree to leave Venice. Is that so?' Filippo nodded. 'Then this ring belongs to you?'

Filippo stiffened. 'I would not give something that was not mine.'

'To be sure, Father. Was it long in your possession?'

'Many years.' Filippo wiped his brow. 'Why does it concern you?'

'It is so . . . unusual. Surely there is no other like it?'

'I hardly think so. Therein lies part of its value.'

Teresa turned the ring slowly in her fingers and placed it on the table between them. The lion's ruby head was blood-dark in the lamplight; its tiny gold eyes and the gold ring in its mouth gleamed. Filippo took another piece of chicken.

'What if I were willing to help you,' Teresa said, 'to see that I Favolosi leaves Venice forever, as you wish.'

'Did Paolo send you for that purpose?'

'I shall tell you the truth, Father. Paolo did not send me. I act solely on my own in this matter. But if I am willing to help you – let us take some wine and discuss what may be done. I am a lover of wine.' Teresa lifted one of the glasses.

Filippo licked his lips, then did the same and drank. 'It has a pleasant taste.'

'Yes, does it not?'

Filippo drank again. He shifted on the stool, looked fixedly at the ring, and said, 'I must ask something. Do you yourself wish to leave Venice?'

'Where I am is not a matter of moment, so long as I am with I Favolosi.'

'Ah.'

'I too must ask something. How do you know the name of my mother?'

Filippo drank again. 'I . . . saw her at one time.'

'Tell me what occasion brought you together.'

'I did not say we were together!'

'Where did you see her, then?'

'Why do you wish to know of such matters?'

'Should a daughter not wish to know all she can of her mother?'

Filippo drained his glass and set it down firmly. He took a breath that swelled his belly and placed both hands flat on the table. 'Then she should know that her mother was a sorceress, who performed conjuration, *herbaria*, healing with prayers not approved by the church, and *maleficium*! A woman who practised evil.'

'And you should know,' said Teresa, her voice a silk-soft contrast to the loud righteousness of his, 'that the wine you have drunk is poisoned and that you will die before this night has ended, probably within the hour, in retribution for what you did to my mother.'

Filippo's eyes grew huge, his cheeks quivered, his hands met and clasped; but the rest of him stayed motionless as if a sword pinned him where he sat.

Teresa said, 'Do you believe what I have told you?'

'I do,' Filippo whispered. 'May the Lord God have mercy on your soul.'

'On both our souls.'

Filippo bowed his head. 'Yes.'

'Good! You admit that you were her accuser, that you had her imprisoned so you could take your pleasure with her – after which you left her to die.'

'She died of . . . an illness.'

'Yes! After you had her charged and thrown into prison, because you lusted after her!'

Filippo lifted his head. Teresa was standing, her shadow looming on the wall behind. 'It is true,' he said. 'I placed the accusation into the lion's mouth.'

'Why?'

'Because the woman was evil.'

'Do not dare to say such things of my mother!'

'They are true. The one I serve told me so.'

'Do you speak of God?'

'Of he who bade me post the accusation. The man who is now Bishop Palma.'

'Do you do blindly whatever he bids?'

'I serve His Excellency gladly, not blindly. He had proof of her evil.'

'What proof?'

'Did she not force men to come to her by using her

charms and incantations and all manner of Satanic means?'

'If they came to her, it was of their own will!'

'Did she not practise love magic? Could she not cast spells to make men lose their potency? Did she not brew potions that—'

'She knew many spells and potions, but she did nothing that was evil. Nothing!'

'Was she not a courtesan, displaying her body at her windows, so that men were unable to resist its lure?'

'That does not constitute evil. What is evil is to imprison a woman, then go to her cell, wearing a mask so no one can know your identity, and force yourself upon her.'

The two of them stopped suddenly, as if realizing simultaneously how their voices had risen in pitch and fervency. The flame of the oil lamp seemed to throb with the echoes.

Filippo's cheeks and shoulders trembled. 'I . . . did lust after your mother. It is true. I saw her only twice – once at her window and once in her cell. She cast a spell upon me. Her . . . physical being incited in me thoughts I could not banish. They tortured my body and sent my soul near to Hell, where it has hovered all the years since then, for no matter what penance I do or what prayers I utter, I cannot scourge those thoughts of the . . . pleasure they carry. Because of her I have committed the sin of lust, but never upon her body, only in my mind. I never touched the woman.' With a sigh he added, 'Not once.'

Teresa made a sound of disbelief.

'You are right, it does not matter, for whether lust is committed in the mind or in the flesh is all one.' Filippo looked down at his clasped hands and the festering finger. 'I am loathsome in the sight of God, a wretched sinner. Yet never did I touch your mother's flesh. Never. I swear it by my love for our Lord God Jesus Christ and His blessed mother the Virgin.'

Teresa's gaze bored as if trying to pierce his skull. Then she leaned down, picked up the ring and said, 'What of this? The man who raped my mother in her cell wore this ring.'

'I . . .'

'You see! You cannot deny it.'

Filippo twisted on his seat. 'It was . . . How do you know that which you are charging?'

'My mother told me of it. She described the ring, told how it scraped against her naked flesh as the man forced himself upon her.'

'You are lying. He would not do such a – you are the witch's daughter, and you lie about him to exact her revenge upon him.'

'Upon whom? Have you not admitted the ring is yours?'

Filippo looked at it for a long time. 'When she died, it was not mine.'

Teresa put her hands into her hair and slowly pulled them out. 'Do you lie, priest? Facing death, do you lie?'

'No. And you, daughter of the witch, have you lied?'

'No.'

They looked at each other, her chin thrust out, his trembling.

'Whose ring was it, then?' she said. 'Whose? Tell me!'

Tears filled Filippo's eyes. 'My bishop gave it to me, in secret sign and seal that I . . . that we together . . . had done God's bidding in charging the woman and ridding His church of her evil presence.'

'And he never told you what he had done to her?'

Filippo gave a sob and twisted on the stool. 'I must see my brother before I die. Please, I ask it in God's name, bring my brother to me.'

Teresa hesitated. 'Who is he? Where does he live?'

'Why, he is Paolo.'

'Paolo?'

'Did you not know? Ah!' cried Filippo. 'I feel your poison begin to work. Please – bring my brother to me!' He got to his feet and stood swaying, like the flame of the lamp.

'Lie upon the bed,' Teresa said brusquely. 'I shall fetch him. The inn is not far.'

CHAPTER TWELVE

She went quickly down the stairs and into the *calletta* that seemed an extension of their narrowness. The moon was low and full, like an orange ready to eat, lighting her way under *sottoporteghi*, over a bridge, and along a canal.

Paolo's brother. Paolo's brother. Her footsteps pounded the words into her mind, but not her comprehension. How could the man to whom she had given poison be Paolo's brother? 'We are from the same village in the Veneto' – that was all Paolo had said. He had not even hinted that the man was his brother, Paolo's brother. That was not part of the plan, not at all.

The plan had come full-blown into her mind almost from the moment she saw the ring. Everything had appeared by magic before her eyes, as if inscribed on a page in the Formulary, the book in which her mother had written her potions and remedies . . . and poisons. That part of the plan Teresa had nurtured for years: She would destroy her mother's killer with one of her mother's own poisons. She had chosen hemlock, which paralysed the breath, because, according to the Formulary, it worked quickly, in no more than an hour, and, more important, it made death appear to be natural. She had gathered quantities of it beside a stream, just before they returned to Venice, and made the strongest possible infusion from it. Every time she had thought of using it, she had imagined a snake dying of its own venom, and her face felt as warm as if two glasses of wine had slid down her throat at once. She had never imagined that the man would be Paolo's brother; or that he would not be the sole destroyer of her mother – not the man who had violated her in her cell. Everything was so complicated, when it should be simple. When the snake should die of its own venom, and not be Paolo's brother.

Yet . . . what matter if he was? He said he had put the accusation in the lion's mouth. He admitted he had wanted to destroy her mother. He confessed to lusting after her, *wanting* to rape her. He was guilty, if not the most guilty.

Teresa stopped short; a cat was crossing in front of her. She watched it glide, like a gondola through water, into a slit of an alley, then hurried on. She no longer saw the streets, or even the moon. As vivid as if painted by Tiziano, she saw the black cat lying beside her on the bed in the boudoir, where her mother sat before a dressing-mirror, wearing a loose, low-cut robe of figured red velvet and several strands of pearls, pulling a double-sided ivory comb through her waist-length hair. 'Is this life not better than being a player?' she said. Teresa had no memory of answering, only of listening and watching the slow voyage of the comb through the heavy waves of red hair. Occasionally it would reach out to run through the coat of the cat stretched on one of the bed's velvet pillows. Her mother would pull the silky strands of fur from the comb and form them into a little black ball, looking around the room with a smile of satisfaction. The chest along the wall was of rare wood; a perfume-burner supported by two carved female figures stood in a corner; the wood of the dressing-mirror was inlaid, and on the stand beside it were a walnut comb case and silver pots of cosmetics. The house had belonged to a woman who died, Teresa's mother had explained when they packed up their belongings and left Bruno and Isabella. Someone who admired her mother had procured it for them to live in. That admirer, or friends of his, would visit from time to time, and people would come there to purchase the potions and elixirs they had used to buy from the players' wagon. 'It will be a much better life for you, little one. We shall live here in safety and comfort,' her mother had said, and offered no further explanation. Teresa had asked for none, not only because she was young but because her mother's manner was, as always, so calm and certain that one would no more question her decisions than ask the ground underfoot why it lay there with such solidity. Indeed, her mother's wisdom was as fundamental to Teresa's existence as the stability of the ground.

On the day that had just leaped into memory, when Teresa's gaze had wandered up to objects she had looked at hundreds of times before, they seemed new to her, so that she blinked repeatedly, expecting the motions of her lashes to restore the familiar unimportance of the satin canopy billowing above the bed and the paintings of naked women and men decorating the ceiling, in which the women's legs were slightly spread and their hands occupied in touching two things: their own nipples and the swollen flesh protruding from the men who bent over them. Always before the scenes had seemed merely like those painted on backdrops for a scenario, but no longer.

'What is it, little love?' her mother said. 'Does something trouble you?'

'Why are those pictures on the ceiling?'

'They were here when we moved into the house, do you not recall?'

'Yes, but why not have them taken away and other pictures put there? Of ladies in beautiful gowns or perhaps a pretty garden.'

'Yes, I could do that, but it is wiser to keep what is there.'

'Why?'

Her mother pulled her comb through the cat's fur again, slowly. 'Because I am a courtesan, and the men who visit me like to see the pictures.' She held up the comb in gentle admonition. 'Do not ask why, little one. I would tell you, but you would not understand my explanation, not for several years.'

'Mother, what does it mean to be a courtesan?'

'Why, to be admired – like these pearls, which the laws forbid to us but which some of us wear in defiance – and given generous gifts in return for doing favours for the men who give the gifts.'

'What favours?'

'Ah.' Her mother had pulled the black cat hairs from the comb and balled them between her fingertips. 'That depends on the man. There is a merchant who asks me to spy on a rival, and another who likes me to read poetry to him. To tell you the truth, Teresa, and I shall always tell you the truth' – her mother had tapped her lightly on the nose with the comb and smiled – 'most of the men who visit me do so because they wish to take pleasure from my body. That is what is difficult for one of your age to understand.'

In silence Teresa had watched the cat twist on to its back, as boneless as bread dough. 'I thought the men came for spells,' she said.

'Did you, my little love? Perhaps you are right, for beauty is a spell of a kind, or so they sometimes tell me.' Her mother had begun combing her hair again. Its red waves shone in the light. 'And some people do come only for spells, but usually they are women who want to make some man love them more, or better, or who hope to conceive a child or defeat a rival in love.'

'Or heal someone,' Teresa said, for it seemed suddenly important to show there were things she did understand. 'Remember, I helped you with the lotion for epilepsy. I prepared the rue and the laurel.'

'So you did, my lovely little one. You are my greatest helper, and I could not live my life without you.'

The cat had yawned and stretched in mute ecstasy. Teresa had wanted to do the same.

She looked up; she was near the inn. The moon was even riper in a sky almost dark. The priest's breathing would be laboured now. He had admitted his share of the guilt. Why could she not rejoice in the prospect of his death?

He came to the cell, came here . . . Her mother's voice had been strange, almost like the sounds Teresa had heard when the players once passed a trap into which a deer had fallen . . . *masked face, but his hands, his hands . . . pushed himself into me . . . ring cutting and scraping my breasts . . . a lion's head of rubies . . . O my girl, my sweet little helper . . .* All Teresa had been able to think of were the pictures on the ceiling; in her mind the men were wearing lion's-head rings and what protruded from their naked bodies was a sword.

The priest must have told her the truth, for no man would tell lies on his deathbed. If the bishop was the more guilty of the two, must she destroy the bishop as well? She started towards the door of the inn. 'I shall find him and make him pay,' she said, but instead of soothing her, the familiar words lay crosswise in her throat, like bones.

She ran into the inn courtyard and up the stairs to her room. A candle burned on the stool beside the bed where Susanna lay, staring at the ceiling.

'Is everything settled, then?' she asked.

'Yes,' Teresa said. 'No. Not entirely.' She grabbed the candle and went to the chest that held her potions and preparations, but nothing seemed to be in its proper place, including her fingers.

'Has something gone wrong?' Susanna asked. Teresa was silent. 'May I help you in any way, since I presume you are still engaged in trying to help me?'

Teresa shook her head, forced herself not to rush, and finally found the object she sought. She shoved it into the pocket of her jacket and replaced the candle on the stool. 'Has Paolo returned?' she asked.

'I do not know,' Susanna said coolly.

'Did you not go out together?'

'We did not.'

'He must be here!' Teresa cried and ran into the hall.

She pounded on the door of his room, and when he opened it, she was so overcome with the dearness of his odd, sharp face, which it seemed she had never truly seen before, that she could only stare until he said, 'Well? Yes? What is it?' She knew how he once would have greeted her – 'Hel-lo, little redhead,' making a song of the word 'Hello' – and she wanted to cry. Would he ever say it again? Would he forgive her? Why was everything so complicated?

'Paolo, you must come with me,' she said. 'The priest wants to see you. The priest who says he is your brother.'

His eyes grew as wide as Arlecchino's. 'He told you that?'

'He told me because he is dying and wishes to speak with you.'

'Dying?'

'Paolo, I . . . I have poisoned him.' She tensed, expecting him to shout or grip her arms, perhaps even strike her.

He merely narrowed the gaze that had been so comically wide. 'That is how you remove the threat to

Anna and to the company – by killing a man?'

'No. Without his knowledge of her, we will all be safe, but that was not my true reason. He is the man . . . one of the men . . . who destroyed my mother. I know because of the ring he gave you. I have waited for years to find the man with that ring and kill him.' She waited. 'My mother, Paolo. My mother!'

'Let us go at once.'

They walked rapidly but in silence. When they reached the house where Filippo lay, Teresa stopped and faced Paolo. 'I did not know he was your brother. I swear it by everything sacred to me.'

'Do you mean that had you known, you would not have used the poison?'

The question thrashed about inside her. 'I . . . cannot say, Paolo.'

He nodded. He was so unlike Paolo, so grave.

When they reached the door of the room, Teresa feared to open it, lest the priest be dead already.

He was alive, still on the striped mattress on the trestle bed, his breathing loud as wind. Teresa moved one of the stools to his side and placed the lamp on it. His face was the colour of a linen sheet, and sweat soaked his hair and made runnels on his cheeks. 'Paolo,' he wheezed. 'You are here.'

'Yes, Filippo. I see that matters go badly with you.'

'The woman has poisoned me. I know not with what substance.'

'Hemlock,' Teresa whispered.

Filippo's smile was a gargoyle's. 'Socrates and I.'

His chest heaved. 'Paolo, I must . . . save you.'

'I regret that I have not been a good brother,' Paolo said. 'Since we met again, I have done nothing as you wished me to do it.'

'I must save us both. Bring our souls . . . my soul . . . to the Lord Jesus Christ.'

'Surely God will welcome you into His kingdom, you who have lived your whole life for Him.'

'I am loathsome to Him . . . as to myself. I must save us both.'

'But you contend I cannot be saved unless I renounce that which has the most meaning in my life – performing on the stage.'

'Players . . . defy God's . . .'

'We are not evil, Filippo.'

His hand went to his throat. His fingers clawed, as if to open a passage for air. 'My brother . . . help me . . .'

'Father!' cried Teresa, deciding only in that moment. 'I shall help you. I have brought an antidote – look.' She pulled from her jacket the flask she had scrabbled for in the chest in her room. 'It contains a powerful root to relieve your breathing and counteract the poison, and quantities of rue, which is a good emetic. Take it. Drink it.' She thrust the flask towards Filippo, but his head rolled away. Then he looked back at her and said, 'Why give poison – if you do not wish it – to do its work?'

'You are Paolo's brother.'

'Ah.'

'And if you are not the man who violated my mother—'

'I did. Many times. In my thoughts.' Filippo's chest pumped again. 'I am . . . lowest of creatures, vilest . . .'

Paolo took the flask and said, 'Come, brother. Drink what Teresa has brought.'

'Better to die. Deserve . . . to die. I am vile . . . loathsome.'

'Do not speak foolishly.' To Teresa, Paolo whispered, 'Are you certain of this antidote? Will it work?'

'I . . . believe so.' That was all she could say. She had never used it, had only seen the potion in the Formulary, her mother's hand noting that it 'acted to expel certain poisons and caused one to vomit profusely'.

'Loathsome,' Filippo repeated. 'The flesh . . . impure . . . ever tempted . . .'

'That is no reason to die!' Paolo cried. 'You can beg forgiveness, you can do penance, you can—'

Filippo held up one hand as if to bless his brother, but only one finger rose, blistered and swollen. 'Struggled always. Satan too strong. Want peace . . . peace in Christ.' His eyes rolled to Teresa. 'Her daughter . . . forgive you.' A fight for air. 'You punish my sin . . . release me from this wretchedness.' One hand gripped Paolo's arm. 'Promise me . . .'

'What, Filippo?'

'Abandon the life of . . . lewdness . . .'

'Come,' Paolo said briskly. 'Drink this antidote. You shall have many years left.'

'Don't want them. O Christ, forgive me!' When Paolo attempted to force the potion past his lips, Filippo pushed it away with sudden strength, so that the flask fell to the floor.

As they watched the liquid pool from it, Paolo whispered to Teresa, 'Can you fetch more?'

'There is no more.' She did not even know why she had prepared it or why, having done so, she had not brought it along with the poisoned wine. Had she doubted herself even as she revelled in avenging her mother? 'He will die, then,' she whispered. 'Soon.' She lifted her eyes from the liquid on the floor and found Paolo gazing at her.

He nodded as if he understood something – perhaps everything – and then turned to his brother. 'Have you made confession today?'

'Yes. Every day.'

'Shall I send for your bishop so that you may receive the final sacrament?'

Filippo twisted in a struggle that seemed to be for something more than air. 'No. If he went to her . . . his ring . . .' His eyes closed, then flew open. 'Susanna Bardi . . . he will force her back to her husband. I do not believe he is right. Do not want her suffering . . . on my soul.' He fixed his fading gaze on Teresa. 'Atone. Save her in . . . my name.'

How could she tell him that the poison had been meant, in part, for just that purpose? 'I . . . I shall,' she said.

Filippo nodded. Then the nodding turned into a rolling of his head, and he began muttering. Teresa realized that he was making a sort of confession, his words barely audible, so interspersed were they with struggles for breath, like steam escaping from a cauldron lid: 'Blessed Mother of God . . . sins of the flesh . . . forgive me, Father . . . forgive Thy most loathsome . . .' His eyes flew open. He clutched Paolo's wrist. 'Love God! Love Him! Mother sent me to serve Him, but I failed. You must love Him. Save us! Abandon wickedness. Love Him!'

That burst of clear speech was his last. He clung to Paolo's wrist while his face grew dark and his body arched and buckled, seeking air; he was like a cask on a rolling sea, tethered by a single rope. Teresa thought it the longest span of time in her life, watching him, waiting. If God had wanted to punish her, He was surely succeeding. She tried to hold in her mind a picture of the last time she had seen her mother, face bright with fever, hair dark with sweat and filth, hands picking at her stained dress. *Had me charged . . . came to the cell, came here . . . God, let me live so I may kill him . . . kill him . . .* But the reality of the priest's dying pushed aside her mother's image and words, as a stone shatters a reflection in the water. Teresa could not watch his face. Instead she looked at his sandalled feet which were grey with the dirt of the streets. A bony growth on the side of one toe slanted it to the right. She tried to think of a snake poisoned by its own venom, but the snake turned into Fra Filippo's foot, moving back and forth feebly, as if it too sought air. Had her mother ever killed anyone? Teresa wondered. Had she actually prepared one of the poisons in her Formulary and put it into a glass of wine and listened to it squeeze a man's life from him?

She saw that Paolo was bending over his brother,

making the sign of the cross. Then he began wiping Filippo's forehead with his sleeve. His hand was knocked away by a huge shuddering, after which came limpness, and finally a silence more awful than the choking it replaced.

Paolo shook his head slowly, sighed, then folded his brother's hands across his chest and closed his eyes. 'He is gone,' he said, as if the words were required to convince himself.

'Yes.'

There was another span of the dreadful silence, which Teresa could not break. She had lost the capacity for speech and action, and could only wait, like a marionette, for Paolo to pull her into life.

'Well,' he said finally, 'we cannot leave him here, like this. What had you planned to do with him?'

'We cannot leave him here,' Teresa echoed.

'That is a certainty. What arrangements have you made?'

She felt her cheeks burning. She realized that ever since she had first vowed to find the man and kill him, the future had ended with his death. Beyond it lay nothing but the fact of having achieved it, which somehow would alter the world and transform everything into happiness.

But she was not happy, and the corpse lying on the striped mattress would not dispose of itself.

'I . . . have made no arrangements, Paolo.'

He lifted both eyebrows almost as high as those on his Arlecchino mask. Then he blew a stream of air through his mouth and said, 'We must remove his body. We must take him to a place where he will be found soon, so that he will have a proper burial, and where he will not . . . be uncomfortable.'

'We could take him to his church.'

'That is a good idea. But how?'

'We might wrap him in a blanket.'

They tried to do so, but Filippo's dead weight made it impossible. Frustrating though the situation was, there was relief in the dry, careful act of discussing various alternatives, which forbade expression of anything else. They might be planning a scenario, Teresa thought. But with a scenario, she would be laughing at Paolo's antics.

At length they decided to support Filippo between them, each putting an arm around his waist, as if he were too ill to walk. They got him into position, and while Paolo held him for a moment, Teresa put out the lamp. They then started down the stairs. Filippo's feet thumped like a badly played drum and, when they reached the street, scraped toes-down in the muck. His head hung, bobbing, and his wet hair fell forward over it, so that instead of his face, there gleamed the white circle of his tonsure, like a miniature of the moon.

How strange it was, Paolo thought as they went slowly and sideways through the alleys, that he could not summon up any childhood memories of Filippo, could not separate him from that sea of eleven sibling faces. If one's brother died, should one not be counting a rosary of memories? He held Filippo's left arm over his shoulder, the hand dangling beside his ear; they were closer in death than ever in life. The one picture he could recall was of a brother – Filippo? Carlo? Pietro? – on a hot day cramming so many berries into his mouth that their juice stained his cheeks and lips and ran redly down his chin. Coming upon him, Paolo had at first thought it was blood and had begun to cry, whether for love of his brother or fear at the sight of blood, he could not recall. How strange was the country of childhood, where landmarks existed but one could not remember what they denoted.

He and Teresa started up the slope of a bridge, Filippo's weight pulling at them like wet sand. Wondering whether Teresa would be able to sustain it the entire way to the church, Paolo glanced over at her; her lower lip was locked under her teeth, and her breathing came nearly as hard as Filippo's had. It was impossible that she had poisoned him, yet of a certainty she would not lie about such a matter. Paolo had always thought of her as a child, albeit a resourceful and determined one; he had never imagined that behind her pretty features and blunt manner lay a consuming desire for revenge. Her face, it seemed, was more of a mask than any carried in I Favolosi's trunks. Perhaps, he thought, all faces were masks; and hearing himself entertain such a metaphysical speculation, would have banished it with one of Arlecchino's capers, except that the dead weight of his brother forbade Arlecchino to appear.

'I must stop for a moment,' Teresa said.

'Very well.'

They rested at the top of the bridge without releasing their burden, so that the dead man still joined them. When Teresa's breathing was easier, she said, 'Did you love him greatly, Paolo?'

'No. But he was my brother.'

'Yes.' She swallowed. 'Do you . . . hate me, Paolo?'

He considered. 'No.'

'I did try to save him. You saw that I did.'

'Yes.'

'But he did not wish to be saved.'

'Except by God.'

'Nothing is as I expected it to be. I thought I hated him, and I do – I did – but when he spoke of loathing himself – he seemed to hate himself more than I hated him. Is that not strange?'

Paolo had not put the thought into words, but she was right. He nodded.

'I do not understand,' she said. 'Why would a person feel such a way? You do not loathe yourself, do you, Paolo?'

Something – perhaps it was the plaintiveness in her voice, or the sad weight between them of the brother he could barely remember – brought into his mind a memory of the day he most wished to forget: the day in the cypress glade. 'I hate my face,' Anna had whispered, and his entire being had understood. 'I am a foolish-looking fellow,' he had confessed to her just before they . . . Even in that confession, he had not loathed all of himself – only his ridiculous face and body.

How strange it was that Filippo the priest, who had

given his life to God, should despise himself more than the brother who had given himself to the stage.

Teresa turned to look at him over the sagging corpse. 'I think he must have committed dreadful crimes, of which we know nothing.'

She was wrong, Paolo thought. However weak Filippo had been, he was not an evil man. She needed to believe she was right, for she had poisoned him.

'Perhaps,' he said.

She sighed again. 'You are certain you do not hate me?'

'I am sorry for you.' After a moment he added, 'I cannot fully understand why you did it – how you could do it. Is it not a frightening thing, to send a man to his death?'

'Yes. Yes, it is.' Her voice cracked like glass. 'I did it to avenge my mother, and partly also for you – because of Anna. I did not know he was your brother!' He did not reply. After a moment she said, 'Let us go on, then.'

They adjusted Filippo's body between them and descended slowly off the bridge and on to the path of stones beside the little canal.

When they reached the church, it was empty and dark save for pale smears of light from some votive candles. They dragged Filippo's body to the altar. 'Let us lay him with his face down,' Paolo said, 'so it may seem that he collapsed here.' After they had done so, Paolo made the sign of the cross over him, and Teresa did the same.

'Goodbye, brother,' Paolo whispered. '*Requiescat in pace.*'

As they made their way back to the inn, it seemed that the weight of Filippo's body was still with them.

'I shall keep my promise to him,' Teresa said. 'If there is any further threat to Anna from the bishop, I shall make certain he does not find her.'

Paolo said nothing.

'That will please you too, will it not, Paolo?'

'Do not concern yourself with Anna and me!' It came out so harshly that he added quietly, 'Naturally I shall be glad if Anna is safe.'

They exchanged no further words.

Bishop Palma was awakened shortly after dawn, his servant speaking in soft but urgent tones. He dressed at once, quickly, and went to the church, believing a mistake must have been made.

There was a body before the altar, and when Palma turned it over, he felt an instant's relief because the face that looked up at him seemed strange. In the next instant he realized why: It was so naked of the deference he was used to seeing that it took him a moment to identify its absence.

'It appears he came in very early and collapsed here,' said the sacristan.

'Yes.'

'God's will be done.'

'Amen,' said the bishop mechanically, but he was feeling two things: rage that his devoted servant had been taken from him, and the beginnings of doubt that the will had been God's.

CHAPTER THIRTEEN

Of Privilege

Let Europe have its barons, earls, princes, *comtes, marquises*. Venice has only one title: *nobilomo*, patrician of the Most Serene Republic.

In the title resides all power and the responsibility to use it with wisdom and justice for the glory of the Republic. He who fails to do so is at the mercy of his fellow *nobilomi* – unless they see fit to treat him with justice instead.

'Good morning, Lady Anna. I am sorry to disturb you.'

'Good morning. I did not expect . . .'

'But now I must call you Lady Susanna, must I not?'

'It does not matter.'

'Then I shall continue as I began, with Lady Anna. May I speak with you?'

'Do you and Isabella need new opening and closing lines for a scene?'

'We always benefit greatly from your great knowledge of literature and exemplary taste in its expression, but I did not come for that purpose.'

'I am attending to something, to some tasks. I am sorry.'

'Why be sorry? Be hospitable instead. You have

scarcely left this room for several days.'

'I wait to learn whether Teresa has been able to do as she said and remove the threat against me, and therefore against all of you.'

'We wait for that knowledge, too. But why wait alone in your room?'

'I believe it is simpler for everyone.'

'Still, I should like to speak with you.'

'For what reason?'

'Perhaps I wish to help with your strenuous tasks. Or perhaps I merely wish the pleasure of your company.'

'Signor Luca, I fear you jest with me.'

'I? I am one of the Lovers, not the *zanni*. Ah. I see I have distressed you – your cheeks have gone red. No, Lady Anna, do not turn away. I do not intend to embarrass you, only to speak with you.'

'Why do you concern yourself with me?'

'To tell the truth, I did not come with a reason. Do I need one? Is it not sufficient that I like to speak with you?'

'If you truly wish to come in, you may.'

'Thank you. Teresa is not here, I see.'

'She went out early this morning.'

'Then I shall sit on the bed and inquire after your health, like a proper guest.'

'I am well, Signor Luca.'

'Splendid. I too am well. Well. Well. Well! You stand and stare at me in silence, as if you wish me to leave.'

'I . . . No.'

'Health is a great gift and doctors are fools. That is my opinion.'

'I do not disagree.'

'Have you had experience of doctors? Of course, you must have. As a daughter of the Bardi, you would receive the most modern medical treatments.'

'They did little good, as you see by looking at me.'

'Lady Anna, I believe you dwell too much on such matters. Let us speak of others. Hmmm. I see nothing in this room from your life in the Bardi palace, not even some of the books that must be the source of your wide knowledge. Did you have many of them?'

'Yes. Many.'

'Tell me of your life as one of the Bardi.'

'Why?'

'So I may hear of what I cannot attain – of uncounted riches and servants who honour one's wishes before one has the sense to wish them. Surely it is a pleasant way to live?'

'Indeed.'

'Are the Bardi riches truly uncounted?'

'A spice trader counts his wealth carefully, I assure you. Signor Luca, your questions cause me to suspect that you came to learn what you can of my family, for purposes I do not know.'

'I merely speak whatever wanders into my head. What I say matters little – I came only to be certain all is well with you. So, once again we are silent. How is it, Lady Anna, that a conversation with you is often more silence than speech? A pleasant silence, however.'

'I am sorry. Signor Luca, I have not thanked you for speaking on my behalf when I made my plea to the company.'

'One cannot consent to furthering a lady's misfortune. One can only admire her courage in escaping it.'

'Thank you. I . . . It was difficult to speak of the particulars of my life.'

'Then that stupid Fiorenza, bursting in with her tale! I hope you were not too distressed. But I see that you were. Why? She has told a lie more than once. And if she spoke the truth . . . If you and Paolo are able to give each other pleasure – whose affair is that but your own?'

'But I— We do not—'

'Now you are as crimson as a Venetian sunset. Your scar stands out against it like a sliver of the moon. But perhaps you prefer me not to speak of it? Let me say rather that men and women are made to give each other pleasure and should not pay heed to others' interference. Paolo is a splendid fellow. If you and he make each other happy, I can only wish you well.'

'He . . . We are not . . . We do not make each other happy, Signor Luca.'

'No?'

The door flew open.

Teresa stood there, stared at the two of them, and said, 'Have you heard the news? It is everywhere this morning. They say Fra Filippo is dead.'

Luca got to his feet.

'Dead!' Susanna cried. 'Teresa, was it your doing?'

'They say he died in his church, before the altar. Anna – Susanna – the danger is now over, for you and for I Favolosi.'

At the Bardi *palazzo*, in the living quarters, the floors were being polished. Slaves worked with soft cloths and jars of wax, rubbing the diagonally cut bricks or squares of porphyry or brilliant *terrazzo* patterns to make them glisten as if the sun were upon them no matter what the hour. The shine on the floors of a *palazzo*, often matching the designs on its ceiling, was a matter of pride to the household.

The slave Ludis walked past two young men working on the stairs, the muscles of their naked shoulders and backs bunching like clusters of fruit. When she had first come to the Bardi, she had also done menial tasks, but soon she had moved up to the kitchens and for many years had been personal attendant to Signora Bardi. At forty she was still beautiful, and her dark face, with its broad cheekbones and large eyes, was as impassive as on the day she had entered the household. All her fury and pain at being captured by pirates on her nineteenth birthday had been vented by the time she reached Italy and sealed behind an expressionless face. If she could do nothing else, she swore, she would prevent her captors and owners from knowing what she thought and felt.

Although she had closed her face and heart, her eyes and ears stayed open, so that there were few matters in the Bardi household about which she did not know a good deal, sometimes more than the Bardi.

The one being who had touched her was Susanna. When the child was scarred for life, Ludis had gone to her narrow bed, turned her face into the pillow and wept. Understanding the burden of the scar in a way she could not fully explain, she had told the child of being captured, of finding her life as a princess of Circassia wiped away like a figure drawn in sand, in the hope that the child would take some comfort. When she married and left, Ludis had grieved silently. When Susanna escaped from her new husband's home, Ludis had felt not only pride but something that had taken months to accept: inspiration. If the scar-child, as she thought of her, who was now the scar-woman, had had the courage and the will to leave, perhaps she, Ludis, could find the strength and the means to do the same, and make her way back to the life she had once known. When Susanna came in disguise to see her mother, Ludis's hope had flared into a vow. She made a plan and waited for the proper moment to put it into action. In the spring, she had told herself, in the spring.

The spring had come, but still she had not acted. There was always a reason – uncertain weather, or a fluttering in her innards that might presage an illness, or the presence of too many strangers in the house. Still, she had begun to wonder whether her thoughts and feelings had been sealed away for so many years that they had dried up completely, like figs left too long in the sun; whether she had become a slave in spirit as well as fact.

She made her way through the floor polishers and reached the Signora's chambers. The Signora was sitting by the window in a state of distraction, with one of her little caskets of jewels open on the table beside her.

'Ludis!' she said. 'There is dreadful news. Have you heard? Fra Filippo is dead. They found him lying before the altar in his church. Such a good man, he was, and taken so suddenly, with no sign of illness.'

'Truly, Signora, a great sadness,' Ludis said.

'Our Bishop Palma is very upset. He depended on the father, to whom he had given the task of finding my Susanna. One wonders now whether she will ever be . . . Ludovico will no doubt . . .' With each of her unfinished thoughts, the long handkerchief in the Signora's hand lifted and shivered.

'Do you still wish to look through your jewels this morning?' Ludis's face and voice gave no sign that suddenly – be it the mention of Susanna or the warmth of the breeze at the window – her spirit had swelled with resolve.

The Signora said, 'I know I must see which need repairing and cleaning, but I am too . . . Another day, Ludis. Put them away, please.'

'Yes, Signora. May I bring something to ease your distress? Perhaps a glass of lemon water?'

'Yes, thank you.'

The Signora patted her face with the handkerchief. Ludis took the casket of jewels, but before putting them away, she removed three rings and two chains and slipped them into the pockets of her skirt. In the kitchens, she told one of the younger slaves to carry lemon water up to the Signora, and took a loaf of newly baked bread and a wedge of *caciócavallo* cheese. She went with her usual stately grace down the stairs, calling the attention of the polishers in the main hall to a patch of brick floor that had been missed.

It was afternoon before her absence was noted, and night before the Signora, at Antonio's insistence, checked her jewels and discovered that some were missing. Antonio cursed and vowed the damned woman would not get far.

A single white candle burned in Andrea Palma's study. In the draughtless air, its flame was straight and steady. Like the numeral one, Palma thought, staring into it. Like a constant reminder that he was alone.

Filippo had been laid to rest that afternoon. Palma had officiated, and even as he had been intoning the Latin words in his most sonorous voice and moving his hands and bowing his head in motions as familiar as breathing, even as he was devoutly hoping Filippo was now at peace in the embrace of God the Father, other thoughts had persisted, like the organ notes beneath the chanting of the choir. Could someone have caused Filippo to die? Could that someone be the daughter of the witch? Was Filippo's death connected to the task Palma had given him? Had Filippo completed that task, or did the threat of the daughter still remain? Above all, how could he, Andrea Palma, learn the answers to those questions? While the censers swayed, the voices swelled, and the many dozens of parishioners shifted and murmured and crossed themselves, Palma had struggled with the questions and with the three emotions that had not left him since he learned of Filippo's death: anger, fear, guilt.

They were with him now, shadows lurking just beyond the light of the white candle. Something else was there as well, some feeling that squeezed at his heart in a ceaseless demand for recognition. He sighed and turned aside, and in that moment – before his reason recalled the truth – he glanced at the door, expecting Filippo to enter. The other feeling burst into fullness, and he knew its nature: grief, which tore him in two as easily as if he were a sheet of the paper on which Filippo had used to sit before him and write in his liquidly beautiful hand. He was alone now, in a way he had not been for many years. The worried, cherubic face that had so often looked at him as if he were already a cardinal, and that death had robbed of its deference and trust, would never gaze at him again. The comfort of having someone know the secrets of his life was gone. The relief of sharing certain burdens without having to name either their nature or their weight could never be experienced again. Andrea Palma put his face into his elegant hands and wept.

There was a discreet knock at the door.

Palma lifted his head. The one of the candle confronted him again, but he wiped away all trace of tears and said, 'Yes?'

The servant who entered had humility so deeply carved into his posture that he seemed incapable of standing straight. 'Begging your pardon, Your Excellency, but a messenger has just brought this letter and says it is of great importance. Seeing the light of your candle, I thought I could knock.'

'Yes, yes,' Palma said and held out his hand. 'What messenger?'

'I do not know him, Your Excellency. I believe it was just an urchin of the streets.' The servant bowed deeply and backed out the door.

Palma broke the seal, held the paper near the candle, and read:

> Fra Filippo sought the whereabouts of Susanna Bardi and found her. If Bishop Palma would know where she is, let him look to the troupe of actors known as I Favolosi, who, lodging at the Inn of the Three Bells, perform for the Polani. Susanna Bardi has been with the players for many months.
>
> One Who Has Knowledge of Her

Palma read it again, then a third time. Could it be a jest? He decided not. He smiled. The letter was a sign that God approved of all he had done, for why else would God send him this knowledge now, when he badly needed to learn whether the threat of the Laurano woman's daughter had been removed? He looked to the shuttered window, wondering how soon he could give orders for Susanna Bardi to be taken from the inn and brought directly to him. He would talk with her, and, wielding the authority of the church and the skills of a subtle questioner, he would learn not only whether Filippo had persuaded the players to leave Venice 'forever' but also whether the red-haired woman had spoken to anyone of matters pertaining to her mother's death.

Then he would restore Susanna Bardi to her husband and family, and place Antonio even more securely in his debt.

'Let me look upon your face,' said Isabella, 'so that it shall be my last sight.'

'And when you awaken,' said Luca, 'may it also be the first.'

'Beloved one!'

'Angelic one!'

'Then let the potion be given into my hand.'

I Favolosi, at the Polani palace, were playing the scenario of *The Lady Who Was Believed Dead*, in which the Lovers planned for Isabella to escape marrying an undesirable man by taking a potion that put her into a deathlike sleep.

'Let the potion be given into my hand!' Isabella repeated.

Teresa, playing her serving-maid, had the goblet. She held it out partway, as she had done many times in previous performances. Her arm and hand would move no farther. She could not move at all. Isabella stared at her, eyes flashing impatience, then anger.

'Give me the potion!'

The voice Teresa heard was Isabella's but the figure was Fra Filippo's. She was handing poison to him.

'The potion!' Isabella demanded. Rustles came from the audience.

Luca rescued her. 'Your serving-maid freezes with fear of harming you,' he said. 'Give me the draught.' He took it from Teresa and gave it to Isabella, who held it to her lips for a long time, then uttered a nearly endless sigh, waved her hands as gently as if they were scarves, let the goblet fall to the floor, and sank after it, gracefully.

The audience murmured its appreciation.

'Now,' said Luca, 'that great fool, her father, cannot marry her to the still greater fool he has chosen for her. Leave me alone with her,' he said to Teresa. 'Your work is finished.'

Teresa nodded and managed finally to move and make her exit.

'What is wrong?' Bruno was after her soon as she was behind the curtain.

'I felt ill,' she whispered.

'That does not excuse you! I feel ill many a time, but you do not find me failing to do my scenes.'

'I am sorry,' Teresa murmured and moved away from him. Paolo turned in her direction, but he was behind the mask, Arlecchino in every angle of his body, ready to lope out for the next scene. She stood by the table where the properties were laid and huddled within herself, knowing what had happened, but not what to do about it. Since the priest's death, she had moved through her days and nights as if she were a painting: a convincing surface, with nothing behind it or within it. She herself had been one of those who looked at the painting, existing only on the outside. In the scene, her feelings had been jarred alive, and her body paralysed with the knowledge that the priest had died – that the death hidden in his wine had been not simulated but real. As Isabella 'died' so elegantly that the audience nearly clapped, she could see nothing but the priest panting and thrashing and choking. Would he be with her forever? Was she, not he, the snake poisoned with its own venom?

She began to shake, and put her head in her hands.

'Teresa, what is it?'

She turned and saw Pedrolino, mask lifted to reveal his concern. 'I am all right,' she said, although the thought of anyone being kind to her threatened to bring on tears.

'If you need anything—' He smiled weakly, as if it were he, not she, who was having difficulty controlling his face. 'Can you finish the performance?'

She saw Bruno watching, scowling. 'I shall finish it,' she said.

She was in only three more scenes. Miraculously she was able to walk on and off and say what was needed, but in the fewest possible words, for any elaborate improvising was beyond her.

When the performance was over, Isabella came towards her with tight eyes and mouth, and she saw that others wanted to ask her questions, so she said loudly, 'I am ill. I am going to the inn at once,' and made her way out of the *palazzo*, still in costume, her face still painted.

Outside, everything was black and grey and silver,

stones and moon and water, and as she walked along, the canals' endless shiver and the constant shift of clouds seemed personifications of her inner state. She did not think of danger, no matter how dark the passageways; she paid little attention to the occasional soft scurryings across her path; she reached the inn as she had left the *palazzo*, prisoned in her agitation.

In the inner court, two men were speaking to one of the servants. She was walking past them, uncaring, when her attention was pricked by the words 'the Signora Rossi' and then snared by a mention of 'Bishop Andrea Palma'. She stopped and went quite still, listening.

One of the men said, 'Do not pretend ignorance. We know that Signora Rossi, who was Susanna Bardi before marriage, is with the players who lodge here.'

'She is?' said the servant, scratching his head. 'I don't know her.'

'Do not pretend ignorance. She is the lady with a scarred face. His Excellency has ordered her brought to him, and things will go badly with you if you do not take us to her at once.'

Teresa's next awareness was of standing beside the servant saying, 'Let me help these men, for I know you have much to do.' He gave her a grateful look and went off.

'Signori, as one of the players, I can assist you,' she said. 'I heard you ask for the lady. I can go to her room and send her to you, if you wish.'

'We do wish. Be quick about it, if you please. And no tricks.'

She nodded and ran up the stairs to her room. Susanna was indeed there, asleep. Despite Teresa's assurances to her and the entire troupe that they were all safe, Susanna had not yet resumed her part in the company's activities.

Teresa looked at her sleeping form, and for a moment, before she could do what she had determined, she heard Fra Filippo, as clearly as if he were in the room: *Atone. Save her in my name.*

As if she had heard it too, Susanna stirred on the bed.

Andrea Palma waited in his study. He knew he should have taken no action until the morning, but he had. If God decided to punish him for the urgency of his desire to settle the matter, so be it. He had sent for the two men, who were more refined and less desperate than *bravi*, although not completely distant from them in spirit, and who had performed tasks for him in the past on a few occasions requiring slightly more persuasiveness than his own purely verbal skills could provide. According to his hourglass, the men should have succeeded by now, or else be coming to report their failure.

Impatience was not a desirable quality in a bishop, or in anyone dedicated to the service of the Lord God. Filippo had had infinite patience. He would wait months, even years, for a prayer to be granted or a sinner to repent. 'Your Excellency,' he would say, 'the will of God is manifested in such time as He sees fit, and we have no conception of how He reckons time, do we?' The bishop felt a moistening at the edges of his eyes and wiped it away impatiently.

A knock at the door. 'Enter!' he called.

The servant who was permanently curved into humility came into the room. 'The men have returned,' he said.

'Is there a lady with them?'

'Yes, Your Excellency.'

'Ah.' The bishop swallowed his relief. 'Bring them to me.'

The servant left the room.

For an instant, Palma thought he was about to suffer another of his crushing, inexplicable attacks of guilt, but the feeling passed, leaving only a memory of cold sweat on his forehead. He stared into the shaft of the candle's flame, clasped his hands, and prayed, willing himself not to count the moments until there should again be a knock at the door.

The count was eighty-five.

The men entered, holding the woman firmly between them. She was veiled and shawled, but her body spoke of anger and resistance.

'Did you have difficulty persuading her to come?' the bishop asked the men.

'Yes, Your Excellency, once she realized where we would take her.'

'Release her,' said the bishop. He held out one hand. 'Take this for your trouble.'

The moment their hands released her, the woman strode away from the men, who took the proffered coins and left quickly.

'Signora Rossi,' said the bishop, 'I rejoice to have found you at last.'

'I did not wish to be found. You have no authority to treat me in this manner.'

'I have the temporal authority granted me by your husband and family, and the much higher authority of our Lord God, who requires us not to abandon our duties of responsibility.'

A silence of several moments. 'How did you find me – when I have taken every precaution to avoid that possibility?'

'I received a letter telling me where you were.'

'A letter? From whom?'

'I do not know, Signora, although I suspect it may have come from one of the players to whom you joined your fate. If so, it is a manifestation of your folly in doing so.' There was no reply. 'Please sit here, Signora, across from me, so we may talk more comfortably.'

'What could you have to say that will give me comfort?'

Palma raised his eyebrows. 'Do you forget, my daughter, that you speak to a bishop of the Holy Catholic and Apostolic Church?'

'I cannot forget it when he has had me brought here against my wish.'

'When was your last confession?' She did not reply.

The bishop leaned forward and looked past the candle into the shadows where she stood. 'If I had ever had any doubts that you should be returned to your duties as the wife of Ludovico Rossi, they would be dispelled by your manner, which differs greatly from what I remember, no doubt because of your acquaintance with the players. I should like to hear of them and of the time you spent with them. If you share your knowledge with me, I will counsel your husband to show mercy to you.'

'Why do you wish to know of the players?'

'It is the duty of God's servants to learn of those who undermine our work.'

She did not reply. Almost to himself, the bishop said, 'I barely can believe I am speaking to the woman I once knew.'

She had heard; she came forward and took the chair opposite him. 'You are not.' She pulled off the shawl, then the veil.

Years of dealing with the world without revealing himself to it came to the bishop's rescue. He held the shock within him, keeping it from his face and forcing it instead into his blood. If only he had told Filippo the woman was a demon, he thought, then Filippo would have had her destroyed without argument or compunction.

Calmly he said, 'You are the daughter of the witch.'

'And you are the man who had her imprisoned falsely in order to satisfy your lust.'

'Is that what you believe?'

'That is what she told me.'

'I do not think so.'

'She told me of the man who came to her cell and took his pleasure with her. She described the ring he wore. Fra Filippo told me the ring was yours.'

The bishop's heart had become galloping hooves,

but he would not allow his reason to fall under them. Even as she held up the ring, he noted her admission that she had spoken with Filippo.

'In charging your mother,' he said, 'I merely acted for someone she had wronged. Your mother was a courtesan and a sorceress. She practised *herbaria* and *maleficium*. She cast spells. She had to be accused and brought before the Tribunal of the Holy Inquisition, which is careful to ensure just treatment to all.'

'The accusations against her were lies.'

'Your mother was the liar. I shall name one of her lies you cannot dispute. She swore that her child had died, yet here you are.'

'Yes. Here I am.' The woman smiled, and in that gesture the mother was reincarnated, denying to the bishop that she was a witch while confirming it with every motion that invited him to place his hands upon her, upon all the soft places of her body.

'I have come to tell you this,' said the daughter. 'Susanna Bardi is no longer in Venice. You cannot return her to her husband or family. If you try, I have ways to make certain that the Council of Ten learns of the crimes you committed against my mother.'

The bishop felt a dizzying lurch within him. His scalp was suddenly as damp as if a wet cloth lay upon it. 'No one will believe your tale,' he said. 'The very invention of it demonstrates your own wickedness, which is as great as was your mother's. I shall have you accused in the same way she was.'

'On what charge?' said the defiant woman – mother

or daughter, the bishop was no longer certain which. He put his fingers to his eyes.

Suddenly the keenness of his reason returned, and with it came an idea so clever that his dizziness retreated before it. He put his hands on the table. 'You have admitted that you spoke with Fra Filippo,' he said. 'You have his ring. I shall have you charged with causing his death, by means of the heretical witchcraft you learned from your mother.'

CHAPTER FOURTEEN

Of our Natures

Composed are we all of the four elements – fire, water, air, and earth – which, as God sees fit to combine them in us, constitute our humours: yellow bile, black bile, phlegm, or blood.

The balance or disharmony among them gives us health or disease, and creates our natures. Yellow bile makes choler; black, melancholy and wisdom. Phlegm produces apathy and calm; blood – ruddiness, optimism, cheer.

Who among us has not found that balance shifting at times, or wished for it to do so?

The bells woke Susanna, as they often did. In Venice they sounded as they never had out in the countryside, or perhaps anywhere else, as if the water over which they rang kept their metal throats moist. Seeing that Teresa was already up and gone, she lay beneath the coverlet, drifting with the random bell-calls, imagining that they pushed her back and forth as the canals pushed a gondola. When she was very small, she had thought the bells were set ringing by dwarfs who lived in their towers and played games by swinging back and forth upon them.

After a while she brought her mind back to the present, knowing she must rise soon, confront her situation again, and try to resolve it. If the death of the priest truly meant she was safe, she must resume her acrobatics and other duties in the company. But how to be certain she was safe, beyond any doubt? And how to learn what role Teresa played in Fra Filippo's death – for although Teresa refused to say anything more than, 'God has answered my prayers,' it was not credible that all she had done was pray. In fact, Susanna had never seen her pray about anything in all these months.

She winced, hearing the inner voice that seldom allowed her to delude herself, certainly not for long; whether it was a scourge or a comfort, she had never decided. She rose from bed, went to the window, and opened the shutter. The soft early light bathed her face, and the bell-sounds moved as close as her thoughts. The truth, she admitted, was that she stayed in the room not to think and plan but to avoid talking to the company, for behind their faces, like a leer behind a mask, lay knowledge of the cypress-grove afternoon. She leaned against the window frame. The rough wood pressed into her cheek, near the scar. How odd to have conquered the fear of revealing her scar, only to find another reason to avoid facing people.

When Luca came to her room, she had badly wanted to tell him Fiorenza's tale was invented. The knowledge that she would be lying – and so would be disloyal to Paolo – had sat upon her tongue and silenced it. 'Paolo is a splendid fellow, and if you and he can make each other happy . . .' There had been no regret in his voice, only good humour.

She turned from the window to the basin and ewer to wash her hands and eyes and teeth. Would she ever cease missing her little cakes of Milanese soap and the scented water her servants brought and the separate little room for her private close-stool? Propped against the ewer was a note. It was hard to read, as if scrawled hastily in poor light.

> Anna, You are discovered. Bishop sent his men for you. I did not wake you for I knew you would keep me from going in your stead and claiming to be you. Hide yourself, for when bish. learns who I am he may send for you again. I do this in the dead man's name, for his sake and mine. If I do not return by midday, pray for me. Teresa.

Susanna put down the note, splashed cold water on her eyes, read again. She wetted her fingers and began to rub her teeth vigorously. How did the bishop know where she was? Had Fra Filippo told him – or was it someone else? Someone in the troupe?

She thought of Luca, coming to her room and asking about her life with her family. His friendliness could have been a mask over his desire to learn more about her so that he could betray her presence to the authorities. She recalled his snake-hisses while telling tales around the fire in the countryside; she heard his moans while making love to Isabella in the cypress grove. What madness allowed her to hope he had any interest in her besides the need to advance his fortunes? Had he not told her that he had lived in a fine house, making love to its mistress so that he might learn his letters and eat well?

Her finger was hurting. She saw that she had rubbed it on her teeth with such force that she had drawn blood. She put it into the basin and watched red tendrils curl into the water. No, she thought, it must have been her mother who told the bishop where she was. She tried to recall exactly what she had told her mother on that strange visit, and then it struck her that she was hoping her own mother had betrayed her, so that it could not be Luca.

She pulled her hand from the water and dried it. When she had dressed, she had no memory of putting on the garments. Teresa's note filled her thoughts and left room for nothing else but the certainty that she could not deal with it by herself.

She went along the hall to stand before Paolo's door. They had never had the talk for which she had gone to his room on the morning Fra Filippo saw her. She raised her hand to knock, then lowered it and backed away. Suddenly the door opened and Buffa burst into the hall. He saw her and began running in three-legged circles. She was bending down to rub his head when Paolo appeared behind him. She looked up. From that angle his nose and chin were like the points of two spears. 'Paolo, I must speak with you.'

'So,' he said, 'you have come to like Buffa, have you?'

'Why, yes, I have.' She did not know which was more surprising: discovering that Paolo was right, or having him ask the question. 'You knew I did not care for Buffa?'

'I always know how people feel about my three-legged stool. I observe that those of us who are not handsome or beautiful either have a special fondness for him or else wish to avoid him.'

'If you thought I disliked him, why did you ask me to feed him for you?'

Paolo smiled. 'Perhaps I knew you would come to see his virtues.'

What an odd conversation to be having, Susanna thought, in light of their circumstances. Was he trying to avoid a discussion of the cypress grove? Or indicating they could forget it without discussing it? She got to her feet. 'We must speak, Paolo.' His expression grew wary. 'It concerns Teresa. She has done something I find difficult to believe and impossible to address.'

'What?' he said sharply.

A door nearby – to Bruno and Isabella's room – rattled as if about to open.

'Come into my room,' Paolo said. 'No, no, we cannot do that.' His eyes swam with a panic Susanna understood. He did not want Isabella to find the two of them together. He grabbed Susanna's hand and pulled her downstairs, Buffa hopping behind them. 'We can go for a walk,' he said.

'I would prefer not, please.'

'Very well, in here. We can pretend we are discussing an acrobatics routine if . . . That is what we can pretend.'

They sat at one of the long dining tables. With Buffa at his feet, Paolo filled a glass from a jug of lemon water and took a round, dark loaf from a basket of bread. He broke off a piece and closed his large lips over it.

Susanna handed him Teresa's note. He chewed as he read, but soon his jaws stopped and his eyes grew large. 'Madness,' he said. 'Madness.' He wiped his mouth and added softly, ' "I do this in the dead man's name, for his sake and mine." ' His face softened.

'I do not understand those words,' Susanna said. 'Do you?'

Paolo put his head in his hands.

'Forgive me,' she said. 'I do not even give you a moment to contemplate. Fra Filippo was a threat to me,' she added, 'yet I am sorry he is dead. He used to hear my confessions.' She waited; no response came. 'You chose not to tell the company, but I know he was your brother. Accept my sympathies for the grief you must feel, especially since you cannot share it with anyone.'

'How do you know we were brothers?'

'Do not forget that the day you and he found each other was also the day you rescued me.'

'Ah, that is so. Outside the convent.' Paolo lifted his head to look at her, and for almost the first time since the cypress grove his gaze held no awareness of that afternoon. 'Filippo and I barely knew one another, and the little we knew pleased neither of us. My grief is that my grief is not deeper.' He sighed heavily. 'Still, to have died as he did . . .'

'You know how it happened?'

'I was . . . Did they not say he died in his church, alone in the darkness?'

'Surely it is a good thing to die in one's church?'

'You are right. Surely it is.'

Susanna waited for him to say more, but he turned away and drank deeply of his lemon water. 'Paolo, what shall I do about Teresa? She has gone to Bishop Palma pretending to be me, and she has not returned. What could she hope to achieve by such a ruse?'

'As she says, she wished to help you, to give you time to escape.'

'Can I simply run away and leave her in danger – a danger I have caused? No. I cannot.' Paolo was silent. 'Shall I tell the others what she has done?'

'Perhaps it would be best to wait until midday, as her letter instructs you, and see whether she returns by then.'

'And if she does not? Is there not a performance tonight?' Paolo nodded. Susanna clasped her hands. 'Why does she take such a risk for me, who may share her room but neither her thoughts nor her love?'

'I . . . cannot say.'

'I suspect you mean you will not. Why is that so? Forgive me, Paolo, I do not wish to offend you. I wish us to be friends, as we were before that afternoon when we—' His gaze hardened into a wall, but she could not allow her words to be crushed against it. 'Can we not say that each of us has glimpsed one of the other's secrets, and let those secrets return to their hiding places?' He flushed. 'Please, Paolo.

Let us vow to forget what happened.'

'When everyone else will not?'

'I know, but . . . I care for you, Paolo, as I hope you care for me. Can we allow the treasure of our caring to be lost?' She put a hand on one of his.

'Good morning to you, Lady Anna. And Paolo.'

Her hand jerked away. 'Good morning,' she said, barely audibly, without turning round. She took Teresa's note and put it in her pocket.

'Do I intrude?' Luca asked.

'No, no,' Paolo said. 'We were only discussing an acrobatic routine.'

Luca sat beside him and reached for some bread.

Paolo tented his fingers and raised the tent high above his head. 'I was explaining to Anna – excuse me, to Susanna – that however desirable her suggestion might be, neither of us is able to execute it.'

'How can that be?' Luca said. 'In all of Italy there is no Arlecchino more agile and no pupil more apt.' He dipped the bread in oil and ate, his teeth white against its darkness. 'This morning I am going to the Rialto. Why not come, Paolo? We can see the painters' efforts in the Merceria, and the orange market, the man at the Sign of the Rose who makes tables inlaid with gems . . .'

Paolo brought his hands down. 'Not today,' he said.

Buffa barked as Umberto shuffled into the room, rubbing himself awake, and headed for the table. Paolo scratched Buffa's head. 'As to the other matter,' he told Susanna, 'I repeat that one can only wait.'

'I suppose you are right,' she said miserably.

The waiting was not long. Bruno had called for a rehearsal meeting after lunch, and even as the troupe was noting Teresa's absence and Susanna was gathering her courage to tell them of the note, the landlord of the inn came into the room, jowls quivering with excitement or fear or both, and said, 'Friends, there is news. The red-haired Teresa – such a woman was just taken before the Tribunal of the Inquisition and charged with killing the priest, Fra Filippo.'

Paolo shot to his feet, a single arrow from the motionless group. In a moment Bruno rose slowly and said, 'Are there witnesses or evidence against her?'

'They say that it is Bishop Palma who denounced her, and that on her person was discovered a ring belonging to the dead man.'

Silence cloaked the players. Finally Isabella spoke. 'It will be as it was with Ginevra. They will question us all, and only God knows what else they will do.'

In the upper reaches of the Doge's palace, the floor of the wooden passageway creaked not only with actual footsteps but with invisible ones. In the cell, three of the walls were too close, and the fourth was made of iron and bars. The dimness plucked at the eyelids, making one squint continuously in the hope, or fear, that someone was approaching. Nothing in the surroundings was as bad as the tales that came into one's mind: of the place in the lagoon where fishing was forbidden, because prisoners were sometimes thrown into it; or the dungeons below, where they might be strangled; or the pillars of the palace, from which they could be hanged by one leg.

It had happened too quickly. Teresa had had no time to prepare her spirit. From the moment she had made her decision, scrawled the note to Susanna, and, shawled and veiled, gone down the stairs and haughtily told the bishop's men, 'I am Signora Rossi. What business have you with me?' it had seemed that she was in a performance – not only because she was indeed playing a role, but because the action moved with the speed of a scenario. Where was Arlecchino? And Pedrolino with his cow-eyes always upon her, which had made her uncomfortable but for which she now yearned? Where were Il Dottore and Pantalone? Thinking of their faces nearly forced a sob from her.

She sat on the narrow bed and cradled her arms. The men had gripped her too firmly – she still felt the digging of their fingers – but the bishop had been as polite as a slave, while demonstrating that he was master.

By good fortune it is Tuesday, so the Tribunal will meet. I shall speak to the Inquisitor as soon as it is light and persuade him to investigate your case at once. Until then you will remain here. I shall have food brought to you. When she screamed that she would tell the Tribunal what he had done to her mother, he merely repeated, *I shall make certain that no one believes such a tale.*

The Tribunal had sat on a platform, six men like a row of large, dark birds, with several more persons beside them, one of whom took down her answers.

Do you confess to placing an unholy spell upon the priest Fra Filippo, to cause him to fall ill and die?

No.

Did you use the words of the Eucharist or of any benedictions while planning to cause his death?

No.

Did you invoke demons to aid you in causing him to die?

No.

Do you say prayers or use crucifixes while making your concoctions?

No.

Do you perform with a company of players who sell your preparations?

Yes.

Do you employ spells and incantations for the purpose of healing persons of their ailments or of ensuring the fulfilment of their fleshly desires?

I . . . I have healed people.

When did you last attend Mass?

I am not certain.

When was your last confession?

I am not certain.

How did you come by the dead man's ring?

He gave it to us, to our troupe, and they let me hold it.

The questions were put by the Inquisitor. His voice was like an oar creaking in its iron lock and his face, although soft and wrinkled, was as fixed as marble in its rectitude. She had felt as if she were trying to cross a raging stream on slippery rocks. How could she say she had no knowledge of potions when half of Venice had seen them being sold in the Piazza, when the Tribunal could, and doubtless would, send its officers to her room? How could she be certain Fra Filippo had not told the bishop where he was going and for what purpose? Could the bishop possibly know what she had done, or was his accusation only invented?

Are you the child of Ginevra Laurano, who lied to this Holy Office by swearing you had died?

Yes.

Did you acquire your unholy knowledge from her?

It is not unholy.

With that, she had found the courage to lift her eyes to the robed figures and say, in her clearest voice, that Bishop Palma had accused her out of malice and spite.

For what cause would Bishop Palma feel malice towards you?

She had tried to say it: 'He falsely accused my mother so he might rape her in her cell. He fears I will speak of it'; but Fra Filippo had slid into her mind, as in the scenario with Isabella and Luca – writhing, gasping, dying.

For what cause would Bishop Palma feel malice towards you?

What if she accused him and no one believed her, because he would see they did not? She would be put to death, or to the torture. Her innards had collapsed into water. 'I . . . do not know.' The fear had turned to shame.

How could revenge have seemed so sweet for all the years of planning, and be as bitter in the execution as the juice of a hundred lemons?

This Holy Office is vigilant to ensure that accusations do not come before it for malicious, self-serving, or impious motives. The charge against you shall be investigated thoroughly and witnesses sought and questioned. Until such time as we need to examine you further, and to hear any defence you put forward, the gravity of the charge ordains that you be held in prison.

For how long? It seemed to Teresa that she had been imprisoned for months already, but perhaps it was only minutes. There was no time in the cell, no air – only a smell like that of a long-dead animal – and no peace, for it was to this place in the Doge's palace that she had come on her two visits to her mother.

My child, my little love, my lovely little one . . .

'Mother,' she said into the dimness. 'I wanted to make them suffer for hurting you, but I am the one who is suffering. Help me. Help me!'

'Hello?' A woman's voice was calling softly from somewhere close.

'Who is it?' Teresa ran to the door. 'Who is there?'

'In the next cell. A prisoner, like you. Are you unwell?' The voice was as comforting as a soft hand.

'No, I . . . Yes, I am ill. The walls are pressing on me. There are screams inside me. I do not think I can keep them inside. If I cannot breathe the air of the streets and see the sky, I shall die.'

'There are many things one believes one cannot endure, yet one does. Why have they put you here?'

Teresa hesitated. 'I am charged with *maleficium*. And you?'

'I stole jewels from my mistress to escape from a *palazzo* where I was a slave. They caught me before I could sell what I had stolen. I have no hope, for I am guilty. Are you?'

Teresa could not reply at once; she was crying.

'Poor Teresa,' said Pedrolino, cupping his chin in his hands which rested on the table.

'Little redhead,' Paolo said, as if she were there.

Next to him, Umberto sighed.

After the landlord had brought the news, the company had collected itself and tried halfheartedly to discuss the evening's performance. When the landlord reappeared later, with the announcement that Teresa had been arrested and put in prison, all pretence of rehearsal had ceased.

'Do you not think,' Susanna said, 'that we should try to save her?'

'Save her?' Pedrolino sat upright as if jerked, his hair flapping. 'Yes! We must save her! At once!'

'Spoken like a fool,' said Giulio.

'But that is what I am – a fool. Does it mean I can never speak sense? How can we be I Favolosi without Teresa? Therefore, should we not save her?'

'Brave words,' Giulio said. 'Here is another word: how?'

'I . . . do not know how.' Pedrolino looked at Susanna.

'I do not know either,' she said.

Bruno dug fingers into the thicket of his beard. 'There is nothing we can do. As we learned with her mother, we are helpless. We told the officials Ginevra was not a sorceress, but instead of helping, it only called us to their attention, so that we found it prudent to leave Venice.'

'Taking her daughter with us,' Isabella added. 'And because of the two of them, mother and daughter, we did not return for years.' She looked across the table at Luca, who was silent. In a corner Buffa worked on a bone.

Umberto said, 'People like us – players – cannot influence the Tribunal.'

'Poor Teresa,' Pedrolino said. His hands and chin sank back to the table.

Susanna cleared her throat. 'Could we not at least try to help her? Perhaps we could persuade Signor Polani to intercede for her.'

'We?' Isabella made the single word a chorus of disapproval.

'You are right,' Susanna said. 'It would have to be you and Bruno.'

'You suggest we ask our patron to address the Tribunal of the Inquisition in order to rescue one of our number?' The deed was rendered impossible in Isabella's naming of it. 'One of us who acted as she did solely because of you?'

'How *did* she act?' said Bianca, who had not spoken before.

Everyone turned to her. She had listened to the discussion with pursed lips, Fiorenza beside her, the two of them turning from speaker to speaker like cats watching a flight of birds until suddenly Bianca shifted in her seat and blurted her question.

'What do you mean?' Susanna asked.

'Teresa said she would remove the threat you caused. We do not know what she did to remove it. Therefore, how do we know she did not kill the priest, as they charge?' Bianca crossed herself. 'It is a great sin to kill a priest.'

'Ah,' said someone; it seemed like everyone.

Isabella leaned down the table. 'Bianca, today there is a better head upon those shoulders than upon any others.'

Bianca nodded in satisfaction.

'Paolo,' said Bruno, 'you know her best. Tell us what you think she did.'

He looked around the group. The cords that bound him to all of them, the common awareness of mood, mind, and body that was crucial to performance and nurtured by the forced intimacy of their lives, seemed to have loosened. 'You stare as if I were a stranger,' he said lightly, 'or had turned green, or changed into a lizard.' He smiled. No one smiled back. 'I may spend time with the little redhead,' he added, 'but I seldom know what she is thinking or planning. No more did I know on this occasion.'

'That is all you have to say on the matter?' Bruno asked.

'No. I say she is one of us. If we can find a way to help her, we must.'

The two men regarded each other in silence. Then

Bruno rose, locked his hands behind him, and strode Captain-like back and forth several times. When he stopped, he faced the group and said, 'There is no need to continue this discussion because there is nothing to be done for Teresa.'

'We leave her to the mercy of the Tribunal?' Susanna asked. She looked around the room. The only eyes that did not turn away were Luca's.

Isabella said, 'My dear Bruno, what you say is true, but whether or not Teresa was involved in the death of the priest, that is how she is charged. We, as her associates, will be regarded with suspicion. We must think how to protect ourselves.' She shook her head sadly. 'Despite my sympathy for one who shares life with a man unwillingly, I fear that in the name of our common good, such a fate must now be considered. Many women do endure it, after all. Earlier I made the suggestion with regret, and now I offer it in pain, but I fear Susanna must return to her husband.' She held up a slim, white hand as if someone had objected, although no one had. 'If she goes to Bishop Palma and says she returns at our urging, not only could she ensure the safety of the company, she could plead with the bishop to urge the Tribunal to show mercy to Teresa.'

Susanna stood motionless, looking at Isabella. The only sound was Buffa's bone-growling in the corner.

Luca's fingers had been dancing silently on the table. 'I do not see why the bishop would be influenced by Susanna's pleading.'

'Surely that is clear,' Bruno said.

'Not to me.'

'Explain it to him!' Bruno ordered.

'Certainly,' Isabella said, 'although I would have thought he could see it for himself. Luca, the bishop will be grateful for her return and will be disposed to listen if she says she knows Teresa well and believes her innocent of any crime. Second, and more important, Susanna is a member of a noble family, and a bishop will want to please them by granting her request.'

'That is well reasoned,' said Giulio's wife.

'No. It is not.' Luca stood and folded his arms.

Isabella's cheeks mottled. 'Why not?'

'Susanna told us the bishop has been searching for her since she ran away. Why should he be grateful to her for returning? More likely, his failure to find her for so long has embarrassed him, and he may be angry with her. As to the matter you say is the most important, I think it will be Susanna's husband and father whom the bishop wants to please, not the lady herself. And since they have no interest in Teresa's fate, why should the bishop try to please them by influencing the Tribunal on her behalf? I see no advantage in asking Susanna to return. Even if I did, I would not be cruel enough to ask it.'

Silence. Everyone looked at Isabella, whose lips thinned into a string, and then at Bruno, whose face grew darker until it seemed he would burst with his own blood.

He did. 'By God, Luca, you take your pleasure with

my wife, yet you do not support her in a matter vital to our future!'

Several members of the company gaped. All had suspected that Isabella and Luca were lovers in life as well as in performance; none had known whether Bruno suspected as well.

'Bruno!' Isabella cried. 'Be quiet!'

'I have been quiet long enough!'

Luca unfolded his arms. 'Very well, Bruno. Here is my reply. I take pleasure if and when it is offered, not otherwise. As to why your wife feels the need to offer it – only you would know.'

'Oh, dear,' said Umberto. Giulio's wife gasped. Isabella's pale green eyes went paler.

Bruno rocked on his heels for a moment. Then he rushed at Luca.

Susanna turned and ran from the room.

'Here,' said the guard. 'Supper.'

Teresa did not move from the bed.

'Eat,' the guard warned. 'Trouble if you don't eat. They don't like it.'

Teresa rose and went to the cell door. In the poor light, through the bars, she saw grey hair and sagging jowls. She took the bowl he put through the opening. 'Have you been here a long time?' she asked.

He nodded. 'Many years. My father before me.'

'Do you remember, about six years ago, a woman who was a prisoner here – a woman with red hair like mine?'

His brows met and locked in an effort to remember.

He shrugged. 'Maybe. Too many people.'

'She was beautiful. Bishop Palma himself came to see her. Do you remember the bishop coming to the cells?'

'Bishop?'

'Please, could you try to remember?'

'Why?'

'I would . . . I would like to hear about it.'

The man frowned as if her explanation was outside his comprehension. He returned to the solid ground of experience. 'Eat. Trouble if you don't.'

He walked away. Teresa stood clutching the bowl, which held pasta and a chunk of bread. She could not imagine eating them, or anything else, but she did not know what the guard might mean by 'trouble'. She pushed her face as far as possible through the bars and called, 'Ludis?'

She repeated the name three times before the reply came, 'Yes? I was sleeping.' Earlier, they had talked for some time through the bars, offering the only comfort possible to prisoners, asserting the value of their lives by telling their tales to each other. 'How can you sleep?' Teresa asked.

'I learned long ago, when I was first captured, that sleep is the only sure way to find peace.'

'Have you eaten what they brought?'

'Yes.'

'I cannot.'

'You must. If you accept one day at a time, you can live through years.'

'I cannot live here for years! I shall die!'

'From your voice, I do not think so.'

'What do you mean?'

'I hear strength in your voice, if not in your words.'

'In you I hear patience. And melancholy.'

'I have had to accept that what happens, happens.'

A long silence. 'Ludis? Are you still there?'

'Yes.' A smile in the voice. 'I cannot go anywhere else.'

'I mean, are you still close?'

'Yes.'

'I must try to eat this food, I suppose.'

'You see? You are accepting. Eat, then try to sleep.'

But it was useless. After she had forced down the pasta, cold and coated with an unidentifiable sauce, and eaten half the bread, Teresa lay on the bed, but each time she closed her eyes, their lids twitched and trembled and fluttered open on the darkness.

When a light appeared she thought she imagined it, but it grew stronger and then turned into a lamp in the hand of the guard who had brought her the food. She got up and ran to the cell door. 'Yes?' she said.

'You ate the food?'

'See, there is the empty dish.'

The man grunted. 'Good. You ate, so I bring her to you.'

'Who?'

'The old woman. Your grandmother.'

'What?'

He took the empty dish and left. Teresa clutched the bars, hanging from them, unable to think, even to conjecture what might be going to happen.

At length the light reappeared at the outer edge of her vision and slowly grew. 'This one,' said the guard's voice. 'She is in here.'

'Teresa?' said another voice, cracked and strange.

'Who is it? Please, who is it?'

'Grandmother Anna. Do you not know me?'

'Holy Mother,' Teresa whispered.

The door to the cell was unlocked. 'I come back later,' said the guard.

When his footsteps had creaked away, Teresa said, 'Anna! How can you be here? Why are you here? Did you find my note? I told you to hide.'

The bent figure straightened and pushed back shawl and veil. 'I came to ask questions. Why did you go to the bishop pretending to be me? You knew the pretence could not be sustained for long, and you risked angering him.'

'I did it to give you time to run away.'

'Why jeopardize yourself for me? I do not even think you have any special liking for me.'

'I did not, in the beginning.'

'Why?'

'I suspected you were from a noble family. I knew you would bring trouble to us. Besides, you were weak and afraid. I like people to be strong. When you began to change . . . What made you change?'

'I did not know that I had.'

'Do not be foolish. Would the Anna who first came to I Favolosi have been able to disguise herself and get into this cell? She would have shrivelled in a corner behind her scar and waited for Paolo to help.'

Neither of them spoke for a moment.

'And now?' Susanna asked. 'Do you still dislike me?'

'I suppose I do.'

'Why?'

'Perhaps because Paolo loves you.'

'Teresa, I swear to you that Paolo and I do not—'

'Or perhaps it is because I like you.'

'I beg your pardon?'

'It is not wise to become too friendly with people. Even Paolo . . . Not even with Paolo.'

Into the silence came the sound of off-key singing, very distant, as if from another world.

'How is everyone?' Teresa asked. 'Paolo and Umberto and Pedrolino and . . . everyone. How are they?'

'They are well.' Something strange was in Susanna's voice. But she changed it at once. 'I must ask you – how did the bishop know where to find me?'

'He said he received an anonymous letter.'

Silence. 'A letter that could have come from someone in the company?'

'Yes, but what matters now is that he knows where to find you. I told him you had already left Venice, but I do not know how long that will keep him from going to I Favolosi. You must leave the city at once. Or else what has been the use of my effort?'

'I repeat my question. Why jeopardize yourself for me?'

Teresa hesitated. 'I also wished to see the bishop about . . . something.'

Susanna took a few steps around the cell. 'What you say is not sensible. There must be things you are not telling me. I must know them, or I can never persuade the troupe to help you.'

Teresa felt a leap of hope. 'They want to help? What can they do?'

'I have no idea, yet. First they must be persuaded – some of them are unwilling.'

'Who?'

'Bianca, among others.'

'That cow!'

Susanna continued as if she had not heard. 'They wonder whether you actually did what you are accused of – killed Fra Filippo.'

'Did . . . What did Paolo say?'

'Why should he say anything?'

Teresa pushed her hands into her hair, as if to straighten her thoughts. 'Sometimes he believes he knows more about me than he does.'

'What is the truth of it, then?'

Teresa shivered. 'The priest died because he wished to.'

'I do not understand. If you do not tell me, I shall leave.'

How cold it was in the cell, Teresa thought, even colder than she had realized. Would Susanna, or anyone else, help her if she told the truth? Why was everything so complicated? Without help, she would be alone in the cold and the dimness and the walls that would not let her walk or see or breathe. 'If I tell you,' she said, 'I place my life in your hands.'

'Are any other hands held out to you?'

'You must swear not to tell the others.'

'I cannot make that vow before hearing what you say.'

'Then how can I trust you?'

'You will have to do so without a vow, Teresa.'

'I do not like you to be as strong as that!'

Susanna gave a small laugh, then said, 'The guard may come soon.'

Teresa wrapped her arms around herself, put her head back, looked at the ceiling. The sentences flowed as easily as water over worn stones as she told of the vow to avenge her mother and of the masked man who had raped her. But when she spoke of her plan for Fra Filippo and the poisoning, her jaw began to tremble and then to jerk, so that she had to lower her head and finally to put both palms against her cheeks in order to hold the words steady. When she finished – when she and Paolo had laid the priest before his altar – she was crying, on Susanna's shoulder, sodden with the relief of telling it, and of feeling Susanna's arms around her. 'I do like you,' she sobbed. 'And I trust you.'

She stopped crying, realizing how still Susanna was.

She pulled away to read Susanna's face. But the dimness and the veil hid it. 'I have told you everything,' she said. 'Do you still wish to help me?'

Susanna said her name several times, in a way that might be pity or could be revulsion.

'I tried to save him! He wanted to die! He admitted

he had put the accusation in the lion's mouth. He confessed that he had lusted after her! He wanted me to save you. I swore to do it. I wanted to! Can't you believe me?'

'I believe you.'

'Then . . . ?' Teresa clenched her fists. 'I knew you would not understand!'

'I have not said I don't understand.'

'You understand but you have no understanding. You think you could never do what I did because you are a Bardi. You do not know what your family is capable of. Your own father visited my mother many times.'

'My father . . . and your mother?'

'Yes! Many times! I hated the men who came to see her. That is why I did not like you at first – soon after you came I learned you had some relationship to the Bardi. I followed you one day. I saw you enter their house and stay for some time. And just today I learned more about the Bardi and your father.'

'What do you mean?'

'A slave from your parents' home is in the next cell, imprisoned for escaping and stealing some of your mother's jewels. She spoke of you, and I told her I knew you. She is fond of you, I think.'

'Do you mean Ludis? Here?'

'In the next cell. She told me things about your father and his good friend, the bishop who raped my mother.'

'What did she tell you?'

'She heard your father and the bishop talking about

my mother, saying the Republic must be rid of her.'

'My father was involved in—?'

'If you do not believe me, go to the door and call to Ludis. Then do as you like about me. I cannot bear it here! What has been the use of all I have done? Mother, why did you have to die?'

Teresa flung herself on the narrow bed. It offered no comfort.

CHAPTER FIFTEEN

Of Heresy

The Church must be ever vigilant against heretics, from the Northern devil Martin Luther and his writings to those diviners and magicians who offer worship to demons and use sacramental objects in their divinations, such as holy oil, the relics of the Saints, water, candles, or consecrated olive branches, or any other sacred or consecrated thing.

Sitting at his breakfast after early Mass, Bishop Palma peeled an orange and waited for Antonio Bardi. Parting the bright skin from the fruit, he reviewed all he had done. To use Filippo's death as the means for removing the threat of Ginevra Laurano's daughter – that was a great satisfaction. Not merely because the plan was clever but because it was just.

The papal nuncio had agreed that Teresa Laurano must come before the Tribunal at once. 'To destroy the good Filippo by the use of *maleficium* . . . that will require a full *procèsso*.'

'You may recall,' Palma had said, 'that her mother, who appeared before the Tribunal some years ago, was not only a player and later a courtesan but also a sorceress. No doubt she passed her skills on to her child, who has now turned them to this terrible purpose.' The nuncio's head had swung in fervent denunciation so that his white beard moved like a pendulum.

Unfortunately, one could not talk to him without suffering his sly accusations that Venice was insufficiently set against the threat of Protestant doctrine. One had to nod and assure the nuncio that one was irrevocably anti-Protestant. Never mind that at certain dinners with families like the Bardi one had to soothe their visiting trading partners from the north of Europe – Protestants all – by implying that Venice was not intolerant, that she sympathized with the Reformation and its challenge to the absolute authority of the church. Men like Antonio Bardi made such adjustments necessary. The bishop corrected himself. It was life that required the adjustments. Bardi was merely one of the vessels through which life made its demands and offered its rewards.

Palma had spoken not only with the nuncio but also with the other two ecclesiastics on the Tribunal, letting them know – subtly, of course – that he could have no motive for accusing Teresa Laurano except the desire to bring Filippo's destroyer to justice.

It was a hollow threat the redhead had uttered – *Do not try to return Susanna Rossi to her husband and family. If you try, I have ways to make certain that the Council of Ten learns of the crimes you committed against my mother*. What ways could she possibly have? Still, there was no harm in being prudent. Palma could easily wait until she was found guilty before pursuing the matter of Rossi's wife. Ludovico and the Bardi had waited many months already. They could wait a few weeks longer, at most. Their gratitude would be no less.

Palma took a strip of peel from his orange and laid it on the table. The mother's hair had held something of that colour, but buried in its softness had been something darker as well, something evil. 'I wish to see the woman before I consent to charging her,' he had righteously, and truthfully, told Antonio Bardi. 'Stand by her house one night,' Bardi said, 'and watch for her to come to her window.' Dressed plainly, Palma had gone, taking Filippo with him. The shutters had opened, and there she had stood, leaning slightly towards the *calle*, stroking a black cat lying on the sill, her face a perfect expression of the divine order and beauty of God's world but the fiery hair that flowed down her naked shoulders calling one's eyes to the place where, just above a low bodice, peered the rosy buds of her nipples. She had looked out into the clear, warm night and smiled, and Palma had felt so strong a need to place his fingertips on those buds, and his hands over the white fields from which they grew, that its cause could only have been maleficent magic. *Maleficium*.

He pulled off the lacy white webbing covering the orange, took one of its sections, and sucked it into his mouth. How sweet was the juice. How sweet.

Filippo had understood. They had never discussed

it, but Palma had seen that understanding in Filippo's eyes, twisting like a flame.

'Signor Bardi is here,' said a voice. Palma looked up at his servant and, behind him, Antonio's dark presence.

'I want nothing to eat or drink,' Bardi said, waving aside his offer and refusing as well to be seated. 'I am busy this morning. I want only to know what is so urgent and private that I must come to your house. Have you found my daughter?'

Palma tented his fingers. 'Regrettably, not yet. Filippo was close to learning something of her, but he died before he could acquire the knowledge or communicate to me the path for acquiring it.'

Bardi scowled and muttered something else before saying, 'I am sorry to hear of the priest's death. He was devoted to you.'

'And I to him.'

Bardi hunched his broad shoulders. 'Why have you summoned me?'

Palma cleared his throat, where the taste of orange was still strong, and said, 'Ginevra Laurano.'

'Why mention her name, after so many years?'

'She has returned to haunt us.' When Bardi crossed himself, the bishop added, 'I do not mean that she lives again. I mean that she had a daughter, who is now in Venice and possesses too much knowledge of the past. However, I have accused that daughter of using heretical witchcraft to cause Filippo's death.'

Bardi sat down as if pushed.

'We must see that justice is done,' Palma said. 'I

have spoken to the ecclesiastics on the Tribunal, but a word with its secular members would come better from you.'

After a silence, Bardi said, 'By God, I begin to regret using my influence for you in the past.'

'Did you not receive fair value in return?'

The two men regarded each other. Bardi's eyes were the first to look away.

Susanna was preparing to go downstairs, where I Favolosi would be waiting for her. Earlier she had gone to Bruno and Isabella's room. Bruno was alone, in a sullen humour, wine hanging on his breath. 'Look here, you have already caused us more trouble than the authorities.' When he heard what she wanted, he had grudgingly agreed to call the company together. 'I do not wish to be the cause of any more fighting,' she had said. Bruno had grunted in reply.

She smoothed her hair, pinched her cheeks, and tucked her veil in a pocket. Before leaving the room, she looked again at Teresa's bed, on which she could almost see the desperate figure she had left in the prison – who was in prison because she had tried to save Susanna and surely therefore deserved to be saved herself. Yet to poison a man, a holy man, was an awesome crime, although the attempt to save him stood in Teresa's favour. Susanna had been struggling to weigh matters against one another, wishing for the wisdom of the Jesuits at their new college in Rome. When she learned that her own father had not only visited Teresa's mother but might have played some role in her death – when a brief, whispered colloquy with Ludis confirmed what Teresa said – she had known she would indeed try to help Teresa, no matter what the redhead had done. She did not quite put it into words – did not want to; it lay in her throat, below the level of language. Saving Teresa would somehow help to punish her father for the things he had done, and not done: for the march around the table under the Mantuans' chill gaze, for the marriage to Ludovico, for her mother's unhappiness, for his rages, made all the more frightening by their unpredictability.

She had said none of that to Teresa. Only, 'You should tell the Tribunal everything, not only the story of your mother's death but how you tried to save Fra Filippo from the poison's effects. The Tribunal will surely be merciful to you.'

'Never! I cannot confess that I gave poison to the priest! The bishop is too powerful. He will make certain no one believes anything else I say, and I will be strangled and thrown into the lagoon!' Teresa had flung herself back upon the bed, drowning in her sobbing, and in her shaking body Susanna had recognized the helplessness and fear that used to possess her own.

After her slow, dark journey back to the inn, during which she never once considered that *bravi* might lurk in the shadows, Susanna had slept little. Pacing the room much of the time, she had discarded half a dozen ideas, including asking Paolo to go before the Tribunal and tell what he knew. That alone would not be enough – Teresa was surely correct about the power of the bishop. In the early hours of the morning, passing the shelf that held her acrobat mask, she had felt the call of its blank face, had taken it up and slipped it on. Her body had shifted to its commands, and her mind, in the strange, constricting freedom that always came with the mask, had peered down new roads, and she had known what to do.

She looked at the mask now, back on its shelf, smiled at it for reassurance, opened the door, and went down the stairs.

'If you want,' she said to them, 'I will return to my husband.'

In the babel of their reactions, she saw disappointment on Luca's face – because he could not now benefit from betraying her to her family or to the bishop? 'I promise to return,' she continued, 'but I attach a condition. I have a plan for helping Teresa. If you help me execute it, for I cannot do it without you, when it is finished, I will return to Ludovico Rossi, if that is what you want me to do.'

Would they believe her, after the vehemence with which she had said she would never go back? Would she truly go, if they told her to? She looked at their expressions – frowns, puzzlement, a sly smile or two of pleasure – and knew she would have to go if they asked. If she did go, she would find a way to leave again, or else to kill Ludovico. In the next moment she realized she had vowed to kill a man, and meant it. Teresa, she thought, would understand.

'Have we not made it clear,' said Isabella, 'that we

do indeed want you to return to your husband?'

'Not all of us,' said Paolo.

Bianca sniffed.

'Most of us.' Sitting beside Bruno, Isabella put a hand on his arm and stared at Susanna, at the scar.

Pedrolino stood. He clutched his guitar, as if for support, but his manner was calm, as if he were doing exactly what he wished. 'I want to help Teresa. What is your plan for her?'

'Yes,' said Luca. 'Tell us your plan. I should like to hear it.'

Isabella regarded him icily, and Bruno gave off antagonism like fumes of wine. Umberto was blinking and rubbing his eyes. The others' faces, so mobile in performance, were stiff with caution.

'I think you know,' Susanna said, 'that the Tribunal is alive to the possibility of malicious motives behind an accusation and, when it finds them, has been known to dismiss the charges in question. Teresa has told me, that in accusing her, Bishop Palma has such a motive. My plan is to help her by revealing that motive to the authorities.'

' "Revealing"?' said Bruno. 'What do you mean by that word?'

'I mean that we . . . you . . . should do that at which you are all so skilled – perform.' She waited, watching Giulio's and his wife's brows rise in a unison that would have been comic in other circumstances.

'I do not understand,' said Paolo. 'How can Arlecchino reveal anything to the Tribunal?'

'And how,' said Giulio, 'do you know anything of the bishop's motives?'

'Last night, in disguise, I went to see Teresa in prison.'

'Without consulting or telling us?' Isabella said.

'Would you not have prevented my going?'

Isabella shrugged.

'Teresa told me a story I believe none of you know – that Bishop Palma was responsible for accusing her mother and that when Ginevra Laurano was imprisoned, he went to her cell and raped her.'

Quiet in the room. Unblinking, staring quiet. Susanna folded her hands. The was a clawing sensation in her breast; she realized she had eaten nothing all day. Or perhaps the feeling was not hunger.

Isabella said, 'I do not know that I believe such a tale.'

'It is true,' Paolo said quietly.

Fiorenza looked at her mother before addressing him. 'You say that because of Anna. You say what she wants because she is your lover.'

Paolo flushed, but he swallowed and said, still quietly, 'I swear it is true. I learned of it while . . . while talking with the priest one day.'

Another silence.

Luca said, 'Tell us your plan, Susanna. I wager it is a good one.'

She made herself look at him. 'I propose that we – rather, some of you – arrange through the Polani to perform before an audience that includes members of the Council of Ten. It can be announced as the scenario of *The Woman Who Was Falsely Accused.* I shall write it – I have most of it in mind already. It will enact the story of Ginevra Laurano and the bishop. When it finishes, someone will step forward and announce that the scenario is true.'

'By God,' said Luca, 'that is splendid. To use a scenario in such a way – by God, there would be a performance!'

'*Brava!*' said Pedrolino. 'Teresa will be saved after all!' He clapped, but no one joined him.

Bruno said, 'Who would be willing to play the parts?'

'Yes,' said Giulio's wife. 'Who would play Teresa and the bishop?'

'I had hoped Giulio would portray Andrea Palma.'

'Never!' said his wife.

'Perhaps Umberto, then?'

Umberto squirmed in his seat, muttered his dead wife's name, was silent.

'As to Ginevra Laurano,' Susanna said, 'only one person could do the role justice. If Isabella wore a red wig . . .'

'She could do it indeed,' Luca said.

Isabella rose in her seat, nostrils working like tiny bellows. 'I will not do it. What if the audience does not take kindly to the performance? What if we are sent to prison to keep Teresa company? I might help her by doing something reasonable, but this is not reasonable.'

'Perhaps not,' Luca said, 'but would it not be splendid?'

'It is a mad idea. We cannot entertain it even for a moment. Rather, we should consider the woman who suggests it. Why should we do this in exchange for her returning to her husband? Why do we need to bargain with her? She belongs with her husband and family, and I say we take her at once to Signor Ludovico Rossi so we may be left in peace.'

'By God,' said Luca, leaping to his feet, 'if you do that, I shall leave I Favolosi. At once! Now!'

'You would not do that.'

'I would.'

They glared at each other, two beautiful profiles skewed with anger.

'I say we let him go,' said Bruno.

'No!' Susanna could not stop herself.

'We need Luca,' Giulio said. 'A good Lover is not so easy to find.'

'Hah!' That was Isabella.

'Giulio is right,' Paolo said. 'We cannot do anything that would cause Luca to leave us.'

Several other voices agreed so firmly that Bruno turned around in surprise.

'I am so weary,' Isabella said through her teeth, 'of discussing what to do about this woman!' She shook out her sleeves as if they were banners and swept from the room.

Paolo started after her, turned at the door and said, 'We must help Teresa. I will do whatever I can to make a success of Susanna's plan.' He ran out. Buffa trotted after him.

Bruno scowled, made a fist, and punched it into his

other palm. Susanna could see the muscles of his wiry torso moving beneath his shirt.

Luca said, 'How many others are willing to try what Susanna suggests?'

Pedrolino raised his hand. After looking around the room, so did Umberto.

'There you are,' Luca said. 'Four of us, including Paolo. Tell us more of your scenario, Susanna.'

'There must be a woman to play the role of Teresa.' She looked at Fiorenza, determined to accept her help if she would offer it, but Fiorenza shook her head violently. Bianca who was not even a reasonable possibility, sniffed and patted her daughter's hand.

Luca said, 'It seems you are the only one left to do it.'

'I?' Susanna looked at the face in the frame of golden hair, the brown eyes smiling as much as the fine, full lips. 'I? No. No. I cannot.'

Luca shrugged. 'Then we have no choice but to put a red wig on Pedrolino.'

Pedrolino gave a yip of alarm.

'What idiocy,' said Giulio's wife. 'Whatever else Ginevra Laurano might have been, she was a great beauty. Men's eyes were always upon her. Pedrolino in a wig, indeed! Come along, Giulio. Let us leave to themselves all who wish to continue this ridiculous conversation.'

Susanna watched them leave, followed by others, until only Umberto, Luca and Pedrolino were left with her. Luca said, 'I believe you must play the role, Lady Anna, or else your plan is doomed.'

She felt her scar throbbing, even though she had not thought of it for hours. Even though it never throbbed. Her fingers went to it. 'I cannot.'

'We will help you,' Luca said. 'I will help you. You have already done more difficult things.'

'I have not. You do not understand.'

'Ah, well, perhaps I do not. You can explain it to me. Or shall we agree to abandon Teresa?'

'Please, Isabella,' Paolo said. 'Please let me speak with you.'

Leaving not only the meeting but the inn, Isabella had stormed out to the *calle* and into the nearby *campiello*. In the soft, bright light her hair was a new shade of gold, and though her back and neck were stiff with anger, the outline of her body was a lovely series of curves.

Paolo ran ahead of her, circled in an Arlecchino caper, and said piteously, 'Lady, if you do not speak, I shall have to hang myself.' He began to do a *lazzo* of despair, miming first that he was the hangman, hulking and scowling, and then the accused, who whimpered and shook so badly that his shanks knocked against each other. Two children passing with their mother ran to look at him, laughing like little bells.

Isabella stopped. An ill-fitting smile appeared. 'Oh, very well. You know I cannot resist Arlecchino. What do you want?'

Paolo stood. 'I . . . he . . . we! We ask you to grant us one favour.'

'And it is?'

'That you do nothing to force Susanna to return to her husband but instead help with her scenario.'

The smile changed shape. 'That is two favours, neither of which I care to grant. Why do you wish to protect her? I know the answer. You love her.'

'No,' Paolo said. 'I do not love—'

'Why do you lie to me? You sleep with her, do you not? Did Fiorenza not tell the truth?'

Retorts would have flown through his mind, Paolo knew, if it were anyone but Isabella. He looked down at the tips of his boots, which lay like mute tongues. 'Does one always love a person one sleeps with?'

Isabella's mouth tightened before she spoke. 'If you do not love her, then why take her side?'

'Can one not take another's side without love?'

'Do not fence with me, Paolo. I am not in the mood. I should merely like to know why you defend a woman who has placed us all in jeopardy. Every moment she stays here adds to our danger.'

'I . . . do not know,' Paolo said miserably. 'I feel sympathy for her.' He realized the children were still there, waiting for him to caper again.

'Ah. Sympathy,' said Isabella. 'What of me? I thought you loved me.'

'You . . . you . . .' How to keep from stammering? He bit his lip, then said, 'You believe so?'

'I know so.'

'But . . . how?'

'My dear, a woman always knows such things. It does not take any particular necromancy. I have known you loved me since the day you ran after our wagon and begged to come with us.'

'You have known?' Within him Paolo could feel Arlecchino waiting to caper and deny that he loved her. The children were staring at him, their eyes shiny and brown and hopeful. 'And did you . . . Do you . . . Were you offended?'

'Why should it offend me to be admired and loved?'

'I do not know. Go away!' he said to the children, but they did not move. Within him, Arlecchino pushed hard; it was as if their roles had reversed and he, Paolo, was now the mask and the costume that covered the inner fool. 'No!' he said.

'What do you mean?'

'I mean . . .' He looked at the children. One of them smiled, and the smile opened his heart like a knife. 'I will tell you. I will say it! Isabella, you cannot imagine how I love you. Your beauty has nurtured me every day since I met you. No woman is as splendid as you, as charming, as fine a player. You are all a woman could be, or desire to be. I have said your name to myself a thousand times, and each time it fills my mouth with a taste of honey. You are the sun of my days, and the moon of my nights. No one can love you as I have done – as I do.' He heard his words, the madness of them. He saw the children staring at him in puzzlement, one with a finger in her mouth, but he did not care about them, or anything else, even what Isabella had done with Luca, because she was smiling at him. 'Do you—' he said. 'Could you possibly—'

'If you love me so much . . .' The sentence hung

unfinished, tantalizing as a half-revealed breast.

'Yes, my dearest Isabella?' He could barely believe he was saying such words to her – not in a performance, saying them as Paolo.

'If you love me so much,' she said, 'then you would help me make Susanna return to her husband and remove the danger to us.'

One of the children, the boy, giggled. Paolo wanted to turn to him and box his ears, but he could not hurt a child. 'Isabella,' he whispered, 'I have admitted that I love you.'

'Yes, my dear Paolo. Therefore, I ask you to show that love by helping me with Susanna.'

'Show?'

'If you do, I shall be very pleased.'

'Pleased?'

'No one else will need to know, if that is what troubles you.'

'Troubles?'

'Will you do it, or will you merely stand repeating my words to me?'

Somewhere within him, Arlecchino was laughing. Or perhaps it was the two children. Paolo licked his lips, which had gone dry. 'I fear I cannot help you, Isabella.'

'Why not?'

'I . . . do not know.'

'I do. It is because in spite of your pretty speech you care more for Susanna than you do for me.'

'No, no, I— Does it matter to you, how I feel?'

'Certainly. It puzzles me greatly. I believed I could

count on you, but now I see I was mistaken. You prefer that creature with the scarred face. That is a pity. A great pity.'

Isabella turned and walked away. Arlecchino gave a cry and then was silent. The children's mother called to them impatiently.

'A great pity,' Paolo murmured.

The shutters were drawn against the brilliant afternoon. The dim light was cut by an occasional hard knife of sun, as a sleeve was cut and inset with ribbons of silk. The room was a small one, at the rear of the inn near the kitchen, where Luca had arranged for the five of them to discuss and rehearse Susanna's scenario. No one could find Paolo, however, so the rest of them had talked through everything and parcelled out the roles. Umberto would be the rich merchant: 'None of Il Dottore's Latin!' he had exclaimed. 'But then I must wear the Pantalone mask. How will I persuade Giulio to loan it to me?'

Susanna had to soothe him repeatedly, telling him not to worry about the mask, they would solve that problem later – all the while wondering if he would truly be able to play the role. It was an invention based on what she had heard from Teresa, and then from Ludis, about her own father.

Paolo and Pedrolino would be *zanni*, as usual, in the early scenes, and when the enactment began of the actual plight of Teresa's mother – called only the Woman – they would double in small roles, including a priest and a prison guard.

'I? A priest?' Pedrolino said. 'Paolo would do it better than I.'

'Careful,' Luca said, mock-threatening, 'or we shall put the red wig on you after all.' Luca would enact the bishop, who first made the accusation against the Woman and later, masked, went to her cell to rape her.

All the while they were planning it and adjusting it to their number, there were little drum-rolls of panic beneath Susanna's calm descriptions and summaries of scenes. *I cannot do this*, she thought. *I must do this. Teresa risked much in order to save me. I must do this for her. I cannot do this.*

At length all decisions were made, except those involving Paolo and the most crucial one: the actual giving of the performance, which should take place as soon as possible. 'We might rent a hall,' Umberto said. 'But how to ensure that members of the Council of Ten are in the audience?'

'The Polani could arrange the performance in their palace,' said Pedrolino.

'Certainly,' Luca replied. 'But how do we explain the audience we need? Can we take the Polani into our confidence? I am doubtful.'

There was a collective sigh. 'Let us think on it and meet again tomorrow,' Luca said. 'For now, Susanna and I have work to do. We must discuss how she is to be costumed and begin rehearsing her performance.'

I cannot do this, she thought. As soon as Pedrolino and Umberto left, she said, 'I have not yet thanked you for allying yourself with me.'

'Now you have,' Luca said. He squared his shoulders and clapped once. 'Let us begin.'

Hastily she said, 'You conducted matters very well.'

'I had a fine scenario to work with.'

'You would make an excellent *corago*.'

'I too have thought so.' Luca smiled. 'A *corago*'s task is to make certain the roles are properly executed. Let us waste no more time, Lady Anna, and begin. You believe you cannot play the role of a great beauty all men desire, is that the difficulty?' She could barely nod. 'Stand up, please.'

She had to obey.

'What did you think of as you stood?'

'Why – of nothing. Of getting to my feet, as you asked.'

'Very well. Now, please, walk slowly around the room.'

She forced herself to do so.

'What were your thoughts as you walked about?'

'I had no thoughts in particular, except to finish walking.'

'There is the first lesson,' Luca said. 'You pay no heed to the body God gave you. You regard it simply as a means for transporting the soul through this world, as little more than a horse or a wagon. You stare at me, but I know that what I say is true. The secret of beauty is to believe one has it and to rejoice in its possession.'

'But I do not have it!'

'Then you must behave as if you do. I speak seriously. Do you believe all great beauties are truly beautiful? Some have serious flaws – eyes too close, teeth crooked, chin pointed, forehead or neck too short – but they conduct themselves as if they were beautiful in all respects. They walk through the world, or stand or sit, as if they deserve the admiration of all eyes. Therefore, they command it. Watch Isabella. It is true that God gave her beauty, but it is also true that she believes in her beauty. I assure you that if she did not, if she were indifferent to it, people would not acclaim her as they do.'

'Is the same true of you?'

'Of me? I suppose it must be, although I tell you in candour that I seldom think of my face, except to thank God for bestowing it upon me.' Luca frowned. 'I suppose I learned very early to conduct myself with pride – perhaps when I was wearing the blue smock at the fairs and smiling at women, to separate them from their coins. Now I no longer need to think of such matters, which take care of themselves.' He regarded her speculatively. 'Whereas you have thought largely of whether people are looking at the scar.'

How could he speak of it so casually – as no one else ever had?

'Do you know, Lady Anna, you might have had beautiful eye patches made, of silk or velvet, sewn with jewels, and gone about the world as The Great Beauty Who Wears An Eye Patch.' He laughed. 'Did you ever have such a thought?'

'No.'

'What did you think of?'

'Chiefly of matters of the mind and spirit – of the

beauty of Petrarch's words or Tiziano's painting, or the matters discussed by Pico della Mirandola or Machiavelli or Erasmus.'

'That is what we must change,' he said. 'I do not mean you should not think of such matters, for they create in you a beauty of spirit, but you must also think of the physical beauty you do possess – the long neck, the round chin, the high forehead. For our purposes today, you must fill your mind with such thoughts. Now then,' he said, brisk again, 'walk around the room once more, thinking as I have advised you.'

I cannot do this.

'You must try,' he said. 'For Teresa.'

Susanna locked her arms over her breasts.

'No, no. Let your hands fall to your sides. Your hands are beautiful. Think of them as you walk.'

She would have to try. Her hands fell to her sides. She began to walk. 'Hold your neck high,' Luca said. 'Your neck is beautiful. Think of your beautiful neck and hands and chin.'

She was trying, but her hands felt like two sacks, and her neck was stiff. *I cannot do this.* Perhaps for someone else, but not for Luca, not while he watched. She heard him say, 'Think of nothing but the beauty you do possess, nothing else,' and those words forced the memory upon her of walking around a table, wearing a velvet dress, while the Mantuans watched. Her hands dug into the cloth over her thighs, so they could not go to the scar. Just when she felt in control, she began to weep.

'Lady Anna! Sit down, sit here, calm yourself, do

not weep, please do not. I would not hurt you for any consideration in this world. Please forgive me for a fool.' She might have wept for an hour if Luca had not eventually said, in his distress, 'I shall fetch Pedrolino. He will do the role. He is not unattractive, and with a red wig . . .'

'He would be even uglier than I,' she said.

'Do not use that word, I beg you!'

'But he would be.' As suddenly as she had wept, Susanna began to laugh. The more she forbade herself, the less she could stop. Her breasts ached with the force of the laughter, which brought more tears, until she did not know what state she was in, wretchedness or merriment. Luca stood, bewildered.

Finally she was able to control herself and face him. 'I am a poor pupil.'

'No, I am a thoughtless *corago*. In my wish to help you, I forget the pain you must feel.'

'Why do you wish to help me?' A pointless question, for he could only lie.

'I like and admire you, Lady Anna. I have profited by your knowledge and taken pleasure in observing you change from a frightened woman who shrank against walls to one who is now leading the effort to save Teresa. Have you not seen my feeling? I have made no attempt to hide it.' A stripe of sunlight came through the shutter and disappeared into his hair, and his brown eyes looked at her as earnestly as a child's.

'I do not understand your feeling,' she said. 'And I find it difficult to accept what I cannot understand.'

He looked at her for a long time, his gaze now that of a man. 'Well,' he said finally, 'we can continue, if you like, and I shall be more considerate. Or shall I fetch Pedrolino?'

She rose. 'Let us continue.'

'Very well.' He rose too. 'I do not change my argument, only my methods. It is still true that the secret of beauty is belief in it. I ask you once more to walk about the room, but this time I leave your thoughts to you.'

'I might do better if I wore my veil, or my mask.'

'Perhaps, but would you not be hiding behind them?'

'Perhaps, but in the performance I must wear something to cover my . . . my face, or no one will believe in me.'

'If you require mask or veil to believe in yourself, then put it on.'

He could not, of course, have said anything more calculated to make her decline. 'I accept the challenge to do without.'

'Good.' Luca sat down again and folded his arms. 'Do not speak to me, but do anything else you wish. I shall respond to the language spoken by your face and body. Whatever I say and do will be governed by what they say and do.'

I cannot do this. Cannot.

'Begin walking,' he said.

So she did.

She prayed for the mask; behind it, she had done many things she could not do otherwise. She tried to imagine she wore it, telling her body to move as it had on the afternoon she and Paolo— Her thought collided with the reality of Luca's presence. She had used the mask to pretend that Paolo, poor Paolo, was Luca. Her body went as awkward as that of a woman nine months gone.

She heard a great yawn, and looked at Luca. His head was rocking sleepily from side to side. *Look at me. I order you to look at me.*

His eyelids began to close.

She went closer to him and with one hand swept her skirt from side to side, imitating the motion of his head.

His head ceased rocking. His eyes opened and looked at her.

She walked away slowly, her back towards him, knowing that her body moved gracefully. When she had gone several paces she looked at him over one shoulder, with the good side of her face. He whispered, 'Who are you, lady?'

She smiled too, shook her head in negation, and began to circle in front of him slowly. She felt one hand rise to cover her scar – not in shame but rather as if it were a fan. Her fingers spread over the bad eye, and her body half turned, so that she was aware of the profile her breasts were offering to him.

'*Brava, bellissima,*' he said, and got to his feet.

She stepped back quickly, but smoothly; she seemed to move on a carpet of water, undulating, smiling, inviting, forgetting all doubts of him and of herself, willing him to do as she wished and come to her, believing that he would, that the scene she had imagined a thousand times would be enacted in truth.

He moved towards her.

Fear returned in a jolt. He stopped where he was, a distance away. 'Do you fear me?' he said softly.

'No,' she whispered. 'I fear myself.'

'Why?'

She shook her head and turned away, but only partially, feeling the need in her breasts and allowing it to show.

'You must learn not to turn away when a man reveals that he desires you.' He came closer and reached out a hand. She took it.

He pulled her against him, put both hands on her face, and kissed her. His mouth was soft but impatient. She resisted for a moment, then ceased. He slid one hand down to her breast. She sighed deep within herself, and let her head fall back, neck revealed to his lips.

The pleasure was so intense, as if her body was sliding into warm, scented oil, that she feared she would moan.

Instead, she heard the door open.

She pulled herself up from a place as deep as the lagoon and turned to see Paolo, gaping at the two of them.

'I . . . I . . .' He said it again and again, as if plucking the same note on a lute string. Finally he found other words. 'They told me you wanted me. But I see I am not wanted. Forgive me.'

'No, no,' Luca said. 'Perhaps I should ask your forgiveness.'

'Why?'

'Please!' Susanna cried, trying to gather her thoughts and her senses. If Luca apologized to Paolo, she would scream. If she had to rehearse now with Paolo, as if nothing had happened, she would faint. 'Thank you for your help, Luca,' she said, wrapping fragments of composure about her and heading for the door. 'Let us all meet later today and continue working.'

CHAPTER SIXTEEN

'O supreme generosity of God the Father. O highest and marvellous felicity of man. To him it is granted to have whatever he chooses, to be whatever he wills.' – Pico della Mirandola

I Favolosi, most of them, were eating breakfast. Conversation was sporadic, interrupted by the sounds of chewing of bread and fruit and cheese. The troupe's easy camaraderie had been silenced, replaced by the awareness of division. All troupes had fights; it was impossible to live in such forced closeness, without the edges of temperaments growing sharp and sometimes slicing one another. Fights typically involved the sharing of earnings or the inequitable assignment of roles or living space. Now I Favolosi was facing something different: a split in ranks over how much each of them was willing to risk in order to help another. The trust and mutual dependence they took for granted in performance had been whipped away, like a cloth removed from a table by a magician, but the cups and plates left behind were rocking, not standing solid.

'Pass more bread,' said someone who was thinking,

If I were in prison would you leave me there, with nothing but crusts and water?

'This day promises to be hot,' said another, while thinking, *Will we come together again when this matter is resolved?*

The sound of these unspoken thoughts ran below the chewing jaws like a continuo. Buffa, at Paolo's feet, seemed to hear it, for he rose repeatedly, cocked his ears, and barked until Paolo reached down and fed him.

'What is the matter with that dog?' said Fiorenza, thinking, *I would not mind being rid of the animal, but then Paolo would be gone as well, and how can we survive without Arlecchino?*

'Buffa is not happy,' Paolo said. Everyone knew what he was thinking.

Silence, except for a knife sawing at a hard crust.

'Luca,' said Giulio carefully, 'will you still play with us at the Polani two nights hence?'

Luca looked up from his food and shrugged. 'We shall see.'

Feet shifted below the table, as if their owners could speak only by such means. People looked at Bruno, but his lips remained closed, as pink and moist in their nest of beard as young birds, and his eyes stared straight ahead.

After some moments Bianca said, 'Where is our dear Isabella this morning?'

Bruno pushed away his plate, still silent. As if she had only been waiting for someone to ask, Isabella swept into the dining room. She wore a green silk dress, and her hair, freshly golden, fell in long waves.

'Good morning,' chorused several voices, but she brushed them away with a gesture. 'I have an announcement.' She waited until everyone's eyes lifted to her, even Paolo's and Luca's, before she continued, honey-sweet, 'I shall speak with Signor Polani. The performance we give in two nights will not be the one we discussed. Instead, those of you who wish to do so will present *The Woman Who Was Falsely Accused*. I shall tell Signor Polani that, for the performance to have its full impact, the audience must include the bishop and some members of the Council of Ten.'

Silence. Even the feet below the table had lost their power of speech.

Finally Luca rose. 'Why are you offering to do this, Isabella?'

'To help the five of you disgrace yourselves and leave the rest of us free to please our patron.' She spoke viciously now, and with pleasure.

Watched by everyone, Luca turned to Bruno. 'She will take this action with your approval?'

Bruno's lips opened like a beak awaiting food, then closed. He nodded.

'I see.' Mockingly Luca added, 'We accept your gracious offer of help.'

They tried to make Susanna's hair redder, but it only turned paler, more golden. So they took the only red wigs they had – comic ones – and sent Pedrolino all over Venice to find a wigmaker who could shape them into something appropriate and do so in a day. He did, but charged them a good deal of money. 'I will pay for it,' Paolo said, almost stoically. When Umberto and Luca tried to remonstrate with him, he held up both hands and walked away. There was also the problem of covering Susanna's scar and the eye it distorted. As a great beauty, she could not wear her featureless acrobat mask, nor did they wish her to cover her entirely with a veil. Finally Luca devised a veil of thin lace that left the tip of her nose free and sloped downward from it, framing her mouth.

The greatest problem, however, was that of things unnamed. Paolo was in a melancholy humour, as none had ever seen him. The joy and foolishness of Arlecchino had drained away, and the others worried whether it would return to the man soon and to the player by performance time. The moment rehearsal was over, he went off by himself and seemed especially to avoid Susanna and Luca. Susanna was glad that he did. She knew she should speak with him, but could not think what to say. He made her feel shame because she had wanted – still wanted – to tell Luca, 'Paolo and I are not lovers, I do not love Paolo, I have nothing to do with Paolo.' But if she said it, then she would have to tell Luca why she and Paolo had lain together in the cypress grove. Perhaps Luca did not wish to speak of such matters either, for he talked only of the performance. She began to wonder whether what happened between them had been a dream. If it had truly happened, then had their actions been merely a rehearsal? To her, they had seemed real, but he was a skilled player. Could a player be so convincing that no one could tell he was pretending – not even the player himself?

Pedrolino and Umberto noted this behaviour, wondered, and over a bottle of wine shared the fear that they had allied themselves with an ill-fated undertaking. Neither told the other how deep that fear went.

On the morning of the performance, two men presented themselves at the inn, their jaws and eyes heavy with moral authority. They were from the Tribunal of the Inquisition, the notary and a commissary, come to search the room of the accused and question certain of her fellow players. By chance Pedrolino was on the stairs and heard them speaking to the landlord; he flew in panic to Luca, who ran to Susanna's room and advised her to hide. 'Where?' she said blankly.

'In the chest in Pedrolino and Paolo's room.'

'Chest!' she cried. 'I forgot about Teresa's chest! Look, there it sits, full of herbs and oils and all she uses to prepare her potions and charms. Why didn't I empty it and hide everything? Why did I forget it until this moment?'

'There is no time,' Luca said. 'The men are on their way up the stairs. If you do not want to be found and questioned, you must hide.' She hesitated. 'Come!' He grabbed her hand and pulled her into the hall.

In his room, Paolo was sleeping; he sat up, hair skewed to one side like a frozen wave, but grasped the situation at once. He opened the chest, threw out some of its contents – costumes, pots of cosmetics, old masks – and helped Susanna crawl inside. With her skirt wrapped around her like a winding-sheet, she craned her head and saw them both looking at her, Paolo and Luca, until Paolo threw an old cloak over her and the anxious ovals of their faces were blacked out. She heard Paolo close the lid and say, 'I shall sit upon it if the men come in here.' She heard Luca's reply: 'Good. Pedrolino, stay here too. I shall make certain that no one betrays her presence here.' The blackness of the chest made her sight useless but her other senses keener. Her nose pulled scents deep into her throat – sweat, dust, and something like rotting apples – and her ears filled with the beat of her blood even as they heard every creak of the floor and rustle of the mattress when Pedrolino and Paolo moved about. Neither spoke, and when Buffa suddenly barked, Susanna was so startled that she had to bite on the cloak to keep from crying out. Soon she heard what the dog must have heard: feet coming along the hall and the voice of the landlord, indistinct but so fearful and obsequious it seemed to be wringing its hands.

Veronica Bardi was lying on her bed, for the shock of Ludis's betrayal and capture still made her feel the need of much rest, when the slave who had taken on Ludis's duties brought her a letter. 'It just came by messenger, Signora.'

She sat up, pressed the backs of her hands to her forehead, then opened and read the letter:

On no account should the Signora Bardi and her

husband fail to attend the banquet this night at the *palazzo* of the Polani and to remain for the performance by the players of *commèdia*, for thereby all the Bardi, including the husband of their absent daughter, will learn something of particular interest to them.

One Who Wishes to be of Assistance

Veronica studied the words, trying to decide or imagine who would have reason to send such a message. The invitation had come some time before, but neither she nor Antonio had regarded it with any urgency. It was understood that he might decide not to attend at the last moment, as he often did, pleading something more urgent, which he always declared to be a matter of the spice trade. Veronica was never certain he told the truth. Sometimes she feared he merely preferred to be with one of his courtesans, most probably Almond-Eyes, but on the several occasions on which she had found some pretext to seek him out in his offices on the lower floors of the house, he had indeed been there with some stranger or other – men in odd clothes, with skins either as pale as frost or as dark as molasses. 'Veronica my dear,' he always said, as deferentially as if she were a royal visitor, 'may I introduce to you . . .' and there would follow some outlandish name, so full of consonants that it sounded like a series of coughs or, if the man was from the East, as susurrant as water lapping at a gondola's oars.

Veronica called for the new slave to bring her one of the loose robes she wore in the private rooms of the *palazzo* – why could the woman not do so as quickly and smoothly as Ludis? – and went in search of Antonio. He was not in his rooms; his bed had not been slept in. She returned to her own quarters, changed into a dress of brown silk, and went down the central stairs.

He was in his office, ledgers spread before him and his heavy brows knotted in a frown. 'What do you want?' he said when she paused in the doorway. Veronica knew at once that he had been with Almond-Eyes, for his voice held the combination of irritation, satisfaction, and guilt that she had long learned was unique to the mornings after such nights.

She went to him and held out the letter. He took it with a snap of his wrist, read, then looked up at her. 'Who has sent us this?'

'I have no idea. I thought perhaps you could tell me.'

'How should I know anything of it?'

'Bishop Palma has said nothing to you regarding Susanna? Do you think . . . Might this letter mean she will be found?'

'By the Lord God, when she is found, she will answer for all the trouble and shame she has caused us.'

'You would not treat her cruelly, would you, Antonio?'

'I would treat her justly. If that be cruelly—' He shrugged.

Veronica sighed. 'We will attend this evening then? You will not decide to . . . go elsewhere?'

'We will attend.' Antonio reached for his quill.

'Should we make certain Ludovico is there as well? He is mentioned in the letter.'

Antonio did not look up. 'As you like.'

'I do not like. I have never liked him, as you well know.'

That brought Antonio's gaze back to her. 'See that he is there this evening.'

Veronica started for the door, then turned, pulled by the question that often hung on her lips and by the desire to hear him confess. *Where did you go last evening?* But the fear that he would answer, and she would have to live with the burden of certainty, stopped her, as usual.

'What is it now?' he asked.

She had been so fixed on suppressing the forbidden question that another escaped without her consent – just as, determined to keep the dog from slipping outside, one forgot to watch the cat. 'What sort of pact do you have with Ludovico?'

'Pact? What do you mean?'

'Nothing. It is nothing.'

Antonio thrust the quill into the inkwell like a dagger and stood. 'Tell me why you asked such a question.'

'I do not know.'

'Tell me.' His voice was menacingly quiet.

Veronica's hands reached for each other. 'Very well. At one of our dinners, I once heard the two of you speak of a pact. And only a week ago, I heard him use the word to you again.'

'He referred to his marriage – his offer to marry Susanna.'

'Why does he speak of it as a pact?'

'Because he is an idiot!'

'Then why did you marry our daughter to him?'

'Because no one else would have her. Leave me now, so I may do the work that maintains this establishment and all its luxuries.'

'Very well, Antonio.' Veronica left the room with more dignity than she had entered it. She knew she had touched on something Antonio wished to discuss even less than his courtesans, but could not see what to do with the knowledge.

The commissary and the notary emerged from Teresa and Susanna's room with identically satisfied smiles on their otherwise dissimilar faces. No one knew precisely what they were taking away in their black monk's cloth bag. Luca, who had posted himself in the hall, heard one of them refer to 'the Formulary found in the chest'. They announced that they would speak with the troupe's leader, and did so for over an hour. Afterwards, wiping his streaming face with a red kerchief, Bruno told the others that they had asked many questions about Teresa's mother as well as Teresa herself. 'They asked why we had lied about Ginevra's child being dead. Isabella gave a splendid performance – dabbed at her eyes and said Ginevra had begged us not to reveal her daughter's existence, and we had felt so sorry for our fellow player that we honoured the promise. She was heartbreaking, but the faces on the two officials never changed. One of them wrote for a long time in a black book, and the other asked about Teresa's potions and elixirs. Did she evoke demons or draw circles and diabolical signs or use any consecrated objects? I said not that I knew, but then, I never stood around watching her preparations. Isabella took to her bed after the men left, and she's not coming out until they are gone from the inn.'

They spoke with Luca, asking many of the same questions. Over and over he replied that he had never watched Teresa's preparations and had been concerned only with selling the results. They asked about Teresa's performances. Did she reveal her breasts and backside? Depict certain bodily functions? Join in making sport of the clergy? Allow male players to touch her body, put their hands beneath her skirts, and so on? Under the weight of their gaze, everything done in innocence and good humour grew black, like paper turned to cinders.

The officials asked to speak with the Arlecchino of the troupe. In Paolo and Pedrolino's room they repeated many of their questions. Paolo answered as shortly as possible, Arlecchino silent and shrivelled in his breast. How often did she go to Mass? asked the notary. Did she make confession regularly?

Pedrolino, who had remained silent, suddenly stood, clenched his fists, and cried: 'Teresa Laurano is good! She could not be guilty of any crime!'

The two officials turned to him; the notary, nearly as thin as Paolo, with a long, ascetic face as pale as a candle, said, 'Do you wish to become a witness for the defence?'

'Defence?' Pedrolino said weakly.

'The accused may present a defence, if she wishes, with the aid of one of the doctors in canon law who plead in our ecclesiastical courts.'

'I . . . do not know,' said Pedrolino. 'I only know that she is good.' He sank back on to his mattress, and the questioning of Paolo continued.

When the officials had gone, Paolo went to the chest and lifted the lid. Susanna's hands clutched the edge of the wood and she stumbled out, legs and arms stiff and her face dead white with strain and fatigue. A muscle jerked near her bad eye, aggravating its distortion. She sat on Paolo's bed and put her face in her hands. The two men looked at her, watching her shoulders move in spasms.

'Anna,' said Pedrolino, 'I mean, Susanna, shall we still perform for the Polani tonight?' He waited. 'Why do you not answer?' Another pause. 'Paolo, she looks dreadful. Do you think she will be able to perform?'

'I cannot say.'

'You must make her answer.'

'How can I do that?'

'I do not know, but you must. She is your lady.'

Paolo bit his lips. When he did speak, the words came out as if weighed with stones. 'I have no lady. Susanna is not my lady.'

'But . . . but . . .'

'No. I am not.' Susanna's head was still in her hands. 'Paolo and I were friends. We did favours for each other. One day, a great favour. Since then our friendship has rotted like fruit. Curse Fiorenza for her tale.

Curse all who believe her. Curse the two of us for stupidity.' Her shoulders shook again.

'Yes,' Paolo said. 'Curse us both.'

Her head lifted. 'How long should we do so? Forever?'

'No. Not forever.'

'How long, then?'

He touched her shoulder. 'Let us curse briefly and then be friends as before.'

'Do you truly wish it, Paolo?'

'I do.' He held out both hands.

She took them and rose slowly. 'Then I can perform this evening.'

They embraced each other.

'I am glad, Lady Anna,' said Luca's voice. They all turned to see him in the doorway, watching. 'But there is little time. We must hurry.'

They snatched up their properties and costumes and made ready to leave. The rest of I Favolosi watched them go in silence, except for Giulio, who wished them well. 'Look here,' Bruno said. 'If you fail tonight . . .'

'Yes?' said Luca. 'If we do?'

Bruno shrugged and glowered.

The five of them left the inn and headed towards the Polani palace. Clouds turning red and orange hung high above them like silk pillows. Luca walked alone, behind Paolo and Susanna, watching the shadows they cast in the coppery light.

He did not care whether they were lovers, he thought. Every man and woman was entitled to pleasure; he believed that as devoutly as anything he heard in church, perhaps more.

He did not know what to make of himself. He had been intrigued by Susanna from the first; she had been like certain people he had seen on his travels – fascinating because they were different. In France he had met a man of amazing height and talked with him for several hours, trying to capture a sense of how the world would look from such a parapet. And there had been a holy man in the north of Spain who, wearing only a loincloth, had squatted on a rock hot enough to blister his skin and talked hoarsely of the manifold sins of the flesh, in such detail that one could only assume he had once committed them. Such people, Luca knew, would stay forever in the theatre of his mind. Perhaps he had thought Susanna would be the same. But she had behaved in unexpected ways, losing her fear, taking matters into her own hands, refusing to be governed by the angry mark that pulled at her eye. She was no longer an object of curiosity; he liked her. Nothing more. Yet when they rehearsed alone, he had felt a desire for her that had nothing to do with the stage. She had been real beneath his fingers, warm and silky, and if Paolo had not interrupted and she had been willing, the scene would have played to a finish that Luca was sure would have pleased them both. And the satisfaction would not have been solely of the flesh, of that he was sure as well, although he did not know what to make of his certainty. Instructing her in the art of seductiveness even as it was aimed at him had been in itself seductive. Touching her and feeling her breath on him like a sweet little wind had been different from the many times he had found pleasure with women, but he did not know why. It was as if a new spice had been brought from the East and added to a familiar dish. Why should he desire this woman in a way different from others? Why had he told her that her hands were beautiful when they were not, particularly – they were rather square, like a boy's? Why did he now find himself looking at them often? He was not used to questioning his pleasure, merely seeking it.

He had gone about his tasks for the performance with a puzzled half-smile he did not even realize was on his face until he met Isabella in the hall and she said, 'I see you have become so great a fool that you have acquired the look of one.'

He had stopped short. Her words, which usually fell on him offstage as heedlessly as summer rain, had coruscated in their own unpleasantness. He had asked her, sincerely, 'Do you care never to do anything but insult and injure?'

'Oh,' she said. 'Oh, my. I can recall a time when you were very interested in what else I could do.'

'That is true.' He had folded his arms.

Slowly she flushed. 'I take it that time is now over.'

'I believe that is our mutual desire.'

She had taken a shuddering breath, as if readying to attack him for using the word 'desire', but instead she had walked away.

He had watched her, knowing they had lain together many times but unable to recall any detail of their encounters except that she had a small, dark mark in the pit of one arm. He could not even remember which.

Ahead of him, Susanna stumbled. Paolo steadied her.

Why should he care if they were lovers? There were more serious matters to consider, such as whether they would all fail and be sent to prison or a worse fate. He loved a challenge, but still, it was madness to have accepted this one. How had Susanna persuaded him to do it?

In the Polani banquet hall, below the *candelieri*, thirty guests chatted of the spice trade, the upcoming regatta, the plan to replace the decaying Rialto bridge with one of stone. The floors were strewn with sweet-smelling herbs, which the servants' feet crushed as they moved about, releasing a constant fragrance, and when the guests opened their intricately folded napkins, a small bird flew from the space within each. Wings beat wildly in freedom and disappeared through the open windows, after which the diners began consuming their brethren – partridge and quail – as well as sausages, pig's brains, and truffles, followed by fruit and sweet cakes of many kinds.

Outside the hall the players waited. Luca paced, thinking of his first entrance as the bishop. Umberto fussed with the Pantalone robe and mask that Giulio loaned him at the last moment – 'If they can help Teresa . . . But do not tell my wife.' Paolo, in Arlecchino mask and costume, twirled his *batte* in intricate loops.

Pedrolino silently plucked his guitar like a rosary. Susanna walked in slow circles, reciting poetry to herself. No matter how deeply each was occupied by private worries and thoughts, all were aware of one another, their tension forming a net in which they squirmed together like captured fish. Luca broke stride now and then to put a reassuring hand on Umberto's shoulder or make an unnecessary adjustment to Susanna's veil, Paolo whispered a *lazzo* to Pedrolino, Susanna nodded to Umberto and Luca as they passed her.

The noise of clearing away the feast began; all too soon it ended. Wordlessly the players took one another's hands, their fingers both transmitting tension and seeking release from it. Then Luca said, 'Arlecchino, go!' Paolo opened the door and bounded into the hall, to laughter and applause.

He loped back and forth on the stage, head sinking into his shoulders and rising again like an apple bobbing in a tub. Suddenly he stopped and gaped at the audience, astonished to discover them; the laughter that had been rolling along with him came to a roar. He shrugged, sat down, and did the *lazzo* of the cat, scratching his ear with his foot, stretching out with his rear in the air, then perfectly imitating the way the animal cleans itself with its tongue. Much applause. He stood, bowed, stretched his hands over his head, frowned, rubbed his stomach, and went into the *lazzo* of hunger, searching frantically for something to eat, chewing on his shoes, his *batte*, and finally on his fingers, as if they were drumsticks.

Much laughter and more applause.

It was time to be serious. He said to the audience, 'Ladies and gentlemen, tonight we perform for you something new, something different, which will have only this one performance. Yes! Only you will see the play we have created. Then it will be gone forever.' Murmurs of surprise and appreciation. 'Is it comical? Tragical? Historical? All of those, and one thing more as well, which you shall not know until we tell you.' He held up both hands for quiet. 'We present now the play of *The Woman Who Was Falsely Accused.* Our scene is Venice, and our matter concerns a beautiful veiled woman who captures the heart of a man but does not return his love, so that he is driven to accuse her falsely. May our humble efforts give you pleasure and enlighten your thoughts.'

He bowed and left the stage. Pedrolino entered with his guitar and sang a plaintive song. Umberto strode out, his gait not as confident as Giulio's would have been but his costume and manner nonetheless suggesting that he was a rich Venetian merchant. After some comic business with Pedrolino, as his servant, he spoke at length of his love for the beautiful courtesan whose name no one knew. Then he quitted the scene. It was Susanna's time to enter.

For the first several minutes she knew nothing except the beating of her heart. No doubt she opened her lips and spoke, for there did not seem to be silence, but she had no awareness of doing so and might as well have been a creature painted on a backcloth. Then

Umberto re-entered and responded to her, and she regained some sense of herself, felt her body move and heard her words to Umberto, the merchant, telling him she could not be his because she was a courtesan, who belonged to all, not to any one man. Gradually she began to feel more confident, and by the time of the first scene with Luca, who was dressed in a bishop's robes, she was, wonderingly, even beginning to feel some pleasure in what she did. She dared to look at the audience. Her courage fled, for she saw her father.

Although nothing in her scenario hinted at his name, she had known she was implicating him in the role of the Pantalone: a merchant who conspired to silence the courtesan because she spurned him. He was not meant to be there, in the audience. She had not asked for him. The bishop, and some Council members, yes, but not her father. How had he come there? She told herself that he could not know who she was, that the half-veil and wig protected her, but surely he would know her voice. In a moment he would call her name. She saw her mother beside him, and on his other side, Bishop Palma. The enormity of what she was doing took her breath. Had not the Archbishop of Milan recently declared that players must not be allowed to use church garments of any kind? Her scenario would destroy them all. She had known it was a possibility, yet she had not felt it like the weight of a horse toppling on her. She realized she had stopped speaking and was standing still, a statue except for the eyes staring through the lace of the veil at her parents and Palma.

Luca, as the bishop, said, 'Lady, beauty such as yours can come only from God.' Then in a whisper, lips barely moving: 'What is wrong? You must speak!'

'My father,' she managed to whisper back, 'is here.' They could not go through with the scenario. They must change it, make it simple and innocent, with no suggestion that a Venetian merchant was involved in the crime.

Luca, the bishop, was circling her, studying her. Luca himself whispered, 'Look only at me. Think of no one else. Think of our private rehearsal.'

Slowly her gaze went to him. Reflections of many candles lit his eyes, which were looking at her with desire, but it was the bishop's desire, the bishop who was looking at the Woman. Yet it might also be Luca's desire. It was the bishop's, but he is the bishop, whom your body must entice even as your words deny him. Think only of him, no one else, only him.

She cleared her throat. 'Your Excellency,' she said, 'if you admire me, let it be from afar.'

'Distance is a cruel punishment, lady.'

'Distance is . . . God's law between us.' Her body began to lose its stiffness.

'I am the interpreter of God's law,' he said.

'And I the interpreter of man's wishes.'

He moved a step closer. 'Then you know what this man wishes.'

She moved away. 'I cannot grant such wishes.'

The words began to fly, back and forth like a ball. She threw them without thinking, letting responses flow into her mind and then from her lips. He was smiling at her, a Luca-smile behind the bishop's and when they ended the scene, she walked off with a smile of her own. From behind the side-curtain that covered their entrances and exits, she heard him improvising the bishop's thoughts, brilliantly. When he too walked off, there were murmurs of displeasure from the audience. Had they begun to suspect which bishop was being depicted? Or did they dislike the portrayal of any bishop? She was going to ask Luca, but he put a finger to his lips and took her hand. He held it through the next scene, a comic one between Arlecchino and Umberto, the merchant, moving his fingers slowly over and around hers so that she barely heard what was being improvised on the platform and knew only that there was laughter, in which she wanted to join.

From then on, the scenario moved more and more swiftly, with no comedy to halt its propulsion. Umberto and Luca conspired to accuse the Woman of sorcery. She was taken by a guard – Paolo in a different mask and costume – and put into prison. In what seemed only a few moments, a man who wore a black mask over his eyes – but was clearly Luca – ordered the guard to admit him, entered the cell, and began to advance towards her. 'I shall have you, damnable woman. I have had you brought here to do as I wish, my pleasure shall be your duty, you cannot turn away from me now—'

'No, no,' she said. 'Do not touch me, I beg you in God's name, please.'

'You shall do as *I* please!' He put his hands on her shoulders and pulled her to him.

'Bishop!' came a cry from the audience. 'Did you do that? Did you take your pleasure with her?'

Luca froze, half-crouched above Susanna. She could not speak either. It must be her father, calling out. She had planned to trap the bishop but had caught her father instead. Soon he would be upon the platform, pushing Luca aside, grabbing her, punishing her.

But he did not come. Instead, after a moment so silent that even the candle flames were still, the diners began murmuring. Luca moved back as if in a dream. Susanna sat up, looked to the audience, saw a man standing, the focus of all eyes – saw that he was not her father. It was her husband. 'Ludovico!' she exclaimed, before she could caution herself.

'Hah!' he cried back. 'Who are you, that knows my name?'

She looked at Luca, but for once there was no message or guidance in his eyes, only amazement. She lifted her veil.

'Look! There she is – my wife!' Ludovico came towards the stage, pushing aside chairs and people. 'Bishop, there she is, right there before us. Why did you not find her? Bardi, why did you not return her to me? She is mine, by our pact! I demand that she return to me at once!'

At the edge of her vision Susanna saw Paolo, Pedrolino, and Umberto come from behind the curtain, masks off, eyes wide. Luca returned to life. He leaped from the platform and grabbed Ludovico, who thrashed in his arms like a huge-bellied fish, croaking, 'My wife! I demand my wife!'

'Help me here, someone,' Luca called.

Signor Polani came to life as well and beckoned to two male slaves, who ran forward, took Ludovico between them, and headed for the door. Some of the diners rose in confusion.

'Wait!' Luca cried. 'Stop, everyone, at once!' His voice, trained to cross distance and penetrate corners, had the desired effect. 'We have not finished! Let us tell you why we have performed this scenario for you and why you are the only ones to see it.'

The room quieted. Even Ludovico stopped twisting in the slaves' grip.

'Arlecchino?' said Luca, and waved him forward.

Paolo came to the edge of the platform and began the speech they had carefully planned, for once leaving nothing to improvisation. His voice faltered in the opening words but soon grew calm and strong. '*The Woman Who Was Falsely Accused* is not merely a scenario. It is comical and tragical and historical but also, as I promised you, one thing more, which you shall know now: it is an accusation. By this means, rather than by posting a letter in the lion's mouth, do we send it to the members of the Council of Ten, some of whom we know to be present. We charge that one of our number, Teresa Laurano, who suffers now in prison, was charged by Bishop Andrea Palma for malicious motives. We have just shown you the explanation of his malice. The Woman in our scenario is the mother of Teresa Laurano, and because Teresa knows the truth of her mother's imprisonment, the bishop had her sent before the Tribunal of the Inquisition, charged with causing the death of a priest by heretical witchcraft.'

He stopped. His words hung in the air like *candelieri*.

'This is blasphemous.' Andrea Palma had remained in his seat, expressionless, but now he rose and said, in the voice that had filled the stone caverns of many churches with its power and beauty, 'If ever there were doubt that players, by their nature as well as their actions, deny and defy the God who has created them, here is proof of their blasphemy and wickedness.'

Paolo lifted his chin like a lance. 'Your Excellency knows that we have shown the truth about the malice of his motive, just as he knows we were driven to this means because his power and influence would otherwise prevent anyone from giving credence to what we say.'

Everyone, including the players, was looking at the bishop and at the figure who rose from the other side of the dining tables, a member of the Council.

Before either of them could speak, Ludovico roared, 'Bardi! Why did you send the bishop to do your work? I did not sign your marriage contract so that he could take his pleasure!'

It took many attempts by Luca, joined by Signor Polani, to quiet the uproar among the diners so that the member of the Council of Ten finally could say, 'The Council will investigate the charges we have heard tonight, and investigate them fully.'

CHAPTER SEVENTEEN

> Many people of both sexes give themselves over to diverse incantations and devilish superstitions and by their venery and vain rites procure many wicked things, destroy men, animals and fields, induce grievous errors, whereby they spread great scandals . . . – Papal bull of 1501

The Venetian Tribunal of the Inquisition had one purpose, one voice, and six pairs of ears and eyes.

Its purpose was to recognize and condemn heresy in all its forms and manifestations. Its voice was that of the Inquisitor, who put virtually all questions to the accused and witnesses. Its ears and eyes belonged to him and to the five other members. His two fellow ecclesiastics – the papal nuncio and the Patriarch of Venice – worked to ensure that the needs of the Holy Roman Catholic and Apostolic Church were served; and the three secular members, called the Tre Assistenti, represented the Council of Ten. They safeguarded the interests of the Republic and made certain the Tribunal did nothing to threaten Venetian political or commercial interests. There were also a notary, to record testimony, and a fiscal. All of them were elderly, grey with a wisdom and authority that laid a common stamp upon their lips, fine or full, their noses, straight or bent, and their eyes, clear or rheumy. They knew they were feared and respected by men. They believed they were loved by God.

They sat at a raised table in the private church near the Piazza San Marco where their business was conducted in months of warm weather. Only with obdurate defendants did they meet in the torture chamber. The church was cool and damp, as if the lagoon lived in its stones. The light from its windows fell in pale colours, stained by the scenes depicted on their glass, and candles and censers flickered in the many corners. Before the Inquisitor lay a copy of the book on which the Tribunal relied. The *Directorium Inquisitorum* had for two centuries guided Inquisitions everywhere on proper procedures and on the recognition of heresy.

Two of the Assistenti had attended the Polani banquet and had described the scene to their colleagues, who had heard of it by other means as well, for the tale had begun spreading through the city only hours after it was over. The next morning Andrea Palma had spoken privately to each of the ecclesiastics on the Tribunal, acknowledging that he had had Ginevra Laurano accused of heretical witchcraft – he said he had actually told his clerk to take care of the matter – but assuring them that the tale enacted by the players could only be based on the ravings of a sick woman. Did the record not show that Ginevra

Laurano had died in prison of a high fever?

'He spoke of his innocence with utter conviction,' said the nuncio.

'When the players enacted the accusatory scene,' said the Patriarch, 'did he exhibit signs of guilt?'

'Not that I observed,' said one of the Assistenti who had been there.

Nonetheless, the players' accusation had to be addressed and quickly. The Holy Office could not seem to ignore something known to all of Venice.

They sent for Antonio Bardi.

His rage at having to come before them was barely controlled, lying on his skin in red patches like sunset on a puddle. In his gullet burned the knowledge that his own daughter had played a large role in publicly implicating him and thus forcing him to stand where he was – before men he had often invited to dine at his home – answering their questions like a boy at his lessons.

'Did you ask Andrea Palma to have the woman Ginevra Laurano accused of sorcery?'

Antonio badly wished to deny this and make an end of matters, but he could not seem to be obstructing the Tribunal in its holy mission. More important, he did not know what Palma might have told them, or what Ludovico could be trusted to say, or not say. So he clenched his fists and said, 'Yes.'

'Why did you do so?'

'Ludovico Rossi asked me.' *Curse the day*, he thought, *that my fortunes became entangled with his.*

'Why did you feel obliged to do as Ludovico Rossi asked?'

'He was going to marry my daughter.' *Curse the day he came with his offer.*

'What reason did he have to accuse the woman Ginevra Laurano?'

Antonio put a hand on the place where his dagger normally rested, but he had had to surrender it to enter the Tribunal's presence. 'She was a courtesan known for using sorcery. Rossi said she put a spell on him.'

'Did the spell involve prayers or sacred objects?'

'I do not know. I merely agreed to help my future son-in-law.' *May he be cursed for everything, beginning with his birth.*

'Why did Ludovico Rossi not make the accusation himself?'

'I do not know.'

'Antonio Bardi, the Holy Office observes that you involved yourself in this matter with little knowledge of its nature.'

The choler rose higher, a red bubble waiting to burst. Antonio lifted his chin above it and did not reply.

'Did you yourself know the woman Ginevra Laurano?'

He swallowed and nodded, knowing he could not deny it. *Curse Susanna and the other players.* They had shown 'the courtesan' spurning 'the merchant'. Ginevra had never spurned him. If he had not made the pact with Ludovico . . . if fear of having it known had not tied them to each other's necks . . .

The Inquisitor's voice creaked on. 'Why did you ask Andrea Palma, and not another, to investigate the woman?'

'I believed him best able to do whatever was necessary.'

'He was not then a bishop, as he is now, was he?'

The cords in Antonio's throat tightened like rigging. 'No.'

'Then why go to him?'

The bubble burst. 'Because he was courting my favour. Because the bastard son of a noble house could not become a bishop without the support of families like the Bardi! No man achieves a bishopric in Venice without such support. You know this well. Palma did as I asked because I supported his ambitions!'

There, it was said, the words relieving his rage like the lancing of a boil. Let them remember, the sanctimonious six before him, that Rome did not rule in Venice – that no churchman acquired power in the Serenissima without the consent and contrivance of the noble families.

The Tribunal's lips registered varying degrees of displeasure and discomfort. *Hah!* thought Antonio. Let them see it was useless to humble a Bardi.

He was back in the Piazza, where birds fluttered disconsolately in a sudden rain and few vendors' stalls were open, before he began to feel uneasy.

Ludovico Rossi stood before the Tribunal as if he might slump to the marble floor of the church.

'Why did you ask Antonio Bardi to accuse the woman Ginevra Laurano?'

'Why did you not come forward to this Tribunal when she was charged?'

'What was the nature of your complaint against her?'

'Do you claim that she placed a spell on you?'

He tried to answer, for it would be good to have someone understand why he suffered, but his mind would not function properly. He looked at his hands, which seemed as pale and wrinkled as if he had held them too long in water.

'Did Ginevra Laurano use holy water or candles in her divinations?'

'Did she use them in casting beans or the *cordella*?'

'Do you have knowledge of her daughter Teresa Laurano?'

Ludovico managed to say, 'No.'

All his spirit had left him on the night of the banquet. At first he had been so maddened by what the players were enacting that he had not known what he was saying or doing. He had come to himself only when he felt the arms of the slaves around him like chains, and then he could think only of his anger at the bishop, and at Bardi for involving the bishop, so that he had cried out against both of them. When the uproar finally settled, Ludovico had felt eyes upon him, many needles of disapproval, contempt, and amusement, which punctured him many times, in many places, until the slaves seemed to be holding only half the man they had originally grasped. Someone had helped him to his gondola, and when he reached his house, he had gone to his bed, curled into himself like an infant, and sunk so deeply into a phlegmatic humour that he had refused to see or speak to anyone but the slave who brought him plates of food he barely touched. He had emerged only once, briefly, for an urgent matter pertaining to bills of lading, then returned to the dimness of his room. Whenever he recalled the players' performance, memories of his fury would shake him, but they would roll away like thunder and leave him alone with his humiliation.

'What was the nature of your complaint against the woman Ginevra Laurano?'

'Do you claim that she placed a spell upon you?'

'Do you believe, and have cause to believe, that Andrea Palma had congress with the woman in her prison cell?'

He saw again what he had seen at the banquet: Palma bending over Ginevra, who somehow was also Susanna. His fury rumbled. 'Why should he . . . It is not . . . Why should he . . .'

'Ludovico Rossi, this Holy Office commands you to explain yourself.'

If they knew why he was suffering, they might help him. 'Why should Palma possess her – when she had cast a spell upon me so that I could not?'

The Inquisitor looked at the Tre Assistenti on his left, whose eyes had all grown larger, and the two ecclesiastical brethren on his right, who nodded almost imperceptibly. 'Tell us of the spell and how she laid it upon you.'

'I do not know.'

'You had no evidence?'

'I could not lie with her! There was the evidence! I could not be as a man should be with a woman! Clearly she had placed a spell upon me, which lasted until . . . And if Andrea Palma dared to satisfy himself with her, while I . . .' Ludovico clenched his moist wrinkled hands. Could they not understand, those righteous faces? Did they not see how he suffered?

'Why did you ask Antonio Bardi to accuse the woman for you?'

'So she could not know who had destroyed her! If she knew, she would cast another spell on me!'

'Why did you not accuse her anonymously, in a lion's mouth?'

'I had to be certain the accusation would be regarded seriously.'

'The Holy Office investigates all such accusations. Why did Bardi agree to do as you asked?'

'We made a pact. I signed a contract to wed his scarred daughter, whom no one else would have. For his part he was to see that Ginevra Laurano was accused and punished. But the players say he did not! Instead he sent the bishop to do it. Ginevra Laurano was to be destroyed, not to provide pleasure for the bishop! If Bardi had not gone to the bishop . . .' Ludovico's eyes left the dimness of the cathedral and travelled in moments to the inner country where his thoughts and dreams awaited him. 'If Susanna were with me,' he muttered, with no awareness that logic was absent, 'none of this would have happened. We would be happy together.' Every night, he thought, she would have come to him, or invited him to come to her. She would have wanted him, implored him, to possess her in ways . . . masterly ways . . . and if she did not, he would force her, until she would have begged him . . . to caress her scar, the little, red piece of skin that tugged down on her eye and revealed the lining of the lower eyelid. It compelled him in a manner he could not explain, since he had first seen her. He must have her and the scar, the one making the other beautiful. He must be allowed to touch it whenever he liked, fondle it, feel his own body swell into life at the sight of it . . . He stepped closer to the table and peered at the Inquisitor. 'My wife must be returned to me. Order that she return to me.'

'It is not in the jurisdiction of this Tribunal to issue such an order.'

Ludovico blinked. Had they not heard him? Had he failed to make himself clear? 'But you must,' he said. Susanna could restore him to himself. She who had conspired to humiliate him – by pretending to be Ginevra Laurano! – could undo the effects of her latest actions.

'Remember whom you address, Ludovico Rossi.' The Inquisitor laid a hand upon the *Directorium Inquisitorum*. 'We follow God's law, not men's pleas.'

Had he humiliated himself again, confessed his shame to these men, for no purpose? 'I demand that you return her to me!' he cried. 'I demand it!' He was still repeating the words when guards removed him from the church.

'The progression of past events now seems clear,' said the Inquisitor. 'All began when the woman Ginevra Laurano placed a spell upon Ludovico Rossi so that his male member did not function. He therefore wished to have her accused of witchcraft and destroyed, but not to know he was her accuser. He persuaded Antonio Bardi to do his bidding by offering to marry the disfigured daughter. Bardi, in turn, asked Andrea Palma to take charge of the matter, in exchange – but I wager it was only in partial exchange – for using his influence to see that Palma received a bishopric. Finally, as the last action in the chain, Palma told his clerk Fra Filippo to make the accusation. Ironically, Filippo must have placed it in a lion's mouth, for that, as our records show, is how the accusation was ultimately received.'

'It would appear,' said one of the Assistenti unhappily, 'that the players' accusation is true in most of its essentials.'

'Yes,' said the Patriarch. 'But the central point – that Palma violated the mother and therefore had malicious motivation for accusing the daughter – is not corroborated.'

'How can it be,' said one of the Assistenti, 'if Palma denies it and there are no witnesses?'

The Patriarch stared up into the dimness above his head and put words to a thought shared by the others. 'If Teresa Laurano would . . . confess to the murder of the priest . . .'

'We might put her to the torture,' said one of the Assistenti.

The Patriarch frowned. The Inquisition in the enlightened Republic of Venice resorted infrequently to what was common practice elsewhere.

'Let us question the players,' said the Inquisitor.

'You are the Arlecchino of the troupe known as I Favolosi?'

'Yes, Your Excellency.'

'Did you know the woman Ginevra Laurano?'

'Your Excellency, she had died by the time I joined the players.'

'Did Teresa Laurano tell you how her mother had died?'

'No, Your Excellency.'

'Then on what basis did you present an accusation about the woman's death in your performance at the Polani banquet?'

'It was based on what Teresa had told Susanna Bardi.'

'So you yourself have no knowledge of the truth of the matter?'

'No, Your Excellency.'

'How long has Susanna Rossi been with the players?'

'Since last winter, Your Excellency.'

'Why did Teresa Laurano tell the story of her mother's death to Susanna Rossi, whom she has known only briefly, and not to you, a friend of many years?'

'I do not know.'

Silence. The Inquisitor's hands lay on a book before him. Their veins seemed drawn by a blue brush. Paolo's own hands were wet, yet his mouth was so dry that his teeth stuck to his lips. He had imagined the scene many times in the two days since the banquet. The reality was quieter and calmer but more frightening, for he expected it to change at any moment. His entire body waited for the blow of the question that surely would come: *Do you know anything of the death of the priest Fra Filippo?* In the silence of the church, with the Tribunal as quiet as dead men, he thought he heard the question coming at him already. He pictured Isabella, to bolster his courage. With a sting, he remembered he no longer loved her. He could not, for she was not the Isabella he had worshipped but a strange, cold woman to whom his love meant nothing. He did not know what to do without that love, which had been the anchor of his life for so long, or how, without it, he would answer when the question came.

The Inquisitor leaned forward. Paolo's body tensed. But the question was: 'Do you know it is blasphemy to portray a servant of the church on the stage?'

'No, Your Excellency,' he said almost eagerly, 'I did not know that.'

'Do you know that in northern countries infected with heresy the Holy Catholic Church is ridiculed, so the ignorant may learn false doctrines?'

'No, Your Excellency.'

'Did Teresa Laurano participate in performing tales of adultery?'

'I . . . I suppose we all did, sometimes.'

'Did she show her legs or breasts to entice audiences to buy her nostrums?'

'It was only in fun, Your Excellency. Just to make people laugh and enjoy themselves and forget that life is hard.'

'Do you believe that men should forget this life?'

'Only its difficulties, Your Excellency.'

'Therein lies the evil of the theatre. It denies the Christian social order by substituting an artificial world for the real one and encouraging men to participate in that artificial, lascivious life and to neglect or abandon their contemplation and study of God's truth. Do you accept what I have said?'

'I . . . I do, Your Excellency.'

'Yet you plan to continue in this way of life?'

'I know nothing else, Your Excellency.'

The Inquisitor lifted his hands as if they were consecrated objects and placed his fingertips together. 'If the death of the priest Fra Filippo was caused by unholy means, would you wish to help this Tribunal discover them?'

Paolo's lips were glued to his teeth. He forced them apart. 'Yes, Your Excellency.'

'Then I ask you, by your love of our Lord God and your desire to spend eternity in His bosom, not writhing in the flames of Hell, surrounded by the smoking and spitting of your flesh and prodded by the pitchforks of all Satan's devils, for a man who compounds the sin of enticing his fellow men into the lascivious, artificial world of the *commèdia* by refusing to aid in discovering the means by which the priest died will assuredly be consigned to Hell, I ask whether you can tell us anything of his death.'

Finally, the question. It was easy to answer, for the Inquisitor had said everything needed to strengthen Paolo's resolve. 'No, Your Excellency. I cannot.'

'Susanna Rossi, did Teresa Laurano tell you of the manner of her mother's death?'

'She did.'

'What cause had you to believe she told the truth?'

'Her manner of telling it. Also, I had come to know her well during the months I spent with I Favolosi.'

'During those months did you know her to prepare potions and ointments?'

'Yes.'

'Did you know her to practise love magic and cast spells?'

'She spoke of doing so, but I never saw her.'

'What kind of spells?'

'To cure an aching back or help a woman conceive – things of that nature.'

'Did she recite prayers or incantations or use sacred objects?'

'Never in my presence.'

'Did you believe she possessed supernatural powers?'

'If I had, I should have asked her to remove this scar from my face.'

'Even if she had used heretical means to do so?'

'I might have been tempted, Your Excellency, but I

hope I should have responded as a good Christian.'

'Did she speak to you of the priest Fra Filippo?'

Susanna lifted her eyes to the Inquisitor's and firmly told the lie she was resolved upon. 'No.'

'Have you knowledge of how the priest met his death?'

'I do not.'

'Do you accept the dominion of the Lord God over your immortal soul?'

'I do.'

'Such that you would protect that soul by telling this Tribunal all you know of the matters before it?'

'Yes.' She hesitated, but only for a moment. She had cast her lot with the players on the night of the banquet and could not call back those actions even if she wished. 'In proof of my desire to aid the Tribunal,' she said, 'I tell you of someone who may cast light upon the matters you investigate and confirm part of the accusation we made at the banquet.'

'Who?'

'A slave who served my family for many years was recently imprisoned for theft. Her name is Ludis. She may have knowledge of value to you.'

'Knowledge of what?'

'Of the relationship between Bishop Palma and my father, in regard to Teresa Laurano's mother.'

A long pause. 'Susanna Rossi, I ask you why, as the daughter of a noble house and the wife of a worthy citizen, you chose to run away and lend your presence to the irreligious actions of players of *commèdia*?'

'Your Excellency, as an admirer of the Greek

writers, I have an interest in the matters and methods of the drama. But there is a greater reason. You see the scar that God has placed upon my face. The players treated me as if the scar did not exist. Because they did so, I was able gradually to realize that the true scar was not upon my face but within me.'

'Do you question God's wisdom in causing your face to be scarred?'

She had told one lie already, Susanna thought; telling another could not matter so much. 'No, Your Excellency,' she said. 'I do not.'

When she emerged into the Piazza, bells were sounding the hour of dusk and the rain had stopped, leaving a creeping mist in its wake. She looked about, slightly weak without the tension that had held her rigid, not quite knowing where to go. A figure came from between two of the portals and moved towards her. She squinted disbelievingly: it was Luca.

'Are you all right?' he said.

'I believe so.'

'What did they ask you?'

As she told him, his eyes fixed on her face as if he would draw it. 'Yes,' he said when she finished, 'they asked me and the others many of the same questions.'

'What do you think they will do?' she asked.

'Who can predict the will of those who predict the will of God?'

They looked at the Doge's palace, where Teresa was held. Inside, lamps were being lit. Pale arches of light fell into the Piazza.

'Would you like to have some supper?' Luca said.

'I do not think I am hungry.'

'Then let us walk to the inn.'

He took her arm. Their feet struck rhythms as soft and regular as the lapping of water. The world was made of a hundred shades of grey – mist and stones and dusk reflecting and changing one another. Susanna did not know what to say. Since that night at the Polani palace, she had not allowed Luca into her mind, except as one of her co-conspirators. To concentrate on the situation the performance had created, to decide what to say to the Tribunal, had required all her being. Now the testifying was over and he was beside her, his golden presence silvered by the light, his hand warm on her arm.

'You are trembling,' he said. 'I can feel it.'

'I was frightened of them.'

They crossed a bridge as a gondola slid under it. 'I have been afraid before in my life,' Luca said. 'Once at sea, when a storm came up, so terrible that it turned the whole day black and bolts of white shot from the sky. And once in Spain, when I thought I was walking alone on a road and suddenly felt the points of two knives in my back. But standing before the Tribunal is worse. You can fight a storm with ropes and buckets, or robbers with your wits and strength. With the Tribunal I did not know what weapons to use.'

'Nor I.' She smiled. 'I tried to hold myself as if I had courage.'

He smiled back. 'No matter how gently they speak, one is in their power.'

They walked on. 'I do not like to be in anyone's power,' he said.

'Not even a woman's?' she said, so softly that he asked her to repeat it.

'Not even a woman's.' They separated to walk single file down a very narrow alley. When they emerged, he said, 'Yet women – certain women – do have power. I cannot deny it.'

'Why should you try?'

'So as not to become a captive.'

They looked at each other, faces half buried in the shadows.

'Let us walk on,' he said.

'How did you escape from the knives in your back?' she asked.

'I made the robbers believe that I had no coins.' He laughed. 'I have always been a good player.'

When they reached the inn, Susanna expected to be greeted and questioned on her ordeal, but none of the others was about. Luca took her arm more firmly and led her up the stairs. He opened the door to her room, entered behind her, closed it. She lit the candle. He followed her and put his hands on her face, one thumb resting on the scar. 'I desire you greatly, Lady Anna.'

She wanted to say that she felt the same, that her need of him was a fever in the blood, but instead she heard the question that had been with her since the first time he had shown her a kindness: 'Why?'

'I do not know, myself. It may be your spirit, or your wit, or your courage, or the beauty that lies everywhere in you save here.' His thumb pressed the scar. 'I have concluded it does not matter why.'

'No?'

'I want to be honest. If we become lovers, I cannot say what our future will be. I have never known a woman to whom I cared to be faithful forever.'

'Nor have I known any man.'

'Are we agreed, then, Lady Anna?'

'Do you wish to sign a contract?' she said.

He laughed. Then kissed her as on the day of the rehearsal, but even longer and deeper. His lips moved to her eyes, to the scar, to her throat. He put his hands on her breasts, all along her body, beneath her skirt. 'Let us be naked,' he said. They stripped off their clothing. He turned her so that the candle flame lit her body. 'You are beautiful,' he said, but she did not take in his words at first, for she was looking at his nakedness, which was more nearly perfect than a statue from the Greeks, and more splendid because the flesh was alive, moving with his breath, rising with his need.

In the hours that followed, between the times of pleasure so fierce that it bordered on pain, she wondered how her inexperienced body knew so many ways to present itself to his touch, or to wring from him great cries of satisfaction.

Once, as the candle guttered out, she thought of the Tribunal. If she confessed to them what she and Luca were doing, they would call it adultery and punish her for her sin.

* * *

'Do you know why you are here?'

'No,' said the slave named Ludis. She had been taken from her cell in mid-morning and brought to the church, where she had waited, resigned, until she was led into the presence of the Tribunal.

'We are the Holy Office of the Inquisition in Venice. We summon you solely to give evidence on a matter we are investigating. Your own crime and its punishment are matters for the secular courts and therefore of no concern to us. Do you understand?' She nodded. 'Are you a good Christian, Ludis?'

'I cannot say.'

'What do you mean?'

'Is it not the Christ who must say who is a good Christian?'

The Inquisitor hesitated. The words might have been insolent if the woman's dark eyes and handsome face were not so devoid of life. Neither fearful nor resigned, as prisoners usually were, she seemed beyond feeling.

The Inquisitor said, 'Tell us what you know of the friendship between your master Antonio Bardi and Bishop Andrea Palma.'

'The bishop came often to the Bardi *palazzo*. That is all I know.'

'We are advised differently.'

'You are mistaken.'

'We are told you know something of the bishop and Signor Bardi and the woman named Ginevra Laurano.'

'Who has told you that, my lord?'

'Do not address me as "my lord". We are so advised

by Susanna, of the Bardi house.'

'Susanna! She has come before you?'

'She has.'

The woman's lips softened. She lapsed into thought for a few moments, then raised her head. 'Often I waited upon Signor Bardi and his friends. As a slave, I knew my presence was barely noted. On several occasions I heard Signor Bardi and the man who later was made bishop speak the name Ginevra Laurano. It had no significance to me until one day I came upon them and heard the bishop say that he had been to her cell the evening before and that she was a dangerous woman. I knew I had heard something that could endanger me if my hearing of it were known, so I left the room before the men could realize my presence.'

'You are certain of what you say?'

'I am.'

'You could not have been mistaken?'

'Any of us can be mistaken, but of this matter I am certain.'

'Do you know that the fires of Hell await those who lie to the Inquisition of the Holy Roman Catholic and Apostolic Church?'

'I have no cause to lie.'

Try as he might, the Inquisitor could not make her alter or retract her testimony, which the notary recorded. When he sent her away, she wore the same impassive look with which she had entered and moved with as much dignity as if she were a princess.

The Tribunal watched her leave.

The papal nuncio, head shaking and white beard wagging, said, 'His Holiness will be distressed to hear of these matters.'

'Must he hear of them?' asked one of the Tre Assistenti.

'All that happens in the Most Serene Republic interests His Holiness.'

'Yet this matter concerns only citizens of the Republic.'

'Does it?' asked the nuncio, with the formal politeness that accompanied any discussion of the relationship between Rome and Venice. 'I have admired Andrea Palma as much as anyone here, but he hopes to be considered for a red hat. Therefore I think his conduct in this matter must be known in Rome.'

Silence. The Assistenti looked at one another. They did not want Palma's conduct known anywhere because it involved the conduct of Antonio Bardi, and the reputations of the noble families were their concern.

The Inquisitor said, 'Let us see the bishop again. Perhaps he can help us find a solution to this distressing matter.'

Andrea Palma looked at their faces, as stern and impersonal as if they had not all shared many occasions with him, secular and religious. He shifted his posture to stand even straighter. If it were to be a test of wills between the six and himself, he would be above them, no matter how high they sat.

The Inquisitor said, 'We wish to have further

knowledge of your dealings with Antonio Bardi in regard to the woman Ginevra Laurano.'

That was as expected. 'Certainly,' Palma said. 'Signor Bardi asked me to learn whether the woman practised sorcery and, if so, to see that she was accused of such practices. I found Bardi was right – she was a sorceress, very probably guilty of heresy. I instructed my clerk to see to the matter.'

'Why did you not accuse her to this Tribunal yourself?'

'Sadly, I no longer remember. These events happened years ago, and my many responsibilities do not leave me time to recall the detailed execution of each.'

'We are aware of your responsibilities. We are also aware, because the fact is entered in our records, that the accusation against her was received anonymously in a *bocca di leone*. Why did your clerk choose such a means?'

That, too, was expected. 'I have no idea. Tragically, he is not here to tell us, Teresa Laurano having caused his death by *maleficium*.'

'When did you learn that Ginevra Laurano's daughter, Teresa, was alive and was in Venice?'

'Fra Filippo learned of it and told me, shortly before his death. It is probably for his knowledge of her that Teresa Laurano wanted him to die.'

Silence. The Inquisitor was thinking; his colleagues watched him. He made the fingers of both hands meet at their tips, pair by pair, and said, 'For what motive do you make your accusation?'

'My motive is love of my friend and fellow servant of our Lord, Fra Filippo, and the desire to see an end to such *maleficium* as caused him to die.'

'Do you swear before God that you have no other reason?'

'I do swear.'

The Inquisitor's nostrils pinched as if he had caught the scent of rancid meat. 'Do you swear there is no truth in the accusation made by the players, that you visited Ginevra Laurano in her cell and forced yourself upon her?'

'In the name of my love for our Saviour the Lord Jesus Christ, I deny and repudiate that suggestion. It is a desperate and blasphemous attempt by Teresa Laurano's friends to save her from the justice of this Holy Office.'

'Do you swear you never went to the woman's prison cell?'

'I do.'

A long silence, until the Inquisitor said, 'A witness before this Tribunal overheard you tell Antonio Bardi that you did visit the woman in her cell.'

Palma managed not to rock backwards with the force of the unexpected. Even as his mind raced over the possibilities – Veronica Bardi? Antonio himself? – he heard the confidence in his reply: 'Such a witness is mistaken, I assure you.'

The six pairs of eyes trained on him unblinkingly, as if trying to communicate some thought without giving evidence of its passage.

Clearing his throat, the nuncio leaned forward. 'Let

us review these matters.' By tacit agreement, it seemed, they were going to speak less formally. 'You are aware that the essence of these proceedings must be passed on to Rome.'

'Yes?' Palma did not know why the word came out as a question.

'The accusation of the players, true or false, is so widely known in Venice that Rome must be advised of it.'

'I tell you it is false!'

The six pairs of eyes bored into him.

'Regrettably,' said one of the Assistenti, 'testimony from others corroborates much of it. We are at a loss to reconcile such testimony with your denial.'

'Rome,' said the Patriarch softly, 'will not be pleased.'

'It is a shame,' added the nuncio, 'that a man who has served God with such devotion and distinction will be able to advance no further in that service.'

Silence again, coming in like fog, disorienting Palma. He clung to the watching eyes, waiting for one of the mouths to speak further, but the silence thickened. The eyes shone in it, their message growing like the light of approaching lanterns. They wanted him to speak, to say – what? That he had done as the players depicted? Had lusted for the red-haired woman from the moment he saw her at her window? Had grasped eagerly at Bardi's request to accuse and destroy her – for she had placed her spell upon him, commanding him to have her accused anonymously, so no one could guess at his desire . . . forcing him to go to her cell, and finally ordering him to place his hands upon her body, and enter it, in the act whose recall could still make him shudder with pleasure; no, loathing. Never! To tell such matters would be the end of his power, his virtue, his life. He looked at the six pairs of eyes and shook his head helplessly. Another light appeared in the fog, coming from he knew not where, slowly filling his mind with its strength. *Filippo*, he thought, *my dear Filippo, you stood below her window too, that is true. And you went once to her cell. Yet I cannot do that. Unless you want me to – do you want me to say it, Filippo? Do you want me to be able to continue doing the sacred work of the Lord?* On his left, as if from the loft where the choir chanted, he heard a whisper: *Yes*.

'My friends,' he said. His voice seemed to come from a deep well. 'I see I must confess to you. Your perception is too acute. I can hide the truth no longer. It is true that Ginevra Laurano was violated in her cell. But the violator was . . . was . . . Fra Filippo. Yes. He made confession to me not long ago. Perhaps he knew he would die soon. I had long suspected that he carried some terrible burden on his soul.' The fog was clearing. 'When Ginevra Laurano told her daughter that a masked man raped her in her cell, she spoke truth. I do not know how the daughter came to believe that man was I – perhaps the mother, in the fever that killed her, was herself mistaken, or was in delirium.' He sighed. 'I hoped not to soil the reputation of my dear, dead friend, but I know Filippo would not wish me to suffer for his sin.' He looked at the eyes, waiting.

'Ah,' said the Inquisitor, at last. 'So the players' accusation, true in its larger portrait, is false in its most important detail.'

Palma nodded. Something warm and wet slid from his hair and down his neck. He called on all his will, but could not keep his hand from reaching back to touch the liquid. He looked at his fingers, terrified they would be red. But the liquid was colourless – perspiration.

'This is sad news,' the Inquisitor said. 'Yet the Holy Office is gratified to know of your innocence of the crime of rape, Andrea Palma.'

He bowed his head. There must be no more investigation of any kind, of anyone, for they would look more closely at him, and what he had just said.

The Inquisitor's rusty voice continued. 'What then of your charge against Teresa Laurano, that she caused the priest's death by *maleficium*? If she did not know it was he who had violated her mother, if she believed it was you, why would she wish to harm the priest?'

The marble floor seemed to wave beneath Palma's feet. He gripped his robe and lifted his gaze. 'I . . . Let me explain my reasoning to you.' The cloth in his hands was damp, but an argument was coming to him, as one always did, praise God for his command of words. 'If Teresa Laurano knew how I loved Filippo . . . she could not attack me directly because of my office . . . I feared she had taken revenge by depriving me of Filippo, who was my dearest friend on earth.' *Forgive me, Filippo*, he thought. *Forgive me. Forgive me*. He heard someone sobbing loudly. He looked around; it was himself. He sank to the floor and put his head in his hands. *Forgive me. Forgive me.* The words would not stop, nor the tears, nor the grinding pain of being the creature whose action caused them.

After a while he looked up at the Tribunal. Six pairs of eyes, not hostile, not friendly, merely waiting.

'Perhaps,' he said, 'my grief for Filippo clouded my judgment. I wanted – needed to explain his death. The evidence of the ring, found on her person . . .'

The Inquisitor said, 'We have established that Filippo gave the ring to the players.'

'I see. So there is no true evidence against her. Perhaps the accusation was too hasty. To best serve God's purpose, perhaps it should be withdrawn.'

The Inquisitor nodded.

Palma put a hand on the marble, in order to rise to his feet. From nowhere the crushing sensation came upon him, more powerful than ever in his life, as if he were a beetle beneath a giant palm.

He looked into the years ahead of him, but the hand was always there.

Dimly, from above him, he heard the voice of the Inquisitor. 'Andrea Palma, even as it welcomes your testimony, this Holy Office shares your grief over the sin of Fra Filippo. We note with admiration the piety and humility that prostrate you before us. Rise now, and go in peace.'

Palma wanted to cry out, but he must rise and smile and go. That much, he could will himself to do.

CHAPTER EIGHTEEN
Leaving

Improvising is our life and livelihood, yes. But we cannot live always on a tightrope; we need poles to anchor our flights. So, we learn couplets for concluding a discourse – *chiusette* – and speeches for exiting – *uscite* – to be certain of ending matters with finality and flair.

Ah, for *chiusette* and *uscite* in life!

The little canal was a shifting mosaic. Paolo sat on the edge of the *fondamenta*, watching chips of sunlight rock on the blue-green water. Buffa was beside him, licking the lifted stump of his fourth leg.

It was the kind of day, Paolo thought, on which a man's spirits should reach the clouds, but they were earthbound. 'Ah, Buffa,' he said, 'is there anything we can do for the soul of poor old Filippo?' Buffa's tongue worked busily and said nothing. Why could an animal not have a soul? Paolo wondered. Susanna had once told him that it was a subject of debate among learned persons, but looking into Buffa's wet brown eyes, which filled with love and trust the moment they opened, one had no need for debate. As to Filippo's soul . . . That was a more difficult matter. He had said,

'Bring my soul to the Lord Jesus Christ.' But according to the Tribunal's findings, already known by everyone in Venice, it seemed, the violator of Teresa's mother had been Filippo, not the bishop. Paolo did not believe it. The dying Filippo had confessed to violating Ginevra – but only in his thoughts. Paolo scratched between Buffa's ears. 'I would like to clear his name, but I cannot. Having concealed from the Tribunal that I was present at his deathbed, how can I reveal it now?' He sighed. Should a man go to Hell for his thoughts? Did God see no difference between a man's thinking and his actions? 'If so, Buffa, I shall come to know the Devil well.' He thought of all the times he had lain with Isabella in his thoughts. He waited, expecting melancholy, but a startled expression came over his face. It was not only that he no longer loved her; he no longer wished to lie with her.

'Buffa,' he said, 'can it be so?' He summoned her image. It was not of the beauty he had adored but of the woman indifferent to the passion he had confessed with such difficulty, denying Arlecchino, pulling the words from their hiding places. She had cared only about getting him to help rid her of Susanna. She was not a good person, he thought, as surprised as a child learning that others could be cruel. The good person was Susanna. He must have known it even in the street of whores. He did not want to lie with Isabella, even in his dreams.

He sat quietly, testing and tasting the new sense of himself, studying its chip-reflections in the water. After a time he lifted his gaze. 'Buffa, I shall never again care for a woman in that way.' He stretched his arms and looked about. People passed in a thin stream over a nearby bridge. Men with bulging forearms carrying coils of thick rope. An aproned woman lurched by with a wheel of cheese. Another emerged from a *sottoportego*, setting foot on the bridge, blinking into the sun. Paolo stared, then jumped to his feet and ran. 'Hel-lo, little redhead!' he cried, although her hair was not so red now; it looked as if dirt had been rubbed into it, and her dress was stained.

'Paolo?' she said. 'Is it really Paolo?'

'Yes! It is!' He felt himself grinning at her, his mouth stretching nearly until it hurt. 'Little redhead, you are free!'

She raised a hand to shield her eyes; her fingers were almost grey. 'It was dark. The guard came. I thought he had food, but he unlocked the door. He said the charge was dismissed.' Her hand fell to her side. 'I am . . . free?'

'Yes! Perhaps this is a day for singing, after all. I shall walk with you to the inn. Will you take my arm?'

She nodded – she who had always marched alone, at her own pace. Paolo told himself that soon she would be the Teresa of old, that she needed only a wash, clean clothes, and a glass of wine.

'How is . . . everyone?' she said, as if unable to recall any names.

'Fine, fine. Well, perhaps not entirely fine, for we are divided now. Split in two by what has happened.' He glanced at her. 'Do you wish to hear?'

'Yes,' she said. He did not know if he believed her,

but he told it anyway: from Susanna's asking the troupe to save Teresa, to the performance at the Polani banquet, to the summonses from the Tribunal, to the Tribunal's decision.

She frowned. 'That is why they released me? They decided the bishop did not harm my mother?'

'Yes.'

'They are wrong.'

'Yes.'

She stopped, clutching his forearm. 'I cannot fight them again, Paolo.'

'No.'

'I thought I was an arrow, heading straight to the target, but I struck many other people. And not one of them was the bishop.'

She started walking again, still holding on to him. 'Do you know the worst part of being in prison? Even worse, in a way, than wondering if they are going to torture you or kill you?'

'No.'

'It is having nothing to do but lie there and think about all you have done in your life and whether it was the right thing to do, what it has achieved.'

'Ah,' he said. 'I would not care to contemplate such matters for long.'

They walked on. Buffa saw a bitch in a doorway and skittered over to growl and sniff at her. When Paolo persuaded him to leave her and follow them again, Teresa said, 'The bishop accused me of the very thing I had done – causing Fra Filippo to die. But I do not see how the bishop could know it, do you?'

'No.'

'I lay in the prison cell and asked myself whether God had sent him a vision, whether God wanted me to be punished.'

'What did you conclude?'

'Nothing.' She rubbed her forehead as if it ached. 'I never told the Tribunal what I did to your brother.'

'Nor did I,' he said. 'Nor Susanna.'

'Thank you.' She clutched his arm more tightly. 'I shall think about it forever – what I did and how it served no purpose except to destroy your brother and embarrass the bishop. But only to embarrass him, nothing more.'

'You must not do that,' Paolo said, 'for then you will spend the rest of your life as you have spent the past ten years, thinking of your mother and her tragedy.' As heartily as he could, he added, 'I shall invent some new *lazzi*, and you shall be part of them.'

'I do not know, Paolo, whether I shall still be a player.'

He stopped so short that an old man walking close behind bumped into him, exclaimed, and scurried on. 'But what else would you do?'

'I do not know. That is the other thing I lay and thought of in prison. When the past was too awful to contemplate, I tried to imagine the future.'

'And?'

'I do not know. Yet.' Her pressure on his arm pulled them forward again. 'Besides, with I Favolosi split in two, what troupe is there to join?'

He did not answer. He had been avoiding the question for days.

At the inn, the company crowded around Teresa, even those who had declined to help her. For a while Paolo could almost believe that everything was as before – except that he had never seen Susanna and Teresa embrace each other. Soon Giulio was making sniping remarks to Umberto, and Bruno was shooting hostile looks at Luca. When Isabella came down the stairs and into the inner court where they were gathered, her mouth gave clear signal that mean words would emerge from it. Paolo could not help himself. He went up to her, closer than he had been since their encounter in the *campiello*.

She turned her head, realizing he stared at her. 'What do you want?'

He nodded, satisfied. 'Nothing.' It came to him how truly he meant the word, and he repeated it slowly.

Isabella might have replied, but the landlord appeared, holding a letter above his head. He made for Bruno, his expression grave. The others fell silent. 'This just came, my friend,' he said. 'From the Polani.'

Bruno tore the letter open. Colour rose in his cheeks as his eyes moved down the paper. He rocked once on his heels, then looked up. 'Alvise Polani will no longer retain our services. Nor will anyone else in Venice. The authorities have banished us.'

Isabella seemed the only one capable of speech. 'For what reason?'

'For the lewd and lascivious conduct in our performances.'

Giulio groaned. Bruno kicked angrily at the side of the stairs. 'It is the Tribunal!' Pedrolino cried. 'I have never been so terrified as when I stood before them. They asked about our performances, they asked if I were a good Christian. I wished to be a thousand leagues away from them, even at sea in a galley. I wished I were a dog, a cat, a fish, anything that—'

'Quiet!' Bruno shouted. 'Who cares what you wished? You are part of the reason we are in this predicament.'

'Me? What did I do?'

'You sided with those who brought this trouble upon us!'

'Yes I did! I am glad! I do not wish to belong to a troupe like yours.'

Paolo watched the storm rise around him – rumbles, shouts, cheeks flushing, fists lifting. Umberto and Giulio grappled with each other. Buffa started barking. When Fiorenza shrieked at him to stop, he was ugly and stupid, Paolo ran into the fray.

A voice rose above the others, demanding quiet. Paolo looked up to see Luca on the stairs. 'My friends!' he said. 'And those who no longer wish to be my friends! It seems our differences can no longer be resolved. Therefore I—'

'Differences that you have fomented,' Isabella said.

Luca ignored her. 'Therefore I believe we must split apart in actuality, as we are divided in spirit. I refuse to be driven from Venice, but I am going to leave her of my own will. I shall form a new company of players, of which I propose to be *corago*, and I invite any who wish to come along with me. I ask only – no, I demand – that you come with good will and in good cheer, for I will not allow meanness of spirit.' Silence. 'Who will come, then?'

Umberto scratched his head, shook it, opened his mouth. 'Umberto!' Isabella said. 'Do not be a fool!' Umberto's mouth closed.

'I will go with you.' Pedrolino bounded to Luca's side.

'You traitor,' Bruno said. 'No one will mourn your loss, for your clowning is a poor thing. It always has been.'

Pedrolino turned a deep, painful red.

'I am with you, Luca,' Paolo said quietly. 'I am pleased to remain in such good company as Pedrolino's.'

'Bravo, Paolo,' said another quiet voice – Teresa's.

'Paolo!' Bruno's face was dark with anger and worry. 'Do not be stupid! Who took you from your village in the Veneto? Who trained you? Who made possible your life as a player?'

Before Paolo could reply, Teresa said, 'He has repaid you a hundred times.'

'You!' Bruno swung on her. 'By God, if the bishop's men had taken Susanna instead of you, none of this would have happened!'

'What!' No one could be sure who had cried out, Teresa or Susanna.

Bruno lifted his chin and glared.

'Did you betray her to the bishop in an unsigned letter?' Teresa said.

'Was it you who told him I was in Venice here at the inn?' Susanna said.

Everyone looked at Bruno. He shifted from one foot to the other, and back again. 'Yes, I did! And if Teresa had not intervened, our problems would have been resolved, and we would not now be banished.'

'But we are,' Luca said. 'Who else will join me?'

'I will.' Umberto stepped forward. 'My dear Catarina would want it.'

Luca bowed. 'It will be my pleasure, Dottore.'

'Traitor!' Bruno shouted.

Luca turned to Susanna. 'Lady Anna?'

She stood at one side with Teresa. She wore neither mask nor veil, but her hands were on her skirt, not covering her scar. 'You wish me to come?'

'Indeed.'

'Of course,' said Isabella, with sweet malice. 'Luca will always give welcome to a *lady*.'

'Yes,' he replied, 'provided she behaves like one.' He turned again to Susanna. 'May I have your answer?'

'You wish me to come as a player?'

Luca smiled broadly. 'And as whatever else you like.'

A look went between them – not so much like a handshake as a touching of fingertips. In that instant Paolo saw that Susanna loved the man. *Oh, dear*, he thought. *Does she not know that he is a great flatterer of women, who does not seem to care deeply for any of them?*

Luca said, 'Will you join us too, Teresa?'

'I think not. I think I shall remain in Venice.'

'But you are banished, like all of us.'

'Teresa the player is banished. But I shall not be a player.'

'What, then?'

Teresa was silent.

Luca looked around the group. 'Anyone else?'

'No!' Bruno said. 'Take your leave, and take nothing else.'

'Oh no,' Luca said. 'I will have my share of the Polani purse – we all will – as well as the masks and costumes we ourselves have made or bought.'

'By God! You set us against one another, but you will not suck us dry!'

Paolo smiled, crossed his arms, and leaned back to watch. It would be a good fight, but he was quite certain Luca would win.

The servant who opened the door to Susanna's knock was the same one who had answered when she had come in disguise to see her mother many months before. A lifetime before.

'Signora,' he said, deference masking what surely was surprise. 'Enter, please enter. I shall tell your mother you are here.'

'No, I will go to her. Is she in her apartment?'

The man nodded. Susanna moved past him into the entrance hall. On one side was the familiar bustle of the spice-trade offices and storerooms. With it came a familiar fear – her father would emerge and either dispute or forbid her presence –

but she pushed it aside and went up the central staircase, thinking of what she had discovered about fear: merely because one felt it did not mean one had to be ruled by it.

The light fell through the pierced windows in remembered patterns; her feet knew the height and slope of each stair before touching it. Yet in the familiarity was something strange – as if she had lived there as a different person.

Her mother was at her writing desk. She rose, came forward a few steps, and began to cry. She held Susanna tightly, saying her name over and over. Finally she pulled back and wiped her eyes. 'Your father wanted to bring you from the players, by force if necessary. But I was certain you would come of your own will, and he agreed to wait a while to see if I was right.'

'Is he very angry?' As she spoke, Susanna realized it was the first question she had asked on her previous visit.

'He is. But all that has happened has made him cautious.'

'I would not have expected that result.'

'No,' said her mother. 'Come and sit beside me.' When they had settled in two carved chairs against the wall, Veronica continued, 'It is a blow to his pride, to have all Venice learn of his conduct.'

'Do you think so many disapprove?'

Her mother gave half a smile. 'Those who put their daughters in convents to avoid marriage dowries have been quick to express their shock and displeasure. But it will pass. When it does, Antonio will be the same as before.'

'And you, Mother? Will you be the same?'

Perfumed fingers touched her face. 'I shall be sadder but stronger.'

'How is that, Mother?'

'I have learned it is useless to love your father. That knowledge saddens me, but it strengthens me as well, for when you understand and accept the nature of your life, you are better able to get what you want from it.'

'Mother, you amaze me, and please me as well.'

'Sometimes I please myself.' Veronica took one of Susanna's hands between both of her own. 'Tell me why you have come.'

'For three reasons. First, to see you and tell you I love you.'

'Ah!'

'Then to say goodbye, for I am leaving Venice.'

Veronica put a hand to her throat. 'I feared you would not be coming back to us, but . . . where are you going?'

'South.' Susanna could not help smiling. 'With some of the players.'

'Why do you cast your lot with them? It cannot be an easy life.'

'It is very difficult. Never knowing whether you will be welcomed or run from town by the authorities, never being certain how far a week's purse will have to stretch, sleeping wherever God and man will permit. I am sure I will have times of regret and yearning for the ease and beauty of my life in Venice. I cannot explain it fully, Mother, but with the players, I am . . . free.'

'Of what?'

'Unless I am performing, I can go about freely without mask or veil. I do not care if people see the scar. If it pains them, the burden is theirs and no longer mine.'

Her mother searched her eyes for a long time. 'Is there someone among the players who helped you to achieve this understanding?'

'I have more than one friend among the players, Mother.'

'Excellent. Tell me of the one who matters most.'

'He is the male Lover, although at the Polani banquet, he was the bishop.'

'Susanna! He is a gloriously handsome man.'

'Who therefore could not love me?'

'I do not say that.'

'Perhaps you think it, Mother. Do not protest – I have thought it often myself. But is it not unfair to him to assume that his own beauty makes him judge others only by their appearance? He was able to look at me and see past the scar, but for a long time I could not do the same for him.'

'Does he say that he loves you?'

'Not yet.' Susanna smiled. 'At least I know he will not say he loves me only to gain my money.'

'Is he a man who is able to love a woman?'

'I believe so, although I do not think he knows it yet.'

'Have you lain together?' Susanna nodded. 'My

daughter, what if he does not love you as you love him? I know what it is to yearn for someone whose eyes and thoughts go elsewhere. Such a life lies heavy on the heart.'

'I know, Mother. But I am wagering the future on the joy of the present.'

The door banged open.

'So!' said her father, huge and glowering. 'They said you had come back.'

Her mother stiffened. Susanna said, 'Do you want me back, Father?'

'I want you to make restitution for the trouble you have caused.'

'What do you want me to do? Return to Ludovico?'

'Hah,' said her father. 'He would like that, but I have told him he has no more connection with the house of Bardi. Let him stay in his house and cry how badly he has been used. No one will listen to him.'

'Then what should I do? Surely you do not want me to live here with you?'

'Hah,' he said again.

'I have not come home, Father. I am here to say goodbye. I leave in two days, with some of my player-friends.' He snorted, as if she had said she were going to live with dogs. 'I came for another cause – my third reason, Mother. I ask you to withdraw the charge of theft against Ludis.'

'By God,' said her father, 'you have more gall than a pirate. Why in the name of heaven or hell should I do such a thing?'

'Because Ludis has done me and my friends a great service.'

'Why would such a reason weigh with me?'

Susanna started to answer, but her mother leaned forward. 'Here is another reason, Antonio: because I ask it as well.'

Susanna saw her own surprise on her father's face.

Her mother said, 'All Venice now knows of your conduct with the woman Ginevra Laurano, revelations that cause me grief and embarrassment. I have asked for little in our life together, but I ask you to do as Susanna says. Withdraw the charge against Ludis and grant her her freedom.'

'Never. Why should I free a slave who has stolen from me?'

'You owe it to me, Antonio. You have stolen much from me – my peace of mind, for all the years I have loved you while you preferred your courtesans.'

His colour rose, whether in anger or guilt Susanna could not say. 'You bring this up in front of our daughter?'

'She gives me the courage to do so.'

One hand clutched his dagger. 'I visited Ginevra Laurano because she was spying for me on a rival spice-merchant.'

'I do not think I believe you,' her mother said.

'You know the patriciate often employ courtesans as spies!'

'Is that why you go to Campo Santo Stefano to visit the almond-eyed woman?'

This time Susanna understood. He felt guilt, and anger at her mother for making him feel it. 'I refuse to discuss the matter any further,' he said.

'I accept your refusal,' Veronica said, 'provided you have Ludis freed.'

He paced for several moments.

'Otherwise,' Veronica said, 'I shall leave, and you will lose one of your most prized possessions.'

'I do not believe you. Where would you go? You will not do such a thing.'

'Can you be sure? I could do as Susanna has done. I could go with her.'

Susanna watched the silent struggle between her parents, the quiet demand of her mother's gaze and the furious lance of her father's, knowing she was not its object no matter how much they used her name. Their lives bound them together, but their natures allowed of no harmony.

After a long moment her father said, 'I shall see to the slave.'

'Thank you, Antonio.' Her mother turned in wonder when he had left. 'I cannot believe what just happened.'

'I am witness, Mother.'

'I almost wish he had not agreed, for now I shall never know whether I would indeed have left him – whether my rebellion was hollow or real.'

'I think it was real. I think in freeing Ludis you also freed yourself.'

Her mother took her hands. 'Must you truly go, Susanna?'

'I must. Will you allow me to take some books with me?'

'Of course. You must take some of my jewels and turn them into coins, to ease that difficult life.' Veronica smiled. 'Take the jewels Ludis stole.'

'Thank you, dear Mother.'

'Oh, my daughter!' The slender arms came around her, the soft cheek met her own, the familiar body cradled her. 'When you were ill,' her mother whispered, 'I consulted a sorceress, who did many of the things of which they accused Ginevra Laurano, and then her daughter. I had beans cast, and the *cordella*, anything to help heal you. Perhaps they are the reason you did not die. So I cannot think Teresa Laurano is evil. I am glad she is released, and if you wish to spend your life with her and the other players, do it with my blessing.'

That was the memory Susanna carried with her: the loving voice, the arms that clung even as they released her.

In an hour, Teresa thought, Luca and the others would leave Venice. She would meet them at the Molo and bid them goodbye, and then she would be free. Free of everything and everyone. She could go anywhere she liked, at any time.

But where to go? She used to walk the city – and the countryside – searching for the Man with the Ring, but now there was no purpose. The search had brought her only grief, but she felt incomplete without it, as if a leg had been cut off. What did one do when a leg was missing? Run barking after Paolo, she thought bitterly. She shook her head and continued walking.

Without conscious intent, she went along a little canal, over several bridges, through some narrow arches. She saw a cat curled on a windowsill, mimosa trailing from a wall. When she stopped, she was in the *campiello* where, disguised, she had met Fra Filippo; down one alley was the house where he had died. The sun felt cold on her bare arms. She rubbed them and walked on.

The next time she looked outward, she was at the place she had always avoided on her walks. There were the carved door and the window her mother had used to open in the evenings: *Why do you stand there, Mother? – To show the world my wares;* and the *altana* on the roof, where a woman now sat bleaching her hair in the sun. *I shall never try to be blonde, little one, nor must you. God has given us hair of fire, so let us keep it and use it.*

'Mother,' Teresa whispered, 'I have failed you, and myself. Forgive me.' There was no answer.

She went a few steps but turned back. She pushed her hands into her pockets and felt her handful of coins. She could use them to rent some rooms, small and modest at first but well situated, with a good window opening on to the street. She could find a cat, a black one, and she could find customers to make her rich and powerful, so that she could destroy them. Or perhaps they would destroy her first, as they had her mother. It would not matter which happened, riches or destruction; either way, she would be with her mother, following Ginevra's path.

God has given us hair of fire, so let us keep it, and use it.

She heard another voice, not in her mind this time, calling her name.

She turned. 'Pedrolino! What are you doing? Did you follow me?'

He nodded. He stood in the doorway of the next house, strands of hair falling over his forehead. He seemed very young.

'What do you want?' she said.

He came a few steps towards her, then stopped. 'It is foolish, of course.'

'What is?'

'I am.' He pushed at his hair. 'Pedrolino the fool. Not a very good fool. I know that.'

'You followed me to tell me that?'

'No. I want— Isn't this the house where you lived with your mother?'

'How do you know that?'

'Paolo told me where it was. Are you going to live here again?'

'Yes,' she said, as if the question had been a challenge.

'Please don't, Teresa. Come with us. Don't stay in Venice.'

'Why does it matter to you?'

He coloured, put his hands in his pockets, looked away. 'I think about you all the time. I think I must love you. I know you don't care for me in that way, but I don't mind. Well I do mind, of course. I mean I understand that you don't care for me. But to think of you being here, alone and unhappy—'

'How do you know I will be unhappy?'

He turned to her with a look of astonishment so large that it belonged on the stage. 'You will be lonely. What will you do but think of the past and your mother? Who will make you laugh if you are sad or lonely? Who will eat your suppers with you?'

They were foolish, the things he was saying, so there was no reason for her throat to tighten. She cleared it. 'Perhaps I deserve to be unhappy.'

'Oh,' he said, as if she had offered an argument beyond his grasp. He shifted his feet. 'But, Teresa, could you not be unhappy just as well with us?'

He was so earnest, eyes large below the fan of his hair, that she had to laugh.

'There, you see!' he cried. 'If you come with us, you can laugh at me – and Paolo and Umberto. Whom can you laugh at in Venice? Please, Teresa, please. Do not worry because I love you. I will keep it to myself. Well, I may tell a tree occasionally, but otherwise I—'

'Oh, Pedrolino,' she said. 'What am I to do with you?'

'Come with me,' he said. 'With us. Please.'

She felt relief waiting for her, like a stream on a burning day. She hesitated, then stepped into it. 'Very well. But you must do something for me.'

'Anything! What?'

'Forget your yearning for me and look for someone else.' He drooped slowly, as if he were miming a thirsty flower. 'I am not destined for love, Pedrolino. There is a weight on my soul that may never lift. And I should like you to be happy with someone else. So I will not come unless you try. Will you?'

'Oh, very well,' he said, pouting like a child.

They headed south, with a horse purchased at one of the first farms they came upon and an old wagon for which Luca bargained hard in a town in Emilia-Romagna. For both, Susanna contributed some of the coins her mother's jewels had brought. In Bologna they met a mountebank who would make a fine Pantalone and whose wife could play the older female roles. In Tuscany, heading to Florence, they found a young man who could expertly juggle balls, balance eggs on plates, and paint backdrops, and whose wife sewed finely and could copy sheets of songs for them to sell. In Florence they met a fine Captain and wooed him from another troupe. They made friends with some singers and poets and painters with whom they talked into the night.

Many times Luca told the story of the performance at the Polani banquet and what Susanna had done. 'Imagine – a scenario used as an accusation and a trap for the conscience! Will there ever again be anything so clever?'

Sometimes out in the world, and always in performance, Susanna wore a dark blue velvet eye patch, in the centre of which were sewn some of her mother's pearls in the outline of an eye. When she was alone with Luca, she took it off.

In the warmth of September they set off to Urbino and down to Umbria. The light was hazy and golden, the earth grey-green, the sky huge, and in every distance a town would eventually appear, clinging to a hill like some terracotta creature climbing to heaven. Umberto, apprehensive at first, came to be certain he had done the right thing in leaving Bruno and Isabella and the others – who, they heard, had gone to Mantua with some mountebanks. Paolo behaved as he always had, although in the sun one could see fine new lines in the corners of his mouth. Teresa began making her potions again, but she was not quite the same, they all agreed; no longer restless, but too often melancholy. They had good days filled with coins, and bad days with empty bellies. Whatever the day had been, they talked over supper of how they would be a full-fledged troupe when they found two or three more players, skilled and compatible; how they would learn more splendid verses to embellish their scenarios; how they would find a wealthy, liberal, and intelligent patron; how they would one day be summoned to a court in France or even England. They slept in fields, on straw, in groves of trees. Sometimes Luca and Susanna stayed with the others under the stars, but sometimes they went off by themselves.

One night when they lay together, she pulled away from him in the midst of their passion and asked him if he was happy.

'Yes,' he said, reaching for her. 'Yes, yes.'

'Do you still feel you are a man who is free?'

In the moonlight, she could see that he was startled. 'I have not thought of it for some time.'

'Ah,' she said, and smiled.

At first, as a member of the troupe, she merely did

acrobatics and beat the drum to announce their arrival in the towns, but soon Luca said, 'When we do scenarios, you must be the female Lover.'

'I?'

'Who else?'

'Teresa.'

'No.'

'I am not skilled enough.'

'Did you not play *The Woman Who Was Falsely Accused*? By nature you speak with elegance, and I shall teach you everything else.'

'But . . . There is no Innamorata who goes about in a velvet eye patch.'

'There will be,' he said. 'You will become famous for your wit, your beauty, and your eye made of pearls. And I shall be famous too – as the man who loves you.'

'Ah,' she said, and smiled.

The first time she performed the Female Lover was in a short scene, in the square of a small town. Arlecchino capered madly beforehand, stick-fingers waving in absurd gestures, head bobbing as he strutted and twirled his *batte*, his *lazzi* executed with the combination of skill and abandon that was uniquely his. The Lovers' scene pleased the crowd, which parted with a goodly number of coins. Afterwards the rest of the players clustered around Susanna, telling her she had done well.

'Your improvising is becoming good,' said Paolo. He could not help feeling a proprietary interest in her, for was he not the one who had first suggested she perform with them, who taught her her first skill, acrobatics? He felt someone tugging on the patch-strewn jacket of his costume. Busy with Susanna, he ignored the pressure for a time, but finally he turned around.

A young woman stood there, fifteen or sixteen perhaps, her eyes dazed.

'Yes?' he said.

'You . . .' She struggled. 'I never saw such things as you do.'

'Oh?' He could not think what else to say. She was looking at him as if he were the most splendid creature in the world, as if he were Luca. He recognized the look – doubtless it had been on his own face when he had chased after Bruno and Isabella and begged to go with them.

'I want to learn what you do,' she said. 'I want to come with you.'

'Ah, well . . .' He thought it would be only fair, and kind, to wipe the look from her pretty face. He reached up, undid his mask, and swept it off.

She looked up at him. He waited, but her expression did not change.

'I want to come with you,' she said.

More Compelling Fiction from Headline:

EV THOMPSON

His exotic new saga

Blue Dress Girl

A stirring tale of adventure and a moving and tender love story played out against the exotic background of China at one of the most turbulent periods in its history.

Fleeing from the busy port of Canton to avoid scandal and danger, blue dress girl She-she is caught in crossfire and rescued by Second Lieutenant Kernow Keats of the Royal Marines. Instantly moved by her fragile beauty, the young man takes She-she to Hong Kong, to the home of missionaries Hugh and Hannah Jefferies, where she can regain her strength. As she comes to know the handsome hero, the girl's gratitude becomes love – and her feelings are returned.

But a love affair between a Chinese peasant girl and an English officer seems unthinkable in 1857. And as the Taiping rebellion gets underway, Kernow is torn from She-she's side to do his patriotic duty. Can their great love cross the chasm of race, class and background that divides them?

'Thompson enjoys working his backdrop – lots of chaps fighting on boats, warlords, pirate raids, skirmishes and bloodshed...' *The Sunday Times*

'It will keep you turning the pages and certainly appeal to the vast readership who enjoy top quality historical novels.' *Sunday Independent*

Don't miss E.V. Thompson's poignant saga *Wychwood*, also available from Headline.

FICTION/SAGA 0 7472 4136 8